Lady of the Reeds

Lady of the Reeds

Pauline Gedge

Lady of the Reeds was first published in
Canada by Viking Penguin as *House of Dreams*.

Copyright © 1994 by Pauline Gedge
All rights reserved.
First U.S. edition, 1995,
published by
Soho Press Inc.
853 Broadway
New York, NY 10003

Library of Congress Cataloging-in-Publication Data

Gedge, Pauline, 1945–
Lady of the reeds/Pauline Gedge.
p.   cm.
ISBN 1-56947-072-3 (alk. paper)
1. Ramses II, King of Egypt—Fiction.   2. Concubinage—Egypt—
History—Fiction.   3. Egypt—History—To 332 B.C.—Fiction.
I. Title.
PR9199.3.G415L33   1995
813'.54—dc20   95-14837
                                                                            CIP

Manufactured in the United States
10   9   8   7   6   5   4   3   2

Lady of the Reeds

Chapter 1

My father was a mercenary, a blond, blue-eyed giant of a man who had drifted into Egypt during the time of the troubles when the Syrian Chancellor Irsu held sway and foreigners ranged where they would, looting and raping. For a time he lingered in the Delta, taking work where he could, for he was not himself lawless and would have nothing to do with the bands of wandering predators. He herded cattle, trod grapes, sweated in the mud pits where bricks were made. Then, when our Great God Ramses' father, Osiris Setnakht Glorified, wrested power from the filthy Syrian, my father saw his chance and joined the ranks of the infantry, marching through the towns and villages scattered along the length of the Nile, routing and pursuing the disorganized groups of pillagers, executing, and arresting, and played his part in the restoration of a Ma'at that had been enfeebled and almost eclipsed by the febrile creatures who had grappled for the throne of Egypt for years, none of whom were worthy to be called the Incarnation of the God.

Sometimes the drunken vermin my father's troop exterminated were Libu from his own Tamahu tribe, similarly fair-haired and light of eye, who had come to the Two Lands not to enrich it nor to build an honest life but to steal and kill. They were like rogue animals, and my father destroyed them without compunction.

One burning afternoon in the month of Mesore the troop pitched their tents on the outskirts of the town of Aswat, north of holy Thebes. They were dirty, tired and hungry and there was no beer to be had. The captain sent my father and four others to requisition what stores might be available from the headman. Passing the entrance to one of the mud houses they heard a commotion within, women shrieking, men shouting. Fearing the worst, their instincts for trouble honed by many weeks of petty warfare, the members of the troop pushed into the tiny, dark hallway to be met by a crowd of half-drunk men and women swaying and clapping with delight. Someone forced a mug of beer into my father's hand. "Give thanks! I have a son!" a voice floated over the mêlée. Drinking greedily my father wove through the throng to come face to face with a tiny, olive-skinned woman with elfin features, cradling in her bloody arms a snuffling bundle of linen. It was the midwife. It was my mother. My father took a long look at her over the rim of his mug. In his strong, placid way he weighed, considered. The people were warm in their happiness. The headman offered the troop a generous amount of grain from the town's meagre supply. The women came to the tents and washed the soldiers' soiled linen. Aswat was beautiful and quiet, traditional in its values, its cultivable land rich, its trees shady, and the desert beyond was unsullied.

On the day the troop was to continue its march south, my father sought the house where my mother lived with her parents and three brothers. He took with him the only valuable thing he possessed, a tiny gold scarab on a leather thong that he had found in the mud of a Delta tributary and had taken to wearing around his sinewy wrist. "I am on the business of the Good God," he told my mother, pressing the scarab into her little brown palm, "but when I have served my time I will return. Wait for me." And she, looking up into the mild but commanding eyes of this tall man whose hair was as golden as sunlight and whose mouth promised joys about which she had only dreamed, nodded dumbly.

He was as good as his word. Wounded twice in the year that followed, he was at last discharged from the army, paid, and allotted the three arouras of land he had asked for in the nome at Aswat. As a mercenary he held the fields on the understanding that he was available for active duty at any time and he was required to pay one-tenth of his crops into the coffers of Pharaoh, but he had what he wanted: Egyptian citizenship, a piece of land and a pretty wife who was already a part of the life of the town and who was able to make his task of winning the trust of the local people easier.

All this I learned, of course, from my mother. Their meeting, their immediate attraction for each other, the taciturn, battle-weary soldier and the wiry little village girl, was a romantic story of which I never tired. My mother's family had been villagers at Aswat for many generations, minding their own affairs, fulfilling their religious obligations at the small temple of Wepwawet, the jackal God of War and the totem of their nome; births, marriages, deaths weaving them and their neighbours into a tight garment of simplicity and security. Of my father's forebears she knew little for he never spoke of them. "They are Libu, from over there somewhere," she would say, waving her arm vaguely in the direction of the west with all the indifference of the true Egyptian for anything and anyone beyond the borders. "You get your blue eyes from them, Thu. They were probably herdsmen, wanderers." But watching the light from the oil lamp slide over the sheen of sweat on my father's powerful shoulders and well-muscled arms as he sat cross-legged on the sandy floor of our reception room, bent over some piece of farm equipment he was mending, I doubted it. Far more likely that his ancestors had been warriors, fierce men who surrounded some barbaric Libu prince and fought for him in an endless round of tribal depredations.

Sometimes I daydreamed that my father had noble blood in his veins, that his father, my grandfather, was just such a prince who had quarrelled violently with my father and forced him into exile so that, wandering and friendless, he had at last found his way to the blessed soil of Egypt. One day a message would come, he would be forgiven, we would pack our few belongings onto the donkey, sell the cow and the ox, and travel to a far court where my father would be welcomed with open arms, with tears, by an old man weighed down in gold. Mother and I would be bathed in sweet oils, clad in shimmering linen, draped in amulets of turquoise and silver. All would bow to me, the long-lost princess. I would sit in the shade of our date palm and study my brown arms, my long, gangly legs to which the dust of the village always clung, thinking that perhaps the blood that pulsed almost imperceptibly through the bluish veins of my wrists might one day be the precious pass to wealth and position. My brother, Pa-ari, a year older than I was and much wiser, would scoff at me. "Little princess of the dust!" he would smile. "Queen of the reed beds! Do you really think that if Father was a prince he would have bothered with a few paltry arouras in the middle of nowhere, or married a midwife? Get up now and take the cow to the water. She is thirsty." And I would wander to where Precious Sweet Eyes, our cow, was tethered. She and I would take the path to the river together, my hand on her soft, warm shoulder, and while she sucked up the life-giving liquid I would study my reflection, gazing into the Nile's limpid depths. The slow eddies at my feet distorted the image, turning my waving black hair into an indistinct cloud around my face and making of my strange blue eyes a colourless glitter full of mysterious messages. A princess yes, perhaps. One never knew. I never dared to ask my father about the possibility. He was loving, he would sit me on his knee and tell me stories, he was approachable on every subject but his past. The barrier was unspoken but real. I think my mother, still loving him desperately, held him in awe. The villagers certainly did. They trusted him. They relied on him to take his share of the responsibilities of village administration. He helped the local Medjay to police the surrounding area. But they never treated him with the easy familiarity of a genuine villager. His long, golden hair and his steady, startling blue gaze always proclaimed him a foreigner.

I fared little better. I did not particularly like the village girls with their giggles, their simple games, their artless but boring gossip concerning nothing more than village affairs, and they did not like me. With a child's suspicion for anyone different, they closed ranks against me. Perhaps they feared the evil eye. I, of course, did not make my life among them any easier. I was aloof, superior without intending to be, too full of the wrong kind of questions, my mind always ranging further than the boundaries they understood. Pa-ari was more easily accepted. Though he too was taller and more finely made than the other village children, he was not cursed with blue eyes. From my mother he had inherited the Egyptian brown eyes and black hair and from father an inborn authority that made him a leader amongst his schoolmates. Not that he chose to be a leader. His heart was in words. A mercenary's land grant could be passed to his son providing the boy followed in his father's profession, but Pa-ari wanted to be a scribe. "I am content with the farm and I like village life," he told me once, "but a man who cannot read and write is forced to rely on the wisdom and knowledge of others. He can have no opinion of his own about anything that does not pertain to the physical details of his daily life. A scribe has access to libraries, his heart expands, he is able to judge the past and form the future."

At the age of four, when I was three, Pa-ari was taken by Father to the temple school. Father himself could neither read nor write and had to rely on the village scribe to tally his crops for the annual taxing and tell him what he owed. We did not know what was in his mind when he took Pa-ari's hand and led him along the sun-baked track to Wepwawet's precincts. Perhaps he thought of nothing more than ensuring that his heir would not be cheated when it became his turn to plough the few fields supporting us. I remember standing in the doorway of our house and watching the two of them disappear into the white freshness of the early morning light. "Where is Father taking Pa-ari?" I asked my mother who was emerging behind me, a flax basket laden with washing in her arms. She paused, hefting the load onto her hip.

"To school," she replied. "Run back and fetch the natron, Thu, there's a good girl. We must get this done and then take the dough to the oven." But I did not stir.

"I want to go too," I said. She laughed.

"No, you do not," she said. "For one thing, you are too young. For another, girls do not go to school. They learn at home. Now hurry with the natron. I will start for the river."

By the time my mother had finished slapping the wash on the rocks beside the water, rubbing the coarse linen with natron while she gossiped with the other women who had gathered, my father had returned and gone back to the fields. I saw him bending, hoe in hand, green spears of wheat brushing his naked calves, as I trailed after my mother up the path from the river to the house. I helped her drape the washing over the line strung in our reception hall, open to the sky like all the others in the village, and then watched her fold and pound the dough for our evening meal. I was quiet, thinking, missing Pa-ari who had filled my days with games and small adventures among the papyrus fronds and weeds of the riverbank.

When my mother set off for the communal oven I ran in the opposite direction, left the track that meandered beside the river and followed the narrow irrigation canal that watered father's few acres. As I drew near he straightened and smiled, shading his eyes with one broad, calloused hand. I came up to him, panting.

"Is something wrong?" he asked. I flung my arms around

his solid thigh and hugged him. For some reason that memory has survived in me, bright and vivid after all these years. Often it is not the momentous occasions that cling, the times when we say to ourselves—I will remember this for as long as I live—but tiny, inconsequential happenings that flick past unremarked, only to surface time and again, becoming infused with greater reality as time draws us further from the original event. So it was for me then. I can still feel the soft mat of hair on his sun-blackened skin against my face, see the faintly stirring carpet of young crops so green against the further beige of a desert shimmering in the sun, smell his sweat, reassuring, safe. I stepped back and gazed up at him.

"I want to go to school with Pa-ari," I said. He bent, and taking a corner of his short, soil-powdered kilt, wiped his forehead.

"No," he replied.

"Next year, Father, when I am four?"

His slow smile widened. "No, Thu. Girls do not go to school."

I studied his face. "Why not?"

"Because girls stay at home and learn from their mothers how to be good wives and tend babies. When you are older your mother will teach you how to help babies come into the world. That will be your work, here in the village." I frowned, trying to understand. An idea occurred to me.

"Father, if I ask Pa-ari, could he stay home and learn to help babies come and I can go to school instead of him?"

My father seldom laughed, but on that day he threw back his head and his mirth echoed against the row of wilting palm trees that grew between his land and the village track. He squatted and enfolded my chin in his large fingers. "Already I pity the lad who sues for you in marriage!" he said. "You must learn your place, my little sweetheart. Patience, docility, humility, these are the virtues of a good

woman. Now be a good girl and run home. Keep your
mother company when she goes to fetch Pa-ari." He planted
a kiss on the top of my hot head and turned away. I did as I
was told, scuffing the dirt as I went, obscurely insulted at his
laughter, though I was too young to know why.

I found my mother peering anxiously down the path, a
basket on her arm. She gestured to me impatiently as I came
up to her. "Leave your father alone when he's working!" she
said sharply. "Gods, Thu, you are filthy and there is no time
to wash you. Whatever will the priests think? Come." She
did not reach for my hand, but together we walked past our
acres, past other fields, all thick with crops, the wandering
line of palms on our left, the tangled river growth on our
right, cool and inviting, with the wide reaches of the silver
river glimpsed intermittently through it.

After some minutes the fields stopped abruptly, the shrubs
to our right straggled into nothing, and Wepwawet's temple
was there, its sandstone pillars soaring to the unrelieved
blue of the sky, the sun beating impotently on its walls.
From the time of my birth I had come here on the God's
feast days, watching my father present our offerings, pros-
trating myself beside Pa-ari as the incense rose in shimmering columns above the closed inner court. I had watched the
priests moving in solemn procession, their chants falling
deep and awesome in the still air. I had seen the dancers
swirl and dip, the systra in their delicate fingers tinkling to
draw the God's attention to our prayers. I had sat on the
temple watersteps, my toes in the gently sucking Nile, my
back to the paved forecourt while my parents were inside
with their petitions. To me it was both a place of exotic
mystery, forbidding in its secrecy, and the focus of Ma'at in
our lives, the spiritual loom to which the various threads of
our life were firmly attached. The rhythm of the God's days
was our rhythm, an invisible pulse that regulated the ebb
and flow of village and family affairs.

During the time of the troubles a band of foreigners had come. They had camped in the outer court, set huge fires in the inner court. They drank and caroused in the temple, torturing and killing one of the priests who tried to protest, but they had not dared to violate the sanctuary, the place none of us had even seen, the place where the God lived, for Wepwawet was the Lord of War and they feared his displeasure. The village headman and all the adult men had armed themselves in righteous anger and had descended upon the brigands one night as they slept beneath Wepwawet's beautiful pillars. The women spent the following morning washing the stones free of their blood and no man would ever tell where the bodies were buried. Our males were proud and brave, fit followers of the Lord of War. The High Priest had made a sacrifice of apology and restoration, reconsecrating the holy building. This was before my father and his troop camped beyond the village and went in search of beer.

I loved the temple. I loved the harmony of the pillars that led the eye up to Egypt's vast heaven. I loved the formality of the rituals; the odour of flowers, dust and incense; the sheer luxury of space; the fine, floating linens of the priests. I did not realize it then, but my appreciation was not for the God himself but for the richness that surrounded him. Of course I was his loyal daughter, I have always been that, yet I cared less for him than for a glimpse of a different existence that set me to dreaming.

We turned onto the paving and made our way across it, my mother and I, passing between the pillars and into the outer court. Several other mothers waited there, some standing, some squatting on the stone, talking quietly. The outer perimeter of the court was honeycombed with small rooms, and from the dimness of one of them came the sound of boys' voices raised in a sonorous chant that broke into an excited babble as my mother and I came to a halt. She greeted the women cheerfully and they nodded to her.

Presently a tumble of children disgorged from the chamber. Each carried a drawstringed bag. Pa-ari came up to us panting, his eyes alight. Something clinked in the bag. "Mother, Thu!" he shouted. "It was fun! I liked it!" He collapsed onto the floor, folding his legs under him, and Mother and I settled beside him. Mother opened her basket, producing black bread and barley beer. Pa-ari accepted his meal gravely and we began to eat. Other mothers, sons and smaller children were doing the same. The court was alive with chatter.

As we were finishing, a lector priest approached, his shaven skull gleaming in the noon sun, the gold of his armband sparkling. His feet were impossibly clean in his white sandals. I stared at him, bemused. I had never been so close to one of the God's servants before. It was some time before I recognized the scribe who farmed land on the eastern side of the village. I had seen him topped with curly brown hair, streaked with the mud of the Inundation, I had seen him weaving his way down the village street, drunk and singing. I knew later that the God's men were also farmers like my father, giving three months out of every year to temple service, wearing fine linen, washing four times a day, shaving all body hair regularly, performing the rites and duties appointed by the High Priest. My mother scrambled to her feet and bowed to him, signalling to us to do the same. I managed to describe a clumsy little obeisance. I could not take my eyes off the black kohl around his eyes, the bony surface of his skull. He smelled very good. He greeted us kindly, and put a hand on Pa-ari's shoulder.

"You have an intelligent son there," he said to my mother. "He will be a good student. I am happy to be teaching him."

My mother smiled. "Thank you," she answered. "My husband will come tomorrow with the payment."

The priest shrugged lightly. "There is no hurry," he said. "None of us is going anywhere."

For some reason his words touched me with cold. I reached up and tentatively drew a finger down the wide blue lector's sash that enfolded his chest.

"I want to come to school," I said timidly. He gave me a brief glance but ignored my words.

"I will see you tomorrow, Pa-ari," he said and turned away. My mother gave me a little shake.

"You must learn not to put yourself forward, Thu," she snapped. "Pick up the scraps now and put them in the basket. We must be getting home. Don't forget your bag, Pa-ari." We began to straggle out of the court, joining the thin stream of other families wending their way back to the village. I sidled close to my brother.

"What's in the bag, Pa-ari?" I asked. He held it up and shook it.

"My lessons," he said importantly. "We paint them on pieces of broken pottery. I have to study them tonight before I go to bed so I can repeat them in class tomorrow."

"Can I see them?"

My mother, doubtless hot and irritable, answered for him. "No you cannot! Pa-ari, run ahead and tell your father to come in for his food. When we get home you are both taking a nap."

So it began. Pa-ari would leave for school at dawn every day, and at noon my mother and I would meet him with his bread and beer. On God's days and holidays he did not study. He and I would slip away to the river or back onto the desert, playing the games that children devise. He was good humoured, my brother, seldom disappointing me when I made him pretend to be Pharaoh so that I could be his queen, trailing about in a tattered, discarded length of linen with leaves twined in my hair and a vine tendril into which I would tuck stray birds' feathers around my neck. He sat on a rock for a throne and made pronouncements. I issued commands to imaginary servants. Sometimes we tried to draw the other children into our fantasies but they quickly became bored, leaving us in order to swim or beg rides on the patient village donkeys. If they did join in, they complained bitterly that I was always the queen, and they did not get a turn to order me about. So Pa-ari and I amused each other, and the months slipped by.

When I became four, I once again begged my father to let me go to school and was again met with a firm denial. He could ill afford to let Pa-ari attend, he said. The fee for me was out of the question and besides, what girl ever learned anything useful outside her own home? I sulked for a while, sitting sullenly in a corner of our reception room, watching my brother's head bent over his bits of pottery, his shadow moving on the wall behind him as the lamp's flame guttered and swayed. He did not want to play Pharaoh and his queen any more. He was forming a bond with some of the village boys with whom he shared the schoolroom and often he would get up from the afternoon sleep and vanish, joining them as they fished or hunted rats in the granaries. I was lonely, and envious, but I was eight years old before it occurred to me that if I could not go to school the school might come to me.

By then my mother had me firmly in hand. I was learning to prepare the bread that was our staple, to make soups with lentils and beans, to broil fish and prepare vegetables. I did our laundry with her, stamping on my father's kilts and our thick sheath dresses, slapping the linen briskly on the glistening rocks, enjoying the showers of water that flicked against my hot skin, the feel of the Nile silt between my toes. I rendered tallow for the lamps. I mastered her fine bone needles, mending my father's kilts with meticulous care. I went with her when she visited her friends, sitting cross-legged on the dirt floors of their tiny reception rooms and sipping the one cup of palm wine she would allow me while she gossiped and laughed, discussing who was pregnant again, whose daughter was being courted by whose son, how the local tax assessor's wife had sat too close to the head-man's son, the hussy! The voices would flow over and around me, encasing me in a kind of stupor so that I often felt I had been there for ever, that the quiver of dark liquid in my cup, the grit under my thighs, the slow rivulet of sweat coursing down my neck, were all parts of a spell hold-ing me prisoner. Several of the women were heavily preg-nant and I stared furtively at their misshapen bodies. They were part of the spell also, magic that would keep me one of them always.

Sometimes my mother was summoned to deliver a baby during the hours of darkness. I paid little heed to those infrequent disturbances. I would vaguely hear her exchange a hurried word with my father and leave our house before I settled deeper into a contented sleep. But just after my eighth Naming Day my apprenticeship with her began. One night I opened my eyes to find her bending over my pallet, a candle in her hand. Pa-ari was curled asleep on his side of the room, oblivious. There were whispered voices out in the reception room. "Get up, Thu," she told me kindly. "I am bidden to Ahmose's confinement. This is my task and one day it will be yours also. You are old enough now to help me and thus begin to learn the duties of a midwife. You need not be afraid," she added as I struggled up, fumbling for my sheath. "The birth will be straightforward. Ahmose is young and healthy. Come now."

I staggered after her, still in my dreams. Ahmose's husband squatted in a corner of the reception room looking uneasy and my father, bleary eyed, squatted with him. My mother paused to retrieve the bag that always sat in readiness by the door and went out. I followed. The air was cool, the moon riding high in a cloudless sky, the palms spiking tall against the dimness. "We should get a live goose and a bolt of linen out of this," my mother commented. I did not reply.

Ahmose's house, like all the rest, was little more than an open-roofed reception room with steps at the rear leading to sleeping quarters. As we padded in our bare feet through the door, we were greeted distractedly by the woman's mother and sisters who lined the walls, squatting on their heels, a jug of wine between them. My mother shared a joke with them as she led me up the steps and into the couple's bed-chamber. The small mud brick room was cosy with a woven rug on the floor and hangings on the walls. A large stone lamp burned by the pallet on which Ahmose crouched, a loose linen shift folded about her. She looked different from the young, smiling woman I knew. There was a sheen of sweat on her forehead and her eyes were huge. She reached out a hand as my mother set her bag on the floor and approached her.

"There is no need to panic, Ahmose," my mother said to her soothingly, taking the clutching fingers in her own. "Lie down now. Thu, come here."

I obeyed most unwillingly. My mother took my hand and placed it on Ahmose's distended abdomen. "There is the baby's head. Can you feel it? Very low. That is good. And here his little buttock. This is as it should be. Can you discern the shape?" I nodded, both fascinated and repelled by the feel of the shiny, taut skin stretched over the mysterious hill beneath. As I withdrew I saw a slow ripple pass over it and Ahmose gasped and groaned, drawing up her knees. "Breathe deeply," my mother commanded, and when the contraction was over she asked Ahmose how long she had been in labour.

"Since dawn," came the reply. Mother opened her bag and withdrew a clay pot. The refreshing odour of peppermint filled the little room as she removed the stopper, and briskly but gently pushing Ahmose onto her side she massaged the contents into the woman's firm buttocks. "This will hasten the birth," she said to me as I stood beside her.

"Now you may squat, Ahmose. Try to remain calm. Talk to me. What is the news from your sister upriver? Is all well with her?"

Ahmose struggled into a squatting position on the pallet, her back resting against the mud wall. She spoke haltingly, pausing when the contractions gripped her. My mother prompted her, watching all the time for signs of any change, and I watched her too, the huge, frightened eyes, the bulge of veins in her neck, the straining, swollen body.

This is part of the spell also, I thought with a surge of fear as the feeble light from the lamp played on the figure crouched in the corner, trembling and occasionally crying out. This is another room in the prison. At eight years old I was probably too young to have actually expressed in those words the emotion that flooded me, but I remember sharply and clearly the way it tasted, the way my heart lurched for a moment. This was to be my lot in life, to coax terrified women in dim village hovels in the middle of the night, to rub their buttocks, to insert medicaments into their vaginas as my mother was now doing. "That was a mixture of fennel, incense, garlic, sert-juice, fresh salt and wasp's dung," she was instructing me over her shoulder. "It is one remedy for causing delivery. There are others but they are less efficacious. I will teach you to blend them all, Thu. Come now, Ahmose, you are doing very well. Think how proud your husband will be when he returns home to see his new son cradled in your arms!"

"I hate him," Ahmose said venomously. "I never want to see him again."

I thought my mother would be shocked but she ignored the words. My legs were shaking. I slid to sit cross-legged on the warm mud floor. Two or three times Ahmose's mother or one of her sisters would peer in at us, exchange a few words with my mother, and go away again. I lost track of the passage of time. It began to seem to me that I had been drifting in this ante-room to the Underworld for ever, with the sweet and pleasant Ahmose now transformed into a demented spirit and my mother's shadow looming distorted over her like some malevolent demon. My mother's voice broke the illusion. "Come here!" she ordered me. I scrambled up and hurried over to her reluctantly and she handed me a thick linen cloth and told me to hold it beneath Ahmose. "Look," she said. "The crown of the baby's head. Push now, Ahmose! It is time!" With a last wail Ahmose did as she was told and the baby slithered into my unwilling hands. It was yellow and red with body fluids. I knelt there stupidly, staring at it as it flailed its little limbs. My mother tapped it smartly and it let out a breathless howl and began to cry. She passed it carefully to Ahmose, who was already smiling weakly and reaching for it. As she settled it against her breast it turned its head, blindly nuzzling for food. "You need not worry," my mother said. "It cried 'ni ni,' not 'na na.' It will live. And it is a boy, Ahmose, perfectly formed. Well done!" She swept up a knife, and I saw the pulsing cord in her slimed fingers. I had had enough. With a mumbled word I left the room. The women outside sprang up as I pushed past them. "It's a boy," I managed, and they surged towards the stairs with shrieks of joy as I fell into the cool, vast air of dawn.

I stood leaning against the wall of the house, eagerly sucking up the clean odour of vegetable growth and dusty sand and a faint whiff of the river. "Never!" I whispered to the greying, palm-brushed sky. "Never!" I did not know what I meant by the vehement word, but in a confused way it had something to do with cages and fate and the long traditions of my people. I ran my fingers down my boyish chest, across my concave little stomach under the enveloping sheath, as though to reassure myself that my flesh was still my own. I dug my bare toes into the film of sand that always drifted in from the desert. I gulped at the tiny wind presaging the slow

rising of Ra. Behind me I heard the women's voices, chattering excitedly and incomprehensibly, and the baby's intermittent thin protests. Soon my mother came out, bag in
hand, and in the first light of the day I saw her smile at me.

"She is worried about the flow of her milk," she remarked
as we set off for home. "All mothers share the same concerns. I left a bottle of ground swordfish bone with her, to be
warmed in oil and applied to her spine. But she need not
worry. She has always been very healthy. Well, Thu," she
beamed. "What did you think? Is it not a wonderful experience, helping to bring new life into the world? When you
have attended more births, I will allow you to minister to
my women yourself. And soon I will show you how to com-
bine the medicines I use. You will become as proud of your
work as I am."

I gazed ahead to the quiet ribbon of the path with its line
of trees now swiftly gaining definition as Ra prepared to
burst over the horizon. "Mama, why did she say she hated
her husband?" I asked hesitantly. "I thought they were
happy together."

My mother laughed. "All women in labour curse their
husbands," she said matter-of-factly. "It is because their husbands are the cause of the pain that traps them. But as soon
as the pain stops they forget how they suffered and they welcome their men back to their beds with as much eagerness
as before."

Traps them... I thought with a shudder. Other women
might forget the pain but I know I never will. And I know I
will not make a good midwife though I will try. "I want to
learn about the medicines," I said, and did not need to go
on, for my mother stopped walking and bent to hug me.
"Then you shall, my blue-eyed darling. Then you shall," she
said triumphantly.

I did not realize until much later how profoundly the
experience of that night served to focus the discontent with

which, I am certain, I was born. All I knew at the time was that I was repulsed by the sheer animality of childbirth, did not envy Ahmose the life of constant care the arrival of the baby would mean, and shied away from the deep stirrings of panic the event represented. I felt guilty because my mother seemed delighted at my interest in the whole process, an interest that did not extend beyond a fascination for the potions, salves and elixirs she mixed and brewed as part of her profession. Of course I felt proud when she ushered me into the tiny room my father had built onto our house where she measured out her herbs and prepared her concoctions, but the pride was a part of my whole urgent need to learn, to acquire knowledge, for knowledge, as Pa-ari had said, was power. That little room was always redolent with the aroma of fragrant oils, of honey and incense and the bitter tang of crushed plants.

My mother could neither read nor write. She worked by eye and hand, a pinch of this, a spoonful of that, as she had learned from her mother. I would sit on a stool and watch and listen, filing everything away. I continued to attend village births with her, carrying her bag and soon passing her the medicines required before she even asked for them, but my distaste for the process of parturition never left me, and, unlike her, I remained unmoved at a child's first cry. I have often wondered if there was some serious lack in my make-up, some gentle component of femininity that did not take root when I was myself in the womb. I struggled with my guilt and tried very hard to please my mother because of it.

I soon became aware that my mother's work entailed more than just the task of midwife. Women slipped into our home for other reasons, some of them whispered furtively into my mother's understanding ears. She did not discuss specific secrets with me but spoke about them in general ways.

"An abortion may be procured by a crushed mixture of dates, onions and acanthus fruit steeped in honey and applied to the vulva," she told me, "but I think that this treatment must be supported by a potion of harsh beer, castor oil and salt drunk at the same time as the outward salve is used. Be very careful if you are asked to prescribe for this, Thu. Many wives come to me for such a purpose without the knowledge and consent of their husbands. As my first duty is to the wives I do my best to satisfy them, but you must always be able to keep their requests to yourself. It is better to prevent conception than deal with it after the damage is done."

My ears pricked up at this. "How can you prevent such a happening?" I asked her, trying not to sound too eager.

"Not easily," she retorted, unaware of the importance of my question. "I usually suggest a thick syrup of honey and auyt gum in which acacia tips have been soaked. Crush the acacia first, and after three days, throw them away and insert the syrup into the vagina." She gave me an oblique glance. "This can wait," she said abruptly. "You must learn to assist the beginnings of life before you study how to prevent it. Give me the pestle resting in that dish, then go and see if your father has come in from the field and wants to wash."

I think that my father must have compelled her to take her own advice, for not long after this conversation with my mother I heard her and my father arguing one night when I could not sleep for the heat of Shemu. Their voices had begun as a low murmur and then risen in anger and I listened while Pa-ari snored.

"We have a son and a daughter," my father said sharply. "It is enough."

"But Pa-ari wants to be a scribe not a farmer. Who then will till the soil when you are too feeble? And as for Thu, she will marry and take the skills I am teaching her into her husband's household." I could hear the fear rise in her, being expressed as anger, and her tone grew shrill. "There will be no one to care for us in our old age and I would be ashamed to trust to the kindness of our friends! I obey you, my husband. I do not become pregnant. Yet I grieve for the emptiness of my womb!"

"Hush, woman," my father commanded in the way that prompted immediate obedience from us all. "I do not plant enough crops on my three arouras to support more mouths. We are poor but we have dignity. Fill the house with children and we increase our poverty while sacrificing what little independence we enjoy. Besides..." His voice fell and I had to strain to catch the words. "What makes you think Aswat is as peaceful and secure as it seems? Like all women you see no further than the path to the river where you carry the washing, and your ears open only to the gossip of the other wives. The men here are not much better. They direct the pedlars and wandering workmen to the women, to buy or to hire, and do not listen to their tales, for they are insular and suspicious of all who were not born here. But I have seen this Egypt. I do not spurn the strangers who come and go. I know that the eastern tribesmen are trickling into the Delta, trying to find land for their flocks and herds, and in the Delta there is trouble. It may come to nothing, or it may mean that the Good God may call upon all his soldiers to leave their fields and defend their country. How would you fare then, with babies to feed and your midwifery to perform as well? If I was killed the land would revert to Pharaoh, for as you say, Pa-ari is not likely to follow in my footsteps. Ponder my words with your mouth closed, for I am weary and need to sleep." I heard my mother mutter something else and give a resigned sigh, and then there was silence.

When my father's voice had died away I lay on my back, gazing into the pressing dark heat of the little room, and imagined the foreigners he had spoken of sifting slowly across the fertile soil of the Delta, a place I had never seen and barely heard of, spreading out, oozing southward along the Nile towards my village like the black mud of the Inundation. The vivid picture excited me. Suddenly Aswat shrank in my mind from being the centre of the world to a very small backwater in a threatening vastness, yet I did not feel lost or in danger. I wondered what they were like, these sinister people, what the Delta was like, what blessed Thebes, home of Amun the King of the Gods was like, and I was in a boat floating down the Nile towards the Good God's fabled northern capital when I fell asleep at last.

Chapter 2

As I have said, I was eight years old when the inspiration came to me that if I could not go to school, the school should come to me. It was at about the same time that I began to work with my mother and my days were full of obligatory household chores but the need to learn was a constant ache, a kind of mild desperation that returned to nag at me in the few idle moments I had. My plan was simple. Pa-ari would teach me. He must know almost everything there was to know by now, seeing that he had been trudging along to the temple school for five years. One afternoon when our house and indeed the whole village drowsed under the fierce heat of Ra's summer scorching and Pa-ari and I were supposed to be resting, I dragged my pallet close to his and peered into his face. He was not asleep. He was lying on his back, both hands behind his head, and his eyes had followed my movements in the half-light. He smiled at me as I bent over him.

"No, I won't tell you a story," he said loudly. "It's too hot. Why can't you sleep, Thu?"

"Keep your voice down," I told him, settling back. "I don't want a story today. I want a big, big favour from you, dear Pa-ari."

"Oh gods," he groaned, rolling onto his side and propping himself on one elbow. "When you use that wheedling tone of voice I know I'm in trouble. What is it?"

I studied him as he continued to smile at me indulgently, this brother whom I adored, this lordly young male who had begun to make pronouncements in Father's assured way that brooked no argument. I kept no secrets from him. He knew how much I disliked helping Mother with birthings, how fascinated I was with her potions, how lonely I felt when the other village girls turned from me with smirks and giggles on the few occasions when I tried to play with them. He knew also of my need to be the daughter of a long-lost Libu prince out of that same loneliness. I assumed no haughty airs with him and he, in turn, treated me with a gentleness unusual between brother and sister. I touched his naked shoulder.

"I want to be able to read and write," I said, the words tumbling out in a breathless spate of anxiety and embarrassment. "Show me how, Pa-ari. It won't take you long, I promise!"

He stared at me, taken aback, and then his smile broadened. "Don't be silly," he chided. "Such learning is not for girls. It's precious. My teacher says that words are sacred, that the world and all laws and all history came from the pronunciation of divine words by the gods, and some of that force remains enclosed in hieroglyphs. What use would such power be to an apprentice midwife?"

I could almost taste the things he was saying, feel the excitement of such mastery. "But what if I don't become a midwife?" I said urgently. "What if one day a rich merchant is going by in his golden boat and his servants lose an oar and they have to put up overnight right here at Aswat, and I'm down on the bank doing the washing or even swimming and he sees me and falls in love with me and I marry him and then later his scribe falls ill and there is no one to take down his letters? Dearest Thu, he might say, take up the scribe's palette, and then I am struck dumb with shame, for I am nothing but a poor village girl without learning and I can see the scorn on his face!" I was quite carried away with my own story. I felt the shame, saw my unknown husband's pity, but then all at once my throat dried up. For part of the story was true. I was indeed a poor village girl without learning, and the realization was like a stone growing heavy in my heart. "I am sorry, Pa-ari," I whispered. "Teach me, I beg you, because I want to understand the things you know more than anything on this earth. Even if I remain nothing but a village midwife, your labour would not be wasted. Please."

A silence fell between us. I looked down at my hands lying curled in my lap and I knew he was regarding me steadily. I could almost hear his thoughts, so motionless was his body.

"I am still only a nine-year-old schoolboy," he said quietly after a while, speaking without moving. "I am nothing more than the son of a soldier farmer. Yet I am the best student in my class and if I choose I can go to work for the priests of Wepwawet when I turn sixteen. The written word will assure me a position as a scribe if I want it one day. But what would the written word do to you?" He reached across the dimness and took my hand. "Already you are not satisfied, Thu. Such knowledge will only hurt you further."

I grasped his fingers and shook them. "I want to read! I want to know things! I want to be like you, Pa-ari, not help-less, without choices, condemned to stay in Aswat for the rest of my life! Give me the power!"

Helpless...condemned... These were adult words coming from some part of me that did not know I was only eight years old, unformed and gangly and still in awe of the giants who ruled my world. Tears of frustration came to my eyes. My voice had risen and this time it was Pa-ari who warned me to be quiet with a swift finger to his lips.

Wrenching his hand free he held it up in the universal gesture of submission.

"All right!" he hissed. "All right. May the gods forgive me for such an act of foolishness. I will teach you."

I wriggled with joy, my earlier misery forgotten. "Oh thank you, dearest!" I said fervently. "Can we begin now?"

"In here? In the dark?" he sighed. "Honestly, Thu, you are tiresome. We will begin tomorrow, and in secret. While Mother and Father sleep we will go down to the river and sit in the shade, and I will draw the characters for you in the sand. Then you can see my pieces of pottery, but Thu," he warned, "if you do not concentrate I will not bother with you for very long. Now go to sleep."

Happily, obediently, I pulled my pallet back to its place and collapsed on it. Now I was engulfed in weariness, as though I had walked a long way, and it was the greatest pleasure to close my eyes and surrender to unconsciousness. Pa-ari's breathing had already deepened. I had never loved him more.

I prayed constantly and incoherently through the following morning that no village baby would choose that afternoon to be born, that I would not have to wait to use one of the communal ovens to bake the bread for our evening meal and thus fall behind with my other work, that Pa-ari would have a good morning at school and not be too grumpy and tired after his barley cake and beer to keep his word. But all went well on that momentous day in the middle of the month of Epophi. He and I paraded meekly to our room and sat tensely waiting for our parents to succumb to the stupor of the hour. It seemed to take a long time before their intermittent comments ceased and Pa-ari signalled me to get up while he carefully lifted the bag that held his precious bits of clay so that the pieces did not clink. Together we stole out of the house into the blinding white heat beating up at us from the deserted village street.

Nothing stirred. Even the three desert dogs, the colour of the beige sand that had spawned them, were sprawled motionless under the thin shade of a straggling acacia bush, their endless hunt for food forgotten. The portals of the crude grey houses were dark and empty. No birds sang or flitted in the drooping river growth and our bare feet made no sound as we ran towards the water. It was as though all living things but the two of us had been spirited away and the village would stand untenanted under Ra's dazzling bright gaze for ever.

The river had not yet begun to rise. It flowed beside us with a turgid majesty, brown and thick, its banks exposed, as we picked our way to a spot out of sight of the village and the road that ran between water and houses. There was no grass in the place where Pa-ari turned aside, only a hollow of soft sand beneath a sycamore. He lowered himself to the ground and I joined him, my heart racing with excitement. Our glances met.

"Are you sure?" he asked.

I nodded and swallowed, unable to answer aloud, and his head went down as he opened the drawstring of his bag and tipped its contents in a pile beside his knee.

"You must learn first the symbols of the gods," he told me solemnly. "It is a matter of respect, so pay attention. This is the totem of the goddess Ma'at, she who brings justice, and her feather stands for truth and the correct balance of law, order and rightness in the universe. Her feather is not to be confused with the Double Plumes of Amun, he who resides in great splendour and power at holy Thebes." He handed me a branch. "Draw for yourself now." And I did so, enthralled, captivated, and something inside me whispered, now you have it, Thu. Now it is here, within your grasp. Aswat is not your world any longer.

I learned quickly, soaking up the information as though my soul had been the parched, cracked earth of Egypt itself and Pa-ari's symbols the vivifying deluge of the Inundation. I mastered twenty names of the gods that day and I pictured them in my mind as I went about the evening's tasks, whispering them to myself over the lentils and dried figs I was helping my mother prepare for our meal until she said tartly, "If you are speaking to me, Thu, I can't hear you, and if you are saying your prayers I wish you would wait until your father lights the candle before the shrine. You look tired, child. Are you well?"

Yes, I was well. I hurried through my meal, earning another reprimand from Father, for all I wanted to do was climb onto my pallet as soon as possible so that I could sleep, and make the next afternoon come all the faster. That night I dreamed the symbols, all golden and glittering as they swept across my vision, and I summoned and dismissed them at will as though they were my servants.

I did not lose that enthusiasm. As day followed day, Epophi giving way to Mesore and then the New Year and the blessed rising of the flood water, and I realized that I was not going to fall ill, the gods were not going to punish me for my presumption, Pa-ari was not going to abandon me, I ceased to gulp frenetically at my lessons. Pa-ari was a patient teacher. The jumble of beautiful, closely packed signs on his pottery pieces began to make sense and I was soon able to chant to him the ancient maxims and nuggets of wisdom of which they were composed. "A man's ruin lies in his tongue." "Learn from the ignorant as well as from the wise man, for there are no limits that have been decreed for art. There is no artist who attains entire excellence." "Spend no day in idleness or you will be flogged."

Writing them was a different matter. I had no paint and no pottery. Pa-ari's teacher dispensed such things at the temple school and collected what was not used after class and Pa-ari refused to try and steal the tools I needed. "I would be disgraced and expelled if I was caught," he objected when I suggested stuffing a few extra bits of clay into his bag. "I will not do it, even for you. Why can't you use a stick and some smooth wet sand?" I could, of course, and I did, but with bad grace. Nor could I draw the characters with my right hand. I reached for everything with my left including the stick, and after seeing the results when I tried to use my other hand,

Pa-ari gave up trying to force me to change. I was a clumsy, laborious writer but I persevered, covering the banks of the Nile with hieroglyphs, practising with my finger on walls and floors, even drawing in the air as I lay on my pallet at sunset. Nothing else mattered. My mother exclaimed over my new docility. My father teased me because I fell so often into silent reveries. I had indeed become biddable and quiet. I was no longer so restless and dissatisfied, for the realities of my outward life were completely subordinate to my inward existence.

I no longer cared that the village girls shunned me. I felt superior to them, hugging my precious literacy to myself like some magic talisman that could protect me from every threat. The small ceremonies that made up our daily life— the marriages and deaths, gods' feast and fast days, births and illnesses and scandals—were no longer manifestations of my prison. When I accompanied my mother to visit her friends, to drink palm wine and listen to the women's chatter and laughter, I did not feel trapped. I had only to withdraw a little in my mind, to go on smiling and nodding at them while I silently spelled out the names of the herbs I had crushed and steeped for my mother's salve that morning, and I would watch her berry-brown, animated face while she told some story, watch her broad smile come and go, watch the lines around her eyes crinkle, and think, I know more than you do. I do not need to be sent to the herb-gatherer to say the name of the plant you barter for. If I wanted I could write the name, and the number of leaves, and the price I expected to pay, and then I could go and dangle my feet in the Nile while I waited for a reply. Yes, I was arrogant, but it was not the cold arrogance of spite or assumed importance. I did not imagine myself to be better than the family I loved or the women who passed in and out of our house with their jokes and their troubles, their courage and their uncomplaining stoicism. I was different, that was all. I had always been different, as Pa-ari knew himself to be different, and that awareness made me all too eager to secretly flaunt the thing that hid my insecurity.

So the time went by. When he was thirteen and I was twelve Pa-ari graduated from pottery and paint to papyrus and ink, and on that day my father gave him a man's kilt of snowy white linen of the sixth grade that had come all the way from the flax weavers' market in holy Thebes. The linen was so fine that it clung to my admiring fingers as I handled it. "You may wear it to school," father told him with, I thought, a tinge of sadness. "Beautiful things should be used, not laid away for special occasions. But learn to clean it properly, Pa-ari, and it will last a long time." Pa-ari embraced our father, then stood back awkwardly.

"I am sorry that I love words more than the soil," he said, and I saw that his fists were clenched behind his back. Father shrugged.

"There is no need to be," he replied gently. "Blood will out, my son, or so they say. Your grandmother was a word-woman, and wrote and told stories. If the Good God calls me to war again I will bring back a slave to work the land."

"Who did she tell the stories to?" I broke in, enthralled with this unexpected revelation, but I might as well have saved my breath. Father smiled that slow, enigmatic smile of his and ruffled my hair.

"Why, to the members of her family of course," he said, "but do not imagine that we need to hear any stories, my Thu. Midwifery and healing are more useful skills for a woman than the ability to entertain."

I did not agree but dared not say so. I took Pa-ari's kilt and held it to my face, marvelling at the tightness of its warp and woof. "It is worthy of a prince's body," I whispered, and my father heard me.

"It is indeed," he agreed, pleased, "but know, Thu, that there are five grades above this and the linen worn in the

King's house is so light that one can see the outline of limbs through it." My mother sniffed loudly, my father laughed and kissed her, and Pa-ari snatched his prize and retired to wrap it on.

Later, when we had swum and eaten and then wandered out behind the village to watch Ra set over the desert, he unrolled his first lesson on papyrus from its thick linen covering and spread it out on the sand for me. "It is a prayer to Wepwawet," he told me proudly. "I think I have done it very neatly. The scribe's pen is much easier to use than the thicker paint brushes. My teacher has promised me that soon I may be allowed to sit at his feet outside the classroom and take dictation for him. He will pay me! Think of that!"

"Oh, Pa-ari!" I exclaimed, running my fingers over the smooth, dry surface of the paper. "How wonderful!" The letters, graceful and symmetrical, were as black as night but the light of the westering sun that flooded the surrounding desert was dyeing the papyrus the colour of blood. I rolled up his work carefully and handed it back. "You will be a great scribe," I told him, "honest and clever. Wepwawet will have a jewel of a servant in you."

He grinned back at me and then lifted his face to the hot evening breeze that had sprung up. "I might be able to get you some papyrus of your own," he said. "Once I begin to work for my teacher I will be supplied with enough to carry out my duties, and if I write very small there will be an occasional sheet left over. If not, I can perhaps buy you some. Or you can buy your own." He lifted a handful of sand and dribbled it over his bare shins. "Doesn't Mother sometimes share her payments with you, now that you have become so proficient at your job?"

His question was completely innocent, yet all at once the old familiar feeling of despair rose up in me with such speed that I began to tremble, and with it came a sudden sensuous awareness of everything around me. The splendour of Ra's glorious colour, red-orange against the churned hillocks of the endless sand; the unscented, dry wind that teased my hair away from my face and blew tiny grains from Pa-ari's idle fingers to cling to my crumpled sheath; the sound of my brother's quiet breathing and the rise and fall of his chest—all these things combined with a panic that made me want to jump up and begin to run, run away across the desert, run into the greedy, flushed arms of Ra and so perish. "Gods," I blurted, and Pa-ari glanced at me sharply.

"Thu, what is it?"

I could not answer. My heart was thudding painfully, my hands jerking, half-buried in sand. Grimly I fought to regain my composure, and when the emotion began to ebb I put my forehead against my knees.

"I'm twelve years old," I said, my voice muffled against my own warm skin. "Nearly thirteen, Pa-ari. What stupid dream have I been wandering in? I became a woman several months ago and Mother and I went to the temple with the sacrifice and I was so proud. So was she. Before long you'll be having your own babies, she said to me, and still I thought nothing of it." I lifted my head and met his eyes. "What use has it been to me, all this learning? I was so caught up in the wonder of it, the joy of mastering. The prison doors are opening, I told myself, but not once did I pause to ask what lay beyond." I laughed harshly. "We both know what lies beyond, don't we, Pa-ari? Another prison. Payment, yes. Mother often rewards me. I mix the medicines, I keep her bag filled and in order, I soothe the women and wash the babies and bind the umbilical cords and all the time I am studying with you, I am learning so much..." I gripped his arm. "One day some young man from the village will come to our door with gifts in his hands and Father will say to me, so-and-so has sued for you, he has this many arouras or so many sheep, it will be a good match. What can I say?"

Pa-ari pulled himself out of my grip. "I don't understand what is happening," he protested. "You frighten me, Thu. When such a thing occurs, you say no, if it is not what you want."

"Do I?" I breathed. "I say no. And time goes by, and then another man appears, perhaps not quite so young as the first, and I say no again. How many times can I say no before the men stop coming to our door and I become the kind of woman the other women make fun of and scorn? The dried-up old crones who are a burden to their families and a disgrace to themselves?"

"Then at some moment you say yes, and resign yourself," Pa-ari said. "You have always known that your fate was to be the village midwife and, if you are lucky, to marry and enjoy the fruits of your labour with a good husband."

"Yes," I said slowly. "I have always known this, and yet not known it. Does that make sense to you, dear one? Not known it until now, this moment, here on the sand with you. I cannot bear it!"

He continued to regard me. "Then what do you want, Thu?" he enquired softly. "What else are you fitted for? It is too late to apply to the temple as one of Wepwawet's singers or dancers. You must start to dance at six years old and besides, the girls who dance do it because their mothers danced. This self-pity does you no credit. Life in the village is good." I ran a distracted hand through my hair and sighed. The terrible weight of despair was leaving me.

"Yes it is," I agreed, "but I don't want to spend the rest of my life here. I want to see Thebes, I want to wear fine linen, I want a husband who does more than come home covered in sweat and soil at the end of the day to eat lentils and fish. It is not a matter of riches!" I cried out passionately, seeing his expression. "I am not sure what it is, except that I must get away from here or I will die!"

A tiny smile came and went on his face and I knew that

for once he did not understand, could not share in the storm of apprehension that had whirled me about. His ambitions were small, comfortable and realistic. They suited his quiet temperament. Pa-ari was not given to idle dreaming. "Surely you exaggerate," he rebuked me mildly. "It will take more than the disappointment of a life lived here to kill you, Thu. You are an obdurate young woman." He scrambled to his feet and reached down to pull me up beside him. "Ra has descended into the mouth of Nut," he commented, "and we must go home before full darkness catches us. Do you have any plan that will deliver you from the so-smothering womb of Aswat?" His tone was bantering, so that I did not want to discuss the matter with him any more.

"No I don't," I replied shortly, and strode ahead of him, back towards the fields and down the dusky path that led into the evening quietness of the village.

But my cry of agony in the desert, genuine and unfeigned, did not go unnoticed by the invisible powers that govern our fates. Sometimes in life a moment of pure anguish rising from long turmoil can arrow with great force into the realm of the gods who pause in their mighty deliberations and turn towards the source of the disturbance. So it is Thu, they say. What ails the child? This is no ordinary grumble. Is she not happy with the fate decreed for her? Then let us weave for her another destiny. We will put before her the map of an alternative future so that she may choose it if she wishes. Thus unperceived dó the slow-wheeling fates reverse and begin to grind along another path, and we do not realize until the years behind us have lengthened that we have chosen to be carried with them into a new direction.

Of course I did not reason thus at the time. It was only later that I saw, I felt, the mysterious shifting that had been set in motion in my life by my desperate outburst that day. I resumed my studies with Pa-ari. What else could I do? Pointless or not, they were my drug, the balm with which I tried to soothe my indignation. Yet I believe that from that moment on my old destiny began to wither like a seedling pushed aside by the stronger, more ruthless thrusting of a tall weed, and my new one began to take shape.

Three months went by, and then one scorching afternoon I heard a piece of intriguing news. My mother and her closest friend were sitting outside our house in the shade cast by the wall, the beer jug between them next to a bowl of water into which they dipped squares of linen to cool themselves. I was stretched out some way from my mother, lying on a flaxen mat, my head propped on one elbow as I lazily watched them wring out the linen over their brown thighs, their sheaths rolled up around their hips and their arms glistening with water. Beyond us, across the baking expanse of the village square, the dusty river growth stood bowed and without a stir and I could not glimpse the river itself. I was in a dreaming, not unpleasant stupor induced by the heat and this precious, unaccustomed moment of sheer idleness. I had turned thirteen and my body had begun to acquire the first tentative curves of full womanhood to come. I was contemplating these changes, aware of the small valley damp with sweat between my breasts, the modest hill of my hip against which my other hand rested. The women's voices rose and fell, a pleasant litany of meaningless gossip in which I had little interest. Occasionally my mother passed the sopping linen to me and I drew it over my face but neither of them addressed me directly and I was glad. I sipped my own beer, my thoughts moving from the delights of my body to Pa-ari, kept late at school to take private dictation from his teacher, and then to my father who had gone to a meeting of the village elders. His crops had been harvested and the land lay dead in the summer fire. He was often bored during these months. He had never yet been summoned to work on one of Pharaoh's building projects for his bread and onions as so many were, but then the word from outside was that Egypt was still too impoverished to erect any great monuments. My mother and her friend were discussing the terrible famine that had cursed us during the time of the Syrian usurper Irsu, before the Good God Setnakht and his son Ramses, our present Incarnation and the third to hold that illustrious name, began to put the country back into the way of true Ma'at. The subject of the famine often came up in the summers, spoken of with worried speculation before the village women moved on to lighter topics.

"It was predicted, you know," my mother's friend was saying. "The oracle at Thebes warned the Osiris One and his evil foreign Viceroy before it happened, but I suppose there was such disorder in the country that no one took any notice. You don't care about famine when you are about to be slaughtered in your bed."

My mother gave a non-committal grunt and leaned back against the wall, wiping her neck and the depths of her considerable cleavage. I saw her eyes close. She disliked sensational conversation, preferring to dissect the small failings and harmless secrets of her neighbours.

"I hear that an oracle is coming to Aswat," the other woman went on, "a very famous Seer consulted by Pharaoh himself. He wants to commune with our own oracle, the Lord Wepwawet's I mean of course, here in our temple."

"What about?" my mother murmured with a sigh. Her eyes remained closed.

"Well it seems that Great Horus is building a fleet of ships to go trading to Punt and the Red Sea and even the Indian Ocean and with Wepwawet being a God of War the King needs to know whether or not it will be safe to send them out." She turned to my mother and spoke conspiratorially. "After all, Ramses has had to go to war three times in the last twelve years. He can't want his ships set upon when they're coming back, loaded with the treasure he so badly needs!"

My mother opened her eyes. "And how do you know what our Divine Incarnation needs?" she said sharply. "That is not our business. Finish your beer, impertinent one, and tell me how your sons are doing in school."

Her friend was not abashed. She was my mother's favourite companion because she could not be daunted. She had straightened and taken breath to resume the onslaught when I interrupted her.

"This Seer," I said. "When is he coming? How long will he stay? Will he give readings for the villagers as well as consulting with Wepwawet's oracle?" I was strangely excited, my lethargy gone.

She smiled at me, her teeth a sudden white flash in the bronze of her face. "I don't know," she admitted, "but my husband says he will come within the week. The priests have been cleaning and praying as though Pharaoh himself was going to appear. Ask Pa-ari. He'll be able to tell you more."

"Don't get any foolish ideas, Thu," my mother said easily. "Even if the man agrees to read for people here in the village, his fee will be high and you, my little bleating lamb, will not be considered." To soften her words she refilled my beer cup and gestured for me to drink. "You could hardly offer him your services as an apprentice midwife!"

I grimaced at her, shrugged in silent agreement, then drank, but my thoughts were suddenly busy. What could I offer such a man to induce him to gaze into my future and tell me once and for all whether I would ever leave this place? The women were laughing kindly at me, then they turned back to each other. My mother's friend said coyly, "I hear that a certain man came to see you late one night to obtain a handful of colocase. Oh I know you won't talk, my dear, but the implications are quite delicious."

I was not interested in the desire of the man in question to cure his sterility. I was no longer listening to the increasingly drowsy conversation. Rolling onto my back I put my hands behind my head and gazed up into the harsh blueness of the sky. I would have to confirm this snippet of information with Pa-ari, make sure it was not a tale that had grown larger and more distorted in the telling. And if it was true, what payment could I offer a mighty Seer? What would he accept? I had nothing of any value—three sheaths, a simple bone comb to hold back my hair, a necklet of yellow-painted clay beads, a pretty cedarwood box my father had brought home for me from Thebes one year and in which I kept a few precious things, feathers and oddly shaped stones that had caught my fancy, dried flowers and the shrivelled but still beautiful skin of a snake I had found beside a rock in the desert. I was sure that none of these would do. Idly I wondered what I could steal, but the thought was fleeting, not serious. Even the mayor of the village, rich by our standards, having a slave and ten arouras of land and three haughty daughters who flaunted their coloured linens and pretty hair ribbons, was poor beside the nobles and aristocrats who could pile gold and silver at the feet of such a man. I sighed. What could I do?

The shade was shrinking. Ra had moved in the heavens, and his hot fingers had begun to caress my feet, his touch both welcome and burning. I sat up and pulled in my knees. As I did so, an audacious idea came to me, an idea so scandalous that it took my breath away. I must have gasped, for my mother shot a glance at me. I stood, and not meeting her eye I said, "I will walk along the river path and meet Pa-ari." She did not protest, and I set off briskly across the blinding dust of the square.

Once under the thin shadow of the trees my pace slowed. I met no one on that suffocating, timeless afternoon, and if I had I would not have noticed them. What could I offer? Myself of course. My virginity. It was worthless to me anyway. I was not saving it for some worthwhile village simpleton,

for some undeserving husband, as the other girls were. I had
heard their whispers, seen their sidelong looks when one of
the boys swung past, light gleaming on his brown skin over
the muscles farm work kept taut. I saw further than they. I
saw those fine boys twenty, thirty years hence in the person
of their fathers, their clean muscles all knotted, their backs
bent, their hands gnarled and thickened and their faces
grooved by the remorseless sun and grinding labour. Only
my father, out of all the village men, seemed to care for his
body, drawing his bow and swimming purposefully in the
river so that his spine stayed straight and his muscles long.
Yet even he had begun to show the rigours of his life. No.
That was not for me. I would trade my body for a glimpse
into my future, and count the loss well spent. Men liked
young girls, I knew. I had heard them talk, heard their lust-
ful laughter when the beer jugs emptied on village feast
days. I was not unattractive, with my budding breasts, my
long legs and small hips, and surely the startling fact of my
blue eyes would titillate a man who was probably used to
such exotic sights in Thebes and the Delta but who would
not expect to see one here. My mother would die of shame if
she knew. My father would beat me. I would be a disgrace in
the village. My heart began to pound.

I had reached the temple precincts. Wepwawet's sacred
home stood graceful and white in the dazzling sunlight, and
I found a patch of shadow just off the path and sat on the
ground, studying the building with the mixture of delight
and awe that it had always inspired in me. I would have
liked to perch on the edge of the stone canal and dangle my
feet in the water but the sun was too hot, and besides, the
water was at its low summer ebb. No sound came from the
walls, or from the sad growth around me. I waited.

After a long time I saw Pa-ari appear under the pylon
leading to the outer court, skirt the end of the canal, and
walk towards me. He was dressed, as usual, in a white kilt

and nothing else. His feet were bare. The bag he carried was no longer full of pieces of pottery for he now used a scribe's palette, pots of red and black ink and brushes of various sizes that belonged to the temple and had to stay there. He was tall and beautiful, my brother, his body a uniform brown, the colour of the earth, of the desert at twilight. He strode proudly, uprightly, his head raised, the sheen of light and heat on his thick black hair, and I thought with a shock, he is one of them, my Pa-ari, one of the village boys the girls giggle over. He is one of them, but oh, I pray that he will not shrink and wither, that he will remain erect and full of sap no matter what. I came to my feet and stepped out onto the path, unaccountably shy for a moment. He saw me and his rather solemn face broke into a smile.

"You must be very bored, Thu, to have nothing better to do than crouch under a tree," he said as I swung into step beside him. "Has something happened at home?"

I shook my head and hugged his arm. "No, but I heard today that a great Seer is coming to Aswat. Is it true?"

"Why yes, it's true," he said, surprised. "The First Prophet himself only knew yesterday, when a message arrived from Thebes. News travels fast in small places." His tone was ironic. He looked at me and then away to where the limp palms towered over our heads, dividing the path from the wasteland of the empty fields beyond. "Let me guess," he went on. "My Lady Thu is anxious to meet this man. She wishes, as always, to have her future spelled out for her like a child on his first day at school."

I scuffed at the dust, watching it puff over my naked toes, both flattered and annoyed that I was so transparent to him. "It is something like that," I admitted. "What are the priests saying?"

"They are saying that this man will arrive three days hence, that he will stay aboard his barge except when he is consulting with the First Prophet, that he will be guarded by royal troops, and that he will not receive any villager but the mayor who will convey Aswat's respectful greeting to the Lord of the Two Lands." His eyes returned to the path ahead. "Therefore, Thu, I suggest you forget about him. While he is here I have no classes or duties in the temple. We can go eeling and have lots of lessons." All at once he came to a halt and pulled open his bag. "I have something for you," he explained. "Here." He drew out two sheets of papyrus, smooth and crisp, and thrust them into my hands. They were followed by a tiny sealed clay pot. "Powder for ink, and a brush my teacher threw away. It's well used but you can squeeze some more life out of it. I was given the papyrus and the ink as a reward for good work," he finished proudly. "I want you to have them."

"Oh, Pa-ari!" I managed, overwhelmed, clutching the precious squares to my chest. "Oh, thank you! Can I try some letters now?"

He held the bag open and reluctantly I slid the treasures back inside. "No you can't," he said firmly. "I'm tired and hungry and very thirsty. Tomorrow morning, if Mother doesn't need you. We can sneak away to our spot under the sycamore."

I thought no more about the visiting oracle for the rest of the day.

Chapter 3

Three days later I was standing with Pa-ari in the crowd of excited villagers when the Seer's barge turned into the canal and laboured the short distance from the river to the watersteps. I had seen royal craft before, usually fast boats flying the imperial colours of blue and white and carrying Heralds with messages for the Viceroy of Nubia far to the south. They would pass Aswat swiftly, cutting the water and disappearing to leave nothing but their wash rippling against the bank. The great barges weighted down with mountainous granite from the quarries at Assuan also went by but rarely, for little building was being done. It was said that at one time the river was busy night and day, thronged with commerce, thick with the pleasure ships of the nobles, choked with Heralds plying to and fro on business for the hundreds of administrators and officials who ran Egypt. Watching this barge bump against the watersteps I was seized with nostalgia for a time I had never known, and fear for the slow eclipse of my country of which until that moment I had been only dimly aware. The village dreamed on, self-contained, but when talk of outside events did begin, the words were all of what had been in a glorious past, of present threats and future disasters. I will ask Pa-ari to read the history scrolls, I decided, jammed against him in the crush of excited bodies. I want to know this Egypt from a different vantage point than the village square.

The craft was painted a spotless white. Its mast was polished cedar, as were its oars, and from the top of the mast the imperial flag was shaken sporadically by the intermittent, dry breeze. The planking curved sweetly from prow to stern, and fore and aft curled inward in the shape of fanned lotus flowers, each painted blue, the petals picked out with gold that glittered intoxicatingly in the sunlight. The cabin amidships had heavy, tightly drawn curtains of some material into which gold thread had been woven, for they also sparkled in the bright day. Sumptuous red tassels hung from the cabin's frame, waiting to tie back the drapery. High in the stern, the helmsman clung to the vast steering oar and ignored the exclamations and cries of the people.

The soldiers ignored us too. Six of them stood on each side of the cabin, tall, blackbearded foreigners with watchful eyes that peered out from under their horned helmets to disdainfully contemplate the sky above our heads. They wore long white kilts that concealed all but the shape of their massive thighs, and beneath collars of studded leather their chests were bare. They were equipped with swords and great round shields. Our father once looked like that, I thought with a rush of pride. He defended Pharaoh. He fought for Egypt. But then I wondered just what these men here today were supposed to be defending the illustrious oracle from. Us harmless villagers? Attacks from the banks of the Nile on his journey to Aswat and back to Pi-Ramses? I saw one of the soldiers shift his weight from one splayed, sandalled foot to the other. The gesture made him suddenly human, and I decided that the escort was simply for pride and show. Was the oracle arrogant, then, as well as famous? It was important for me to know.

A ripple of anticipation went through the watchers as the curtains of the cabin twitched and were drawn aside. A we'eb priest appeared, tied back the drape, and bowed to the figure who emerged. I held my breath.

The ripple subsided quickly and the silence of shock took its place, for the thing that came out of the dimness of the cabin and paused on the deck was a wrapped corpse, walking like a man. It, he, was swathed from head to toe in white wrappings. Even his face was hidden far back in the shadow of a voluminous hood, and the cloak that enveloped him covered his hands as well. The hood came up, turned from side to side, and I was sure that the unseen presence within was measuring us all.

The man stepped up onto the ramp that had been run out between the boat and the stone facing of the canal. I glimpsed a foot bound in white bandages and suddenly felt faint. The Seer was diseased. He had some terrible disfiguring illness that made him too monstrous for ordinary eyes. I would abandon my mad scheme. This was too much. Besides, the sheer daylight reality of the boat, the trappings, the sweating soldiers, had shattered my stupid daydreams. I noticed then that Wepwawet's High Priest with his acolytes had come out from beneath the pylon, wreathed in thin streams of incense, and was waiting to receive the God's strange guest. I turned away.

"Where are you going?" Pa-ari whispered.

"Home," I answered curtly. "I don't feel well."

"Do you still want me to find out how long the Seer is staying?" he pressed. "I go to school with the acolytes. They'll tell me."

I hesitated, pondered, then nodded. "Yes," I said resignedly. It was no good. Even if the man had three heads and a tail I wanted an end to the aimless not-knowing. I would stiffen my resolve. Pa-ari's mouth came close to my ear.

"Remember, Thu," he muttered. "You have no gift."

I swung to meet his gaze, which told me nothing, but I had the distinct impression that he suspected the thing I was determined to offer. Leaving him I slipped through the throng and began to run towards the village. The day had become oppressive, and I could hardly suck in the turgid air.

Pa-ari and my mother returned to the house much later, and I was severely scolded for not preparing the evening

meal, seeing I had been home alone. But even Mother was
caught up in the disturbance caused by the notable's visit,
and did not punish me. I took our cow down to the water
and then milked her. We ate bread and cold soup in the last
red light of the day, and then Father surprised me by asking
for fresh water. I brought it to him, then sat on the floor and
watched while he meticulously washed himself. Mother was
twisting wicks for the lamps and Pa-ari was cross-legged in
the doorway, brooding over the darkening square beyond.
Then Father called for his sandals and a jug of our best palm
wine. I scrambled to obey and Mother looked up suspiciously from her work.

"Where are you going?" she enquired.

He ran both hands through his wet, blond hair and
smiled in her direction. "I am off to seduce one of the
mayor's nubile daughters," he joked. "My dearest sister, your
jealousy is delightful. Really, I am going to indulge in soldier's gossip with the Shardana. I have had no contact with
men of my own kind for a long time. Do not wait up for
me."

"Hmm," was her comment, but I could see that she was
pleased. He took the sandals from me gently, slipped them
on, and hefted the jug of wine. "Pa-ari!" he called to the
huddled form of his son outlined between the lintels.
"Would you like to come with me?"

The invitation was a surprising honour, for Pa-ari would
not be reckoned a man to share in other men's affairs until
he turned sixteen. He jumped up at once. "Thank you,
Father!" he crowed. "I would like that very much!" And
then they were gone. Pa-ari's excited voice faded and the
night fell.

My mother was asleep long before the two of them came
home, but I was not. I sat on my pallet with my back against
the wall in the room Pa-ari and I shared, fighting drowsiness, until I heard their unsteady footsteps turn into the

house. Father's heavier tread stumbled straight into my parents' bedroom. Pa-ari came fumbling for his mattress in the darkness.

"It's all right," I hissed at him. "I'm awake. I want to hear everything, Pa-ari. Did you enjoy yourself?"

"Very much." His voice was laboured and I could tell that he was slightly drunk. He sank onto his pallet with a gusty sigh and the air was full of wine fumes for a moment. "The Shardana are formidable men, Thu. I would not want to face them in battle. I was in awe of them, but Father sat with them before their tents and laughed and drank and spoke of things so foreign that I was reduced to silence. He is a great man in his own way, our father. Some of the stories he told tonight, of his exploits in the time of troubles! I could hardly believe them!"

"Well what of the soldiers?" I broke in sharply. I was jealous of the unfeigned admiration in Pa-ari's voice. I wanted him to love and admire no one but me. "Where are their tents? How many of them guard the Seer at night? Is he on his barge or elsewhere? How long is he staying?"

There was a silence. For a while I was afraid that Pa-ari had fallen asleep, but then I heard his mattress rustle as he found a new position. "I called you obdurate once." The words came quietly from his unseen mouth but their tone conveyed his expression, sad, disappointed. "I think you are ruthless also, Thu, and not always very likeable. You do have a gift, don't you? Something shameful, dark. Do not lie to me. I know."

I said nothing. I waited calmly. Everything in me had gone cold, a kind of dead peacefulness, while our relationship hung in the balance. Would he help me or would he turn aside, just a little but enough to sunder the closeness we had always shared, and define our affection in other, less forgiving terms. I heard the anger and sorrow in his voice as he at last gave me the information I needed.

"There are two tents, set up on this side of the temple wall. Two soldiers stand guard over the Seer, who sleeps in his cabin on the barge. The rest stand down. He will be here for two nights and will cast off for Pi-Ramses at dawn on the third day. If you take to the river and swim up the canal you should be able to accomplish your desire. The guards are really for show."

I did not thank him. I sensed that he would be insulted if I tried. But the coldness in my ka had gone and I felt obscurely dirty. After a long time I said tentatively, "I love you, Pa-ari." He did not reply. He was either asleep or had chosen to ignore me.

All the next day I thought about what I would do. The village remained largely deserted, the people hurrying to the temple in their spare moments to try and catch yet another glimpse of the sinister figure who had glided under the pylon and into their imaginations, but my father slept late and then went out onto the desert for reasons of his own and Pa-ari disappeared with his friends. Mother and I retreated to the relative coolness of her herb room and busied ourselves in grinding and bagging the dozens of leaves that hung drying from the ceiling. There was little conversation and I was free to make plans, each more fantastic and impossible than the last, until I was ordered sharply to soak the lentils for the evening meal and stop daydreaming. With an inward sigh, part hopelessness and part recklessness, I did as I was told. I had discarded all flights of fancy and decided on a direct course of action. I would go simply, nakedly, to my fate. After all, what was the worst that could happen? Arrest, and an ignominious march back to my father's door.

Father came home at sunset, blood caking his chest and dried in rivulets down his arms. A dead jackal was slung across his shoulder, and more blood dripped from its mouth and nose down my father's sinewy back. He tossed it outside the door, together with his bow and two soiled arrows. "I'm hungry!" he shouted into my mother's horrified face. He was laughing. "Don't begrudge a man an afternoon's sport, woman! Thu, bring beer to the river immediately. I am going to wash off this carrion's remains and then I will drink and eat and then you and I," he planted a kiss on my mother's silently protesting mouth, "will make love!"

He set off for the river at a lope and later, watching him splash and plunge about in the water, I understood that the time he had spent with the soldiers had freed him to briefly be the man he had laid aside, willingly but perhaps regretfully, when he chose my mother as his wife. He was fine, my father, straight and honest and strong, yet in my arrogance I pitied him that day for the choices he had made.

We all ate together, sitting cross-legged on our mats with the food on a cloth before us while the sun dropped behind the desert. My mother lit a lamp. Father said the evening prayers to Wepwawet, our totem, and to Anhur and Amun and mighty Osiris, his voice reverential but still full of happiness. Then he and my mother walked out under the stars and Pa-ari and I went to our room. He busied himself with arranging his pallet, his back towards me. "It is the Seer's last night," he remarked non-committally at last, his face still averted. "Have you come to your senses, Thu?"

"If you mean am I going to meet my destiny tonight, yes I am," I replied loftily. The words hung between us, fraught with a dignity I had scarcely intended, and I finished lamely, "Please don't be angry with me, Pa-ari."

He had lain down and was motionless, a dark column on the pallet. "I'm not," he said, "but I hope they catch you and whip you and drag you home in disgrace. You know that none of us has actually seen under all those grim white wrappings, don't you? What if he's not human? Aren't you afraid? Good-night, Thu."

Half the hours of darkness seemed to pass before I heard my parents return, but it cannot have been that long. Pa-ari was soon asleep. I listened to the comfort of his regular, slow breathing and beyond that the watchful silence of a summer night, hot and still. Yes I was afraid. But I was learning that fear can make your spirit sick. It can turn you into a shuffling thing inside and it can feed on itself like a disease until you cannot move, you no longer have any pride. And without pride, I thought darkly, what am I? A jackal howled, the strident, agonized sound very faint and far away, and I wondered if it was the mate of the beast father had killed. I heard his step and my mother's low, coquettish giggle. I wondered if they had lain down together on the warm, dusty earth of the fields or in deep shadow by the Nile. When the house had settled I rose and crept outside.

The air embraced me, fingering my naked limbs and lifting the hair from my neck. The moon rode high and full and I paused to pay it homage, raising my arms to the son of Nut, goddess of the sky, and to the stars, her lesser children, before entering the shadow of the path leading to the temple. Here a little of my exaltation at being out and free and alone left me, for the black palm fronds above my head stirred with a secret fretfulness and I remembered that the spirits of the neglected dead could be thronging the dense moon-shadows, watching me jealously. The path itself had lost its cheerful daytime face and now wore another, dreamlike, pale and magical, a road to somewhere I could not foresee. But that is why I am here, I told myself stoutly, keeping my eyes on my feet while the palms whispered a warning and their laced shadows crept up my body as I walked. I must foresee. I must know.

I sensed rather than saw the greyish blur of the two huge tents that had been pitched up against the temple wall and I came to a halt, poised for flight, my heart suddenly pounding. But there was no sound, no movement. Ahead and to my right the lovely prow of the Seer's boat curved indistinctly. It, too, was still. The river was very low and the canal half-empty. Sweat broke out along my spine as I crouched and ran across the path to the shelter of the river growth. Peering through the branches I saw that Pa-ari had been right. A soldier stood at the curtained door of the cabin, looking in my direction, and I had no doubt that his fellow was stationed on the other side. Very well. I would swim and climb. As I turned towards the river a great tide of excitement rushed up inside me and I wanted to sing for the joy of it. I was smiling and gasping with delight as I slid into the black, moon-rippled water.

I was a very good swimmer and could move without greatly disturbing the surface. Revelling in the silken coolness, the polite resistance of the Nile, buoyed by that strange exaltation, I reached the canal and turned cautiously up it, feeling the stern of the boat grow larger until it towered above me. My fingers found wood and then I rested a moment, my wet cheek against the sweet-smelling cedar. I no longer cared about anything but the thrill of my adventure. Something in me was being fulfilled at last and it grew and blossomed and I knew, hanging there with my mouth caressed by the river, my eyes on the broken sky-road the moon was making all around me, that I would never be the same. "Praise to you O Hapi, source of Egypt's fructifying power," I murmured to the dark expanse of water, then my fingers found a grip and I pulled myself from the God's arms.

The ship's construction was such that the planks were overlaid one upon another. It was child's play for me to climb the side. I had some difficulty at the top where the lip curved inward but once I had anchored myself on this I had only to roll quickly onto the deck to find myself in blessed shadow.

For a long time I lay curled against a pile of rope, my brown body blending with its shape as I scanned the length of the craft. It looked eternal in the deceptive moonlight, as though the cabin was receding even as I assessed the distance. Everything was black or grey or sombre-hued. I saw the two guards, one gazing into the bushes and the other, at the rear of the cabin, watching the temple and the path that continued on to the next village. What must they have felt, standing lookout in such a boringly peaceful place? Foolish? Angry? Or were they so dedicated to their work that it made no difference to them where they performed their duties?

My skin was beginning to dry. Cautiously, lying flat on the deck, I set off to crawl towards the cabin. Only the glitter of the moon in my eyes could give me away, for the rest of me was the colour of the polished wood over which I moved and if one of the men happened to glance my way I would simply lie frozen until his attention passed. My knees and elbows began to ache but I ignored the small pain. I made no sound. I scarcely breathed. And all the while that pulse of intoxication throbbed with my blood. I felt omnipotent, a hunting animal sure of its prey. The soft brush of drapery against my outstretched fingers brought me to myself. I half rose, lifted the heavy hanging, and stepped inside.

The interior of the cabin was very dark and I stood, stilling my breath while I took my bearings. I could just see the dim form of a cot against the opposite curtain-wall and a bulk of huddled sheet on it. Cushions were strewn about, vague humps, and a table containing a lamp was close by the bed. The thing under the sheet was utterly motionless and quiet and I wondered for a moment if the cabin was in fact empty. I also wondered what to do next. All my will had been bent on getting this far, and now that I had achieved my goal I was mystified. Should I approach the cot and lay a hand on the sleeper, if he was there? But what would I feel under my fingers? The firmness of a male shoulder or something horrible, unidentifiable? And what if I should startle him and he should wake with a cry and the guards rush in and slay me before they could see that I was just a village girl? Enough! I told myself sternly. You are not just a village girl, you are the Lady Thu, daughter of a dispossessed Libu prince, are you not? The old fantasy made me smile but did not cheer me for long. I was beginning to feel a presence with me in the little room, as though the thing on the cot was aware of me standing just inside the drapery and was watching my thoughts. I shuddered, my own awareness going to the time that was passing. I must do something. I took one tentative step.

"You may stay where you are." The voice was deep but oddly toneless and the sheet rustled. He, it, was sitting up but I could see nothing beyond the outline of a head. I withdrew my foot. "You have either bewitched my guards, or in the manner of all peasants you have the ability to slither and creep into places where you are not wanted," it went on smoothly.

At least the voice was human. Yet my apprehension did not lift. I was angry at the words but I reminded myself of why I had come. "I did not slither or creep," I replied, annoyed that my own voice shook. "I swam and climbed."

The figure sat straighter. "Indeed," it said. "Then you can swim and climb your way back to your hovel. I judge by your voice you are a young female. I do not make love spells. I do not concoct potions for use on heedless lovers. I do not give incantations to avert the wrath of parents driven to distraction by lazy or disobedient children. Therefore go. And if you go immediately I shall not have you thrashed and carted home in disgrace."

But I had not come this far to slink away suffering from my own private disgrace. I had nothing to lose, now, by standing my ground and I spoke through the cloud of unease that still troubled me. "I don't want any of those things," I retorted, "and even if I did, I could probably do them for myself. My mother is rich in herb lore and so am I. I have a request, Great One."

This time the voice was amused. "Only Pharaoh is the Great One," he answered, "and it is impossible to flatter me.

I know my own worth, but it seems that you have an inflated opinion of yours. How rich in herb lore can an unlettered urchin from this backwater of Egypt be? And how unique a request can she put forward? Shall we see? Or shall I go back to sleep?"

I waited, my hands sliding to clasp each other behind my back as though I was about to be reprimanded. The air in the cabin was close, faintly perfumed with jasmine. The smell made me feel slightly dizzy. My knees and elbows were now throbbing, and water was still dripping from my hair and running between my breasts and down my spine. I supposed that there might be a puddle at my feet. I peered through the cloying dimness, striving to see that head more clearly yet for some reason dreading to do so. The sheet whispered again. The man stood up. He was very tall. "Very well," he said wearily at last. "Make your request."

My throat went dry and I was suddenly thirsty. "You are a Seer," I managed huskily. "I want you to See for me. Tell me my future, Master! Am I condemned to live out my days in Aswat? I must know!"

"What?" he responded with tired humour. "You do not ask for the name of your future husband? You do not want the number of your children or of your days? What kind of a village brat are you? A nasty, small-minded, unsatisfied one perhaps. Consumed with greed and arrogance." There was a silence in which he went very still. Then he said, "But perhaps not. There can also be simple desperation. What is your gift? What can a kneader of the Aswat dung possibly offer in exchange for this mighty revelation she so blithely demands? A handful of bitter herbs?"

This was the heart of the matter. I swallowed. My throat hurt. "I have only one gift precious enough in my eyes to present to you," I forced out, and got no further, for at that he began to laugh, sitting down on the cot. I could see his shoulders shake. His laughter was raw, a painful sound, as though he was not used to mirth.

"I know what you are about to say, little peasant girl," he choked. "I don't need the water and the oil to predict your offer. Gods! You are poor, your hands and feet are coarse with labour. At this moment you stink of river mud and you are doubtless naked. And you thought to offer yourself to me. Supreme arrogance! Insulting ignorance! I think it is time to take a look at you." He bent, uncovering a tiny brazier in which a coal glowed faintly, illuminating nothing but the hands that cupped it. I tensed. There was something wrong with those hands, something terrible. He leaned to the table where the lamp was, and suddenly the room burst into light. The disordered cot was of darkly polished wood inlaid with gold, its feet like the paws of an animal. The linen rumpled over it was finer than anything I had seen, transparent and glowing white. The lamp flooding the cabin with radiance must be white alabaster. I had never seen this stone before but I knew about it—how brittle it was, how it could be ground so thin that you could see the outline of your hand through it, or a picture painted on the inside of a bowl or lamp. The floor covering on which I stood was red...

And so were his eyes, the pupils red as two drops of blood, the irises glittering pink. His body was the colour of the sheet he had wound about his waist, white, all white, and the long pale hair that fell to either side of his face to rest upon his shoulders was white too. The lamplight found no glint of gold in it, no sheen of colour on his body. The whiteness was so stark that it reflected nothing back. I was looking at death, at a demon whose only life lay shockingly in those dreadful red eyes that had narrowed and were watching me carefully.

Thank all the Gods my hands were behind my back, for before I could stop myself I was feeling for the amulet my mother sometimes lent me. It was of the Goddess Nephthys giving power to the chen sign that protected the wearer

from all evil and I wished I had stolen it before setting out
that night. But it was not on my wrist. Now I was defenceless
before this monster, this creature from the Underworld, and
I knew in a flash that if I showed horror or any fear he would
order me killed at once. Those blood-filled eyes told me so.
My fingers twined around each other in an agony of effort
not to scream, to remain still, to hold that loathsome gaze.
He sat immobile, staring back at me, and then he smiled.

"Very good," he said softly. "Oh, very good indeed. There
is courage beneath that impudent exterior. Come closer. My
eyes are weak." On legs trembling with fatigue I walked up
to him, and as I grew closer the smile faded. He searched my
face and as he did so his self-control seemed to falter. "Blue
eyes," he muttered. "You have blue eyes. And delicate features and a lissom body, finely jointed. Tell me your parent-
age. Guard!" Now I did let out a shriek but the time of my
danger had passed. The soldier's shadow appeared on the
drapery.

"Is all well with you, Master?"

"Yes. Bring a jug of beer and send to the temple for honey
cakes." The shadow faded and I heard footsteps on the
ramp. "Sit here beside me," the Seer invited, and I sank
onto the cot. My terror was fading but not the repulsion I
felt, and I could not look away from his face. I was
exhausted. "Your gift is refused," he went on with a half-
smile. "I don't lust after girls, or women either for that matter. I learned a long time ago that lust interferes with the
Seeing. But I do not grieve. Power is more satisfying and
lasting than sex."

"Then you will not See for me!" I broke in with despair.
For answer he took my palm and his alien, bloodless forefin-
ger traced the lines on it. His touch was cold.

"You have no right to disappointment," he retorted, "for
what are you? I did not say that I would not divine for you,
merely that I refused your gift—such as it is. You have an

inflated view of your own worth, little peasant girl. Blue eyes," he murmured to himself. He placed my hand back between my naked thighs and pulling another sheet from the cot bade me cover myself. "Few men have seen me," he went on. "My servants, Pharaoh, the High Priests when I stand before the Gods to do my homage. You have been honoured, peasant, though you do not know it. Some I have killed for catching me unawares. You knew that, didn't you?" I nodded. "Never forget it," he said harshly. "I value loyalty above all else, because of what I am."

"And Master, what are you?" I dared to ask. He examined my face again before replying, his expression inscrutable. The lamp sputtered and I saw the tiny flame become doubled and leap crimson in both of his eyes.

"I am not a demon. I am not a monster. I am a man," he sighed, and in that moment my revulsion began to die. Genuine pity took its place, not the scornful pity I had felt for my father by the Nile but a gentle adult emotion. I shed a little, a very little, of my overwhelming selfishness. His sigh was soon spent. "Give me your forebears," he ordered crisply and I did so.

"My mother is a native Egyptian, the midwife in Aswat as her mother was before her," I explained, "but my father, who is now a farmer, was a Libu mercenary. He fought for Pharaoh Osiris Setnakht Glorified against the invaders and if our present Horus of Gold demanded it he would fight again. He is very handsome, our father." He leaned forward.

"You have a sister, then?" I shook my head.

"No, a brother, Pa-ari. Father wants him to inherit his arouras when he dies but Pa-ari is going to be a scribe. He is very clever."

"So you are the only daughter? And I suppose that you will be a midwife also?"

I twisted away from him. It was as though he had pressed the point of a knife against an open wound. "No! I don't

want to! Always I have wanted something else, something
better, but already I am trapped! I am my mother's apprentice, I am the good daughter, I will be the good wife to some
good village man, good, good, good, and I don't want any of
it!" He reached out and took my chin in his cold grasp,
turning my head. My blue eyes seemed to fascinate him, for
he studied them again.

"Calm yourself," he said. "Then what do you want?"

"Not this! I wanted to go to school but Father refused, so
Pa-ari has been teaching me to read..." He folded his arms. I
noticed that he was wearing a heavy gold ring, a serpent
winding lazily around his finger.

"Indeed? You are full of surprises, my beautiful peasant.
Oh? You did not know that you were beautiful? Well perhaps if I were your father I would not tell you either. And
you say you can read. Here." He rose, and going swiftly to a
chest against the side wall he opened it, withdrew a papyrus
scroll, and thrust it at me. "Tell me what this says."

I was unrolling it as the guard returned. The Seer's attention left me as he commanded the refreshments to be placed
just inside the curtain, and I had a chance to look at the
words. They were closely packed and very elegantly drawn
so that I was tempted to sit there and admire the penman-
ship but I did not want to fail this test. By the time the man
had picked up the tray and returned to the cot I had
skimmed the contents of the scroll. I looked up at him hesitantly. He gestured.

"Well, go on!"

"To the Eminent Master Hui, Seer and Prophet of the
Gods, greetings. Having upon your command journeyed to
your estates in the Delta, and having sat down in council
with your stewards of land, of cattle, of slaves and of grain, I
assess your holdings at this harvest thus. Of land, fifty
arouras. Of cattle, six hundred head. Of slaves, one hundred.
Of grain, your granaries are full. Of wine, three hundred and

fifty jars of Good Wine of the Western River. In the matter of the disputed boundary of the flax field with your neighbour, I have entered into an appeal for judgement with the mayor of Lisht who will hear the pleadings within the month. Touching upon..." He twitched the scroll from my hand and let it roll up.

"Very creditable," he commented wryly. "So you did not lie. Your brother achieved this miracle? Do you know that very few women in the harem of the Great God can count the number of their fingers, let alone read? Can you write also?" I could see the beer and cakes on the edge of my vision.

"Not well," I blurted. "I have had nothing to practise on."

He must have sensed the direction of my attention for he flicked a hand to the tray and bade me eat and drink. True to my mother's stern training I poured for him first, offering him the cup and the dish of cakes. He refused both and sat watching me as I gulped the beer and bit with relish into the cakes. They were lighter and sweeter than any I had tasted at home. I tried to chew them slowly. He continued to regard me, one foot up on the cot, an elbow resting on his knee and his cheek against his knuckles, then he got up, returned to the chest, and pulled out another scroll. This one he unrolled himself.

"What would you prescribe for a headache that has been intense and very sharp for more than three days?" he asked. I stopped eating and blinked at him, all at once aware that I was being tested. From the time he had lit the lamp and seen my blue eyes he had been probing me. I answered without too much trouble.

"Berries of the coriander, juniper, poppy and sames plants, crushed with wormwood and mixed in honey."

"How do you administer?" I hesitated.

"By tradition the head should be smeared with the mixture, like a poultice, but my mother gets better results if the patient swallows it by the spoonful." That cracked, dry laugh filled the cabin again.

"Your mother may be a peasant but she possesses some wisdom! And what may be used to make the met supple?" I stared at him. The met involved the health of all the nerves and blood vessels.

"There are thirty-six ingredients to the poultice," I replied. "Must I list all of them?"

"You are impertinent," he chided me. "Can you handle the poppy?"

"In all ways."

"Do you know what to do with antimony?" I did not. "Lead? Lead vitriol? Sulphur? Arsenic? No? Would you like to learn?" I lowered my beer cup.

"Please, don't make fun of me," I begged, stifling a sudden urge to cry. "I would very much like to learn." He tapped the scroll against the ghostly white of his forearm.

"Thu," he said gently, "I saw your face in the oil three months ago. I was divining for Pharaoh, my mind upon him, and as I bent over the bowl you were there, the blue eyes, the sweetly curving mouth, the sultry black hair. Your name whispered through my mind, Thu, Thu, and then you were gone. I do not need to read for you. Fate has presented us to each other, for reasons that are as yet unknown. My name is Hui, but you will call me Master. Would you like to learn?"

Three months ago! My pulses raced. Three months ago Pa-ari and I had sat in the red sand of a desert sunset and I had cried out my frustration. The gods had heard me. A shiver, light as a drifting blossom, went through me and I was filled with awe.

"I am to be your servant?" I breathed. "You will take me away from here?"

"Yes. I leave at dawn. The orders have already been given to the crew. You must agree to obey me in all things, Thu. Do you agree?"

Feverishly I nodded. Now all was happening with the speed of an approaching khamsin. The storm had not struck, but its imminence appalled me. Is it really what I want? I asked myself frantically. The choice is here. After so long, it has come. Do I hold out my arms to embrace it or do I run home to the babies and the herbs, the palm wine and gossip, village dust between my bare toes and Father making the nightly prayers in our little house, his blond head bent in the candlelight, Pa-ari and I in the delightful stolen hours, knee to knee... Pa-ari...

Now I did weep. Fatigue and excitement, fear and tension had taken their toll. Hui made no move until I had finished, then he rose.

"Go home and tell your father to be at the foot of the ramp an hour before dawn," he said. "Come with him and bring whatever you wish to remember of Aswat. If he refuses, you must stay here, for come what may I must sail with Ra's rising. Go now. You have two hours."

I was dismissed. Stumbling, I pushed aside the drapery and started down the ramp. The air smelled good after the close confines of the cabin, fresh and full of the things I realized now were more precious to me than I had supposed—Nile mud and dry grasses, the tang of the dung-laden dust and the clean odour of the desert. I did not run back to the village. I walked, sobbing all the way.

Chapter 4

Sunrise was still only a subtle thinning of the hot darkness when Father and I came to a halt at the foot of the ramp leading onto Hui's barge and faced the guard's challenge. We had not spoken to each other on the path that was taking me away from everything I had known. My mother had woken grudgingly to my urgent prodding. She had lit a candle, and by its feeble light had sat on their pallet, her hair disordered and her eyes swollen, while I poured out as much of my disjointed story as I wanted them to know. Father had been immediately alert under my hand, in the way of seasoned soldiers. He listened non-committally, his expression going from confusion to mild annoyance to vigilance as I tried unsuccessfully to convey the urgency I felt. When I had finished I crouched before them, fists and jaw clenched in the knowledge that the sun was coming, Ra was about to be reborn from the belly of Nut, and once his fire touched the eastern horizon beyond the river my hope would be gone. Father took a corner of the coarse kilt he had discarded on the mud floor the night before and calmly and deliberately wiped the sweat from his forehead and the back of his neck. "You have been crying," he remarked. His voice triggered a flood of mixed recrimination and solicitude from my mother.

"You naughty girl," she said vehemently, "running about under the moon and stirring up trouble like a whore! What about the soldiers out there? You could have been raped or worse! You are possessed! Are you sure you weren't just dreaming, my sweet? A dream, yes? Young girls have strange fancies sometimes. You dared to speak to the Seer, you impudent child? How could you shame us so?" In her agitation the linen that had covered her slipped to her corrugated waist. Her generous breasts were quivering with panic and indignation. At once my father lifted the sheet and unconsciously she grabbed it to her chin.

"Woman, be silent," he ordered, and she closed her mouth, glaring at us both. He searched my face, then nodded. "I will come," he said quietly, "but Thu, if you are simply playing one of your games with us or if you dreamed a wish to trouble our kas I will thrash you until the blood runs. Wait for me outside." I scrambled to my feet, and as I turned towards my room I heard my mother say, "You are wrong to humour her, my husband! She is wayward and fanciful! We must marry her off as soon as possible and put a stop to her dangerous silliness!"

Pa-ari had obviously been wakened by the sound of her furious voice. I groped for his hand and held it tightly as I sank beside his pallet. "Oh, Thu," he whispered. "What have you done? I tried not to fall asleep. I wanted to wait up for you but somehow... What happened?"

Quickly I told him everything except that the Seer was under the special protection of the gods, not for the pathetic witlessness that rendered a person sacred but because of his grotesque body. He put his arms around me and we clung to each other, my mouth buried against his neck, my nostrils inhaling the musky odour of his skin that I had come to associate with trust and companionship and loyalty. "So you are to have your chance," he said, and I could hear the smile as he spoke. "My funny little Thu. Send word to me of how you fare as soon as you can."

I did not want to release him. I wanted to take the path, climb onto the barge, sail to the Delta, still entwined safely in his embrace. But I pulled away and went to my pallet, feeling for the cedar box that held my treasures, lifting the basket that contained my best sheath and a few other pieces of linen. "I will not need to hire a scribe," I replied. "I can write to you in my own hand, and you must write back, Pa-ari, for I will miss you above all. Farewell." Clutching my possessions I went to the doorway.

"May the soles of your feet be firm." He gave me the ancient blessing, and I carried the words and the sound of his voice in my heart as I slipped out of the house to find my father already sniffing the strange deadness of the air that always preceded the dawn. He did not acknowledge me and we set off across the village square in silence. I did not look back. I had already vowed that I would never set foot in Aswat again.

The guard looked tired and his manner was irascible until he recognized my father's voice. "What, no palm wine to break your fast this morning?" he joked as he approached the curtained cabin. I heard him question the being within but the reply did not travel to the end of the ramp. He lifted the drapery and nodded. We crossed onto the barge and entered the cabin.

The room was full of shadows. The only light came from the small brazier the Seer had used much earlier to light the lamp, which was now out. The scent of jasmine invaded me but this time I welcomed it, drawing it deep into my lungs as a harbinger of change. Dimly I perceived the now familiar outlines of table and chest, cushions and cot.

The creature sitting on the cot rose and became a column of greyness, folded, swathed, enveloped in voluminous linens. I was startled when my father bowed. I had not thought to do so the last time I stood here. The voice that issued from the bindings, when it came, was muffled.

"Greetings," it said. "I am the Seer Hui. I do not particularly want to know your name. It is not important."

"It may not be important to you, Master, but it is vital to me and, I hope, to the gods. If you do not wish to hear it then I will not speak it. Thu, go and sit down by the far wall." I did so, pride for my father welling inside me. He was not cowed by this threatening vision. His answer had been dignified. "My daughter tells me that you have offered her a position in your household," he went on carefully. "I love her and want her to be happy, therefore I stand here before you to ask in what capacity she is to serve."

"I was under the impression that it was I who summoned you," Hui said dryly. "However, I know your unspoken fear. I have no concubines, nor do I buy the services of whores. Your daughter's virginity is safe with me, indeed, I intend to guard it with a great deal more zeal than you seem to do. Thu is intelligent and ambitious. I will cultivate her intelligence and teach her the proper use for ambition. She in her turn will help me with the preparation of medicines and the pursuance of my studies in the nature and properties of minerals. Once a month she will write a letter to her family. If a month goes by without word from her you may lodge an enquiry with your mayor and have a summons issued against me. In exchange for her assistance I will pay you one deben of silver and I will make sure that the next arouras of khato-land around Aswat will be deeded to you." I gasped. One deben of silver would support nine people for at least a year. My father rounded on me sternly.

"That was not polite," he rebuked me, and turned back, but suddenly I could smell his nervous sweat, acrid and offensive. "Thu is not for sale," he said coldly, "and what you offer is not a dowry. Besides, no farmer in Aswat is near death, therefore no land is about to revert to Pharaoh and become khato. Thu is not for sale!" I thought I heard a chuckle from the bandaged and hooded mouth.

"I am not buying her, you simpleton, I am compensating you for the work she will no longer be able to perform as apprentice to your wife. And do not have the effrontery to question my readings. Within a year, five arouras here will become khato-land. They are yours and I'll add a slave to help you work them."

Father said nothing for a long time. Then he moved closer to the Seer. "You are very eager indeed to take my daughter away with you, aren't you, Master?" he said softly. "Why? The great cities of Egypt are full of noble, gently raised girls as intelligent and ambitious as Thu and requiring less training. What is your true reason?" Hui stood his ground, indeed he also narrowed the space between himself and my father. His gliding step conveyed a polite menace.

"It is not for you to question the wishes of the gods," he said, "but I may tell you that I saw your daughter three months ago in the divining oil. I knew nothing of her save her name until she appeared before me this night, stark naked and dripping wet." Oh you did not need to tell him that! I thought mutinously. You are trying to tease me and annoy him. Father, however, made no response and Hui continued. "I do not attempt to manipulate destiny. I merely read the messages of the gods, impart them as I see fit, and wait for their fruition. I waited to see what the face in the oil might mean. The gods have appointed this night to juxtapose their will with that of Thu." The grey, linen-laden shoulders lifted in a gesture of resignation. "I speak the truth." My father sighed and his body loosened. After a while a faint grin came and went on his face.

"I refuse the silver," he said, "but I will take the land—if it becomes khato. And the slave."

"So." Hui walked to the table and picked up a scroll which he offered to my father. "You test my skill as a Seer, peasant. You do it with more subtlety than I would have expected, and with some wit, therefore I will not turn you into a toad on the spot." He rasped out an abrupt laugh. "This holds my promise to you. The offer of the silver remains on the document should you ever have need of it. Thu! Rise and bid your father farewell!" He lowered himself onto the cot and watched impassively as I scrambled up. The agreement had been made. The scroll was in my father's hand. The Seer now commanded me.

I looked up into my father's face, so familiar, so dependable. He took my chin in his big, rough palm and studied me for a moment. "Are you sure that this is what you want, my Thu?" he asked me quietly. "You can still change your mind and come home with me." I fell against him and hugged him tightly.

"No," I answered against his chest. "If I go home I will always wonder what fate I had refused. Say a farewell to Mother for me. I could not do so because she was upset. Tell whoever leads Precious Sweet Eyes to the river to drink that she does not like to stand in the mud opposite the village. She prefers the sandy shoal a little to the north. Tell Paari..." Father disengaged himself from my arms and put a finger to my lips.

"I understand," he said. "I love you, Thu." He kissed the top of my head, bowed to Hui, and walked to the curtain. It shushed closed behind him. I heard his greeting to the guard, his heavy footfall on the ramp, then he was gone.

I had been unaware of the activity outside the cabin, so wrapped was I in the events within, but now I heard running feet, the thud of ropes flung down, sharp orders being given. The loud scrape of wood on wood signalled the drawing in of the ramp, and the barge gave a shudder. Hui and I looked at one another. I was still clutching the basket and the box to my chest.

"Is that all you want to bring?" he asked incredulously. I nodded.

"It is all I have."

"Gods!" he exclaimed. "Is it clean? I want no lice or fleas in here. Oh for Set's sake don't start crying again. If you wish to watch Aswat disappear into the dawn you had better go onto the deck. We are at this moment sliding down the canal and will turn north immediately. I am going to sleep."

I did not want to see Aswat vanish. I could not have borne the pain or the excitement. The Seer had shed his cloak and hood and was untying his white hair. I thought for one dreadful second that he was going to order me onto his cot with him but he pulled a shirt over his head, tugged off an ankle-length skirt, and unbound his feet. My head was spinning with weariness.

"Well," he said impatiently, lying down and pulling a sheet over himself. "Are you going?"

"No," I whispered. It was an effort to speak. "I want to sleep, Master."

"Good! There are plenty of cushions on the floor and you will find more sheets folded beside the chest. I hope you rest peacefully."

I did not think that he was bidding me sleep soundly. He was hoping that I did not snore. Clumsily I gathered up the cushions to make myself a bed against the far wall. I fetched a sheet, and winding it around me, collapsed in a huddle of nervous exhaustion. Faint light was beginning to filter through the few cracks in the curtains, bringing the contents of the cabin into focus. I glanced down the length of the room at the Seer. His eyes were open. He was watching me. I did not want to see a glint of red in his gaze so I turned over and was asleep almost at once.

I awoke in the same position in which I had fallen asleep, after a deep and incoherent dream that I forgot as soon as consciousness returned. Dazed, I reached for the edge of my pallet but felt softness instead. The room was stiflingly hot and diffused sunlight burned around me. I had overslept and Mother would be furious at my neglected chores. Then I saw the cot at the far end, neatly made, and the figure sitting writing at the table, a scribe's palette beside his colourless fingers. He was wearing a knee-length kilt of many pleats that fell softly towards the floor. A necklace of intricately detailed blue and green enamelled scarabs lay against his throat and its counterpoise, a black Eye of Horus ringed in gold, sat in the cleft between his shoulder-blades. The snake ring glittered as his fingers moved. Through half-closed eyes I studied him. Last night he had been mysterious, frightening, ageless, a thing not quite human. Today, as Ra raged beyond the drapery, he was still mysterious but not so frightening, and he was definitely human. Sweat trickled from his white-haired armpits. He had a small bruise on his upper arm, blue-black and threatening on that bleached skin, and he had slipped off one leather sandal and hooked one foot behind the other as he worked. I could only see one-half of his face but the chin line was clean and firm.

"I have turned the sand clock seven times since you fell asleep," he said without looking up. His hand continued to stab at the papyrus. "We have eaten, the rowers have rested, we have slipped past the accursed city, and two crocodiles were sighted on the bank. They are a good omen. There is food and drink beside you."

I sat up. The tray held water, which I drained at once, and beer, and a plate of bread piled with chick peas and slices of duck drizzled with garlic oil. Although the cabin was unbearably hot I fell upon the food with a will. "What is the accursed city?" I wanted to know.

"Do not speak with food in your mouth," he replied absently. "The accursed city is a place of great loneliness and heat and tumbled stone ruins. None will live there although the peasants are allowed to take away the blocks to make grindstones for their grain and to shore up their irrigation canals. A doomed Pharaoh built it and lived there, flouting the gods, but they had their revenge, and now only the hawks and jackals inhabit Akhetaten. Your hands are greasy. There is washing water in the bowl by the wall." Awkwardly tying the sheet around me I rose and dabbled my fingers, then I picked up the beer.

"What are you doing, Master?" I wanted to know. He sat back, placed his pen carefully on the palette, and turned his gaze to me. There were tiny tracks around the blood-filled eyes and a deeply grooved line running from one side of his nose to a corner of his mouth, giving a cynical cast to an otherwise intriguing face.

"You are never to ask me that question," he said coolly, "in fact, Thu, you are to ask permission to speak if you have a question. I examined your belongings while you slept. Put on the sheath. The tattered thing you wore when you returned to the barge with your father has been tossed overboard. When we tie up for the night you can bathe properly in the river. Until then you must go dirty. Go on deck and amuse yourself, but do not gossip and chatter with any of my servants. I have ordered an awning erected against the cabin wall where you may take the shade." I glanced about quickly. My precious box, my link with my family and my childhood, was nowhere in sight but my basket was still propped where I had left it.

"Master!" I blurted. "May I ask a question?" He nodded. "My box..."

"Your box," he said with quiet scorn, "is in the basket. I thought it would be safer there. Now clothe yourself and go." I drew my best and now only sheath out of the basket then hesitated, embarrassed at the idea of being naked before him in daylight. He turned on me impatiently. "If I had wanted to rape you, you stupid girl, I could have done it a dozen times over by now, though what makes you think you are so enticing is beyond me. I made it quite clear last night, when you pranced about without your clothes, that I have no interest whatsoever in your skinny little body. Go!" Mutinously I dropped the sheet and pulled the sheath on over my head.

"I did not prance," I retorted, and sweeping the curtain aside, went out into the blinding sunshine.

The side of the barge was four steps away and I paused, blinking and taking in what I saw. We were moving ponderously but at a good pace in the middle of the river. Sandbanks dotted with ragged palms slid by, and beyond them a collection of mud houses huddled on the edge of dry, cracked fields. A brown ox, knee-deep in the murky shallows, had its head down and was drinking. A naked peasant boy with a stick in his grasp, as dun-coloured as his beast, stared at us as we glided past him. In the distance the desert hills shimmered golden in the heat haze. The sky was white-hot. As I turned rather shyly forward to where the oarsmen moved to and fro and the captain sang the rhythm, the village dropped away to be replaced by empty land cut by a path that meandered beside the Nile. I was disappointed. I might have been looking at Aswat and its environs from my father's fishing boat.

The deck was hot under my bare feet. The oarsmen ignored my progress but the captain on his stool, under his canopy, favoured me with a brisk nod. I walked to where the graceful prow curved up and inward, over my head, and leaned out. Crystal wavelets folded back from the barge's assault, and above my head the flag bearing the imperial colours, blue and white, cracked in the prevailing north wind of summer. The breeze, hot though it was, felt good on my skin after the close confines of the cabin. Ahead, the river made a slow curve and vanished out of my sight so I retreated to the wall of the cabin where, as Hui had said, a white linen awning had been erected for me. Cushions had been strewn on the deck under it. I lowered myself into the shade with a sigh of satisfaction. Now was not the time to think of Aswat, to allow homesickness to invade me. Better to consider how desperately I had wanted to leave, how the gods had answered my prayers. I examined the vague guilt that stole over me as I relaxed, and realized that it was due to unaccustomed idleness. My mother would not have approved of me lolling here on plump satin like a pampered noblewoman while the oarsmen heaved and grunted under my eyes. Soon I will go aft and look at the helmsman on his perch in the stern, I told myself, but indolence had me in its gentle grip and I surrendered to it happily.

Perhaps I dozed, for it seemed that the sun had moved swiftly towards the west when my master called me sharply from beyond the curtain. I hurried to obey his summons, noticing as I did so that the placid, dreamlike shoals and banks of the river were changing. We were slipping by a house the like of which I had never seen before. It had its own watersteps as though the inhabitant was a god, and the tree-dotted land around it was a startling green. That meant many servants to haul water from the shrinking Nile. I glimpsed pillars, white as washed bones, and a portion of stone wall. Casting a glance further forward I saw another estate in the distance. Suddenly I was a foreigner in my own country, an uncouth peasant girl with dirt under her finger-nails and not the slightest conception of how life might be lived by the people in those ethereal mansions. This time, as I came into Hui's presence, I bowed.

He was lying on the cot draped in a sheet, and I could see that the linen under him was soaked with his sweat. I could hardly breathe for the thickness of the air and the stench of his odour under which was a faint hint of jasmine. Fleetingly I was reminded of the lyings-in I had attended with my mother. Many of the cramped mud rooms had smelled like this.

"Master, why do you not come outside?" I blurted without thought. "Ra is sinking towards the mouth of Nut, and soon the breeze will freshen."

"Thu, you have no manners," he muttered. "I told you not to question me. Nor may you give me advice unless, the gods forbid, I decide to ask you for it. I cannot go outside while Ra still rides across the sky. The merest touch of his rays upon my flesh causes me untold agony, as though he had bent down and put his mouth against my skin." He saw the shame of my presumption on my face and smiled. "If I had been born a fellahin like you, my father would have slaughtered me or Ra himself would have taken my life. Sometimes, particularly when I am forced to travel in primitive conditions like this, I wish it had been so. The moon is more to my taste than mighty Ra, and I bear alliegance to Thoth, the god to whom he belongs. We will tie up tonight on the outskirts of his city, Khmun, and perhaps you would like to see the sacred burial place of all the ibis birds brought there to lie under his protection. However." He pointed to the table. "Sit on the floor beside me and read me those scrolls. They are unimportant accounts from my Treasurer and letters from my friend in Nubia and I know their contents. Attempt the words you do not recognize." I picked up the bundle and surveyed him.

"Master, may I say something?"

"I suppose so."

"Let me bathe you. There is water in the bowl, and cloths, and I have much experience seeing to the comfort of women in labour. I could make you feel better." His smile broadened and he laughed aloud.

"That is the first time I have been compared to a broody female," he choked. "Sit, Thu, and do as you are told."

So I sat and spelled out the scrolls, sometimes with ease but more often with a humiliating difficulty. Pa-ari's lessons had not taken me as far as I, in my vanity, had believed. Hui corrected me brusquely but not unkindly, and as we worked the light in the room mellowed slowly to a friendly pink and the barge ceased to rock. At length I heard the ramp run out and we were interrupted.

"Permission to enter, Master. It is I, Kenna."

"Come."

The man who presented himself and bowed wore a simple

white kilt with a border embroidered in yellow. A yellow
ribbon cut across his forehead and trailed down his naked
back. He was shod in straw sandals, wore a silver armband,
and smelled gloriously of saffron oil. I presumed that the servants' boat had also been moored, and surely this creature
with the loftily aristocratic nose and haughty gaze was none
other than Hui's High Steward.

"Speak," Hui ordered.

"The sun is even now almost below the horizon and the
cooking fires have been lit. Will you be dressed and come to
the river so that I may bathe you? An acolyte from the temple of Nun awaits your pleasure on the bank. The High
Priest wishes you to dine with him tonight, if you so desire."

So Kenna was nothing more than my Master's body servant. Then in what clouds of luxury would the High
Steward appear? I felt myself shrink into insignificance. Hui
jerked his head at me. It was a dismissal.

"Find a secluded spot and bathe yourself," he told me,
"then go to the servants' barge and they will feed you.
Kenna, see that she has what she needs after you're done
with me. You can wander about Khmun for as long as you
want, Thu, and after that you will be travelling on the servants' barge. Kenna will resume his customary place here in
my cabin." The body servant shot me a look of sheer malice.
I rose, placed the scrolls back on the table, bowed to Hui,
and pushed past the supercilious Kenna. So I was to be rele-
gated to the servants' quarters. Well what did you expect? I
asked myself furiously as I swung down the ramp. Instant
recognition, my Libu Lady Thu? Respect and deference and
indulgence? Wake up! If you want those things you will
have to work for them. Very well, my thoughts ran on as I
breathed deeply of the evening air and looked about me. I
will work and I will have them.

What I saw drove all irritation from my mind. The barge
rested lightly just within the tip of a wide bay fringed with

acacia and sycamore trees. A little way off, the beach was cheerful with the twinkle of fires and chatter of the servants beside their own craft. I supposed that the oarsemen had joined them, for the oars of Hui's barge had been shipped and now hung high above the waterline. Beyond both boats, strung out along the bay, bathed in the afterglow of a red sunset, lay the largest town I had ever seen. Watersteps led to hidden gardens whose trees leaned over mud walls. Light craft of all descriptions rocked at their moorings. Here and there a road appeared, diving into a palm grove and reappearing only to run past a collection of huts and disappear once more. Behind the houses, the huts and the trees I could just make out the beige pylons and lofty pillars of several temples. Somewhere here, I knew, enshrined in a Holiest of Holiest, was the sacred mound which had arisen first from the primeval floodwaters of Nun, the original Chaos, the place where Thoth, god of wisdom and writing and every scribe's patron, had begat himself and risen upon a lotus flower. I thought of my favourite scribe, my own dear Pa-ari, at that moment, and wished fervently that he could see the home of his god.

Turning, I walked along the bank away from the town and the barges. Here there were donkey paths winding through the parched undergrowth and I took one that brought me out to a secluded marsh. The reeds stood like the brittle spears of some absent army, but once through them the sand was firm under my feet. The sun had gone and the dusk was deepening. The water was no longer pellucid but reflected the darkening sky. Pulling my sheath over my head I waded into its calm embrace. I had no natron with which to wash myself but I did my best, scooping up sand and rubbing myself with it vigorously, running my fingers over my wet scalp. When I had finished I could no longer see the farther bank. The silence around me was absolute. Standing waist deep in the almost imperceptible tug of the current I closed my eyes. "Oh Wepwawet," I prayed, "strong God of War, my totem. Help me to do battle with myself and with the unknown Egypt into which I sail. Give me a victory, and so bring me to my heart's desire." I had not even opened my eyes when a jackal began to howl, startlingly close on the other side of the river, and I shuddered. Wepwawet had heard me.

By the time I returned to the barges, full night had fallen and I was hungry. Skirting my Master's craft where a lamp burned high in the cabin, I trudged grimly towards the crackling fires of the servants. At first I was not noticed as I stepped into the circle of light, then Kenna rose from his stool and came over to me. "I understand that you are to be attached to the Master's household as personal servant and apprentice," he said coldly, without preamble. "Do not think that the title of apprentice gives you licence to take on any airs. You will not last long, so remain humble. You will have less far to fall when you are sent back to your native dirt." He looked me up and down with deliberate insolence. "The Master sometimes has these momentary foibles but he soon tires of playing the generous lord, so beware." He pointed across the sand. "There is lentil soup, bread, onions and beer over there. You will sleep with the others on the deck of the barge. I will have a pallet and a blanket placed ready for you." He marched back to his stool and was soon deep in conversation with a man I recognized as the captain of Hui's barge.

If I had been older, I would have known first that Kenna was marking his territory like a desert dog who lifts his leg against a rock and second that he was desperately in love with his Master and jealous of anyone who might usurp his place in Hui's affections. But I was an innocent country girl, hurt by this man's cruel words. As I ladled soup into a clay bowl and picked up my sliced onions, slapping them onto the heavy barley bread, I fiercely reminded myself of Hui's

Seeing in the divining bowl, of the hand of fate in my life, of the worth I placed on myself regardless of how others saw me. I would get even with him, I vowed. I would spike his wine with enough poppy to make him seem drunk when he went about his duties. I would sprinkle certain salts on his food so that his bowels would turn to water. As he talked he was watching me, his dark eyes alert to my every movement.

Balancing my food I went to join the group of servants sitting by one of the fires. Willingly they made room for me. Their curiosity was friendly. Some were cooks, some scullions to clean the barges and the Master's quarters. The oarsmen were there, and the guards who were not on duty. Their tents were pitched some way away but they were enjoying the conviviality. The guard who had admitted my father and me to the cabin recognized me and had drunk with my father, so that I was greeted kindly. When the night lengthened and the fires began to die, I went with them onto their barge and slept easily beside them on the pallet the disdainful Kenna had provided. I did not visit the ibis burial ground. I did not fancy wandering about this alarmingly big place alone and besides, I promised myself, one day I will come here in state with a hundred servants of my own and Pa-ari with me, and together we will investigate all the marvels of Thoth's sacred home.

I passed the second and third days on the river in the company of the other servants. Hui did not summon me and I did not know whether to be pleased or anxious because of it. My companions did not discuss his deformity. I could think of no other word for his physical grotesqueness. Had he or his mother been cursed before he was born? Or were his afflictions the outward manifestation of the gift of Seeing that had been granted to him by the gods? It was impossible to say.

Kenna remained on the other barge, so it was often a merry gathering under the huge awning of our barge while we slipped steadily north. The villages and small towns, the dead fields and wilting palm trees, the churned desert beyond the cultivated land and the mighty cliffs that protected Egypt, glided past us with a dreamlike dignity and I watched and drowsed, talked and listened, slept and ate, in a rising contentment tinged only slightly with homesickness. Most of the villages we passed resembled Aswat, so that sometimes it seemed to me that the barge was held in a spell of motionlessness while Aswat itself passed and repassed endlessly, a mirage just beyond my reach. But at other times, when I sat in the cool sand at the end of a fiery day and chatted with my fellows while we drank our beer and ate our simple food, Aswat faded into unreality. I was finding an equilibrium.

On the afternoon of the fourth day we came to the plain of Giza and I fell silent, leaning over the side of the barge and staring at the mighty pyramids that dotted the desert. I had heard of them. Father had spoken about them once or twice, but nothing he said had prepared me for their grandeur, their awesome nobility. My companions, who had seen them many times before, ignored them, but I fell to dreaming of the gods whose tombs they were, and wondering what Egypt had been like in that long-ago age. All the rest of that day they delighted and troubled me, and they were still faintly visible when we tied up at the city of On.

Khmun was a camp compared to the grandeur of the home of Ra. We were approaching the Delta and the river was busy with commerce. The quays of On were full of industry. Nobles' estates stood side by side along the river as far as the eye could see, and behind them the great temple of Ra poured a steady stream of incense and chanting into the darkening blue of the evening sky.

The Master had commanded that we tack to the west bank of the river to spend the night. The city sprawled along the east bank and the west was given over to the dead.

I think he did it because he had a grudge against Ra, who would burn him if given a chance, but whatever the reason, we were subdued as we made our fires and shared our meal, thinking of the tombs behind us in the empty and starlit waste of the desert. I did not want to see the city. I did not want to leave the safety of the barge at all. Like a frightened animal curled in its burrow I clung to what I knew and tried to prepare myself for yet another climactic change. My restlessness in Aswat, my bold dreams of escape, seemed the paltry, flimsy fabrications of a child who plays with dolls and is suddenly confronted with a real baby to tend. I longed to reach out for Pa-ari's reassuring hand.

That night, after the fires had died and the desultory conversations of my bedmates had faded, I could not sleep. I lay on my back gazing up at the red Horus gleaming balefully in its net of white constellations. Tomorrow we would enter the Delta and in two days I would see my Master's house. I did not want to consider the future. Nor did I want to dwell on the past. The present was enough. After a while I closed my eyes but it was no good. I pulled on my sheath and left the barge.

A guard challenged me, then let me pass with a warning. I had been told that the fringes of the Delta could be dangerous, that the eastern tribes Pharaoh had defeated three times in battle continued to filter into Egypt past the border forts of Djahi in Northern Palestine and Silsileh and pasture their flocks and herds on land belonging to Egyptians. The Libu of the western desert, who had allied themselves with the eastern people in their attempt to conquer the Delta by force, continued to raid the villages on the edge of the Delta's rich vineyards and orchards. There were murders and thefts and woundings, and the army could not patrol everywhere at once. The Medjay did what they could, but they were trained to police the villages and deal with internal problems. Desert predators were too much for them. All this shocked and troubled me. I had believed that Osiris Setnakht Glorified, our Pharaoh's father, had secured Egypt internally and our present Horus of Gold had driven the foreigners from our frontiers for ever. The increased vigilance of the soldiers as we proceeded northward had been taken for granted by my companions who ignored the added security.

Still, this was not yet the Delta. I was close to the heart of the city of On, far from the fringes of cultivation to east or west. I did not intend to go far, only to wear out my body a little so that I could sleep. I kept close to the river, treading easily through black shadows and the ashen light of the moon.

I had come to an open stretch of sandbank and was about to turn back when I saw him. He was standing waist deep in the silvered water, arms raised, his head thrown back and that lustrous white hair cascading past his shoulders like iridescent foam. Here, bathed in the pale aura of his god, lost in adoration or tranced in Seeing, he was uniquely beautiful and I drew in my breath and paused. Quietly I began to retreat but a twig must have snapped under my tread for he swung about and called to me.

"Are you spying, praying, or seeking adventure, my little peasant? How are you faring, flung in with my menials? Perhaps you are sneaking south to find Aswat again as a poorly trained horse will seek its stable."

I did not yet know him well enough to decide whether or not he was being spiteful. I could not discern his face in the gloom though his body was bathed in ghostly moonlight.

"I came upon you accidentally, Master," I said loudly. "I did not mean to spy."

"No?" His hands went to his hips, hidden under the slow swirl of the dark water. "But Kenna tells me that you are full of questions to your new-found friends. Could it be that my trust in you is misplaced?" This was so grossly unfair that I had no ready answer. I remained silent, and it came to me once more that he was conducting some sort of test. I resented it. "But Kenna is a man of violent prejudices where I am concerned," he went on smoothly. "He does not like you at all."

"Well, I do not like him either!" I shouted back. "He should not judge me upon the evidence of one meeting!" He began to wade towards me. "It does not matter," he commented. "Kenna is only a servant. His opinions do not interest me. Isn't that so, Kenna?" I whirled about. Kenna was standing behind me, the Master's clothes in his arms. His face was a mask as he met my eye.

"That is so," he agreed tonelessly.

"Good." Hui had left the water and was approaching us naked, and I thought with a jolt, why not? For Kenna and I are as nothing, little better than slaves, faceless and without importance. I should have lowered my gaze but I could not. I was mesmerized by the pallid, somehow tainted symmetry of the tight-muscled white belly, the high-rounded buttocks, and the thing that hung between Hui's thick thighs. Embarrassed, intrigued, heated, angry, I could not, in my fourteenth year, recognize the dawning of my sexuality and it is only now, looking back with sadness, that I see the budding of a confused passion that was to colour the rest of my life. I was aware of the sudden tension in Kenna before he stepped around me and began to towel the moisture running like milk down Hui's body. His movements were practised, gentle and impersonal, yet I clenched my teeth as I watched him. Hui watched me. He continued to do so as his servant draped him in linen, leaving only his head bare. When Kenna had finished, Hui dismissed him abruptly. He bowed and vanished promptly into the darkness.

"Are you happy, Thu?" the Master enquired. "Are you regretting your decision to cast your lot with me?" He was looking at me, now, with solicitude. I shook my head.

"Good," he said thoughtfully. "Now, my obdurate little colt, we will sit here on the dead grass, under the dead trees, and I will tell you a bedtime story." To my amazement he arranged himself on the earth, drew up his knees under the thick cloak, and signalled that I should join him. I did so. "I will tell you a story of the creation of all things," he began. "And then you will be able to sleep, will you not? Here. Rest your head against me. In the beginning, Thu, in fact before there was a beginning, the Nun was the all. Chaos and turbulence. And with the Nun there was Huh, the unendingness, and Kuk, the darkness, and Amun, the air…" His voice had a hypnotic quality, deliberately calming and reassuring, but the power of the story kept me listening, at least for a while. He spoke of how Atum, child of the chaos that was Nun, created himself by an effort of the will, and how he brought light to disperse Kuk, the darkness. So sometimes the Atum was Ra-Atum, the phoenix ever new. He told me how Atum, being alone, copulated with his shadow and so begat the gods. Increasingly his tone wove in and out of the fantasies sleep was conjuring in my mind. I was dimly aware that I had slumped against him and his arm had gone around me. Then his voice became a monotonous song. I felt myself lifted, carried, placed on my pallet, the blanket pulled to my chin, and then the blessed oblivion of unconsciousness.

Chapter 5

The thought of those days on the river still brings a lump to my throat, for I was still half a child and hopeful, and trusting in both gods and men. Just beyond On the Nile divided and became the three mighty tributaries and several smaller ones that emptied into the Great Green. Our barges took the north-eastern finger of the river, the Waters of Ra, and as I sat cross-legged on the deck I saw a slow miracle take place. Gradually the aridity and barrenness of summer gave way to the sweetness of spring. The air grew heavy with the scent of growing things. Papyrus thickets crowded the verdant shores, their dark green stems and delicate fronds weaving and whispering in the cool breeze. Everywhere there was fertility. Birds flocked and wheeled, piped and fluttered. White cranes and ibis stood motionless in the shallows, seemingly as bemused at the riotous lushness of the life around them as I was. And there was water everywhere; glinting half-glimpsed through dense trees, lying blue and still in full irrigation canals, rippling with the wash of tiny brown bodies bobbing up and down in the ponds. It was not surprising, I thought as I inhaled the distinctively sweet odour of what I came to know as the fruit orchards, stripped bare at this season, that the foreign tribesmen coveted such a paradise. The cattle that lifted their incurious heads and watched us glide by were somnolent and fat with health. The Waters of Ra became the Waters of Avaris. We passed the temple of the cat goddess Bast in the red glow of a perfect evening, and lit our fires amid a soft but constant susurration of insect song.

On the afternoon of the following day the outskirts of the most beautiful city on earth came in sight. The mighty Osiris One, Ramses the Second, had built Pi-Ramses to the east of the ancient site of Avaris where the ramshackle hovels of the poor leaned drunkenly together around the temple of Set, Ramses' totem, and greeted the traveller from On with dust, noise and filth. I had never seen distress like this. I wanted to avert my eyes, but before I could tear my gaze away a jumbled pile of stones took its place. I learned later that it was the remains of an even older town, its name lost in antiquity. A string of trading barges obscured my view, its crew and ours exchanging coarse insults as it was forced to tack towards the shore to make way for us. Indeed, the river had become thick with craft of all kinds, each bent on appropriating the few open stretches of water, and the air was full of shouted expletives. When the traffic eased, the ruins had gone, to be replaced by the great canal Ramses had built to surround his city-palace. Here we had to wait, for the junction was choked with craft, but after much yelling and swearing a path was cleared for us. We began to drift to the right.

Now my dissatisfaction turned to awe. On our left was a vast and confusing collection of warehouses, workshops, granaries and storehouses, cacophonous with busy life. The canal had widened into a vast pool into which quays extended. Goods of every description were being loaded and unloaded. There were children everywhere, little naked half-wild beings who scampered like rats over the wares and called to each other in shrill voices.

Beyond this, the city showed another character. Gardens and orchards surrounded the white houses of minor noblemen and officials, merchants and foreign traders. The polite peace of a modest affluence permeated them.

After a while the pool narrowed again, and this time it was guarded by armed soldiers in light skiffs. Looking ahead

I saw my Master's captain answer a challenge. The skiffs drew aside and we slid through the small opening into the Lake of the Residence, Pharaoh's private domain. There was not much to see. The southern wall of the palace was far too high to show anything of what was within, and it seemed to go on forever, finally curving away to be replaced by more impeccably groomed gardens. Here there were dazzlingly white marble watersteps against which several large craft rocked. Gold and silver glittered on their sides, their masts, their exquisitely damasked cabins, and each one flew the imperial colours of blue and white. They were Pharaoh's own barges. Seeing the flag Hui's vessel was flying, the guards thronging the watersteps saluted, and then we were past them and the sheltering wall came back to meet us.

When it ended, more estates began, but these were different. I could not see the houses for the walls that enclosed them. Tree branches leaned over towards the water, and the tops of stiff palms spiked against the sky. The watersteps were all of marble, and where they ended there were wide paved courts in front of the pyloned and doubtless well-watched entrances. The people who really mattered in Egypt, the Viziers and Treasurers, the Butlers and Overseers, the High Priests and Hereditary Nobles, lived here. Those people know Pharaoh, I remember thinking as Hui's barge nosed to the bank. I will see people who speak with the Horus of Gold himself.

Servants had appeared, running across the paving to secure Hui's barge and settle the ramp on the watersteps. Behind them a large man came slowly forth from the shadow of the entrance pylon and stood at the top of the steps. I should say glided forth, for he moved with a heavy yet graceful dignity. Everything about him was round, from his thick upper arms gripped by silver armbands to his substantial waist, to the cords of his calves. His bare skull shone. One pendant earring swung against his thick neck.

His fleshy mouth was hennaed orange and the cold eyes that flickered rapidly over the mêlée developing on the water-steps were emphasized with kohl. He spoke one sharp word and my companions, who were pressing and jostling to be first on our ramp, fell back.

Hui emerged from the cabin of his barge. As always when in public he was invisible beneath his white shroud. Striding the ramp and mounting the watersteps he received the big man's short bow and together they walked across the paving, in under the small pylon, and were lost to sight. Kenna and a few of the servants from the house went next, and then there was a concerted rush from the second barge. I found myself swept along with the crowd, off the barge, onto the stone that was hot beneath my bare feet, and through the entrance. The friends of my voyage scattered, obviously glad to be home, and I was alone.

I could hear the activity still going on behind me. The barges were being unloaded. But I stood in my grubby, now tattered sheath, feeling lost and out of place. Two paths ran out from where I stood. One went to the right, plunging under trees towards a wall glimpsed through the foliage. I presumed that it led to servants' quarters, for the people had disappeared along it. The other went straight ahead. All around me trees, shrubs and palms were densely massed, obscuring my view. Flower beds were laid out neatly beside the walkway. I was tempted to follow the faces that I knew, to seek reassurance, but mutinously decided that, seeing no one had told me where to go, I should go where I pleased.

I set off along the central path and soon came to an open area with seats and a fountain that splashed its water into a large circular basin. To left and right the path diverged and on both sides were thorn hedges. Rather timidly I peered over one to find myself looking at a fishpond. Lotus pads floated on its quiet surface and an old sycamore cast its shade on the verge. The other hedge completely enclosed a pool that must be used for swimming, for a small curtained hut had been built at one end and someone had left a linen tunic and an empty cup on its stone edge. Skirting the fountain I continued on. The path took me past a kiosk, a small shrine in which there was a stone offering table, hollowed at one end, and an exquisite statue of ibis-headed Thoth whose tiny black-painted eye stared back at me. I bowed to him as I passed.

Then the trees thinned and I came to a gate before a wide, paved courtyard. The house was before me, its entrance pillars painted white and resplendently embellished with the likenesses of exotic birds and vines that curled up to meet the roof. I could see the rest of the sheltering wall now, running high and forbidding behind more trees to either side of the house and behind it. Set in the wall to the right was a double door that must also lead to a servants' domain—kitchens and granaries probably, and perhaps stables, though I did not think that Hui would like to drive a chariot. Once more I hesitated. Should I march up to the entrance hall and announce my presence? I could dimly see a guard, or perhaps a doorkeeper, sitting on a stool beyond one of the pillars. For a moment I toyed with the idea of making my way home again and having done with all this ignominy. How could Hui have forgotten me, after our vital conversations? Well, they were vital to me anyway.

I retraced my steps, enjoying the cool, dappled shade of the little forest, the green silence in which I moved. Arriving at the fountain I went through the thorn hedge to the pool and settled myself beside its clear depths. I was thirsty and afraid, but I made myself remember my prayer to Wepwawet and how it was answered. The thought consoled me. I could always walk into the markets of Pi-Ramses and hire myself out as a domestic servant. My mother had taught me the value of cleanliness. My services would go to one of the rich merchants whose homes I had admired, and he would have a son. I would be scrubbing the paving before his door and the son would emerge, darkly handsome, lonely. I would glance up and he would see, for the first time, my blue eyes. He would be intrigued, then obsessed. His father would rage, his mother cry, but a wedding contract would follow... So I dreamed, nervous and adrift, while the glinting water netted the sunlight and a curious cat came stalking out of the hedge to sit in the shade and watch me with its unblinking, myopic stare.

A long time afterwards, when my fantasy had run its course and I knew I must do something, a man came hurrying from the other side of the clearing. I rose as he approached me red-faced and out of breath.

"Are you Thu?" he panted. I nodded warily. "Oh, thank the gods!" he exclaimed. "Where have you been? I was sent to find you an hour ago. I thought you might be with the other servants so I've turned the compound upside down." He glanced around the pool. "You are not supposed to be here unless on the Master's business," he reproved me mildly. "These gardens are for the family only. Follow me."

"Family?" I echoed as I trotted to catch up with him. "Hui has a family?"

"Well of course he does," the man replied irritably. "His mother and father are retired to their acres outside On. If you want to know more you must ask him yourself and take the consequences. Servants are never allowed to question their betters unless it has to do with their duties. He does not encourage gossip. You really are a provincial, aren't you?"

That closed my mouth, although I burned with questions. I had thought of the Master as a creature of lofty aloneness, self-sufficient, almost self-generating. But a family? Were they all monsters? The servant had taken a path that ran between the outer wall of the estate and the trees and we had to angle across the blinding expanse of the courtyard to reach the entrance. The doorkeeper on his stool did not acknowledge us.

A short way in under the pillars a huge room opened out. It was dim and cool after the furnace of the outer court. Light poured down in brilliant shafts from several thin windows high under the ceiling. More white pillars were spaced across the gleaming, tiled floor. The furniture was sparse and elegant, a few cedar chairs inlaid with gold and ivory, low tables topped with blue and green faience work, but the walls were alive with scenes of feasting. I had no chance to examine them then. I padded after my escort, whose own sandals slapped busily as he strode. A group of men were clustered beside one of the pillars. Hui was one of them. I could not be sure that he saw me but if he did he made no sign. His hooded head turned and then turned back.

At the far end of the hall and immediately to my left, beyond the wide double doors that stood open, a flight of stairs rose steeply. To my right were other rooms whose doors were firmly closed and between them a guard sat. Ahead was a passage running away to left and right and directly in front of me, twenty steps away, a square doorway led onto a terrace and more gardens before the wall loomed.

But my attention was fixed at once on the man who was rising from behind a desk by the stairs. It was as though a small mountain had chosen to move, for it was the person I had seen above the watersteps. He had been impressive then. He was terrifying now. Unsmilingly he looked down on me, inspecting me from head to dusty toes with those impassive black eyes, then he folded his great arms across his barrel chest and sighed. The earring quivered gently against one pouched cheek. "Go," he ordered the servant with me. The man bowed and disappeared along the passage. "So," he went on resignedly. "You are Thu. You are also a nuisance. This is an efficiently run household, and you are no longer free to go where you please when you want. I have been instructed as to your status and handling by the Master, therefore do not complain about any order you may receive. If you have questions you will put them to me or to Disenk. You will not approach the Master under any circumstances unless he sends for you. Do you understand?" I nodded vigorously. His voice was a rumble of threatening power. "Good," he continued. "Follow me."

He moved with surprising agility to the foot of the stairs and began to mount, his kilt swaying gently about his oddly delicate ankles. Meekly I did as I was told. He had not introduced himself. I supposed I was too much of a nonentity for him to bother. At the top of the stairs there was a dark passage flanked by many doors. He led me almost to the end before opening one of them and gesturing me inside. I blinked. The room was full of sunlight that cascaded through the large window ahead of me. There was a couch of wood, draped in fine linens and cushions. Beside it was a table on which stood an alabaster lamp. Two chairs were arranged haphazardly by the window. A huge feathered fan was propped against one wall. A pair of matching chests also hugged the wall, large, handsome things with bronze fittings. A woman stood in the middle of all this luxury. Slight and tiny, dressed in a spotless but plain sheath, her hair tied high with a red ribbon, she smiled at me and bowed to my companion. "Disenk, this is Thu," he said brusquely. "You can begin by giving her a bath. Scrape off some of that Aswat muck and pluck her eyebrows." He did not wait for an answer. The door closed firmly behind him.

Disenk and I eyed one another through the sun-soaked air. She was still smiling, her hands behind her back, expectancy on her little face. I did not yet understand that a conversation was usually opened by the person of highest rank in a room so I too waited, nonplussed, then to cover my confusion I wandered over to the window and looked out. I was directly above the entrance, and below me one of the men I had seen in the hall was just getting onto a litter. He twitched the curtains closed and the four slaves in attendance lifted it and set off towards the gate and the trees. I decided to speak. "Who is the big man who brought me up here?" I asked. "He told me that if I have any questions I am to put them to him, or to you."

"That is Harshira, the Master's Steward," she answered readily. "He is responsible for the running of the household and the keeping of all the Master's accounts. His word is law."

"Oh." I turned back into the room a little shyly. "Where are my things, Disenk? My basket and my box?" She went at once to one of the chests and lifted the lid.

"They are here, safe. The Master forgets nothing. Would you like to bathe?" She was being polite. The Steward had already commanded her to give me a bath. As if my swim in the Nile every evening was not enough!

"Not really," I said, "but I will if I must. What I want is to be told where I am to sleep. And I want a drink." A small frown creased her unlined brow. She gestured broadly.

"But this is your room," she told me. "You will sleep here."

"Do I share it with you?" I looked about for the pallet on which I supposed I would lie. She laughed.

"No, Thu. It is all your own. I sleep close by. Would you like water or beer or wine? There is also pomegranate or grape juice."

"My own?" I whispered. I had never imagined such space, such opulence. I had presumed that I would be housed with the other servants outside the main grounds. I thought of the room I had shared with Pa-ari. It had seemed large enough, but it would fit in here four or five times over. "I would like beer," I said with an effort, and she opened the door and called. Not much later a small boy appeared carrying a tray. Disenk took it from him and set it by the couch.

"There are raisins and almonds if you are hungry," she said, pouring beer and handing me the cup. "Then we must go to the bath house. Harshira forgets nothing either!" I took the cup and drained it. There was no cloudiness and little sediment in the dark liquid. Immediately Disenk offered me the dish of nuts and dried fruit.

"Are you to be my companion, my guardian, what?" I questioned her as I crammed a handful of the appetizing mix into my mouth. "I would like to know where I stand, Disenk." Once again an expression of pain furrowed her brow as she watched me.

"Your pardon, Thu," she said, distressed, and I thought for a moment that I had somehow offended her. "A lady does not talk with her mouth full. Nor does she take so much food that her cheeks bulge. It is ugly and unseemly." I stared at her, feeling the surge of truculence that always rose in me when anyone gave me advice or a reprimand.

"I am not a lady," I retorted. "Everyone has been reminding me of that fact since I left Aswat. I am a peasant girl. Why should I try to be anything else?" Yet I swallowed hurriedly and resisted the urge to scoop up more raisins and almonds.

"You are very beautiful," Disenk said gently. "Forgive me for upsetting you, but my orders are to refine and civilize that beauty. I hope you will not find my lessons too humiliating. I intend only good."

Her mention of beauty mollified me. No one but the Master had ever called me beautiful before, and that was only off-handedly, in passing. Vanity in girls was not encouraged in my village. It was thought to breed idleness and selfishness in a world where hard work and obedience were admired. Even Pa-ari had done little more than tease me for my blue eyes. "I believed that I was here to assist the Master in his labours," I probed cautiously. "Why must I learn such frivolous things?" Her gaze dropped. Black eyelashes quivered against the fine-grained patina of her skin.

"I am only your body servant," she murmured. "Harshira has not seen fit to acquaint me with the Master's purposes for you. Now if you are refreshed we will go to the bath house."

"My body servant?" I gaped at her incredulously, while wanting also to laugh. "I am to have a body servant?" For answer she smiled again, politely, and going to the door she held it open.

"It is time to bathe," she said firmly.

There were more stairs at the opposite end of the passsage to the one I had ascended, almost outside my door. These were narrow, and led down to a small interior courtyard surrounded by the walls of the house where a date palm spread its stiff shade in complete privacy. One other door led out from it, and to my left as I stepped onto the stone paving of the courtyard was a dim entrance. I followed Disenk into it. The room had a sloping stone floor with a raised slab in the centre. It was damp and cool. Huge urns brimming with water from which a sweet but subtle scent emanated lined the walls, and shadowy recesses held unrecognizable pots and jars. Disenk gestured. "Please remove your sheath," she requested in a tone that I soon came to know as a good-natured command, then she vanished. Uneasily I did as I was told, dropping my worn clothing and feeling immediately vulnerable. A wave of homesickness engulfed me and then was gone. I wanted to step out into the late afternoon glow of sunlight streaming past the doorway of the bath house but was afraid of being seen naked by invisible eyes.

I was hesitating when Disenk reappeared, followed by two female slaves carrying dippers and linen towels and a young man in a loincloth. I shrank back dismayed as he approached me, my hands going instinctively to cover my genitals. His appraisal, however, was completely impersonal. He ran a hand down my calf. "Very dry," he muttered. Lifting my foot, he kneaded it briefly, and here I heard disdain in his words. "These feet are very calloused and rough," he complained. "I cannot be expected to work miracles, Disenk."

"Castor oil mixed with sea salt to begin with," Disenk ordered. "The feet must be abraded. As for her skin, olive oil and honey should suffice."

"But so much body hair," he grumbled, the massive muscles of his shoulders and arms flexing as he lifted my tresses and expertly felt my spine. "Good lines though." I spoke up.

"I will thank you to keep your opinions to yourself," I retorted, though inside I was cringing with shame. "It is bad enough that I am being forced to bathe as though I am dirty when I swim in the river every single day, but I will not stand here and be discussed like a cow being judged in the market-place!" He smiled in surprise, and for the first time he looked me full in the face.

"Your pardon," he said formally. "I am only doing my job."

"Like Disenk," I said, allowing anger to mask my humiliation, and he bowed.

"Like Disenk," he agreed. Going to one of the recesses he selected several pots before leaving the room. Disenk signalled. Still mutinous, I got up on the slab and the slaves sprang to life. Water from the dippers cascaded over me, then hands rubbed me vigorously with grains of a substance I identified as natron. More water sluiced off the salts. My hair was washed and coated in olive oil, then wrapped in a towel. I was dried gently, then led outside. The slaves bowed and vanished as silently as they had come.

Meekly, my skin tingling, I lay on the portable table that had been set up under the palm. Disenk knelt beside me, tweezers in hand. "This will hurt," she told me, "but from now on I will remove the pubic hair twice weekly and the pain will be less. I will shave your legs and under your arms in a moment." I nodded, then looked up at the trembling fronds of the tree outlined against a slowly blushing sky while she set to work. The pain was indeed intense and I supressed the urge to pull away from it. "Your pardon, Thu," she went on, her head bent over my abdomen, the tweezers making pricks of fire, "but you must not swim in the river any more. For one thing, water alone cannot cleanse and soften the skin and for another, a lady does not expose herself to direct sunlight for fear that her colour may deepen and she may begin to look like a peasant. Your colour is too dark. You must stay indoors or walk under the protection of a canopy so that it may become pale and attractive. I will treat your skin with meal of alabaster to hasten the lightening process."

I wanted to kick out and stop the steady throbbing of my tender region. I wanted to grab up my comfortable, shabby sheath and thumb my nose at Disenk and her snobbishness, running out through the house, into the gardens, away from all this nonsense, but the die had been cast and my metamorphosis had begun. Each ruthless manipulation of Disenk's tweezers took me further from my origins, and in the end I accepted my hurt, gritted my teeth, and remained silent.

When she had plucked my genitals she attacked my eyebrows, her tiny, perfect face pressed close to mine, her pink tongue protruding delicately as she concentrated, then she shaved me with a sharp copper razor while another slave held a bowl of steaming hot water at her elbow. At last she rose and I made as if to scramble up but she shook her head, jerking her fingers imperiously at someone out of my sight. The young man was back, looming over me suddenly as he set his pots on the ground. "Better," he observed drily, and I sighed. "Turn over, Thu." I did so. Cool oil slid onto my back, and as his hands descended onto my shoulders I felt every muscle in my body loosen. Perhaps being a lady would not be so bad after all. I closed my eyes.

Much later, tired and hungry again, I submitted to a further washing of my hair, sat while Disenk slipped a pair of papyrus sandals onto my newly softened feet, stood while she wrapped me in voluminous linen, and followed her back to the quiet safety of my room. The sun had long since left my window and the sky beyond it was red swiftly dissolving into darkness. The bedside table had been moved to the window and was crowded with dishes whose odours sent a gush of saliva into my mouth. Disenk removed their covers. There was broiled fish and hot fresh bread, grape juice and sticky figs, leeks in white sauce. I did not wait to be invited to eat but sat at once under Disenk's watchful eye. The fish melted in my mouth and the flavour of the leeks was enhanced by something in the sauce that I had not tasted before. This time I took small portions and strove to be dainty.

There was a bowl of water by my hand, and before reaching for the figs I made as if to drink from it but Disenk shook her head. "That is for rinsing the fingers," she explained, pushing the juice towards me instead, "and when you have done so and are ready to eat again I dry your hands." She lifted a small cloth. Suddenly it was all too much for me and I had to swallow the quick tears that had risen.

"I'm so tired, Disenk," I said. "I know it is wrong to waste food but I cannot finish this meal." She laughed.

"Dear Thu," she replied. "What you do not consume will go back to the kitchen or to the beggars outside the temples of the city. Do not fret. Come." She lifted the table away from me and walked to the couch where she turned down the sheet and stood waiting. "Sleep now. My pallet is outside your door, in the passage, if you wake in the night and need anything." Gratefully I approached the bed and clambered onto it, and she lowered the sheet over me. It was obvious that no prayers were to be said and I wondered who the totems of the house were. Thoth, certainly, for I had seen his shrine in the garden, but to whom was I to pray in order to sanctify my rest? What other gods guarded the inmates of Hui's home through the night? Disenk was lowering the reed mat that covered the window, and the room filled with a slumbrous dimness. She walked to the table. "There is fresh water beside you," she told me, gathering up the remains of my meal, "And I will leave the figs in case you are hungry in the night. Do you wish to be read to sleep?" Startled, I declined. She smiled, crossed the floor, bowed, and let herself out, the door closing softly but firmly behind her.

Drowsily I turned on my side and lay looking into the dusky stillness around me. I knew I should get up and face the south, where many miles and another life away, Wepwawet's temple stood peaceful and gracious at the end of the path beside the river along which I had kicked up the dust with my bare feet so many times. I should perform my prostrations, say the words of gratitude and abasement that I owed to the god who had answered my plea, but I was unwilling to move. My muscles ached pleasantly from the expert massage the young man had given me and my mind, full to overflowing with a jumble of impressions, strange voices, instructions and anticipation, was exhausted. My stomach was full. My eyes closed. Mother always taught us that we must never ask someone else to perform a task we can do for ourselves, I thought as I curled into a ball and savoured the deep softness of the cushion beneath my head. But it seems to me that such virtues are reversed here. A lady is judged by how little she does for herself.

Do not become lazy and complacent, Thu, some part of my heart whispered to me. There may be dangers ahead that only a sturdy peasant girl could face. Swallow your pride and learn from Disenk. Obey those in authority over you. But never forget that your father is a farmer, not a nobleman, and the god who raised you up can just as quickly cast you down. But he won't, I thought firmly. We have a special bond, Wepwawet and I, for he is a God of War and I am a warrior.

Chapter 6

The sound of the window mat being raised woke me the next morning, and as I sat up a ray of strong sunshine fell across my couch. Disenk approached, smiling a greeting, and placed a tray across my knees. There was grape juice again, fresh bread and dried fruits. I drank thirstily with an anxious eye on the window. It appeared that Ra had already travelled across half the sky and I had no right to be still abed. Disenk stood waiting attentively, small hands folded, until I spoke.

"Do I begin work today do you think, Disenk?" I asked her. She answered immediately, and it was then that I began to understand that it was up to me to initiate any conversation with her.

"When you are bathed and dressed you are to report to Harshira," she told me. "Other than that, I do not know. I am sorry."

My heart sank, and some of my appetite left me. I did not particularly want to face the daunting bulk of Hui's Steward. My quarters had very quickly become a womb and this woman a safeguard, but I scolded myself inwardly for my cowardice and dabbled my fingers in the waterbowl as daintily as I could, holding them out for Disenk's ready cloth and noting her pleased expression. I was a fast learner. "Down to the bath house again?" I asked in mock dismay, and her good-mannered smile widened into a grin of pure amusement. For a moment I saw the real Disenk under the strictures of her position.

"Again," she nodded, removing my tray, "and every

morning." She held out a fresh sheet and I slid off the couch to be wrapped in it. "Once I am satisfied with the condition of your body, Thu, the routine will not be as harsh." The papyrus slippers appeared and she knelt to put them on me. "Do not be angry with me," she begged half-seriously. "I only fulfil the wishes of the Master through the words of Harshira." I sighed, and followed her into the passage.

The same bland faces ministered to me in the bath house, and the same young man stroked and pounded at my body. I was shaved again but not plucked, to my profound relief. The process did not take as long as it had the day before and I felt guilty for taking some enjoyment from it. Afterwards I returned to my room to find that a small but very beautiful table had been set up under the window. It exuded the faint, steady scent of cedar wood and its polished surface was cunningly inlaid with gold in the likeness of Hathor, goddess of youth and beauty. Her serene face looked up at me and the sun sparked along her gracefully curving cow's horns as I ran my fingertips over her, marvelling at the workmanship. Disenk indicated that I should sit. Her own hand went to a catch on the rim of the table and half of the top lifted on cunningly concealed hinges to reveal a cavity full of pots, brushes and spoons. Deftly Disenk arranged a selection on the half that remained closed, and placed a copper mirror in my lap. "What are you going to do?" I wanted to know.

"You are very young, and do not require much painting," she replied, "but no one should go about without kohl to protect and beautify the eyes, and the mouth also should be guarded. Each night I will anoint your face with oil and honey, but for the day, simple cleanliness is enough." Her hands were busy opening tiny jars and selecting brushes. She peered into two pots, frowning, holding them against my cheeks, weighing the effect.

"Show me," I ordered. She did so. They both contained powdered khol, one a dark grey and the other green.

"Your eyes are blue," she said, "therefore the green is not for you." While she spoke she had been dropping water into a tiny crucible and adding the grey powder, mixing it carefully with a bone stick carved to resemble a river reed. Her actions were graceful but deft and I wondered for the first time who had trained her, and where, and what her origins might be. "Close please," she commanded. I did so, my eyelids quivering at the unaccustomed touch as the brush passed over them. I felt the slickness on my temples and for just a moment caught a whiff of her breath, an odour of cumin that was far from unpleasant. "You may open," she said. "For your mouth I have red ochre, also brushed. Part your lips a little, Thu." There was a pause, and this time the brush tickled. "Now look at yourself."

I did so, bringing up the copper mirror in some trepidation, then gasped at what I saw. An exotic creature gazed back at me, the dark paint now emphasizing the startling clarity of my blue eyes so that they dominated my face over cheekbones that had suddenly become delicately patrician. My brown skin had a healthy sheen to it. The red mouth was parted in surprise, the lips full and lush. "It's magic," I whispered, and the image mimicked my words. The eyes narrowed seductively then widened. I could not put the mirror down. Disenk chuckled, obviously complimented.

"Not magic, Thu," she said. "Any proficient cosmetician can make beautiful that which is truly ugly, but painting you requires no skill. You are an easy assignment."

Something in her artless words chilled me. Slowly I lowered the mirror. I wanted to ask her what all this pampering was for. After all, Hui had brought me to Pi-Ramses only to be his servant. Or was there another reason? Had he lied when he told my father that he would guard my virginity more closely than Father himself had done? Was I being prepared for his bed? Suddenly I felt suffocated. Disenk was combing my hair in long, sure strokes but her touch no longer seemed pleasurable.

"I am flattered that the Master has seen fit to take such a personal interest in me," I managed clumsily. "Surely not all his servants are accorded this attention." Her movements did not falter. The comb continued to glide through my heavy tresses.

"All the house servants must be physically acceptable and presentable," she pointed out. "Forgive me, Thu, but when I first saw you yesterday I might have mistaken you for a kitchen slave. Many important people come here. The servants must reflect the taste and elegance of the establishment."

I was somewhat reassured but not altogether convinced. Not every servant had a sumptuous room to herself, of that I was sure, for did not Disenk herself sleep in the passageway and was she not, by her own admission, my body servant as well as my teacher? I resolved to question Harshira though the prospect was horrifying. Disenk was binding a blue ribbon round my forehead and arranging its ends to fall one over each shoulder. She reached for a jar, broke the wax seal on it, and using another bone stick she anointed me with the contents, pressing gently under my ears, in the hollow of my neck, against my inner elbows. She stroked it through my hair, and gradually the light but pervasive tang of oil of saffron filled the atmosphere. "There!" she said with evident satisfaction. "Now for your sheath and sandals and you will be ready."

I stood woodenly as she pulled the garment expertly over my head, avoiding contact with my face, and settled it tight to my body. The linen was white and fine, softer than anything I had ever felt let alone worn, even softer than the kilt Father had brought home so triumphantly for Pa-ari. It draped itself around my slight curves as though it had been made for no one else. A slit up one side would allow me to walk and I looked down admiringly but warily at my provocative length as Disenk put the sandals on my feet. "Remember, Thu," she warned me, straightening and regarding her handiwork critically, "you must not lope. The sheath will allow small, polite steps, very graceful, very becoming, and you will soon become used to its restriction. A lady does not gallop." She went to the door and called sharply. A boy entered promptly and bowed. "He will take you to Harshira," she said, and I turned about and left her, feeling as though I was being torn from my mother's arms.

The little slave moved confidently ahead of me along the passage while I teetered after him. My natural stride was long and within a very short time I was in danger of falling on my face as the sheath caught me with every move. At the head of the stairs leading down to the centre of the house I paused. I had had enough. "Wait!" I called to my silent guide, and bending, I examined the stitches in the side of the sheath where the slit ended. They were tight. My mother would have approved of the skill they exhibited. Nevertheless I worked at them until they loosened then I picked several of them undone. The slit was now above my knee but I did not care. The boy was looking at me aghast, as though I had stopped to actually take off the stupid garment. "What are you staring at?" I snapped at him, half in annoyance and half incredulous at my own temerity, and he raised his hands to me, palms skyward, in the ancient gesture of submission and apology and turned away.

I squared my shoulders in defence and anticipation as we came to the foot of the stairs, but the table where the Chief Steward had sat only the day before was empty. The boy marched past it, turned left away from the main reception hall so that we faced the large, open doorway that gave out onto the rear garden and estate wall, then left again along an inside corridor. The distance was not great. A closed door barred our way. He knocked, was bidden to enter, did so, announced me loudly and succinctly, then slipped past me and vanished. I walked into the room.

It was full of light and I realized immediately that it lay directly under my quarters, for I could see the front courtyard with the waist-high wall, the gate and the trees clustering beyond. A gardener was just disappearing into the far shade, tools over his shoulder, and a kilted young man strode casually past the window. I could hear his sandals tapping on the paving. This is a good place for the office of the Chief Steward, I thought, even as I came to a halt and bowed. He can see everyone who comes and goes. Nothing will escape him during the daylight hours. I wonder where he sleeps?

The man himself was sitting, as before, behind a table, but this one was massive and laden with papyrus scrolls of every size. A silver dish piled with wrinkled purple pomegranates sat half-buried to his right hand, a wine jug to his left. Cupboards and chests lined half of each wall from floor to ceiling. The other half was taken up with doors. One, I surmised, led to the main hall and the other surely let into the quarters of the Master and his other important staff members. There my observations ended, for the man himself waved me forward. There was an empty chair beside me but he did not invite me to sit. I resisted the urge to clasp my hands nervously together. His kohled eyes travelled me from head to toe without expression. Both his hands, heavily ringed and surprisingly slim for a man of his girth, remained flat on the desk before him.

"Are you well?" he asked harshly after the moment of silence. I nodded. "Good," he went on in the same noncommittal tone. "Today you will dictate a letter to your family, telling them so. When you have finished you will spend the rest of the afternoon in the company of one of the under-scribes, who will begin to teach you how to write and will assess your reading ability. After your evening meal, which you will take with Disenk in your own room, you will exercise with the Master's physical instructor. Then you will take a history lesson. That is all. Do you have any questions?"

I did indeed. I had a dozen questions, but under his dark, impassive gaze I felt myself quail. Pull yourself together, Thu, I told myself sternly. Pretend you are a princess and this man is nothing, an inferior whose fate you can decide with a toss of your beautiful, beautiful head. I moistened my lips, wondering fleetingly as I did so if I was transferring red ochre from my mouth to my tongue and would end up looking twice as stupid as I felt.

"As a matter of fact," I said, with a poise that surprised me, "I have several. If, of course, it is permitted." My tone was more sarcastic than I had intended and one of his carefully plucked eyebrows rose a fraction. He lifted one finger from the desk as an indication that I might continue. I took a deep breath. "Why must I take a history lesson?"

"Because you are an ignorant little girl."

"I swim in the river every day. Why must I exercise?" Disenk's comment regarding cleanliness had rankled. He did not move.

"Because if you do not exercise you will eventually become unattractively flabby." Unconsciously I stepped nearer to the desk. "Your pardon, Harshira," I said firmly, "but what does it matter whether I am unattractive or not? I am here to assist the Master in his labours, am I not? Yet I am primped and pampered like a...a concubine!" The word came hard to my tongue and I knew, furiously, ashamedly, that I was blushing. The exacting morals of my peasant upbringing ran strong and deep in me in spite of my reckless nature and I could see my mother's disapproving face as she reproved me for wanting to talk about some village woman who had been behaving in an unseemly manner. "Concubine," to my Aswat neighbours, was synonymous with laziness and moral depravity. A man might take a destitute village woman into the bosom of his family, sleep with her, have children by her, but always for the right reasons. Sexual adventure alone was not one of them. His legitimate wife might be barren or in poor health so that she could not perform her household duties. The woman in question would have no other recourse due to her straitened circumstances. When the villagers spoke of Pharaoh's harem it was always in terms of our Ruler's necessity to safeguard the Horus Throne with many potential heirs, ridiculous though the justification might be.

Harshira smiled. His huge cheeks rose. His dark eyes narrowed and for a moment lost their imperturbability. "Did the Master make you any such promise?" he asked me pointedly.

Promise? Promise! Did this man think that the prospect of concubinage was something to be yearned for, anticipated? "Certainly not!" I burst out.

"Then why are you anxious? Or are you, in your vanity, perhaps disappointed? I assure you that your virginity is quite safe in this house. Just do as you are told, like an obedient little peasant. Give thanks for your good fortune, learn while you can, and leave the larger issues to those who know better. Is there anything else? No?" He reached behind him and struck one note on a small copper gong. At once the door on the right opened and a servant came in and stood expectantly. "If he is unoccupied, ask Ani to grace me with his presence," the Steward ordered. The man bowed and left. Crushed, I put my hands behind my back and gazed out the window with attempted nonchalance, seeing out of the corner of my eye that Harshira had placed his elbows on the desk, fingers steepled under his broad chin, and was watching me carefully. Suddenly he laughed, the sound a booming roar that made me jump. "We shall see," he chuckled. "Yes indeed." He poured wine from the jug, picked up the cup, inhaled slowly, then sipped with evident enjoyment. Putting down the cup he unrolled one of the scrolls littering the table and began to read, ignoring me.

I remained still, struggling with my anger. His treatment of me was at such variance with the way I had been catered to by Disenk's small army of servants that I was completely disarmed. It was as though he had set out to deliberately prevent me from fancying myself the lady Disenk was trying to create. And perhaps that is so, I thought darkly, my attention going to the one long golden earring trembling against his bull neck as his head bent lower over the scroll. One holds out the sweetmeats, the other wields the whip. To what end? In what strange school have I found myself? But before I could consider the matter further the door behind me opened. Harshira immediately let the scroll rustle closed and stood. I turned.

The man coming forward, smiling, can only be described as anonymous. It was a word I used for him much later. At the time I merely felt that I must look him over several times before I could form an image of him in my mind that could be retained. He was of average height, neither strikingly tall nor short. His build was unremarkable, his features completely regular, even the lines around his mouth could have been drawn by an indifferent artist carving one face in a crowd of similarly middle-aged men. His wig was a simple black shoulder-length creation. He wore a plain white tunic and a thigh-high white kilt. I would have passed him by in the street without a glance or worse, not known that anyone had shared the path with me. His eyes, like Harshira's, said nothing of what was inside, but unlike the Chief Steward's, they gave no hint of intelligence beneath. He was a man to be forgotten, ignored, a man whose presence would never prompt feelings of inferiority or arrogance. In a room alone with him, one would be entirely oneself. He and Harshira exchanged bows.

"This is Thu," Harshira said simply, gesturing brusquely in my direction. To my surprise, the scribe bowed to me also.

"Greetings, Thu," he said, and his voice was a shock. Low

and melodious, the words perfectly enunciated, it reminded me of the temple cantor at Aswat, whose praises to Wepwawet would fill the hidden sanctuary with strong music and drift over the wall to echo through the inner court. The sound always brought a throb of strange longing to my throat. "I am the Master's Chief Scribe, Ani. I understand that today you are to dictate to me." He turned back to Harshira. "May I take her now?"

"You may. Run along, Thu, and try to dictate a short and coherent letter. Ani's time is more valuable than your words." I gave him what I hoped was a hostile glance but he was smiling at me, the flesh of his face rising into new configurations. I bowed stiffly and followed the scribe out of the room.

We did not go far. A short way back along the passage I had previously walked with the little slave, we entered a door on the opposite side and I found myself facing a more congenial view than Harshira's. Ani's window gave out onto the rear of the gardens. A narrow paved path ran half-hidden between dense shrubbery and the tall trees that grew against the great sheltering wall so that the room was filled with a cool, green light. It contained a desk, several chairs and shelves crowded with hundreds of scrolls. Each shelf was neatly labelled. The atmosphere was quiet and peaceful and I felt myself begin to relax. Ani closed the door behind us and motioned me to a chair.

"Be pleased to sit, Thu," he said kindly. "I will prepare my palette." His manner held none of the arrogance of Harshira's and he moved and spoke with a warm, calm assurance. I sank into a chair and watched him pull his palette across the desk, uncap the ink, select a suitable brush. A sheaf of papyrus lay at hand and he lifted a sheet, opened a drawer, removed a burnisher and began to vigorously smooth the beige paper. His working materials were plain wood, the palette scored and stained, the brushes unadorned, but the burnisher was of creamy ivory inlaid with gold, its handle softly gleaming from years of use. Lovingly he laid it on the desk, picked up the palette, came round, and sank to the floor by my feet. His eyes closed and his lips moved in the silent, ritual prayer to Thoth, patron of all scribes and the god who had given hieroglyphs to his people. I was vividly reminded of Pa-ari, and felt a rush of affection towards this man, now dipping a brush into the ink. He looked up at me and smiled, and suddenly I did not know how to begin. Shyly I cleared my throat, my gaze travelling the room as I hunted for words. He must have seen my dilemma.

"Do not be afraid," he told me. "I am an instrument, nothing more. Think of me that way. Speak from your heart to those you love. Forgive me, Thu, but has your brother the skill, yet, to read your words to your parents?" I admired his gentle tact.

"I suppose the Master has told you all about me and my family," I replied ruefully. "Yes, Pa-ari is already an accomplished scribe, still in school but performing a scribe's duties for the priests in our temple. He will read to my parents. But I do not know how to begin. Or where," I finished helplessly. "There is so much to tell!"

"Perhaps a formal opening would be appropriate," Ani suggested. "'To my loving parents, greetings from your dutiful daughter Thu. May the blessings of Wepwawet the Mighty be on you and on my brother, Pa-ari.' Will that suffice?"

"Thank you," I said. His head went down and he began to inscribe the words, quickly and with an unselfconscious neatness. I cast about in my mind for a place to begin. Should I start with the journey? A description of the house? A proud declaration of the fact that I had been assigned a body servant? No. I must be diplomatic. I must not speak to them as though they were now somehow beneath me. My fingers had tightened on the arms of the chair. I looked down at the spotless, gossamer-soft linen folding over my knees, felt the ends of the blue ribbon stir against my naked shoulders. My tongue tasted the slightly bitter flavour of red ochre.

All at once a full awareness of the strange and wonderful fate that had overtaken me blossomed in my consciousness. Until then I had been moving in a kind of waking dream. The trees beyond the window stirred briefly in a stray puff of wind. I could smell the perfume of the saffron oil anointing my body, the faint sweetness of the cedar wood chair in which I sat. Ani came to the end of the greeting and looked up, brush poised expectantly, and I noticed for the first time the silver Eye of Horus lying against the folds of his tunic. This was my world now, in all its complexity, with all its mysteries and surprises. I was no longer a little peasant girl, running barefooted by the Nile. I inhabited a different womb from which a different person would emerge.

Rising, I began to pace, palms pressed together. "I have so much to tell you," I began, "but first I must say that I love you all and I miss you. I am being treated well, in fact, you would not recognize me now. The Seer's house is a marvel. I have a room all to myself, and in it there is a couch with fine linen…" I had come to the window. I leaned against the casement, eyes closed, dimly hearing the faint rustle of papyrus as Ani worked but was soon lost in the flood of words that poured out. I told them about Disenk and the food and wine. I described Harshira and the frightening, exciting confusion that was the city of Pi-Ramses I had seen briefly from the river. I talked about the fountain and the pools, the other servants, my glimpse of Pharaoh's barge tethered to the marble watersteps of the palace as Hui's craft had drifted past.

Then suddenly I had said it all and I was left with an awareness of my own loneliness. I imagined Pa-ari's face as he read the scroll to my mother and father in the poor light of the tallow lamp. I could hear his steady voice as it sent

my words into the tiny, cramped room. My father would listen intently, silently, his thoughts hidden as always. My
mother would exclaim from time to time, leaning forward,
her dark eyes glowing with admiration or sparking disapproval. But I was here, here, I was not sitting cross-legged
with them on the rough hemp mat, hearing someone else's
incredible adventures with envy and yearning. "I miss you
most of all, Pa-ari," I ended. "Write to me soon." Trembling
with fatigue, empty yet at peace, I resumed my seat. Ani, of
course, made no comment on what must have seemed to
him an incoherent outpouring. The ink was rapidly drying.
Under Ani's coaxing the scroll rolled up. He rose and placed
it on the desk, then covered the ink. He called softly.
Immediately the door opened and a servant came in.

"Clean my brush and mix fresh ink," Ani ordered. "Tell
Kaha to wait upon me." The servant bowed, swept up the
palette, and went away. "The letter will go upriver with one
of the Master's Heralds," Ani answered my unspoken question. "There will be no charge to your family of course. You
will dictate to me again in one month's time, Thu. Ah!" He
beckoned impatiently at the young man who had knocked
and entered. "This is my assistant, the Under-Scribe Kaha.
He is in charge of your lessons. He is inquisitive and rather
rude, which is unfortunate, because he is also mildly intelligent. Kaha this is your pupil, Thu." Kaha grinned and
looked me up and down with a frank curiosity.

"Greetings, Thu," he said. "Ignore the comments of my
master. He is afraid that one day I will surpass him in both
intelligence and competence. I already surpass him in wit."
Ani grunted.

"Begin with the scrolls we have already discussed," he
told Kaha. "Go out into the garden. The child needs air."

"Thank you, Venerable One," I said haltingly as Kaha
swept up a bundle of scrolls from a shelf and ushered me out,
and Ani threw me an absent smile and turned to his desk.

"I don't think I shall ever have the good fortune to become a Chief Scribe," Kaha said airily as we moved down the passage towards the shaft of sunlight cascading through the rear doorway. "I talk too much. I do not blend well into my surroundings. I have too many opinions and like to express them too loudly." We turned left and I blinked, temporarily blinded by the force of the mid-afternoon sun. Kaha clicked his fingers and at once a slave who had been sitting in the shadow by the door sprang towards us, a sunshade at the ready. Kaha then ignored him. The man walked behind us, holding the yellow dome over our heads, its blood red tassels dancing just before our eyes. We rounded the corner of the house and crossed the main courtyard. I wondered if Harshira was at his window, marking our progress, and resisted the urge to glance back and see. "We might as well make ourselves comfortable by the fishpond," Kaha remarked as we paused so that the slave could open the gate. "It will be cool there and we won't be disturbed."

I barely heard him. It was good to be out of the house at last, to lift my face to the blue sky glimpsed above the jerking palms, to feel hot air on my skin. I wanted to remove my sandals as soon as we had left the burning paving of the courtyard but Kaha strode on, down the winding path I had covered, it seemed, a henti ago, until he veered and plunged through an opening in the thorn hedge. The pool lay dark and still, its surface hardly disturbed by the light flutter of the insects that skimmed it. Lily and lotus pads floated, green and elegantly curved. There were, of course, no flowers. It was the wrong season. Kaha lowered himself to the grass. "Bring whisks, water and mats," he snapped at the servant. "Go to my rooms and request papyrus and my second-best palette." He graced me with one of his wide smiles. "Beer would be better," he confided as the man hurried away, "but we don't want our faculties clouded, do we? So you are Hui's little peasant from Aswat." His eyes slid over me, but somehow his scrutiny was not insulting. "They tell me you are sharp-tongued and wilful." I drew in my breath to protest but he went on. "They also tell me that the Master had a dream about you or a vision or something. Lucky you!" He sorted quickly through the scrolls and held one out to me. "None of that is my concern," he said firmly. "I have been given the not unpleasant task of providing you with an education. Not unpleasant, that is, if you do in fact exhibit some intelligence. Here. Read this to me." I took the scroll and unrolled it.

"Kaha," I said slowly, deliberately, "I am rather tired of being described disparagingly as 'the little peasant from Aswat.' Peasants are the backbone of Egypt. Without them the country would collapse in a week. The sweat of my father waters this house and don't you forget it. Besides," I finished rather lamely, "my father is Libu, and he was a soldier long before he took to farming. I do not have a peasant's lineage." He laughed.

"So you object to being scorned as a peasant, not from any pride in being one but because you are convinced that your blood is just a fraction bluer than that of your Aswat neighbours," he exclaimed with unexpected astuteness. "Sharp-tongued, and conceited also. Read to me, Libu princess. If I judge that you love and revere the written word as much as I do, I shall forgive you all your faults." I hated his perception but rather liked his forthright manner. When will this testing end? I wondered, and taking a deep breath I scanned the scroll.

It was the account of a military engagement that had taken place hentis ago, during the reign of some Pharaoh called Thothmes the First. The narrator was one of his generals, Aahmes pen-Nekheb. The language was difficult, colourful and slightly archaic, and I was soon stumbling as I fought to decipher the black characters. Pa-ari's lessons had been less onerous, the simple words making up simple max-

ims regarding morals and behaviour. This scroll was full of
the names of places and tribes I had never heard of, long
words of action, long passages of exposition and explana-
tion. When I stumbled Kaha waited. When I came to a frus-
trated halt he prompted me. "Break down the word into its
holy components," he told me. "Pray. Guess. Enter into the
sanctuary of this work." He did not joke any more. His attitude was attentive, sombre. When I had groped my way to
the end he took back the scroll. "Now tell it to me," he
commanded and I did so, my eyes on the water of the pond
and the darting dragonflies whose wings glittered as they
passed in and out of the reach of Ra's fingers. The servant
had returned, quietly laying out mats for us, setting water
jugs in the grass and fly whisks in our hands. He withdrew
just out of earshot and settled himself under a tree.

"Not bad," Kaha commented when I fell silent, "but you
did not even attempt to remember the number of prisoners
taken."

"Why is that necessary?" I asked rather petulantly, for I
believed I had done rather well. "I am to be an assistant, not
a scribe, and besides, the account is written for all to see and
a scribe takes dictation. He does not memorize and give
back by rote." Kaha gave me a keen look.

"A scribe must be proficient in many ways," he objected.
"Suppose he takes a dictation and the scroll is sent and several days later his master says to him 'Scribe, exactly what
did I say in that scroll?'"

"But do not the under-scribes spend their time making
copies?" I countered smoothly. "The scribe merely needs to
read from the copy." I was obscurely annoyed with him. He
rolled his eyes.

"Thu, you are being obtuse," he sighed. "Sometimes an
official is in conference with another official and needs to
know later what the other official has said, but he has
ordered his scribe not to write anything down." I gazed at

him thoughtfully.

"You mean that sometimes a scribe must have the eyes and ears of a spy."

"Very good!" he responded sarcastically. "And now, if you have sufficiently embarrassed yourself with your presumptuous naïvety, we will continue with the lesson. I have ascertained that you can read—after a fashion. But can you write?" He set the palette the slave had brought across my knees, opened the ink, placed a brush in my right hand. I wanted to excuse myself before I had even begun, to tell him how I had studied in secret, how I had only rarely been able to practise on expensive papyrus, but I pressed my lips firmly together against the rush of despicably self-pitying words, and transferring the brush from my right to my left hand I dipped it in the ink and waited. There was a pause. Glancing up I saw his eyes narrowed, fixed on me in speculation.

"So," he said softly. "The left hand not the right. No one told me that you are a child of Set."

"What of it?" I flashed back at him. "My father also uses the left hand, it is more natural for us, and he is a great soldier and a servant of my god the mighty Wepwawet, the War God, not Set the turbulent, the bringer of chaos! Do not judge me thus, Kaha!" I did not know if I was angry or hurt. I had encountered such prejudice before but not often, and for some reason I had not expected to find it here, in this sophisticated house where the inhabitants did not gather for evening prayers and the day did not seem to begin with any thanks to Amun or Ra.

Once my mother, in a fit of exasperation over something I had done or some argument I had persisted in fermenting, had burst out, "Thu, I sometimes think that Set is your true father, for you stir up trouble all the time!" And once I had been walking across the village compound at sunset on my way home from the fields and I had passed an old man. I hardly noticed him, being tired and hungry and bent on reaching my own door, but he had stopped at the sight of me, pointing, then stumbled and fell in his haste to get out of my way. I was puzzled. The sun-baked square was deserted and I was nowhere near him. Yet as I hesitated, hearing him shout imprecations at me from where he lay spread-eagled in the dust, I saw that the red light of the sinking sun had elongated my shadow until it lay like a misshapen snake across his feet. Then I understood that as a left-handed child, even my shadow brought bad luck, and I had run home in shame and confusion.

Something of those emotions gripped me now as I faced Kaha. He grimaced in apology when he saw my distress, and gave me a little bow.

"It is not something to be ashamed of, you know," he said. "I was taken aback, that is all. Did you know that Set was not always a god of malevolence? That he is the totem of this nome, and the city of Pi-Ramses is dedicated to him?" I shook my head in wonder. Set, to the villagers, had always been a god to placate when necessary, to fear and avoid if possible. "The Great God Osiris Ramses the Second, he of the red hair and long life, was a devotee of Set and built this city to his glory. Set also has red hair—and he may have blue eyes as far as we know," he ended humorously. "So take heart, Thu. If Set loves you, you will be invincible." He drank some water and picked up a scroll. "Let us continue."

I did not want to be a child of Set. I wanted to remain loyal to Wepwawet, my benefactor. The ink had dried on my brush. I bent to the inkwell again, whisked at the cloud of flies that was beginning to gather as the afternoon waned, and prepared to write with a thudding heart.

I did not do so well at the writing. My letters were large and poorly formed, my speed agonizingly slow. Kaha did not tease me. Something had subtly changed in his attitude. He was an attentive and patient teacher, correcting me carefully, allowing me to struggle at my own pace without becoming restless. He had formed a respect for my efforts, I think. After several hours of smudged ink, cramped fingers and frustration he took the brush gently from my stained fingers and lifted the palette from my knees. "That is quite enough for today," he said, offering me water which I sucked down greedily. "The dictation was a difficult one, Thu, but I needed to know where to begin with you. I should return you to pieces of clay on which to practise but I won't. Hui is rich enough to provide you with as much papyrus as you need!" He smiled and I smiled back. "Your reading is quite good. I hear that you have some healing skills also."

"My mother is Aswat's midwife and physician," I told him. "I can write long lists of herb remedies without a mistake but I can see that I am ignorant of all else."

"You will not be ignorant for long," he said slowly. Turning, he signalled to the slave still nodding under his tree. "Go back to your room now, and eat your evening meal. I think we will forgo our history lesson tonight. You are tired, and you still must face a drubbing from Nebnefer."

"I am to be beaten?" I cried in alarm. "What for?" Now he laughed aloud.

"Nebnefer is the Master's trainer," he explained. "He is one of the very few people allowed to see the Master unclothed. I do not think that he will force you to draw the bow or heft the spear but he will expect you to contort your body in many marvellous ways in order to maintain your health and suppleness. Go now." I scrambled upright and kneaded a sudden cramp in my calf.

"If you will give me an old palette and some papyrus I could practise my letters in my idle hours," I suggested, but he shook his head.

"It is not permitted," he said firmly.

"Why not?" He drew up one knee and placed an arm over it. His graceful fingers spread wide and then went limp in a gesture of resignation.

"Your education is to be personally supervised at all times," he pointed out. "On pain of severe punishment I am to make sure that you read or write nothing unless I am present or Ani is present." I folded my arms and stared down at him.

"That's stupid. It makes no sense at all. Does Hui think that I will write nasty secret letters to my family about him?" Kaha smiled.

"Oh, I don't think so. Only the most errant fool would endanger her place here in such a stupid way. No, I imagine that the Master does not want you to pick up any bad learning habits. They are almost impossible to undo. Run along, Thu. Disenk will be waiting." The wry, slightly condescending tone was back. I gave him a mute bow and left him, following the slave who had already raised the sunshade although Ra's fiery rim was barely touching the horizon.

I paced self-consciously a step ahead of him, but as we recrossed the courtyard a thought struck me and I immediately forgot that he was there. How stupid I was indeed, an innocent young fool. Of course Hui need not worry about nasty letters from me to my family. As Kaha had so incisively stated, I would be an idiot to jeopardize my chance for a better life and anyway, how would I go about finding a messenger to convey them? It would be almost impossible for me to slip into the city alone and I had nothing with which to pay a Herald. No. I was being carefully watched, my words and actions weighed and reported. I was not to be by myself. It was doubtless true that Hui wanted only the best-educated staff to serve him. That was obvious and logical. If I was to assist him in any capacity I must be at least as literate as Kaha. The thought was daunting. But there was more, and as I walked along the side of the house towards the rear door, turning the problem over in my mind, I was completely mystified. What was in store for me? I knew now, beyond the shadow of a doubt, that my clumsy, fervent dictation to my parents and Pa-ari would not be sealed and dispatched before being passed under the Master's shrewd eye. Ani his tool, his employee, his Chief Scribe, Ani the necessary repository of his secrets, Ani the invisible man with the seductive voice who could blend so insidiously into any gathering, any background, he would at once have taken the scroll to Hui. A sudden hatred for the Chief Scribe shook me and then vanished. Ani was the perfect confidant. If I were the Master I would do the same thing. Yet why would he waste his time reading the insignificant letter of one of his servants, especially one on whom he had caused to be showered such attention, such care, and who would thus have no complaints to make to her family? To know me better? But why bother to know me better? If I succeeded as a servant, fine. If not, I could go home. Why go to so much trouble over a very disposable young peasant?

I was at my door. The slave bowed me inside and Disenk came towards me smiling. The room was full of the aroma of hot food, and several small, dainty lamps burned steadily, holding back the encroaching darkness. I greeted my body servant absently, stood while she washed the ink stains from my hands and pulled the rumpled sheath over my head, slipped my arms into the voluminous linen wrap she held out, sat while she brushed my hair and then allowed her to lead me to the laden table. All the time my thoughts were tumbling one after another, rolling past Ani and back again, hovering around Hui's enigmatic presence that seemed to pervade the whole house though he was seldom glimpsed. I am being prepared for something other than a lowly assistant, I concluded, but what? The idea excited and terrified me. I did not speak to Disenk as she served me my food, and she remained silent.

By the time I had finished eating, full night had fallen outside and I could see nothing but the tangled clusters of black trees against a slightly lighter sky and one band of lamplight that slanted, yellow and faint, across the court-yard from Harshira's office directly below. Finally I sighed. "What comes next, Disenk?" I said unwillingly. She began to stack the dishes.

"Nebnefer has sent word that he wishes to examine you and speak of your physical training," she replied, "but he will not make you work tonight, and in the future your exer-cise will be taken in the morning, before you bathe. He will come to you himself." How very obliging of him, I wanted to say sarcastically, but I did not.

I watched Disenk summon a slave, watched him remove the remains of the meal, heard, a little later, the knock on the door. Disenk opened at once and bowed to the short, squat man who approached me. His manner and his move-ments were crisp and fresh. I stood and bowed, mockingly removing my wrap before being asked to do so, and he met my eyes and smiled approvingly. I was becoming used to the appraisal of strange men and I did not flinch. His touch was as impersonal as the masseur's had been.

"Good peasant stock," he announced. "But not thick, not heavy. Fine, strong bones, long legs, tight musculature. Well, so it should be at your age. I am Nebnefer, by the way."

"You are the first person here who has had anything com-plimentary to say about my peasant stock," I said drily, and he snorted and pulled the wrap back over my shoulders. I clutched it closed.

"There's more than Egyptian fellahin in you," he told me bluntly, his black eyes darting over my face, "but there's nothing wrong with a peasant's body. Where else do Pharaoh's honest soldiers come from if not from Egypt's fields? You'd make a good runner, Thu, or swimmer, but as it is, all I have to do is keep you firm."

"Then I may swim?" I asked eagerly. He nodded.

"Under my direction, every morning, in the pool. Then you pull the bow, to keep those pretty breasts high. A few

other things. I will see you in the garden tomorrow morning
before you break your fast. Sleep well." He spun on his heel
and left, slamming the door behind him.

...keep you firm...

...those pretty breasts high...

I turned to Disenk.

"I want to see the Master," I demanded. "At once,
Disenk. Go and tell him." She clasped her pretty hands
together, an expression of agony on her face.

"Oh pardon me, Thu," she said in a high, hurried voice,
"but that is impossible. He has guests this evening. They
will be arriving at any moment. Be patient, and I will convey your request to Harshira in the morning."

"I have been patient," I snapped, "and all I get is eva-
sions. I must talk to Hui." She flinched, distressed, at my use
of his name.

"If I go to him now he will be angry," she persisted, her
carefully feathered eyebrows drawing together. "He will not
be disposed to listen to you calmly. Please wait until tomorrow." Her anxiety seemed exaggerated but I supposed that
she was right. I capitulated.

"Oh very well," I said grudgingly. "I will wait for one more
night. But tell Harshira my desire tomorrow, Disenk, for I
am becoming uneasy in this house."

Obviously relieved she began to prattle on about nothing
while she prepared me for bed, and she drew the sheet up
over me and extinguished the lamps with care. Bidding me a
good night she went away and I was left to the shadows and
the sweet redolence of the smoking wicks, and a mind
whose storm of thoughts would not abate.

Disenk had not lied. A short while later I heard voices
and laughter in the courtyard below, and after that the
music of lute and drums and the tinkle of finger cymbals
coming from somewhere within the house. The sounds were
sweet but faint, a faraway enticement to a dimension of life

here of which I knew nothing. I wondered if there would be dancers. The dancers in Wepwawet's temple were dignified and graceful, clothed in the ankle-length linens and thin sandals of ritual and respect, systra in their hands as they moved through the prescribed gestures that praised and importuned the god. I had heard in the village that secular dancers often performed naked, glittering with gold dust, rings on their bare toes, that they could jump the height of a man and bend themselves backward until their heads touched their heels. The music faded in and out as the night wind gusted and the reed mat covering my window slapped against the casement. I wanted to get up and creep into the passage, follow the dull throb of the drums, find the company whose shouts and clapping now wove with the quick, high plucking of the lute. But Disenk slept in the passage and would inveigle me back to bed with her excessive, irresistible politeness. I heard feet running on the paving. An owl cried suddenly, loudly, in the garden. I drowsed.

It was still fully dark when I drifted out of unconsciousness, disturbed by the drunken rowdiness of the guests leaving. "Hey, that's not your litter, that's mine!" a strong male voice shouted, and a woman let out a shriek of laughter.

"Let me share it with you then," she called, her words lazily slurred. "The cushions look soft and yielding and my husband has already left with ours. Harshira, what shall I do?" I came fully awake. The Chief Steward's familiar tone was confident and clear.

"If you will retire to the reception room, Highness, I will order out one of the Master's litters to take you home at once."

Highness? I swung myself off the couch and sped to the window. Lifting back the mat I peered cautiously below. A group of people stood loosely together, lit garishly by flaming torches in the hands of several slaves. A gilded litter sat on the ground, four Nubians before and behind it, waiting for orders. A man in a knee-length red kilt, his gleaming chest afire with jewels, his face heavily painted, leaned non-chalantly against it, grinning. Around them more guests spilled from the main entrance into the torches' light, and more litters were arriving into which they tumbled happily and volubly. Harshira, his broad back to me, was facing a woman whose elaborately pleated sheath was rumpled and wine-splashed. One shoulder strap had torn loose, exposing a sweat-streaked brown breast. The perfume cone atop her long, many-plaited wig had sagged over one ear and the oil from it had somehow been smeared across her cheek, taking a quantity of kohl with it. "Thank you, Harshira," she was saying, one hennaed palm vaguely patting his shoulder, "but I want to go home with the General." The man in the red kilt guffawed. Peeling himself away from his litter he took her flailing fingers, kissed them, kissed her again, this time on her loose mouth, then jerked his head at Harshira and propelled her firmly back into the house.

"The General is going home alone, Highness," he said wryly, his words becoming muffled as he pulled her in under the portico. "You wait here like a good girl and Harshira will attend to you." He added something I could not catch, then he entered my line of vision again, alone. He got onto his litter and his hand, as dazzlingly bejewelled as his wide chest, grasped the curtain. He leaned out. "Good-night, Harshira," he said. "Bundle her into one of Hui's litters and send a guard with her." Harshira bowed. The curtain twitched closed. On a sharp order the Nubians lifted it and set off across the paving, and soon it disappeared into the darkness.

I let the mat fall and slid down until I was crouched under the window. I was shocked and titillated. Everyone got drunk from time to time, I knew that. Drunkenness was a pleasant pastime for those with idle hours to while away. Often my father came home staggering and my mother, in her long afternoons drinking wine with her friends, would occasionally rise with a sparkle in her eye.

But this was different. The nature of the woman's inebriation had shocked me. To get drunk in the village was still to observe the basic proprieties but the princess, for such I judged her to be, given her title, had exuded an air of complete abandonment, uncaring of her appearance, heedlessly flaunting her drunken lust for the man in red. It was as though no one else in the world mattered but herself, nothing had any importance but her own sulky desires. Such selfishness, I thought in envy. Such arrogance! How must it feel to be so rich, so above censure or the moral restraints of ordinary people that one can say and do exactly as one pleases?

Suddenly I longed to be like her, not in her rather disgusting loss of control but in her state. I wanted to dine here as a guest, applaud the dancers, exchange sophisticated witticisms with the noble sitting beside me, flirt with the man in red, pick over my food fastidiously while a slave bent to hear my next command. I wanted to be carried home to my great estate in an elaborately draped litter, give parties myself, perhaps on huge, flowered barges on the Nile. I wanted many lovers. I wanted to be resented and admired. Never never again did I want to be the one feeling the sharp thorn of envy.

Chapter 7

In the morning I told Disenk that I did not want to see the Master after all, that a good night's sleep had allayed my anxieties. It was true that I was not being harmed, in fact I was being cared for scrupulously. Besides, my sight of the drunken princess had given me pause. Hui had connections in very high places. If I behaved myself, if I concentrated on trying to be obedient, one day I might be invited to serve at the festivities of the house. I might even be permitted to meet the Master's aristocratic friends. That was a faint hope, I knew. I was beginning to learn of the gulf that existed between fellahin and noble. Until I had real cause for complaint I would put my vague worries to the back of my mind. I would, however, be vigilant. I would keep my eyes and ears open. Innocent though I was, I knew that such attention was not usually lavished on a minor servant, but I would enjoy it. I would play the game until the Master changed the rules.

My days settled into a rigid pattern. At dawn Nebnefer would come for me and together we would walk through the sleepy house to the pool, its surface always placid and unruffled in the fleeting hush of the hour. I would swim up and down, up and down, while Ra's pink rays rapidly became a bright heat and Nebnefer shouted instructions and admonitions as he strode beside me.

I grew to long for the moment when he left me outside the bath house and Disenk would comfort me with perfumed water, and the masseur's sure hands would soothe me with scented oils, kneading away the soreness of my muscles.

The food awaiting me in my own room would taste like the nectar of the gods. Having eaten, my face would be painted and Disenk would dress me, telling me all the while of fashion and manners, of the methods of setting jewels and dressing wigs, how to get in and out of a litter gracefully, how to address priests and the nobility with the proper deference. I would listen silently, trying not to ask myself how all the prattle could possibly apply to me unless I was lucky enough to catch the eye of some young nobleman.

Once clad I would go to my lessons with Kaha, sometimes in the garden but more often in his tiny office, which was actually an ante-room to the Chief Scribe's domain. In the morning I would read, with increasing fluency and understanding, the scrolls he chose. They usually contained old stories that ended in some moral maxim or other—the kind of tales that all mothers told their children—or were linked to my history lessons of the afternoons. But once in a while they were household accounts, orders for linen or wine, commissions for amulets and other pieces of jewellery.

After the noon meal, eaten in my room, we would change places. I would sit at his desk and labour to write what he dictated. My hand improved slowly. I began to develop a style of my own under his patient tutelage, and I came to trust and admire him. He teased me a great deal, disparaged many of my painstaking efforts, praised me rarely so that I learned to prize and labour hard for those few off-hand words, and consistently called me "little Libu princess." I suppose that he became a kind of substitute for my dear Pa-ari for he was young and energetic and full of fun. Perhaps that was why I never felt physically attracted to him in spite of his eligibility. He was like an older brother, yet to be feared also, for I sensed that his opinion of me carried a lot of weight with his master, Ani, and hence with Hui also.

When my wrist cramped and I had managed more often than not to smear ink over my cheek or down my sheath, we would share beer and shat cakes. Then he would commence my history lessons. He was an entertaining teacher. He recited the king lists each day like poetry, inviting me to choose one pharaoh whose name intrigued me. When I had done so, he would begin the tale of the Osiris One's life, his character, his achievements, his wars and his loves. Once a week he would test my knowledge both verbally and on papyrus. If I did well he would place in my hand a clay scarab, each one a different colour. I kept them in the box I had brought with me from Aswat, and the collection grew.

In the long, warm evenings, after I had eaten formally in my room, waited on by Disenk and expected to behave as though I was at a great banquet, she and I would walk about the gardens or recline by the lotus pond until sunset. Then I would be returned to my room where she would play the lute and sing to me, or teach me little dance steps.

For many weeks I would be tired by the time she snuffed the lamps and bade me a good night. But gradually, as I mastered my lessons and became accustomed to the unvarying routine, I grew restless, and often left the couch where she had dutifully laid the sheet over me. I would raise the window mat and kneel looking out over the dusky courtyard to the shivering trees beyond. The sounds of the city would come to me but faintly, all clamour mixed and muted to a faraway rumble. Sometimes a craft would pass unseen, but I would hear the shout of the captain, the splash of oars. Once a barge drifted by, so brightly lit that its lamps made a wavering glow through the trees. Then there was loud laughter and the babble of many voices, shrieks of mock terror and the frenetic pulse of many drums. I thought of the drunken princess and the red-kilted General as the cheerful cacophony faded and the river was silent again. Were they on board? Had the princess managed to inveigle the General into bed with her or had her lust been nothing more than the vacuous promptings of the wine? I would never know. I was an insect trapped in resin, a piece of flotsam washed into a secret corner of the Lake of the Residence while the current ran on strongly to the Great Green, without me.

Several times I hid and watched the Master's dinner guests arrive and leave, the gaily caparisoned litters and black slaves come and go. Once I thought I caught a glimpse of the General slipping alone across the darkened courtyard but I must have been mistaken. I dreamed of him twice, a romantic figure in red lurking on the periphery of my vision, but I did not allow myself to think of these people much during my waking hours. Although I hated to admit it, they were as far out of my reach as Pharaoh himself, and I did not want to increase the growing agitation my enforced isolation was causing. I no longer knew what fantasies to conjure.

I saw the Master several times, very late at night, gliding like a wraith in the moonlight on his way to the pool with Kenna at his heels. I had no urge to disturb him. Perhaps I was learning a little patience. I half expected him to pause and glance up at me for I had the strong impression that he knew perfectly well I was watching him, but he never did and I was both relieved and disappointed.

Every month I dutifully dictated a letter to my family, knowing that Hui's eyes would weigh my every word. I was tempted to say outrageous things about him but I repressed the childish desire. At first the task brought my family and my old home and the villagers vividly to mind and I would experience a surge of homesickness followed by a tumult of conflicting emotions, but as time went by my family began to lose substance, appearing as increasingly formal and stilted figures to my mind's eye. I received word from them intermittently, or rather, the scrolls would come in Pa-ari's neat, economical hand as they could afford it. My father and mother sent affectionate greetings but obviously did not dictate any news, for the letters' idiom was all my brother's. He wrote of the good harvest, the number of babies born in the village, who had become betrothed to whom, how his studies were progressing. He told me of the life of the temple, in which he was now intimately involved as a scribe, and of one of the dancers, the daughter of a neighbour, who was fast losing the clumsy coltishness of girlhood and acquiring interesting curves. I read this with a sudden lump of jealousy in my throat, for selfishly and illogically I did not want to share my brother's affections with anyone. He did not go out on the desert much any more to watch the sunset, he said. It was not the same without me. He missed me very much. Did I miss him? Or was my new life so full and satisfying that I had no time to think of him? Beneath the friendly words I sensed his concern for me, and wondered if the Master sensed it also, for I was certain that the missives did not come to me fresh. They were naturally unsealed. Peasants did not bother with wax or cylinders or rings for imprinting. I was suddenly afraid, reading Pa-ari's black script. I did not want to have his features become indistinct as time took us away from each other. I did not want him to be frozen in memories, doing and saying the same things over and over in my consciousness because we had no new experiences to share. Yet I knew that I would probably not see him again for many years, if ever. His scrolls, too, went into my box and I reread them often, fighting to keep them all—my clever, impatient mother, my taciturn, handsome father, our lively, inquisitive, earthy neighbours—vital and alive.

So my days followed their appointed pattern. The season of Shemu gave way to Akhet, the time of flooding, heralded by New Year's Day, the first day of the month of Thoth. Everyone celebrated, servants and masters alike. Hui's house and garden filled with the clamour of drunken festivity and the river was choked with the god's worshippers. The noise of the city penetrated my room, but I was not allowed to join the crowds. I was not even allowed into the garden.

Furious and disappointed, I sat at my window with Disenk while the other servants, those with whom I had shared food and comfort on the journey from Aswat and who had received me kindly, congregated happily under the trees and ate and drank to the glory of Thoth. I supposed that they had forgotten me by now. The officials of the household, Harshira, Ani, Kaha and the others, stayed apart from the slaves and kitchen labourers, feasting in Hui's reception hall. Of Hui himself I saw nothing. As a Seer he would have spent the feast day in the temple of Thoth, being consulted by the god's priests with regard to the coming year, and I had no doubt that he had fasted and remained in seclusion to prepare for the occasion, but the day drew to a close without a hint of his presence anywhere.

The month of Thoth passed, and Paophi and Athyr. The flood was high that year. Isis had cried copiously and the crops would be thick and bountiful. The season of Akhet ended with the month of Khoiak, and Peret, the time of receding waters and sowing, began. I was for the first time divorced from the slow, time-honoured rituals that bound the fellahin to the land. In Aswat my father and his neighbours would be out walking the fields every day to judge the quality of the silt spread by the now shrinking river, their feet sinking into the fertile mud, their talk all of what grain should be planted in which plot. Here in Hui's house my own rituals had become just as unvaried, and the only sense I had of the changing months came from the lessening heat and a rise in humidity that brought clouds of mosquitoes into the garden.

Six months after my arrival in the Delta my lessons with Kaha took a new turn. My reading was becoming fluent and my writing improved every day, but it was in the study of history that the change began. One day, sitting in the grass beside the pool in an afternoon loud with the croaking of frogs and hazy with warm, diffused sunshine, Kaha handed me a scroll to recite. He had not begun, as he usually did, with the king lists, but ordered me to read the contents of the scroll aloud. I did so. It was not difficult. "One hundred and seven thousand slaves," I intoned. "Three-quarters of a million arouras, half a million head of small and large cattle, five hundred and thirteen groves and temple gardens, eighty-eight fleet vessels, fifty-three workshops and ship-yards..." I paused and glanced enquiringly at Kaha. "What is this?" He nodded once, brusquely.

"Keep reading." I obeyed.

"One hundred and sixty-nine towns in Egypt, Cush and Syria. For Amun seventy thousand talents of gold and two million talents of silver a year. One hundred and eighty-five thousand sacks of grain a year." The list was short. Kaha gestured but I did not let the scroll roll closed. I reread the figures silently.

"What do you think you have just recited?" Kaha asked. I shrugged.

"It is an inventory of some kind, and seeing that the Great Cackler Amun is mentioned I presume these are his...his tributes." The sheer size of the numbers shocked me. Kaha flicked his whisk irritably at the flies gathering around the water jug.

"You are right. This is a list of all possessions of the gods in Egypt. Listen carefully, Thu. I am going to give you some figures, and when I have finished you are to take up the palette and write them down as you remember them." I took a deep breath and prepared to concentrate. These memory exercises were often difficult and at such times I resented Kaha's blithe ability to recount seemingly innumerable numbers without hesitation. "One person in every fifty in Egypt is temple property," he began distinctly. "One hundred and seven thousand slaves. Of that number, Amun of Thebes owns eighty-six thousand five hundred. That is seven times the number owned by Ra. Say it back to me." I did so, not yet allowing myself to think, only alert to take in and remember what he said. "Good," he went on. "Of the three-quarters of a million arouras of temple land, Amun owns five hundred and eighty-three thousand. This is five times as much as Ra who owns one hundred and eight thousand arouras at On, and over nine times as much as Ptah at Abydos. Of the half a million head of cattle, Amun owns four hundred and twenty-one thousand, in five herds." I closed my eyes, repeating the figures feverishly to myself. "Of the eighty-eight ships, Amun has eighty-three. Of the fifty-three workshops and shipyards Amun has forty-six. In Syria, Cush and Egypt, of the one hundred and sixty-nine towns owned by the gods, Amun has fifty-six. In Syria and Cush he has nine. He is the only god to own towns outside Egypt. Ra has one hundred and three towns. Are you lost?" I opened my eyes and smiled at him, but there was a small twinge of anxiety in the pit of my stomach that had nothing to do with the task.

"You forgot groves and gardens," I pointed out triumphantly. "Of the five hundred and thirteen temple groves and gardens, how many belong to Amun?" He did not return my smile.

"Four hundred and thirty-three, impudent one," he said. "Now give it back to me."

To my amazement and, I think, to his surprise, I went through the exercise without one slip. It was as though his voice had sent the information flying straight to niches in my brain that had been formed and waiting for them. "Holy Isis," I whispered. "The wealth! Seventy thousand talents of gold! And the silver, Kaha! Ten million six hundred thousand deben! I can't…"

"One deben of silver will buy enough food to keep nine people alive for a year," he said bluntly. "At Pharaoh's last tax census the population of Egypt stood at five million three hundred thousand. Amun's yearly tribute of silver would buy food for the whole of this country for nineteen years. He has seventeen times more silver, twenty-one times more copper, seven times more cattle, nine times more wine, and ten times more ships than any other god." His tone was neutral and he was watching me steadily. The twinge in my belly was becoming an ache.

"Amun is a mighty God," I said, whether in agreement or argument I did not know. "You have taught me that many hentis ago when Egypt was in the hands of barbarian invaders, Amun strengthened the hand of the great Osiris One Prince Sekhenenra of Thebes, and with the god's help he drove out the Hyksos and gave the country back to its own people. In love and gratitude the Prince lifted Amun to become Egypt's greatest God. He is deserving of our offerings." I was thinking of Aswat's beloved Wepwawet, and how the people would come on the god's feast days with gifts for him, whatever they could afford. Flowers and freshly baked bread, pigeons, reverently woven linen, sometimes even a whole ox, and the men would each give his time in ploughing, sowing and reaping the little plot of land that belonged to the god.

"Of course he is," Kaha agreed, but I was sure I heard sarcasm in his voice. "But is not Pharaoh the Horus of Gold, Incarnation of the God on earth? Does he not merit our offerings also, and the offerings of the priests who are surely his servants also, because of his divinity?" I did not know where this conversation was going but I was uneasy. I did not want to hear what Kaha was about to say, as though I had some intimation that yet another layer of my innocence was about to be stripped away.

"I suppose so," I agreed cautiously. "Surely Pharaoh is himself a God."

"Then why are the temples exempt from taxation? Why is the state of the royal treasury a scandal and a shame to every Egyptian who loves and respects his King? I have another history lesson for you, Thu. Listen well, and do not forget the numbers you have heard and recited today for they are a disgrace to this blessed country." He spoke without force, without anger, yet with an intensity that trembled between us like a heat haze in the desert. "Pharaoh is entitled to one-tenth of all grain crops and animals from government land, from dues and monopolies, and from requisitions. But he may not touch the vast wealth of the gods. From this one-tenth he must support civil officials and the secular administration of Egypt. He must pay the army. He must support his households and his harems. And he must continually placate the servants of the gods, whose greed is insatiable and whose power is now almost absolute." He had laid aside his whisk and had folded his hands in his white lap. His fingers were perfectly relaxed.

"I do not understand," I broke in. "He is Amun on earth. He is the Horus of the Horizon, glorious in his majesty. He is the arbiter and upholder of Ma'at in Egypt, the embodiment of justice, truth and rightness in the universe. If Ma'at has become unbalanced he must set it right. This does not mean that he, a God himself, should do other gods a disservice."

"He cannot set it right," Kaha objected calmly. "After the time of the Good God Sekhenenra came strong kings who ruled with the wisdom and mercy and power of the gods. They worshipped Amun. Year after year they showed their gratitude to him by pouring riches into his coffers. But the prerogative of appointing his priests they retained to themselves, for they knew that though the God was perfect his servants were not. Thus they achieved harmony in Egypt, the harmony of Ma'at, temple and palace working together for the good of Egypt, with Pharaoh at the pinnacle, answering only to the God himself. But now Pharaoh must answer to the God's servants, and they are arrogant and corrupt. They care nothing for Amun or for Pharaoh. They grow fat. Pharaoh can no longer appoint High Priests, for the office is passed from father to son, as though serving in the temple were a career instead of a responsibility. Other priests of lesser gods give their daughters in marriage to the priests of Amun, and so a net has been woven, Thu. The High Priest of Amun now rules all other priests everywhere. He also rules Pharaoh."

I was shocked and very confused. Father had taught Paari and me to regard Pharaoh as nothing less than a God on earth, all-powerful, all-wise, all-seeing, on whose word the Nile rose and fell, the preserver of Ma'at. The servants of the gods were also all-wise, custodians of Egypt's health, men whose first duty was to enable Pharaoh to carry out the dictates of the gods and to do him homage as the living embodiment of all they held sacred. Pharaoh's word was law, his breath brought warmth and plenty to Egypt. "Why does Pharaoh not dismiss the High Priests, all the greedy ones, and appoint persons more worthy?" I wanted to know. A sadness was welling up in me and I wanted to cry.

"He cannot," Kaha said shortly. "They are richer than he, more closely knit than the officials of his administration, more able to influence those around him than he is himself. They even control the paying of the artisans who work on his tomb."

"But what about the army?" I was thinking of my own father's unswerving loyalty to Pharaoh. "Why can he not summon his generals and have the priests deposed by force?"

"Because an army must be paid, and to pay the army Pharaoh must often ask the priests for the means. Besides, the Egyptian army is now made up of many thousands of foreigners and mercenaries. If they are not paid they will not obey orders. If the priests approve of a royal project, the building of a temple, say, or a voyage to Punt or a trading expedition, they will give Pharaoh their permission. If not, well, he cannot afford their censure. Last year a new calendar of Feasts was inscribed on the walls of Pharaoh's new temple at Medinet Habu. There is now a Feast Day for Amun every three days, as well as the customary days of observance. No one works on those days, Thu. It was a stupid decree and I would like to believe that Ramses had no choice in the matter." He rose and I rose with him. I felt heavy and ungainly. "For our next history lesson I want you to ponder what I have told you and then give me your thoughts on what you would do to restore Ma'at to Egypt. Go now." I bowed clumsily and walked away dazed, as though he had drugged my beer with poppy.

I could not drive Kaha's figures from my mind. With an effort I moved through the remainder of my rigidly ordered day, strolling with Disenk, dining in my room with a formality that was fast becoming habit, taking a music lesson from Hui's lute player who always became impatient with me because of my left-handedness. I tried to tell myself that Kaha could be wrong, that his interpretation of the situation between the Good God and the priests was one man's opinion, but the sadness grew like grey smoke inside me, curling about my heart, stinging in my belly, its fumes filling my brain.

I grieved for the innocence of my parents, the trusting ignorance of the villagers who believed in the omnipotence of Pharaoh and who knew that whatever was wrong, the Mighty Bull would put it right. Could it be that Pharaoh's divinity was a lie, that he was as weak, no, weaker than other men? I shied away from that consideration as from an open flame. I had been taught that the holy Uraeus, the rearing cobra on the Double Crown, would spit venom at anyone who tried to harm the King. Why did not Wazt, Lady of Spells, Defender of Kings, shower these venal priests with her righteous poison? Had Amun overcome her power, rendered her helpless?

I lay on my couch that night unable to sleep. Peaceful shadows painted the walls of my room. The sheets were cool and soft. No sounds drifted on the motionless air. The harmony of darkness and rest was complete. I began to cry, the tears slipping quietly across my temple to soak the pillow beneath. I did not know why I cried but my ka knew. It was for the crumbling of illusion, the destruction of a fond reality whose colours and contours had been dearly familiar to me from the time of my birth. That reality was a lie. Or was it? It had not been a lie in Egypt's past. Surely it was possible somehow to restore true Ma'at, restore Pharaoh's omnipotence and divinity, restore right worship... I put both hands over my mouth and the tears came faster. The sweet fantasies of my childhood could not be restored. They were gone, shredded and blown away in the strong wind of Kaha's words. I was bereft.

The spending of my emotion did not bring exhaustion. Gradually the tears ceased to flow. I wiped my face on the sheet, reflecting half-hysterically how distressed Disenk would be if she knew that I had removed the skin treatment she so assiduously applied each evening, and tried to still my mind but could not. My eyes burned. My body was tense. In the end I rose, and wrapping a linen cloak over my sleeping shift I went out into the passage.

Disenk came awake at once, for as I stepped over her my robe brushed her face. She sat up. "What is wrong, Thu?" she whispered, no trace of drowsiness in her voice. "Are you ill?" She was an efficient watchdog.

"No," I hissed back. "I cannot sleep and I thought I might walk about the house for a while." She was on her feet in a trice.

"I will accompany you." She groped on the floor for her own cloak but I gripped her arm.

"No! Please, Disenk! Just for once let me be alone. I promise you I will not go outside." She was shaking her head even before I had finished speaking.

"It is not allowed," she said firmly, anxiously. "I would be punished. Go back to bed and I will bring you a soothing drink."

It was like trying to force my way through a papyrus thicket. The soft fronds swayed and gave but the stems were stiff, seeming to yield but snapping back as soon as my hand left them. I wanted to shake her. For answer I turned and strode away down the corridor. She gave a small bleat of protest and I heard her light footsteps pattering behind me.

The stairs descended into gloom. I took them absently, passed the Chief Steward's empty table, and entered the passage that ran transversely to the reception hall. At the end of it a faint yellow light wavered over the polished floor. He was still at work in his office. Without bothering to tell Disenk what I intended I approached the door and knocked. Behind me she gave a low exclamation but it was too late. The door was opening.

"Forgive me, Harshira, but I need to talk to you," I said swiftly, before Disenk could address him. He looked very tired. The skin around his eyes sagged and his shaven skull was slick with sweat. He wore only a rumpled kilt and his sandals. But if I had thought to catch him off guard I was mistaken. His gaze sharpened, slipped to Disenk, then back to me. One imperious hand waved the body servant to the floor. The other beckoned me inside. I obeyed and the door was shut.

It was not surprising that his light had not filtered up to me, for the mat had been down over my window and the only illumination in this room came from a small alabaster lamp on the desk. The rest was in deep shadow. Harshira lumbered to his chair and indicated that I might sit also. I did. We faced each other across the littered desk. His features, lit feebly from below and to the side, were like something out of a demon dream, the black eyes sunk in sockets made even more prominent by the exaggerated hollows below, the mountainous cheeks no longer smooth but a nightmare landscape of planes and valleys that slid into new forms as the tiny flame danced in its stone cup. I suppose I looked no better. For some time he regarded me, then he sighed, and pouring wine from the jug at his elbow he pushed the goblet across to me.

"You have been crying," he said matter-of-factly. "Drink." I did so. The violet liquid was dry and refreshing and I drained it quickly. It touched the pain in my abdomen with a different, more earthy fire than the sadness, enclosing and shrinking it. I put the cup on the desk and he promptly refilled it. "Are you going to tell me what is wrong or are you going to guzzle my wine and disappear in silence?" he said wryly. I drank again before answering, then grasped the cup with both hands.

"I am troubled, Harshira," I began, not really aware until later that I had addressed the great man by his name instead of his title, but he did not object. He made no move. Those black eyes of his remained fixed on me. "Today Kaha told me things that have distressed me. I cannot believe them. I do not want to believe them! I need to know if they are true or not." His eyebrows rose.

"What things?"

I told him. As the wine slowed my tongue and deliciously loosened my body I repeated all that Kaha had said. The numbers were still there in my brain, ready to spew from my mouth like some terrible, indigestible fruit. "I do not deny the figures," I finished. "But the matter of the Good God's helplessness—is that merely Kaha's assessment or is it truly a part of what Egypt has become? Tell me, Harshira, for it is as though someone I love dearly has died!" He let out his breath slowly and pursed his thick lips, then he folded his arms and leaned on the desk.

"I am sorry, Thu, but it is as Kaha says," he replied. "For you it is a shock. The common people live and labour far from the labyrinthine weavings of power. Their vision of

Egypt is an ancient and simple one. Without it they would lose heart, and Egypt herself would falter and dissolve into barbarism. They must go on believing that Pharaoh sits at the pinnacle of divine and secular authority and can do no wrong. We live in an age of peculation and greed, dishonesty, ambition and cruelty."

"But it should not be that way!" I burst out. "I have been diligent in my studies of history and I know that it is not right, it has never been right! Do the priests not fear the vengeance of Ma'at? What of their judging when the ka leaves the body? Why does Amun allow such things?"

"Perhaps Amun has withdrawn his favour," Harshira said gently. "Perhaps he, too, waits for a cleansing tide of anger to sweep the country on his behalf and for Pharaoh." I lifted the cup with trembling hands and drank more wine. He broke off until I had swallowed. "You are not alone in your indignation, Thu," he went on. "Many of us hate what is happening, and people like the Master who have access to the palace and the temples are continually trying to counter the insupportable pressure the priestly hierarchy places on the Double Crown. But part of the problem lies with Ramses himself. In battle, in defence of this country, he has been a brilliant tactician. But he does not seem able to fight his enemies within our borders. I expect that Kaha has asked you to put forward a solution of your own. What would it be?" He was speaking to me without a trace of his usual coldness or sarcasm. He smiled at me with a kind of dismal complicity as I hesitated, trying to think past the effects of the wine.

"I have only just heard how things are," I said slowly. "If the great ones cannot find an answer, how can I? I am still aching, Harshira. I do not know. Everything I held to be right is gone."

"Not everything," he contradicted me kindly. "Pharaoh is still on his throne. The foreigners try to force their way past our defences and so far have failed. Egypt has an imbalance but she is still Egypt, glorious and eternal. It is up to those of us who are aware of the true state of affairs to do something about it, and we will." He heaved himself free of the chair and came around the desk. Taking me firmly under my arms he helped me rise. To my dismay I staggered as he let me go. He chuckled drily. "You will sleep now," he said, "and by tomorrow you will have considered the question Kaha has put to you with the objective coolness of a good pupil. You will give a dispassionate answer and argue with your teacher respectfully. Will you not?" I looked up at him through scarcely focused eyes.

"No, I will not," I managed with difficulty. "It will never be a matter of cold discussion for me. I am distraught, Harshira." Now he laughed, but I was not so incapacitated that I could not see the way he was looking at me, with humourless speculation.

"You are drunk," he said, "and that is good. It is just what you needed. Now go with your faithful little escort, Thu, but remember that there are many who care as you do, many who strain to restore the purity of Ma'at, and the members of this household are among the most zealous." He patted me on the back. "Go." I wanted to fling myself into his arms, to feel the reassurance of a father's embrace, but of course I did no such thing. All the same, I thought to myself hazily as I made my way carefully out the door and Disenk rose to pad after me, there has been a subtle change in my relationship with the Chief Steward. He addressed me as an equal.

When I woke the following morning the edge of my distress had been blunted but by no means erased. I saw that I had reacted to Kaha's lesson with the outraged offence of a spoiled child; nevertheless an adult sadness and anger remained. My peasant innocence had gone as surely as the days of my country's ancient innocence, and would not return. I could not calmly ponder a solution to Kaha's question. I was still too emotionally engaged for such an exercise, and all I could picture was a great hand sweeping away all of them, priests, foreigners and Pharaoh himself, so that Egypt could begin afresh. I told Kaha so when we met in his tiny cubicle that afternoon.

"You do not look well," he observed crisply as I sank onto my habitual stool beside him. "You need to fast, cleanse your body."

"I need a better night's rest and a more optimistic lesson from you," I replied tartly. "I am sorry, Kaha, but I have come to no conclusion with regard to the assignment you set me."

"Well let us hope that you have remembered the numbers," he drawled. "Say them." Wearily I did so. They were still there in my mind, clear and black and uncompromising. I thought he was going to rub his hands together when I had finished. "Excellent!" he exclaimed. "Very good, Thu. Your powers of recall are prodigious. Now can you not hazard even a guess as to what might be done?"

I sighed inwardly and made a feeble attempt. "Pharaoh could send to Babylon or Keftiu for gold with which to pay soldiers to overthrow the priests," I offered. "Or use them to confiscate the temples' wealth. He could have the priests murdered. He could enter into a deceit whereby the God appears to speak to the High Priest, expressing his divine displeasure and commanding that his son, Pharaoh, be re-established as the ultimate power in Egypt." Kaha snorted derisively.

"You are indeed not your usual nimble-witted self," he retorted. "Such things have already been considered and broached to the Mighty Bull with cautious tact. He reacted with horror and puzzlement. He will not risk offending Amun, not in the slightest degree. What if it is the God's wish that his servants rule instead of his son? What if the end did not justify the means and Egypt's final fate was worse than it is now? Besides, Thu, Ramses is afraid and tired. He is forty-five years old. He has fought three great battles to keep the eastern tribesmen and the sea peoples from pouring into Egypt and claiming its fertility as their own. Each time he has returned to Pi-Ramses as to a place of safety and peace, a nest where he can curl up after having done his duty and where he chooses to ignore the increasing corruption around him. If he fouls that nest by attempting to change the situation, and if he should fail, he will have no safe place left in which to retire if circumstances force him to go to war again. At least if he closes his eyes he can cling to the pretence that he still rules Egypt and of course the priests give him all the respect and reverence due to his position, even though their words are empty."

"If I were Pharaoh I would risk everything for a chance to restore Ma'at!" I broke in hotly, and Kaha laughed.

"But you are not forty-five years old and scared and tired," he pointed out.

There was a brief silence between us.

"What of the Hawk-in-the-Nest?" I wanted to know. "Has Pharaoh appointed his successor yet? Surely a strong son would do his best to persuade his father that his inheritance must be secure." Before he answered, Kaha seemed to consider. He began to toy absently with a papyrus scraper on his desk, his gaze travelling the untidy, scroll-crammed recesses of his walls. Finally he looked at me.

"Ramses has not yet designated an heir," he said. "The royal sons fall over each other in the harem. Ramses has many women, and several wives, all of them fertile. He is obsessed with the question of the succession but he cannot make a decision. Which of his many fully legitimate sons will make a good Horus of Gold? The priests have their own choices, of course, and pester him with their merits. Ramses knows that if he does nothing there will almost inevitably be bloodshed upon his death as his sons, with their supporters, battle for supremacy. Yet he does not dare to declare for any one of them in case he loses what tenuous power he has. He has tried to weed them out."

"What do you mean?" I asked apprehensively. Kaha shrugged.

"Six of his legitimate princes died suddenly, very close together. The Master believes that Ramses had them murdered. It was a desperate attempt to thin the ranks of potential heirs to the Horus Throne. Ramses cried and beat his breast and they were buried with full pomp, but I do not think he was suffering overmuch." I felt little. The major blow to my gullibility had been struck the day before.

"It was the action of a weak man," I said slowly, "if it is true. Is there no prince left who can shoulder the responsibility of restoring Ma'at?"

"There is Prince Ramses," Kaha replied. He had relinquished the scraper and was drumming his fingers almost soundlessly on the surface of the desk. "He is twenty-six, strong and handsome, but he is an enigma, a man who spends much of his time alone in the desert. No one is close to him, not even his father. His political sentiments are unknown." I was all at once aware of Kaha's intensifying attention fixed on me. His fingers whispered on, tap tap across the wood, and he was still relaxed, but he was waiting eagerly for my response. I stirred on my stool.

"It seems to me," I said bitterly, "that there are no scruples left anywhere in this country but in the remotest villages. Therefore why not commit the final blasphemy? Ascertain the Prince's position. If by some chance his heart bleeds for Egypt, then remove Pharaoh entirely and place his son on the Horus Throne. Of course, those who did so would then become the real power. If the Prince is as gutless as his father, find another legitimate princeling, a baby or child, one who has no conviction, and elevate him to Godhead."

"Your intelligence is truly fearsome for your age, precocious one," Kaha said softly. "But you know that you speak high treason. Anyone entertaining such nefarious schemes would be endangering their immortal ka as well as their body. Who in Egypt would take such a terrible risk? Is there no other way?"

"Seeing that this is merely an academic discussion," I responded bleakly, "I must say that of course there must be other ways, but I cannot think of any. May we pursue another subject today, please Kaha? I am surfeited with the agonies of the King." Immediately his hands were stilled. He straightened.

"Very well," he said, and smiled sunnily. "Today you can practise taking the dictation for a very lengthy and horribly wordy letter from the Overseer of Royal Monuments to the Chief Mason at the quarries of Assuan. I, naturally, will play the part of the Overseer. You are his long-suffering scribe."

The lesson ended on a cheerful, almost hilarious note, but when it was over and Kaha dismissed me I felt exhausted and curiously soiled. I would have been glad to submerge myself in the timeless indifference of the Nile. As it was, I did not return to my room. I wandered out into the garden and sat hunched beneath a thick bush, my chin on my knees, eyes on the play of brilliant light and grey shade just beyond my feet. I was still there two hours later when a flustered servant found me and I was led, unprotesting, to where Disenk waited in the hot dazzle of the courtyard, wringing her little hands and almost weeping in consternation. I did not care. Turning a deaf ear to her words of reproach I followed her into the house.

Chapter 8

So the weeks went by, and although outwardly my routine did not change there was a subtle difference in the attitudes and conversation of the people who dealt directly with me. It was not that they were more familiar in their kindnesses or harsh in the disciplines to which I was subjected. I was not able to isolate just what the shift was, but I felt as though the household had taken me into its confidence, that I was at last a part of its organization. Perhaps it was simply that my own coloration had changed. I was no longer homesick.

The letters I dictated to my family became more stilted as time went on, although I tried to keep them warm and interesting. I prattled on about the details of my life while Ani industriously set down my words, but I said nothing important, for what could I tell them? That the King they idolized was a weak, impotent man? That he was probably a murderer also? That the holy men we were never allowed to speak of lightly were rapacious animals absorbed in their own selfish needs? I wanted to sit down with Pa-ari and share this wound. Pa-ari, however, was far away and judging by his own letters to me, was courting the dancer he had told me about before. We were separated by more than distance. Increasingly our lives were taking very different paths.

It was Kaha with whom I shared the emotions that the day-to-day realities of my new existence brought. I suppose that Disenk should have become a friend, but our relationship was not clearly enough defined. She was my body servant, therefore she was my subordinate. But she was also my teacher and my jailer, under direct orders from Harshira, and I came to resent the pretence that I could command her in any but the most trivial way. The situation must have been trying for her also, and knowing her fastidiousness and her rather snobbish nature, it must have been difficult for her to bow to an ignorant peasant from the desert. I expect that she in her turn resented her position at times but she hid her feelings well, as any good servant should.

I vastly preferred Kaha's male frankness to what I arrogantly saw as Disenk's shallowness. I knew how to talk to Kaha and even Harshira. I did not know how to converse politely with Disenk. Of course, I tended to take women too lightly, and one day Disenk surprised me. I had asked her where she had come from. She misunderstood my question.

"I was Chief Cosmetician in the household of Usermaarenakht, the High Priest of Amun," she told me, much to my surprise. She was mending one of my sheaths at the time, restitching the seam I had automatically ripped so that I could walk more freely. I did this now as a matter of course when I was dressed, and Disenk just as methodically sewed up the seam again. It had become a silent battle of wills. "I was also chief body servant to his wife," she added. Then she fell silent. I had been sprawling on cushions on the floor, watching her. Now I sat up.

"Well?" I prompted her. "Go on, Disenk. What is the First Prophet's household like? What kind of a man is he? How did you come to be working for the Master?"

She had run out of thread. Severing it with one decisive slash of her tiny, sharp knife she reached for another strand. She was sitting at the low table under the window so that the afternoon light could fall on her work and the sun caught her burnished cap of hair as she leaned forward.

"The First Prophet's wife was a childhood friend of the Master's sister the Lady Kawit," she explained, drawing the thread between her tiny hands. "For a time they and other friends of the schoolroom would feast together every month. I would be there to repair their face-paint when necessary. The Lady Kawit praised my work and eventually persuaded me to leave the High Priest's employ and go to her house." She threaded her needle and picked up my sheath. "It was a happy arrangement. But when the Master knew you were coming he asked his sister to relinquish my services. I am now at his disposal." She did not look at me and I got the impression that she felt she had said too much.

"Are you saying that Hui borrowed you from his sister solely to care for me?" I was bewildered. "And what of this sister? Where does she live?"

"The Lady Kawit and her husband have an estate just out of the city," Disenk said calmly. I waited but she had pursed her perfectly painted lips and was plying the needle industriously.

"But are you just as happy here?" I wanted to know. "Were you angry at having to serve me? Will you go back to the Lady Kawit soon?" She smiled at the mild trap I had laid for her.

"I am at the Master's disposal now, Thu," she repeated dutifully and I saw that I would get no more out of her in that regard.

"Were you happy in the High Priest's household?" I pressed. Her nostrils flared delicately. She placed the sheath on the table and smoothed it out, surveying her stitches critically, and I thought that once again she would refuse to reply. She shot me a glance and resumed her work. I noticed that she was sewing over a portion that was already mended. Either Disenk was becoming upset or she was determined that the linen itself would tear before her stitches gave way under my tugging.

"It is not correct for a servant to gossip about her employer," she said primly.

"But don't servants gossip amongst each other?" I shot

back. "And aren't I being prepared for a position as a different kind of servant? Besides, I am not asking you for gossip but for your feelings." She sighed.

"You are a hippopotamus, Thu. You are a battle chariot, rolling over me. No, I was not happy in that place. It offended me."

"Did they forget to use their fingerbowls between courses?" I teased her. Her feathered brows drew together.

"Oh no," she said. "They are very rich, very cultured. The High Priest's father, Meribast, is Pharaoh's Chief Taxing Master and he is also Overseer of All the Prophets of Khmun. The High Priest himself has many influential friends and the house was always full of important people." Once more the knife glittered in the sun, the thread was sliced, and Disenk folded the sheath and began to tidy away her utensils. I smiled inwardly, thinking how this must have pleased her snobbish little heart, but she looked at me solemnly. "But not the right kind of people," she went on. "First, Second and Third Prophets of Amun and Montu and Nekhbet and Horus, dancers and chantresses of the gods, overseers of their cattle and their treasuries. But no princes and nobles, no people of the correct blood. The High Priest and his wife behaved as though they were royal. The house was full of curious and beautiful things. They adorned themselves in silver and electrum. They spoke disparagingly of the royal family. One can inherit power," she finished priggishly, "but power will not confer noble blood. One is born to the nobility or one is not. The High Priest was not. I only thank the gods that Pharaoh has not been persuaded to allow his nobles to marry beneath them." So, I thought. It is as Kaha says.

"You must hate having to serve me," I said drily, and she leapt to her feet, hands fluttering.

"No no, Thu!" she assured me earnestly. "Not at all. I am happy to obey the Master, therefore it is my pleasure to serve you."

"And is the Master a noble?" I said sardonically. She blinked at me.

"But of course," she replied.

She had given me a great deal to think about. I was young, but I was no fool. Had Hui deliberately collected all these malcontents under his roof, or was every nobleman's household as full of dissatisfaction? I had no way of knowing and besides, it had little to do with me. I would eventually perform the duties for which I was being prepared, and leave matters of greater import to my superiors.

The information about Hui's family intrigued me more. Someone months ago had mentioned the fact that he had relatives, but I had forgotten. He had always seemed to be one of a kind, aloof, alone and self-generating, but now there was a sister, the Lady Kawit. What was she like? Was she also a sliver of whiteness, the moon incarnate? Disenk had not said so, but then Disenk was usually a model of decorum.

Occasionally I continued to see the Master pass almost beneath my window as I crouched there in darkness. He was always muffled in linen and trailed by Kenna as he went to swim privately in his pool. I only accosted him once, on the night that Disenk had told me a little of her story. On impulse I leaned out of the window and called him in a low voice, not expecting him to hear, but he came to a halt and looked up. There was no moon then and his face was an indistinguishable blur.

"What is it, Thu?" he called back softly. "Are you well? Are you happy?"

"Yes," I answered, knowing that it was the truth. "But tell me, Master, do you have kin besides the Lady Kawit?" I had taken him aback. I saw him start and recover, then he chuckled.

"Prurient curiosity is not an attractive trait in a young girl," he said drily. "Besides Kawit I have one brother and one other sister." He signalled to Kenna and turned away but I leaned further and forestalled him.

"Master!" I was ashamed of myself and yet burning to know. "Are they... Are they..." He looked back at me briefly.

"No, Thu," he said coolly. "They are not." He continued across the courtyard, a regal, ghostly figure merging into the shadows.

"Impudent child!" Kenna hissed before he too hurried on and I decided, as I let the window mat fall and tiptoed across the room to my couch, that Kenna had probably been employed as an Overseer of Prisoners working the gold mines in the burning wastes of the Nubian desert before he had found his way into Hui's service. I could easily see him flogging and torturing the hapless criminals and licking his lips with pleasure as they gasped for the water that he denied them.

That night I dreamed that I was the one with the whip and Kenna the grovelling slave. He was filthy, terror-stricken and emaciated. He was also stark naked. I awoke in a glorious flush of heat that had nothing to do with Ra's appearance in the eastern sky, my nipples hard and my loins moist, and for the first time I arrived at the pool for my morning exercise before Nebnefer. I felt full of vitality.

In the world outside, the crops were sown, grew to maturity, and were harvested. Shemu began. Egypt died, as she did every year at this season. The ground cracked and turned to dust. Everything living crawled into whatever shade could be found and lay drained and helpless under the sun's fierce onslaught.

At least, that is how it always was at Aswat. Here in the Delta, on Hui's estate, the heat was certainly intense and the air dry. But the watered gardens remained lush and green, the foliage of the trees fragrant and dense. The months slid by. Pakhons became Payni and then it was the beginning of Epophi and my Naming Day. I was fourteen years old.

The morning began with an early rising and a walk to the pool through air that had already lost its fleeting freshness as Ra opened his mouth and breathed fire over the earth. Nebnefer was unusually bad-tempered, standing waist deep in the water with his fists bunched against his hips as he yelled at me to pull harder, go faster, so that by the time I scrambled over the lip and began my stretches I was wondering why I had been born at all. I was, I confess, feeling sorry for myself. At home my day would have begun with extra sleep, and some simple gift would have been placed by my dish as I ate the morning meal. I would have been escorted to the temple with my whole family so that they and I could give thanks for my life and health. I would have laid some precious possession, a favourite toy perhaps or a vial of oils I had mixed carefully myself, at the feet of Wepwawet's High Priest, and in the evening the friends of the family would have gathered to drink wine and eat the special sweetmeats my mother prepared for me once a year. Not that I had enjoyed many friends. On the few occasions when a couple of the village girls had darkened our door for my naming day I had resented the way they gobbled up the treats and depleted my father's meagre stock of expensive wine.

But here, I thought mutinously as a slave held a sunshade over me and I walked back to the house, there is no celebration. No one cares that today I am fourteen years old, the age of betrothal in the village, the age of new womanhood. Sullenly I submitted to the routine of massage, dressing and cosmetic application that usually pleased me, and in my pretty sandals I slap-slapped my way briskly to Kaha's office for my first lesson, pausing to savagely rip at the seam of my sheath. Disenk had surpassed herself. The threads held but the fabric, so fine, so transparent and soft, tore with a tiny ripping sound. I did not consider how only a year ago such material would have filled me with awe and I would have handled it with gentle reverence. Now I ran down the stairs, strode along the passage, and knocked on Kaha's door with nothing in my mind but the rather spiteful thought that Disenk would have a long hour of mending in the evening. Or I would be issued with a new sheath. Perhaps a yellow one this time. I hoped so.

Kaha opened for me, but instead of ushering me within he came out and took my hand. He was smiling. "Come," he said, tugging me further along the passage. "School is over for you, my little Libu princess. Today you graduate from Kaha's lessons." We had come quickly to a pair of imposing double doors where the passage terminated. They gave off the expensive, subtle aroma of Lebanon cedar. Kaha rapped twice, then bent and kissed my cheek. "I congratulate you— I think," he grinned. "You are now in the hands of a much more severe taskmaster than I, whereas I can cheerfully hand you over and spend the rest of my day wandering in the markets of the city. May the gods smile on you, Thu." He turned on his heel and walked back along the passage. I was too dumbfounded to call after him, and, in any case, one of the doors was sliding open. I swung round. Ani was bowing me inside. Rather unsteadily I passed him and the door was closed behind me. I looked back. Ani had gone.

"Do not stand there with one foot across the other like a dazed heron," an annoyed voice commanded. "Haven't you learned anything in the past year? Come here."

Chastened, my heart thumping against my ribs and my palms suddenly wet, I did as I was told. Hui rose from behind the desk. He wore a voluminous white tunic whose many crisp pleats unfolded across his upper arms. His white kilt was also pleated to his knees. Otherwise, his pale flesh was unadorned by jewellery, although his red eyes, those frightening demon eyes, were circled in black kohl. The effect was startlingly magnetic. His stark white hair had been pulled up and back from his face and braided so that it fell in one thick plait between his shoulder blades. Deliberately he placed both palms on the desk.

"Go back upstairs," he said coldly, "and change your sheath. If you tear the seams any more you will sew them up yourself. Is that understood?" I nodded dumbly. "Good. I do not want to see you come in here unkempt every morning. Go." I hurried to do as I was told. Every morning, he had said. Every morning! My life was to change again. I flew up the stairs and burst into my room, eyes shining.

"A fresh sheath, at once!" I shouted at Disenk. "And I promise I will walk like a lady from now on! I am to work with the Master!" She smiled, completely unsurprised, and going to the chest, extracted a garment. I could hardly stand still while she removed the mutilated one. I was ridiculously happy.

Outside his doors again I smoothed the fresh sheath over my hips and pulled the ends of my red hair ribbon to lie on either side of my neck. My hands were clean and I could see no dry skin on my calves and feet. I took a deep breath, knocked, and went in. This time he smiled.

"Much better," he said. "Sit down, Thu. I know that this is your naming day. Therefore I have something for you." Leaving the desk he approached the shelves that lined his walls and I had an opportunity to survey the room. I did not know what I had expected, some outward show of wealth or authority perhaps, the furniture inlaid with gold, chests of gems, but I was a little disappointed. Hui's surroundings were spartan, and differed little from Ani's or Harshira's office. Indeed the window was smaller and higher. Hui's desk was large and imposing and quite bare apart from a rather beautiful white alabaster lamp carved in the likeness of Nut the sky goddess. The stone had been abraded so thinly that the pattern of stars painted on the inside could be clearly seen even though the lamp was unlit. A much smaller desk had been pushed against the right-hand wall beside another door. Half the shelves on the walls were empty. The rest held chests, but by their plainness I decided that they could not possibly hold any household treasures.

Hui turned, and set before me a scribe's palette. It was new, its polish gleaming softly, its surfaces unscratched and unstained. There was the groove for brushes and a sink for an inkpot. It was black. Inlaid upon its writing surface, picked out in delicate lines of silver, Thoth stood. His long, curving ibis beak stretched over the palette he held in one hand. In the other he grasped a pen. The work was so fine that I actually gasped as I rose to examine it. My fingers found no rough spot, caught on no flaw where a brush might trip.

"It is ebony, from Cush," Hui told me, as I caressed it. "Pharaoh's own craftsman fashioned it to my design. It is yours." While I stared at him, agape, he turned to a shelf again and then placed beside the palette a stack of virgin papyrus and a long, thin box, also of ebony. On its lid, traced in silver, were the glyphs for prosperity, health and millions of years. "Your brushes and paper," Hui went on. "Do close your mouth, Thu. I do not need to see the back of your throat at this hour of the day. The box also contains a scraper of ebony, capped in gold of course. Silver is too soft for rubbing papyrus. Are you pleased?"

I could not speak. With a cry I flung myself around the desk and into his arms, hugging him fiercely. For a moment he held me, my cheek against his chest. I could feel the steady drumbeat of his heart. Then he put me gently away. "These are not toys," he warned as I retraced my steps and lowered myself into the chair with trembling knees. "You are now officially my scribe. Your work will be very specific." He seated himself and folded his arms. "Ani is my Chief Scribe. He handles all my letters, the inventories of the household, the details of my estates. But I need someone to be directly responsible to me in the work I do. I am not only a Seer and visionary," he explained. "It is true that I spend much time in the temples, gazing into the oil on behalf of Pharaoh. I also interpret the movements of the Apis Bull and walk beside Amun when he is carried from shrine to shrine about the city in his Holy Barque, while he passes judgements and listens to petitions. I do not need you for that." He stirred on his chair. "You are perhaps not aware that I am also a physician. I treat whomever it pleases me to treat. This includes my family and those of my own household, of course. I have a great interest in both the healing and the destructive properties of herbs and certain chemicals. I keep records of the disease, treatment and progress of everyone I minister to, in those chests." He nodded at the shelves. "Naturally the information within them is utterly private. No one may read them but you and me. Likewise the conclusions I reach in my experiments with the substances for which I trade in many strange places must remain secret. You will attend me whenever necessary. You will take my dictation. When invited, you may question me with regard to my work, for I intend that you should not only write down what I do but understand it also. Why are you frowning?"

"But why not Kaha, or one of the other under-scribes?" I objected hesitantly. "Why me? Is it because I already have a knowledge of healing?" He laughed harshly.

"The knowledge you have acquired from your mother would not even fill a tiny kohl pot," he retorted. "I wanted an innocent, fresh, untrained mind. Intelligence without the weight of prejudice or the often crippling strictures of a common education. You suit my purposes admirably, Thu. You are highly intelligent. You are ambitious, or you would not have forced yourself upon me that night on my barge at Aswat. The only education you have had so far is the crudest of beginnings with your brother and an intense training with Kaha within the guidelines I myself set."

"So you did not see my face in the oil before we met," I said slowly. "You simply seized an opportunity to perform yet another experiment." He unfolded his arms and leaned across the desk so suddenly that I was alarmed. His red eyes narrowed.

"Not true," he contradicted me vehemently. "I am no charlatan. More than that I will not say. But if you work with me I can promise you a future more glorious than you have ever dreamed." He smiled, and the mood in the room changed. "This is your last chance to say farewell to my hos-pitality and go home. You can take the palette with you, of course. I daresay the skills you have learned might be useful as you sit in the centre of the village and hire yourself out to write letters." The scorn beneath the words was obvious.

"You speak of privacy, of secrets," I said. "Are you not afraid to trust one so young and untried as me?"

"I trust no one," he replied flatly. "Do not flatter yourself on that point, Thu. Believe me, I am not relying on any sense of honesty or loyalty you may have." He sat back, then got to his feet. "I place my trust more in your own secret dreams. You know what I am speaking of, don't you? Besides, if your tongue loosens I will cut it out and send it to your father." He waved me up and I followed him to the door by the small desk. I had no doubt that he meant what he said, and for a moment I was afraid. What strange jour-ney was I embarking upon? With Hui's hand on the tiller, where might my craft end up?

Excitedly I stood beside my Master looking down at the intricately knotted cord that held the door closed. I inhaled the muskiness of his perfume, and thought only of the tanta-lizing yet repulsive whiteness of his hands and how I would like to touch them. My fate was sealed.

"These are knots of my own invention," he remarked as he methodically worked at the cord. "They ensure that no

one enters this room without my knowledge. I change them
when the fancy takes me. At night I place a seal over them,
and a guard stands here. You must learn the knots, Thu. Or
invent your own for me to unravel!" He laughed briefly and
the cord loosened and fell away. He pushed the door open.

The smell struck me at once, the sweet, dry pungency of
desiccated herbs, and I inhaled deeply and delightedly, my
mind suddenly alive with an image of my mother bent over
the task of sorting through the piles of dusty plants on the
table before her. But almost immediately I detected another
odour, much fainter, and the room at Aswat fled. This was a
bitter scent, musky and alien and somehow disturbing. I
could not identify it, for it wove with the healthier essence
of the healing herbs. The room was windowless. The only
light was a shaft that penetrated from the office, flowing
past Hui and me as we stood there and throwing our shadows across the spotless tiled floor and up against the table
opposite. As far as I could see, the table too was spotless, an
expanse of what looked like thin marble that stretched away
on either side. The walls were lined with shelves on which
were phials, jars and pots of every size. Under the table I saw
two great stone flagons. "Herbs must be kept in complete
darkness, as I'm sure you know," Hui said. "But when I work
I bring in several lamps." He smiled at me. "The surroundings can be much more congenial than they appear. Any
dictation I give you regarding what goes on in here must
stay in this room. You look troubled, Thu. What is the matter?" I shook off the moment of trepidation and returned his
smile. "Nothing, Master. Are all the containers labelled?"
His grin widened until he looked almost boyish, and I realized that he was happy. I hoped that it was I who had made
him so.

"No they are not," he answered. "If by some incredible
chance a thief managed to pass you and me at work in the
outer office during the day or the guard and the knots at

night, he would have no idea what to steal." He pulled the door closed and his fingers moved busily and gracefully, re-tying the knots. "He would not dare to unstopper the vials in order to hunt for what he wanted. If he got this far he would know that he might die."

"So you have poisons in there?" I responded to his gesture and resumed my seat. I was not particularly impressed. My mother had often pointed out to me the plants that could kill. The beautiful oleander bush, for example, with its lus-cious pink flowers, was particularly virulent. The smoke from its burning wood would make you very sick. Honey extracted from the flowers would kill. So would its leaves, its sap, even water that had been used to keep it alive. The aza-lea dealt death as well. Also the dove's dung, and the castor gourd, unless its juice was heated. Hui nodded.

"Some of them kill upon contact with the skin. Some of them kill if you are stupid enough to lean over the container and take a breath." All at once he seemed to become bored with the subject. He pushed the beautiful palette and box towards me. "I shall expect you to appear tomorrow morn-ing, properly and neatly clad, your hands clean, your face kohled, and your sheath in one decorous piece," he said. "Go away and play with your gift now, Thu. You may do as you please for the rest of the day." I clutched the palette to my breast in both arms and rose.

"I would like to go to the shrine of Wepwawet, if there is one in Pi-Ramses," I said, "and give thanks on my naming day."

"Out of the question," he responded indifferently. "Besides, Wepwawet has no shrine here. Why do you think I travelled all the way to Aswat a year ago?"

"Then I would like to take Disenk and an escort and go about the city."

"No." The feel of the cool ebony under my hands gave me courage. He had cared enough about me to remember my naming day.

"Then let me wander by the Lake and look at the boats. You tell me to do as I please, but there is nothing to do in this house if I am not to study. Why do you keep me so secluded? Are you afraid that I will run away?" He rolled his fiery, macabre eyes, then fixed me with their red stare.

"Why don't you sleep?" he said caustically. "Young girls need much sleep, do they not? Talk to Kaha if he is still here, which I doubt. Go and bother Harshira. Take another massage. Thoth has a shrine in the garden. Make some prostrations to him. Have you no imagination, Thu? The house is full of things to do. And no, I am not afraid that you will run away. You are free to do so if you wish, but if you do, you will not be received back." I walked stiffly to the door.

"I am not allowed in the reception hall, the servants' quarters or the public area of the gardens," I reminded him. "There may very well be things to do, but I am not allowed to do them. It is most unfair." I did not wait for a response. Bowing, I went out. I knew better than to slam the door but I wanted to. I also knew better than to brood on the petty restrictions of my life, for brooding would change nothing.

I went back to my room. Disenk was not there. Throwing myself onto my couch I examined the precious, the magical gift I had been given, my delight in it quickly dissipating my frustration. It occurred to me, as I turned it to and fro so that the thin lines of silver caught the sunlight, that it was an entirely practical thing to give a graduating scribe. It took no account of gender. True, all the scribes I knew or had heard about were male, but that was not the point. Hui had not considered my sex when he had had the palette made. He was concerned only with my proficiency.

The pride I felt at that thought was mixed with a quixotic disappointment. Would I have preferred a piece of jewellery, a hair ornament perhaps, or a bracelet? Something that acknowledged his awareness of my femininity? What would it be like to kiss those pale lips, plunge my hands through that milky hair? I was not ignorant of sex. No village girl, raised in close proximity to animals, could be. But I was fourteen years old. If I had remained in Aswat the young men would have begun to call on my father, sitting on the mat in our reception room and nervously answering his questions while casting sidelong glances at me, glances, I was sure, that would smoulder with desire. There would have been decorous meetings under my mother's stern eye, walks by the river, perhaps even fumbles and caresses under the palm trees during some stolen night assignation. I would have ultimately scorned them all, I knew. My body was maturing, its needs still confused and contradictory as yet. My heart was waiting to be captured for the first time but my life was severely regulated and restricted. The impulses of girlhood, the fey changes of mood and mind, the feverish, formless dreams that invaded sleep, I felt them all but they were stifled by the ritual of my existence. They did not die, of course. Thwarted, they turned inward, gained strength, became an erotic undercurrent to everything I did.

No young men knocked on Hui's door on my behalf. I had no friends with whom to whisper and giggle in the slow, hot hours of Shemu while we lay on our pallets and wove ridiculous fantasies around the unsuspecting village boys. I had only myself, Thu, poised alone at the age of betrothal. No wonder, then, that Hui began to invade my dreams and disturb my waking hours. Ani was too old to interest me. Kaha had become the substitute for my brother. The masseur was a servant. Strangely I sometimes dreamed of Kenna, always naked and cowed, myself also naked and bending him to my lascivious will. But none of them had the exotic, bizarre appeal of the Master and it was to him, secretly and invisibly, that my heart and my body opened.

He knew it of course, used it and played upon it, directing my sexual and emotional nature as he moulded my intellect.

He was cunning and cold, but I will always believe that whatever affection he was able to conjure was for me. We were alike in many ways—but even as I consider those words I begin to doubt. For I came to him a child, rebellious and unformed, a lump of clay that he took and threw on the wheel and fashioned to his own design. His purposes became mine, or rather, mine became his. Who can say how I might have grown if I had stayed in Aswat? Well. Such conjectures are vain and dangerous. We make our choices, and only cowards refuse to shoulder the consequences of those decisions.

The following morning, clad in a dazzlingly clean fresh sheath, a white ribbon entwined in my hair, my face immaculately painted, I knocked at Hui's door and was told to enter. Obediently I did so, bowed, greeted him, set an ink pot in my palette and reached for the papyrus ready for me on the small desk. The door to the inner room was already open, and this time light cascaded out of it into the office. After one appraising glance at my appearance Hui beckoned me inside. "Set your palette on the table," he said. "Your first task will be to learn to recognize the contents of the containers here. I will show you each one, reciting for you the properties of the herb. You will memorize what I tell you, and the following day you will sit in here and write down what you have remembered from the day before. Thus will we work, until you are completely familiar with all of them." I nodded, slid my palette onto the cold marble surface of the table, and waited. He pulled down a jar and removed the stopper. My nose twitched in approval, for the aroma released was strong and bracing. "Have no fear of this," he told me. "You have already noticed that the smell is particularly efficacious. I prescribe its inhalation to patients who are weak from a long and debilitating disease. Other than that, it can be ground up, diluted, and drunk to settle disorders of the stomach." He handed it to me and I pulled out several long, thin, dark-brown whorls of brittle tree bark. "Your mother would find this extremely useful," he remarked as I examined it. "But she could never afford it, for it comes from a barbaric country on the edge of the world. It is called cinnamon." I returned it to him and he passed me a large box. Opening it I saw withered and twisted roots. Again the smell was pungent but weak. "This too must be traded for," he commented. "It is kesso root. You know of the properties of the poppy, of course. This root can also be used to produce a twilight sleep and dull pain. The blossoms of the kesso can be dried and brewed into a tea which will kill tapeworm in the bowels. I have none to show you at present. I am waiting for a caravan to arrive with several other plants I ordered." I closed the box and handed it back to him. He thrust a bundle of large dry leaves at me and laughed. "Kat leaves," he said. "When I have disciplined you severely for some mistake that you will inevitably make, and you are miserable, soak one of these until it grows supple again and then chew it. But only one, dear Thu. It will make you believe that you can conquer the world and then fly into the arms of Ra as he rolls across the sky. And do not dip into my stock too often or you will come to depend upon the effects of the kat for all your well-being. Here." This time a tiny stone vial was held out to me. It was full of a colourless oil that had no odour. "Savin," Hui said. "A curious oil. Do not allow your hand to tremble, Thu, for a drop on your skin will cause it to blister and rot. It is both a friend to women and a terrible scourge. In small doses it will encourage the monthly bleeding to begin. Some women will ask me for it a month or two after some night of indiscretion of which their husbands are unaware. But if taken in sufficient amounts to cause abortion it usually kills. Convulsions, vomiting of a greenish hue, inability to urinate, and finally inability to breathe. Death is slow. It can take days." I passed it back to him with an inward shudder. "I do not distil the oil myself," he remarked as he set it back on the shelf. "It would take too long and the results would not be pure. I buy it in its finished form. I also buy the poppy already ground into powder. Now this I grow myself. It stinks, does it not? Thornapple. I see that you are familiar with it. Your mother assuredly warned you against the beauty of its white or purple flowers. Its only use is death."

The lesson went on, and I was alternately intrigued, excited and appalled. I asked no questions. I was content to concentrate on remembering the information fed to me, the colour and consistency of the oils and powders and roots and leaves, the methods of administration, the safe and unsafe doses. My mother would have been overjoyed to learn what I was beginning to assimilate, but I looked at the shelves and recognized that no village midwife could ever have afforded the exotic things stored there.

At last Hui poured water from one of the large flagons under the table into a bowl and handed me a dish of natron. "Wash your hands," he commanded. When I had done so, he washed his own, then he bent and blew out the lamps. I picked up my palette and we went out into the office. The sunlight seemed pure and limpidly innocent to me and I took a deep breath, watching carefully as Hui retied the door cord. "Now," he said, going to his desk and seating himself, "we will have refreshments." He clapped sharply and immediately the double doors opened. Kenna came in and bowed. He did not look my way. "Bring beer and cold goose and shat cakes," Hui told him. "If there are any pomegranates that have not completely shrivelled away, bring those also." Kenna bowed again and left.

"Master, does Kenna help you in your work?" I asked with what I hoped was ingenuousness. Hui shook his head.

"Kenna cleans my floor and scrubs down the table but he is not allowed to touch the medicines," he told me, giving me a keen glance. "He is an excellent servant in all ways and I would not want him to inadvertently poison himself.

But do not think to give yourself airs, Libu princess, because you may do what is forbidden to Kenna. Perhaps that is because I value his services over your own. Little girls are cheap to replace. Well-trained, mature body servants of Kenna's experience are not."

"I think I will chew a kat leaf now," I said sulkily, and he gave a single great burst of laughter.

"No, you will not. Uncap your ink and prepare to take a dictation."

Obediently I took up my palette and sank cross-legged to the floor at his feet in the time-honoured pose of all scribes. I was not really insulted. He knew me well, this peculiar man, in fact I was impudent enough to imagine that we understood each other. He had gone to a great deal of trouble and expense to have me educated, and although I strongly suspected that the reason he had done so had very little to do with his need for a new scribe, I trusted him. Carefully I laid the gleaming new palette across my knees, uncapped the ink, opened the box and selected a brush. Then I waited. Hui had settled himself into his chair and was leaning back, arms folded. He glanced down at me. "You are forgetting something," he said. Swiftly I ran my eye over my preparations. Everything was in place. The papyrus sheet under my hand was so smooth that it had not required burnishing. Then it came to me. Bowing my head I whispered the prayer to Thoth, gratitude and pride filling me as I did so. I had a right to say the scribe's prayer now. I was a full-fledged servant of the god of language. When I had finished I smiled happily up at Hui.

"I am re-collected, Master."

"Then begin. To His Excellency Panauk, Royal Scribe of His Majesty's Harem, greetings. In regard to the bowel disorder of the Lady Weret, I send by the hand of my Steward a prescription of saffron and poppy. The Lady Weret must fast for three days and take one ro of this mixture four times a day, followed by one piece of bread in rotten condition. Report her progress to me at the end of a week. In the matter of the child Thothmes' eyes, continue the treatment I have previously suggested, adding the rowan wood and honey salve to absorb the exudations and relieve his itching. Put gloves on his hands if he is tempted to scratch himself. With reference to Queen Twosret's somewhat injudicious request, I understand that you are compelled to make me aware of the needs of the royal women. However, I presume that you cautioned her before passing her question to me. Tell her most respectfully that I cannot comply, but I will wait upon her at her convenience to discuss any other problems she may have. My charges for these physics and for my advice will be forwarded to the Royal Treasurer at the palace. By the hand of my Scribe Thu, I am your humble servant Hui, Seer of the gods and Master Physician." He unfolded his arms. "Did you follow, Thu? Let me see what you have done." Wordlessly, smugly, I handed him the papyrus. He nodded. "Good. It is neat, and I see that you have spelled everything correctly. Make a scroll and give it to Harshira to be sealed and delivered. Where is Kenna with the food?" As though the servant had been waiting, there was a knock on the door and he entered bearing a tray. Placing it on the desk he bowed himself out without a word. I was suddenly ravenous, and at Hui's invitation I rose and began to tear at the cold goose.

"Who is Queen Twosret?" I wanted to know. Hui sipped his wine.

"Do not speak with your mouth full," he rebuked me impatiently. "She is one of Ramses' lesser queens, a member of the Peleset tribe. Ramses brought her back from his wars five years ago." Picking up a copper fruit knife he sliced neatly through one of the wrinkled pomegranates on the tray and inspected the contents with distaste. "She is a pretty little thing but rather stupid. Ramses had a daughter by her and has not touched her since."

"You mean that she was a captive?" I snatched up the discarded pomegranate and began to scoop out its contents with a silver spoon.

"Of course that is what I mean. I suppose you think that is romantic. Ramses won a great naval and land battle. He took over three thousand captives as slaves and gifts to his officials and commanders. It is unfortunate that his internal policies are not as sweepingly decisive. If he would regard Egypt as a battlefield and plan his campaigns accordingly we would not be slowly sinking into a marsh of corruption and decay."

I ignored his wry comment on Pharaoh's ineptitude. By now I had heard the same sentiments expressed many times in this house. "What a horrible fate!" I exclaimed, intrigued. "To be rescued, destitute, from the scene of death and carnage, and dragged in chains to Egypt, only to be selected as a wife for the mightiest ruler in the world, that is wonderful." I was digging for the last of the bitter pomegranate seeds as I spoke. "Then to give him a little princess, for which the reward is to be flung aside and forgotten in the harem! That is unforgivable. What was her injudicious request, Master?"

"None of your business, you ridiculous child," Hui said crisply. "And as for a horrible fate, is Pharaoh expected to regularly service every one of his women? There are hundreds of them in the harem. Twosret has hardly been 'flung aside.' As a queen she has her own apartments, and as the mother of a legitimately royal girl she has direct access to the Might Bull whenever she wants. She also enjoys the privileges of a high position in the hierarchy of the harem because she is a queen and not merely a concubine."

"Like the Lady Weret?"

"Like Weret. Does the thought of being a member of Ramses' harem fill you with loathing, Thu?" He was passing his wine cup under his nose, inhaling the bouquet and smiling at me faintly, mockingly. "I would have thought that a luxury-loving creature like you would be envious." The expression in his blood-filled eyes was inscrutable. I swallowed the last of the pomegranate, dabbled my fingers in the fingerbowl, and considered. It had suddenly occurred to me that one of the few ways a peasant girl could leap the chasm of blood and privilege and come to the attention of the mighty existed in the harem.

"Not loathing," I decided. "But to enjoy the King's favour and then be banished from his bed, that I would find hard. I would want to be the most beautiful, the most pampered, the most indulged, always. What do the women find to do with themselves all day if they are not in the palace?" Hui drank and selected a shat cake. He turned it round and round in his white, fastidious fingers.

"They gossip. They eat and drink. They play with their jewels and order new clothes. Their servants bring them the latest cosmetics and lotions. Some of them, however, do not succumb to the enervating influence of the harem. They engage in trade and other businesses. They keep themselves firm in body and occupied in mind. But those women are exceptions."

"Surely," I said slowly, "it cannot be too difficult to keep Pharaoh's affections if one is beautiful enough and clever enough to come to his attention in the first place." Hui bit into his cake, chewed carefully, then cleared his mouth.

"Ah!" he responded. "That is the crux of the matter. Do you have any idea, my Thu, how few women are clever as well as beautiful? In the harem they may be counted on the fingers of one hand. Great Royal Wife Ast-Amasareth is such a one. She, like Queen Twosret, is a foreigner, a Syrian dragged in chains, as you so inaccurately put it, to Egypt after one of Ramses' campaigns. She is no more beautiful than Twosret, but she is intelligent and crafty. She has made it her life's work to know her husband well, his likes and dislikes, his weaknesses and strengths. Next to the Royal Wife the Lady of the Two Lands Ast, she is the most powerful woman in the harem and at court. She keeps her position through constant vigilance and great wisdom."

"Then why is she herself not Chief Wife, if she is so perfect?" I flashed at him, obscurely irritated by his words. He grinned at me.

"Because she is not quite as intelligent or as cunning as Ast," he told me, "and because Ast is the mother of Pharaoh's oldest son. Now if you have eaten and drunk enough and your curiosity has been satisfied we will continue with your lessons. I have no appointments today."

"I would like to see inside the harem," I said, without much hope as I pulled my palette towards me and prepared to work. "Could I come with you one day, Master, when you go to minister to the women?" To my great surprise and delight he nodded, then he came around the desk, and taking my head between his hands he kissed my hair.

"I promise you, Thu," he replied quietly, "that one day I will take you inside the harem. You have my word." He straightened. "Now!" he went on briskly. "It is time for you to learn of the Metu, the channels that start from the heart. There are four to the head and the nose, four to the ears, six to the arms, six to the feet, four to the liver, four to the lungs and spleen, four to the rectum, two to the testicles, two to the bladder. They carry air, blood, mucus, nourishment, semen and excretions. A blockage of blood or mucus can cause illness. Blockage of the rectum can affect the limbs and even the heart itself. The Metu also carry Vehedu, the substances that bring pain. Thu, are you listening? I shall be asking you for this information again tomorrow. Stop wasting my time!"

With a sigh I abandoned my daydreams and turned to my duty with full concentration. One day I would see inside the harem. I was content.

Chapter 9

Two weeks later I received a scroll from my family and a gift for my naming day. I unrolled the scroll and recognized Pa-ari's usual firm, small script but the language puzzled me. Glancing to the end of the letter I saw that my father had dictated it, and I settled down to read it with a lump in my throat. "Greetings to you, my little Thu, on your naming day," it said. "At dawn this morning Pa-ari and I went to the temple to offer thanks to Wepwawet for your continued good health and happiness. I trust that you have done the same. You will be pleased to know that your benefactor has kept his word. Our neighbour has died after a short illness, and five of his arouras have been deeded to me. The slave the Seer promised arrived three days ago. He is a surly Maxyes who has been herding Pharaoh's cattle in the Delta since he came to Egypt as a prisoner of war and I do not think he is overjoyed to find himself in arid Aswat, but he is strong and a good worker. It seems that your Master indeed has the gift of Seeing. Your mother is well and sends her greetings also. Pa-ari has no more lessons and now works every day for the priests. I long to see you." I laid the scroll aside, my eyes filling with unshed tears. They were the first direct words I had received from my father since we had said farewell on Hui's barge and his calm, steady character suffused every line of the letter.

Glad that my family would be more secure, I turned to the gift. It was a small carving of my totem, Wepwawet, and as I ran my fingers over the smooth lines of the wolf-headed god I imagined the hours of patient work my father had put into it, sitting on the floor by the light of the tallow lamp, his big hands enfolding the wood, his knife moving slowly, carefully, his thoughts on his daughter so far away. Many coats of oil had been added to give the wood the soft patina I saw and felt. Wepwawet's ears were pricked up, his beautiful long nose quested, but his eyes gazed into mine with calm omnipotence. He wore a short kilt, its pleats faultlessly represented. In one fist he clutched a spear, and in the other a sword. Across his chest, the hieroglyphs for "Opener of the Ways" had been delicately chiselled and I knew that Father must have taken the time to learn from Pa-ari how to carve the words. Perhaps Pa-ari had sat by him as he incised them into the wood, advising and cautioning.

The statue was a labour of selfless love I knew I did not deserve. Standing it on the table beside my couch I prostrated myself before it, saying the prayers I should have said to the god on my naming day and beseeching him for his protection for my family. I was chastened and ashamed. When I had finished I took up my palette and papyrus and wrote to my father, and for once the words came from my heart. Even though I was now completely proficient I was still supposed to dictate my letters to Ani for obvious reasons, but this time I defied Hui. He could read in my presence what I had written if he liked, I did not care, as long as he allowed the scroll to go south. I wanted to go with it. Not to abandon my life in this house, of course not, but to look once more into my mother's dark, imperious eyes, to be enfolded in my father's vigorous embrace, to sit with Pa-ari and hold his hand while the sun sank, red and peaceful, behind the pure, bare waves of the desert horizon. That longing lasted for the rest of the day.

Before long I had learned the knots that kept Hui's inner room secure and had devised a few of my own. He liked them to be changed once a month. I thought his measures excessive seeing that a guard was also posted in the passage outside his larger office every night to prevent anyone entering but Hui or myself, but he ignored my protests.

I was soaking up knowledge rapidly but cautiously. I had no intention of poisoning myself as I took down one jar or phial after another for examination and record. Each day Hui would question me closely about the herbs and powders he had instructed me in the day before. If I made a mistake he would repeat the lesson all over again, but I seldom made mistakes. Kaha's memory training stood me in good stead.

I also learned a far more sophisticated medicine than my mother could dream of. Painstakingly I drew the channels of the Metu in the body. I listed the symptoms of the presence of the Vehedu. I pondered the Ukhedu, the rot that could be male or female, that caused disease and pain by working its way through the Metu but that could be killed with the proper drops, salves, poultices and incantations. Before long I understood the remedies Hui dictated to me for the women of the harem or for his few private patients, and sometimes I felt confident enough to ask for clarification if I was puzzled by his prescriptions.

By the time New Year's Day, the first day of the month of Thoth, came circling around again, I was standing beside Hui, ready to lift from the shelves whatever ingredient he requested as he wielded the stone pestle or reduced some liquid over an open flame on the marble tabletop that was always cold to the touch. As well as passing him what he needed, I was expected to keep a careful note of what he was doing, and weigh and record the amount of everything used.

Hui was sometimes away, exercising his gift as a Seer in the temples or at the street shrines, and then I was expected to fill the hours in Disenk's company. But one day towards the end of Khoiak, when once again the river had turned most of Egypt into a vast brown lake and the air was cool, I was at last allowed to work alone. As I presented myself in the office, palette under my arm, and bowed, noticing with a sinking heart that Hui was muffled in the linen swathings that protected him from the sun and the contemptuous gaze of the populace, he pushed a sheaf of papyrus across the desk.

"While I am gone you can make up these prescriptions," he said off-handedly. "Be very careful with the one for the Chief of the Medjay Mentmose. He has a bad case of intestinal worms, and the remedy I have devised for him includes powder of the dog button. You will have to grind the seeds yourself. Wear gloves, and wrap your mouth and nose in linen. Add no more than one tenth of a ro to the finished liquid." As he spoke he raised a bandaged hand to push a stray lock of white hair back under his hood, and a flood of love and pity washed over me. Setting my palette on the desk I ran to him and pressed my cheek against his arm, then I looked up. The red eyes gleamed at me briefly from the shadow of the hood. The rest of his face was covered.

"You are more beautiful than many men who walk about free under the sun," I blurted. For a moment he was motionless. He made a sound—whether a grunt of humour or a groan I could not tell because I could not see his features—and gently shaking me off he glided from the room. I turned to the knotted cord on the inner door, my hands trembling. "Thu, you are a clumsy child," I reproved myself aloud as I fumbled with the knots. "You have made a fool of yourself." The door swung open. I gathered up palette and papyrus and went into the heavy blackness.

From then on I took pleasure in the freedom of being alone amongst the strange odours and fragrances. I would light the lamps, close the door, and reach for the first component in Hui's prescription with a lightness I had not felt since the times my mother had let me out of our house after the day's chores were done and I had run barefoot for the riverbank. The whole household knew that the Master's offices were forbidden to them when he was away. No one could get at me, even Disenk. Only Harshira had the right to approach, and that was only to the outer office. I was privileged. I was important. Best of all, I could indulge my delight in the weighing and measuring, the mixing and rendering and pouring, knowing that I had the power of life or death in my hands.

I had, however, forgotten Kenna. It was the sixth day of Tybi, and one of the new feasts of Amun instituted by Pharaoh. Hui had gone to the palace and as was the custom on any god's festival, the servants were not required to work. The house was quiet. I had opened the inner office, a place that had already become my sanctuary, and was just lighting the lamps, when I heard the outer door close. My heart leaped. Hui had returned very early. Stepping confidently into the shaft of sunlight falling across the floor of the large office I came face to face with Kenna. He was carrying a twig broom, several rags and a jug of steaming hot water. He did not seem surprised to see me, nor did he greet me. His face set, lips pursed, he brushed by me and pushed the inner door wide. I whirled after him.

"What are you doing?" I snapped. He set the jug on the marble-topped table with insulting deliberation, dropped the rags on the floor, and turned slowly, the broom in both hands.

"I have come to clean, obviously," he retorted coolly.

"You are not allowed in here unless the Master is also present."

"I am. I can clean whenever the medicine room is open." He waved at the door. "As you can see, it is open now. You undid the knots yourself. Therefore, I can clean." His caustic tone infuriated me.

"You need not address me as though I was a child!" I said hotly. "I am busy today, making up prescriptions for the Master. I do not want to be disturbed. Go away!" He shrugged.

"I do not need your permission to perform my duties here. I will work around you, Highness." The last word was heavy with sarcasm. I glared at him, fighting the instant burst of repugnance he always managed to conjure in me, and suddenly my mind was full of the occasional dreams I had of him that left me hot and restless. Kenna naked, Kenna cowering at my feet with the marks of my whip across his shoulders. Marching by him I hefted the water jar, carried it out, and set it on Hui's desk. Going back I gathered up the rags and threw them after it. I blew out the lamps one by one. Leaning in, I grasped the edge of the door and began to close it. My face was very close to his.

"I have decided not to work today," I said sweetly. "You will have to return at some time when Hui is here." He smiled but his eyes remained cold.

"To hear his name coming out of your common little mouth is blasphemy," he declared in a low voice. "You are arrogant, vain and selfish. Furthermore, you imagine yourself to be far more important than you really are. I shall of course go to Harshira, and tell him that your pettiness is disrupting the smooth running of this household. Then we shall see whose word carries the most weight."

I did not move. The wood of the door bit into my fingers, so frenzied was my grip, and I squeezed all the harder, thinking furiously. I knew he was right. In this matter I had no authority, and I had been stupid to force such a confrontation. Hui would not bother himself with such a frivolous clash but Harshira would have me dragged into his awesome presence and give me a tongue-lashing. I hated to lose to this bitter, self-important man. I thrust my face even closer. "You are in love with Hui, aren't you?" I hissed. "Madly and hopelessly, and you are insanely jealous of me because although you touch his body, wash and dress him, set out his food and fold down his sheets, you do not share his mind. I am the one who knows his thoughts. I am the one with whom he discusses his work." It was cruel, cruel and completely unnecessary, but I was driven by my own unacknowledged jealousy. I wanted to possess Hui myself, to not only work with him in the delicious intimacy of the herb room but to do all those things for him that were Kenna's domain. I watched the man's nostrils flare, his eyes narrow in hatred, and knew I was right.

A dark exultation bloomed in me, loosened my fingers, oiled my spine, and I closed the gap between us. My mouth fastened itself onto his almost before I knew what I was doing. I could feel him go stiff with shock, his lips frozen beneath mine, then they fluttered and opened and for a moment a delirious pang of warmth shot through my stomach and down to my loins. But he twisted away, and as he did so he bit me hard. I cried out, stumbling back against the desk, both hands clapped against my throbbing mouth, and he grabbed up one of the cleaning rags and scraped it across his face. He was shaking.

"You evil little bitch," he whispered. "So you think you share his work, do you? You have no idea what his work really is. As for his thoughts, do not delude yourself. They are deep and strange and far above anything a conceited whore like you could understand." He strode towards me and I shrank back, believing that he was going to strike me, but he began to gather up the things he had brought. "I have served him longer than you have been alive," he went on scornfully, "and I will still be here long after you have gone, for the seeds of your destruction are already sprouting within you, O child of Set. Put on fine linen. Paint your face and strut about. You will never be more than a crude little peasant, and no magic in Egypt can give your blood the invisible tincture of nobility."

"Jealous!" I shouted at him, my lip already swelling, and he had the effrontery to smile again as he turned towards the door.

"No, Thu, my loathing for you is not jealousy," he said over his shoulder as he went out. "I would not waste even such a base emotion as that on someone like you." Then he was gone.

"It is jealousy! Of course it is!" I shrieked wildly at the closing door. "How dare you speak to me like that!" I was the Master's assistant and he was nothing but a body servant, a drudge.

Striding to the inner door I jerked it all the way shut, and I had begun to tie the intricate knots of the cord when all at once I became completely calm. My hands steadied. My breathing slowed. The marks of his teeth are in my mouth, I thought distinctly. I will have to tell Disenk that I slipped and cracked myself on the edge of a chair. I will tell Hui the same thing, but what will Kenna say to him? Will he complain about me? Will he tell the Master the truth, and will he be believed? How secure am I in Hui's life, in his affections? How much trouble can Kenna make for me, now and in the future, if he chooses to start pouring poison into Hui's ears?

Poison.

The knots were complete, lying tangled against the polished wood of the door. I gazed at them unseeingly and gingerly fingered my wounded mouth. I had behaved abominably, reprehensibly, in goading Kenna. I had been unable to control myself but I had learned a valuable lesson in self-discipline and I vowed that nothing like it would ever happen again. Ever. Once was enough. I should have bitten my own lip and remained silent whatever the cost, but it was too late to undo the damage I had done. Kenna was now an open enemy, able to influence Hui against me in subtle, private ways. Therefore one of us must go, and it would not be me. Thoughtfully I made my way back to my room.

Disenk exclaimed in horror over my minor disfigurement, throwing up her tiny hands and sending immediately for salt

water and a piece of fresh meat. Gently and efficiently she
bathed the swelling and made me sit with the meat covering
it until the throbbing had died away. Then she dabbed it
with honey. I was scarcely aware of her ministrations. My
mind was working feverishly, scanning Hui's collection of
noxious powders. Hemlock perhaps. A leaf tossed into
Kenna's salad would loosen his limbs so that he would not
be able to walk well. His eyesight would become weak and
his heart would flutter. The advantage to the hemlock was
that its symptoms would not begin to show for an hour or so,
but although Hui had taught me the plant's deadly properties he had not schooled me in the amounts needed. Too
much and Kenna would die. Too little, and he might
recover after a day or so and return to his Master's side. The
root was harmless in the spring, but did harmless mean that
it would produce no symptoms at all or that it would merely
make one sick? A refreshing drink made from the leaves of
the thornapple? Hui had included the tiniest amount in one
of his prescriptions. But as the thornapple's noxious qualities
were known to every Egyptian physician it was more than
likely that the Master would recognize Kenna's illness. The
dog button? It was the most virulent poison on Hui's
shelves, killing by inhalation, ingestion or contact with the
skin. Hui had described to me in horrifying detail the way I
would die if I was foolish enough to handle it carelessly. But
in tiny medicinal doses it produced no symptoms at all, and
there was no middle ground of mere illness with its use. It
destroyed completely or it did nothing obvious.

While Disenk checked the progress of my lip, her perfect
features as solemn as though I had lost a tooth and would be
ugly for life, I considered and discarded one possibility after
another. The oleander worked too quickly. The bead vine
had to be chewed. Honey from the azalea was a possibility,
but where could I obtain it? My mind felt as hot and swollen
as my mouth and in the end I pushed all thought of Kenna

away. There was time to decide what to do, days if necessary, before the acid words I knew he would spew forth began to be considered seriously by Hui. If they were taken seriously. Perhaps the Master would brusquely command his servant to be silent, to take his complaints to the Chief Steward. But perhaps Kenna was right and my place here less secure than I had imagined. It was all very difficult. I sighed, and Disenk asked anxiously, "Does it hurt very much, Thu?" I shook my head. The real hurt was inside me. Evil bitch. Conceited whore. Common, arrogant, vain, selfish. Was I all those things? Of course not. Kenna had lashed out from the same pain that had stung me. Jerking away from Disenk's feathery touch I told her that I must swim, and together we made our way out into the garden, I to lose myself in the embrace of the water and she to sit on the bank and watch me.

It was easier, in the end, than I had thought. Once a week Kenna appeared to clean the inner office, and while I took dictation or passed ingredients to Hui as he bent over his stained bowls and utensils, the man would sweep and wash around us. Hui seemed hardly aware that he was there, so used was he to the well-established routine, but I watched Kenna closely. Often he would pause halfway through his chores to summon a slave with beer. He would place the cup on the outer desk to drink from when he became thirsty. Sometimes this did not happen, but more often than not he would end his work by wiping the sweat from his forehead and neck, and stand for a moment while he drained the cup. Then he would gather up his tools, including the cup, and leave. He always finished well before Hui and I and was gone as quietly as he came.

After much deliberation I had settled on the love apple with which to revenge myself on Kenna. Along with several other useful plants, Hui cultivated it in a well-guarded corner of the estate near the rear wall. I had not yet used it in any prescription, but Hui had told me that it was a good sleep drug in cases where a patient must be cut open. He also sometimes gave it to women who were barren, perhaps because its peculiar root was shaped like the penis of a man. I had handled the root without gloves and my skin had come out in an ugly rash, much to Disenk's dismay. Its ripe fruit could be safely eaten. Unripe, it killed. What I liked most about it, however, was that in doses a little over the edge of safety it would produce vomiting and diarrhea. The thought of Kenna laid low in this embarrassing manner made me smile. When he began to recover I would give him some more, and I would keep doing so until, weak and rendered completely incompetent for his work as Hui's body servant, he would be sent away.

My problem, however, was simple. I intended to feed the love apple to Kenna in the beer he usually called for. Therefore I could not use any solid part of the plant. He would have to drink his nemesis. I would have to grind the dried stem and a few leaves, soak the result in water, and add that to the beer. I had no idea how much of the tainted water would be effective, nor could I imagine how to experiment with it.

Obtaining stem and leaves was not difficult. Perhaps two days out of the week Hui was abroad in the city or in the temples and I was left to work happily by myself. I simply removed what I needed from the appropriate jar, ground it with mortar and pestle, and transferred it to another container which I filled with water and hid behind other sealed jugs on the highest shelf. I did not know how long to leave it there to brew, but surely a week would be long enough. Besides, I was afraid that if I left it longer it would be discovered and I would somehow have to explain its presence. I dreamed of it night after night, irrationally afraid that I would enter the office to find it gone, to find that Kenna knew all about it and was going to show it to the Master, to find Hui standing there grimly holding it up as I hurried to begin my work. Twice during that week I earned a reprimand from Hui, for I could not keep my mind or my eyes on the tasks before me. All my attention was fixed on the invisible jar nestling in its hiding place.

So great was my anxiety that I had almost decided to retrieve the concoction and toss it out, when Hui greeted me irritably one morning.

"I must go at once to the palace," he told me as he walked past me to the passage. "The Great Lady Tiye-Merenast is ill. There is not much I can do. She is very old and her heart is weak. While I am gone, find her scroll and make up the medicine you will find already recorded there. It is pepper, kesso root, poppy and a drop of oleander juice if I remember correctly." He halted and turned, fixing me with a sharp look. "Are you ill, Thu?" he asked abruptly. "You have dark circles under your eyes. Is Nebnefer working you too hard?"

"No, Master," I replied truthfully. "I have not been sleeping well of late."

"Fast for three days and then go without meat for a further three," he said. "I will instruct Disenk to that effect in case you are tempted to ignore my advice." He smiled absently and was gone. I heard him call for a guard and his litter as I was reaching for the chests of scrolls in the outer office.

I found the instructions regarding the care of Pharaoh's mother without trouble, and leaving the appropriate chest open on the desk and taking the scroll with me I unknotted the cord of the inner office and went inside. I lit the lamps and began to assemble the things I would need. As I was breaking the seal on a new pot of ground kesso I heard movement in the outer office and my heart skipped a beat. It was Kenna of course. I felt him come to stand behind me and I kept my fingers from trembling as I picked up the tiny measuring spoon. I did not look round.

"He has been called away unexpectedly," I said without preamble. "You can clean if you want to."

"How very gracious of you, Majesty," he replied with heavy sarcasm. "Thank you for your royal permission." I gritted my teeth against the equally biting rejoinder that had slipped into my mind with frightening speed and continued with my task. The medicine was for an important royal woman and required all my attention. I heard Kenna return to the passage and shout for his beer. Everything in me came alert but my concentration did not falter. The powders were mixed to the correct proportions and shaken into the waiting phial. A little warm wax sealed it. My hands were still steady. Kenna was weaving his hostile dance around me with the twig broom. He went out and returned with the bowl of hot water, set it on the floor by my feet, and threw his rags into it. I reached for my jar. Kenna was on his hands and knees, sprinkling natron over the floor. I removed the seal.

The smell was immediately overpowering, a rank, disgusting odour of rotting vegetation, and the water was brown. Kenna had not noticed anything. He was rubbing the tiles now, the dissolving natron rasping slightly as his wet cloth crushed it. I lifted Tiye-Merenast's scroll and the jar and stepped into the outer office. The beer had been brought. It sat on the desk, limpidly innocent, cool and inviting to a thirsty man. I glanced back. Kenna's white-clad buttocks were presented to me. His shoulders moved rhythmically. Holding my breath I poured the contents of the jar into the beer. Fleetingly I wondered when to stop. At half? Three-quarters? But water diluted everything and I did not want my disturbed nights, the panic that swept over me now, to be for nothing. I added it all. The dregs were oily and black.

I found that I was still holding my breath as I quickly stood the jar inside the chest that lay open beside the cup of beer, laid the scroll beside it, and closing the lid, moved away from the desk and went to the far wall. As I was replacing the chest Kenna came out. I walked past him, back into the inner office, sure that the sudden weakness in my knees would make me stumble, but he was already lifting the cup and did not even look at me. My heart was now palpitating wildly and I rammed my fist against my chest, forcing myself not to glance his way.

I began to pull jars and phials off the shelves at random, blindly, and I heard his sigh as he set the cup back on the desk with a click. Oh gods, I thought wildly, feverishly. What have I done? He was coming back. He sank to his knees behind me and I believed for one ghastly moment that I had erred, that he was dying at once, but he picked up his cloth and resumed his slow circles on the floor. I was frozen, my fingers stilled among the motley collection of herbs I had set haphazardly about. Then I became aware that he was standing beside me. "I want to wash the table," he said. Numbly I moved aside while he set water on the tabletop, dipped a fresh rag into it, added natron, and began to vigorously push the jars aside. Once I saw him pause, and a frown crossed his face. But he returned to his scrubbing and at last was finished. Giving me a cold stare he removed the bowl and left.

I heard him gather everything up but I could not stir. I was in the grip of the greatest fear I had ever known, but under it flowed a thin stream of excitement. Would he take the cup? The outer door closed and I ran to see. The cup was gone, leaving nothing but a wet circle on Hui's polished desk. I wiped it off with the hem of my sheath, then I went to the chest, retrieved the jar, added water from one of the flagons under the table, swirled it about, stood on Hui's chair, and threw the contents out the high window. It was foolish, I knew, but every outside entrance had its guard or watchman and I did not want to run the risk of being seen carrying anything unusual that day.

Forcing myself to remain calm I replaced all the jars on the shelves, left the medicine I had been ordered to prepare in a prominent place on the table, then blew out the lamps and retreated. I had done it. It had been terrifying, but surprisingly easy. Perhaps Kenna was even now beginning to feel sick, tired, wanting his couch. With any luck it would be a week or two before I would have to look at his sour face again. I was smiling as I ran up the stairs to my room.

He was already very sick by the time Hui returned at sunset. I had spent the afternoon practising my lute music and even attempting to compose a song of my own, applying myself more diligently than usual to the instrument. I would have preferred to learn to play the intricate, sensuous rhythms of the drum, but drummers were almost always men and Harshira had denied my request for different instruction. I felt virtuous as I plucked the strings. I may have made Kenna ill but was I not at heart a good girl, obedient and hard-working? My music teacher congratulated me for my perseverance when she left, and Disenk asked me to sing my composition again.

I was facing an enticing meal of broiled fish with coriander-flavoured leeks and chickpeas when there was a peremptory knock on the door. Disenk went to open it. Harshira leaned in and beckoned to me.

"The Master has sent for you," he said. "You must come at once."

"What is it?" I asked. I did not need to simulate alarm. A pang of fear shot through me at the sight of his solemn face.

"Hurry up!" he commanded, and I left the table. He closed the door behind me and turned along the passage that now held the gathering shadows of the approaching night.

"I have no sandals on my feet," I protested, wanting reassurance, wanting to hear his voice, for deep in my heart I knew where we were going, and why.

"It does not matter," he rumbled back over his shoulder. We came to the foot of the stairs and crossed straight to one of the two doors opposite their foot. He opened it, indicated that I should enter, then shut it again. He had not followed me.

The first thing that struck me was the smell, a foul, primitive miasma of vomit and faeces speaking of flight and terror and death. Choking, I paused for a moment, forcing myself to slowly accept it. Having worked with my mother I was no stranger to the distasteful stench of a sickroom, but this was different. Here the terror was a palpable thing, weaving heavily with the odours of the body and the thin smoke from the half-dozen lamps to fill me with panic. That too I struggled against, pushing it consciously away and looking about.

The room was the same size as mine but it seemed crowded. A pile of soiled linen lay heaped on the floor. Beside it was a large bowl of filthy water in which a cloth floated. Two slaves moved quickly and silently around the couch that stood in the middle of the space, easing fresh sheets under the half-obscured form lying there. Hui sat on a low stool with his back to me, and I was shocked to see that he was naked but for a simple loincloth. His undressed hair tendrilled white and dishevelled down his back and his skin was streaked with sweat. The table beside him was a litter of pots and phials.

In the far corner a priest stood, the sombre yellow light sliding over his shaved skull as he swayed. In his outstretched hand he held a censer-pipe. The spotless crispness of the wide lector sash across his smooth chest and the gossamer linen of his kilt contrasted brutally with the chaos surrounding him. He was chanting, his ritual drone at last piercing the numbness that had fallen on me.

"I know charms that the All Mighty wrought to chase away the spell of a god...to punish the Accuser, the Master

of those…who allow decay to seep into this mine flesh…"
His eyes were closed. The incense curled lazily into the
foetid air but its fragrance was lost.

The words buffeted me like physical blows. I had done
this. The dreadful scene before me was entirely of my own
conjuring. I was the Accuser, the one who had allowed
decay to seep into Kenna's vulnerable flesh. "… Head, shoulders, body, limbs…" the priest was continuing to enumerate
the stricken members as he tried to bind the gods to the
healing of Hui's servant. I was out of my depth, a child who
had waded into the shallows and flirted with the bottomless
darkness, only to be grasped and pulled down to where voli-
tion no longer existed.

No, I thought with such stridency that I was sure the
word had gone shrieking and echoing against the walls. I
was not pulled down! I jumped, I dived, I left the shallows
gleefully of my own will!

"…I belong to Ra," the priest's doom-laden voice sang
on. "Thus spake he: 'It is I who shall guard the sick man
from his enemies…'" I summoned up every ro of courage I
had and went unsteadily to Hui's side.

He barely glanced at me. He was stirring something in a
cup, his pale face tense, and as I came up to him he reached
for a reed straw. "Lift his shoulders and cradle his head," he
ordered brusquely. "These idiots are clumsy and are causing
him distress." I hurried to do as I was told, going around the
couch and easing myself gingerly beside the damp pillow.
Kenna was clammy to touch. Carefully I raised his flaccid
head, bearing the weight of his upper body against my breast
and holding him still while Hui inserted the straw in his
mouth. I could smell his breath, rank and hot. He groaned
and tried to pull away but I prevented him, horrified at how
little effort it took. The dose was too high, I thought fleetingly. Next time I must make it less. Next time…

"What is wrong with him?" I whispered to Hui. He was

stroking Kenna's forehead with the gently loving gestures of a concerned father while he steadied the cup close to the foam-flecked lips.

"I do not know," he replied absently, all his attention fixed on Kenna. "I thought at first that he had eaten something rotten but the symptoms do not fit. It is like a poison. Come, faithful one," he urged. "Try to drink. You must get well, for no one can care for me the way you do."

Kenna groaned. His chest heaved and fluttered. I felt him swallow once, twice, then with a cry he stiffened and vomited over Hui's hands. Immediately the slaves were there with clean water, working quietly and efficiently. Hui sat back and Kenna slumped against me, his cheek turned into my neck. "What are you giving him?" I asked. The man's diseased breath was like the panting of a wild animal, burning my skin, heating my blood. I wanted to throw him away from me.

"I purged him with durra and black alder at first," Hui told me. He was holding Kenna's hand now, his thumb moving comfortingly back and forth over the servant's prominent knuckles. "But when I realized that it was something more serious than stale food I tried to stop the violence in his bowels with garlic and saffron in goat's milk. I can do little more." Now he looked directly at me. "What is your opinion?" I met his gaze and held it with an effort I knew did not show on my face.

"But it must be an Ukhedu that has entered him through bad food or drink, Master," I said huskily. "What else could it be?" He searched my eyes for several long moments.

"What indeed?" he agreed drily. I fought not to look away, remembering with a surge of horror that he was not only a physician but a Seer, and then Kenna began to moan and writhe. I clasped him tightly as his head rolled back and forth. Hui snapped his fingers and a slave bent with bowl and linen. Carefully Hui wiped his servant's greying features.

I felt Kenna's attempt to speak before a word came out. The muscles of his chest tensed, went limp, tensed again, and I too became taut with the need to clap a hand across his mouth. How clear was his mind in this extremity? Had he been able to deduce the cause of his illness? He turned towards Hui and his fingers came up, scrabbling against the other's naked skin. "Bitter," he whispered harshly. "Bitter." A tremor shook him and he sagged in my arms. Immediately Hui took him from me and laid him down.

"He is unconscious now," he said tersely. "It is a good thing. He will not vomit again and he feels no pain." He stood wearily. "Take the stool and watch him," he ordered. "I want to question the other servants and look closely at the things he ate and drank from today. Did you see him, Thu?" I nodded as I walked around the couch and sank onto the stool he had just left.

"He came to clean the herb room as I was making the prescription for the Queen," I said. "It was as it always is." I kept my attention fixed on Kenna's oblivious form, and heard the Master stride across the room. The door closed.

"...I am one of those of whom a God wishes that he may keep me alive..." the priest was intoning. I felt very cold. Behind me the slaves were removing the soiled linen and the bowls of dirty water. Light all at once leaped, sank and steadied as one of them moved about, trimming the lamps. I began to shiver. Kenna was breathing in shallow little gasps, each outgoing breath a whimper. My heart was as frozen as my body. I folded my arms across my knees, hung my head, and waited.

A long time later Hui returned, coming silently to draw up a chair on the other side of the couch and lean against the rumpled sheets, one arm across Kenna's body. The hours dragged by. Sometimes Hui would mouth words I could not catch, prayers perhaps or some strong spell, and once he sighed and touched Kenna's cheek. There was no response.

He took up a sharp pin, pricking the forearm, the neck, drawing down the linen to expose Kenna's lithe, flat stomach and drawing blood there, but Kenna remained insensible.

Hui resumed his former position and an ominous silence fell, broken only by the sick man's tormented breathing. I had ceased to shiver but it was as though my limbs had been formed out of alabaster and it would have required a great effort to move them. I closed my eyes.

Kenna died as the first light of dawn began to battle the thinning glow of the lamps. There was no warning. His rasping breath simply stopped, and the sense of relief in the room was immediate and overwhelming. Hui got up, peering into the calm face. He laid a hand on Kenna's motionless chest and stood there, concentrating, then his shoulders slumped. With a wave of his hand he silenced the priest. "It is over," he said. "Harshira!" With a sense of shock I swung round. The Chief Steward had been standing just inside the door. "Send for the sem-priests to take him to the House of the Dead. Then proclaim to the household that we will be observing the full seventy days of mourning for him. He has no family but us to grieve for him. Thu, come with me." I stumbled as I obeyed. I was stiff from sitting so long. Following Hui through the adjoining door and having it closed behind me I found myself in a very large room of airy proportions.

A neatly made couch strewn with cushions stood on a dais in the middle. The blue-tiled floor gleamed, spotless. On the walls from floor to ceiling, beautifully executed paintings in vivid scarlet, blue, yellow, white and black showed scenes of vines, flowers, fish, marsh birds, sand dunes, papyrus thickets, all flowing one into the other like a pleasant dream. Hui raised the mat over the window and a shaft of pale morning sunlight splashed across the couch, the gilded chair, the small, ornate tables with their cunningly contrived gilded legs that resembled clusters of reeds. On one of the tables I noticed a tall vase and beside it a vial of oil, both flanked by incense burners. So Hui practised his gift in the privacy of his own room I thought, but vaguely, for the opulence of the surroundings rendered me briefly uncomfortable.

Various chests for clothes and cosmetics hugged the walls, but my attention was drawn to a collection of sordid plates and cups laid out on one of the tables. Hui crooked a finger at me and I went slowly to stand over them. He was haggard in the unforgiving daylight, his red eyes swollen and darkly circled, but his glance was keen.

"I have just lost a faithful friend and a devoted body servant," he said without preamble. "These are the things he used today. The food he did not eat went back to the kitchen and was fed to the servants' cats. They are very much alive. He drank goat's milk this morning in the presence of one of my cooks, with whom he spoke for some time. The cook also drank from the same milking. The cook also is very much alive. The water the servants use to quench their thirst is kept in vast flagons here and there about the house. No other servant is even slightly ill. That leaves the beer." He picked up a cup and with a thrill of foreboding I recognized it. Traces of foam had dried inside it. I did not want to touch it but Hui thrust it at me. "The servants draw their beer from sealed jars delivered straight from my brewing hut," he went on in a level voice. "The Under-Steward is responsible for its distribution. Seven servants drank from the same jar yesterday, and one of those cups drawn was for Kenna, at work in the herb room with you. Look into the cup, Thu." Unwillingly I did so. There were dark, viscous dregs in the bottom, a foul-smelling sediment from which I involuntarily drew back. "Do you recognize the odour?" Hui pressed. I shook my head, passing him the cup and placing my hands behind my back. "It is love apple," Hui said. "Kenna was poisoned by someone very naïve and stupid, someone who probably did not know that the love apple works twice as quickly when mixed with alcohol, someone who thought that by the time he became ill all the evidence of his poisoning would have been cleared away. 'Bitter,' he said. I am not surprised. Bitter indeed. Bitter for him, bitter for me." He took my chin in a rough grasp and pulled my head up so that I was forced to meet his fiery eyes. "Kenna had an enemy," he said, still in that flat, level tone, but his eyes were burning, red flames of anger and loss. "He was not an easy man to love, but neither was he petty, and his heart was mine. He grumbled but he meant no harm. Who did not understand this?"

I said nothing. I could not speak. His fingers dug into me remorselessly and I knew that he had found me out. It was over. My work with him, my pleasant sojourn in this house, perhaps even my life itself was over, but no matter what, I would not admit my guilt. I had not intended Kenna to die. I was not a murderer. Trembling, I waited for the judgement. Then Hui released me so suddenly that I staggered back. "Go to your room," he said coldly, quietly. "While we mourn for Kenna there will be no music or feasts here and the only work we do together will be the things that are unavoidable. You look very tired. Sleep now, and may the gods send you a good dream." His mouth twisted and he turned away.

I stood there for a moment, foolishly. You know! I wanted to shout at him. You know what I did! Will you take your revenge in secret instead of denouncing me to the whole of Egypt? I am nothing but a commoner. Who would really miss me if you slit my throat and cast me in the river? Am I to die quietly, unexpectedly, at some moment when you have finished pondering my punishment? He must have sensed my thoughts for he spoke quickly, without turning. "I will find a new body servant and you will continue to learn the lessons for which you have been brought here," he said.

"Now leave my room." I somehow found the strength to do as I was told.

Back in my quarters I ignored a sleepy and confused Disenk, crawling up onto my couch and reaching for the precious carving of Wepwawet that my father had done for me. I cradled it to my chest, rocking to and fro and crying, weeping for Kenna in a torment of remorse. My tears fell for myself also, for my shock, for the contempt I had seen in Hui's eyes.

I hated what I had done and longed to undo it, and bled a little for the man whose life I had snuffed out simply because I was jealous. I would have brought him back if it had been at all possible, and I did not dare to even think about the judgement the gods would assuredly mete out to me. Clutching the warm smoothness of the God of War I sat shivering and staring into the dimness.

Chapter 10

I spent most of the seventy days of mourning for Kenna in my room with Disenk. There was nothing to do and not much to say. Disenk spoke occasionally of a Kenna I had never known, a man who loved dogs and who had captured and tried to tame one of the desert creatures, shy and harmless but traditionally impossible to domesticate; a man whose mother had abandoned him in the streets of Pi-Ramses when he was three years old and who had steadfastly revered Bes, god of motherhood and the family, in the hope that one day he might be reunited with the woman who had cared so little for him.

I did not want to hear these things but I bit my lip and listened in a storm of confusion, guilt, relief and fear. In the long silences, when the heat of the season blended with the unaccustomed hush throughout the house so that it seemed to me as if time itself had died with Kenna and we were all suspended in an eternal limbo, I sat cross-legged on a cushion under the window, staring at the floor, and tried to recapture something of the person I had been. I did not want to examine the emotions that raged in my heart. Hour after hour I pushed them away, but just when I was able to achieve a precarious calm some image would blossom unbidden in my mind and my throat would go dry, my stomach churn. Kenna's shadowed face by the river when the Master swam in the moonlight. Kenna pacing across the courtyard in Hui's wake, obedient and respectful, his head down over the linen he carried. The feel of Kenna's mouth under my own, firmness melting briefly into passion.

Much worse were the searingly fresh memories of Kenna's clammy shoulders slumped against my chest, the feel of his hot, quick breath on my skin. These could not be fought and I sank helplessly under them. They passed, but at night new horrors attacked me as I tried vainly to sleep. I saw the sem-priest in the House of the Dead bend over Kenna's corpse and force the iron hook into his nostril to draw out his brain. I saw his flank slashed with the Nubian stone and the priest rip apart his skin to lift his cold, grey intestines onto the embalming bench. In the end I sent for Harshira, for I dared not approach Hui, and asked that he beg an infusion of poppy from the Master so that I could rest. The medicine came in due course and without comment and I drank it down, wondering dully whether it would be my last act before facing the gods of the Judgement Hall. But Hui did not exact revenge on me and after many hours of drugged unconsciousness I woke sluggishly, swollen-faced and thick-headed, to another day of inactivity and mental torture.

It was as though the house was sealed. No litters disgorged guests, no laughter broke the shimmering emptiness of the courtyard whose paving pattern became as well known to me as the delineations of my own face. Once I thought I heard a female voice below my window but was too lethargic to get off the couch where I was lying. Disenk told me later that the Lady Kawit had visited her brother to express her condolences.

I was not permitted to attend the funeral on the seventy-first day of mourning. I knelt at my window and watched the members of the household drift quietly across the courtyard and in under the trees on their way to the waiting barges. Kenna would be placed in a simple wooden coffin and would lie in the small rock-cut tomb Hui had provided on his behalf. So Disenk told me. There his friends and fellow servants would gather for the rituals of passing. They would eat the funeral feast outside the tomb and bury the remains of the food, and the little cave would be sealed. Disenk, solemn and cool, had wanted to attend but had obviously been instructed to stay with me. I at last persuaded her to come with me into the garden and we sat in the unearthly stillness, not speaking, while the hollow house drowsed, bathed in white sunlight, and even the birds were silent.

Towards evening we went back inside and Disenk prepared a simple meal for me herself. I had little appetite but I ate, just to please her. Later as she was sewing by the light of a lamp and I was moodily picking through the scrolls of time-honoured stories, songs and poems I liked to read for my own satisfaction, I heard the house begin to revive. The courtyard filled with the sound of chatter and hurrying footsteps. Downstairs a door slammed. Disenk looked up. "It is over," she said quietly, and bent to her work again. I heard Hui's voice outside, faint but familiar, and Harshira's deep bass as he answered.

Suddenly it was as though a crushing weight had been jerked from my chest. I took a long, slow breath. It was over. I had not seen my Master for more than two months but it did not matter, he intended to forgive me, life would go on. Where the weight had been there was now the soft, healthy heaviness of a natural exhaustion. I yawned. "Undress me, Disenk," I said. "I think I will go to bed now." She obeyed immediately. I fought my sleepiness until she had finished the usual ritual of massaging my face with oils and honey. Then I fell at once into the blessed dark pit of unconsciousness. There were no dreams.

In the morning, before I had even left my couch, someone knocked on the door. Disenk opened it. A short, powerfully built man stood there. He smiled at Disenk and bowed briefly across the room to me.

"I am Neferhotep, the Master's new body servant," he said. "I bring this for Thu and Disenk. I also bring a message. Thu is expected to attend the Master for work as soon as she has completed her personal tasks." Thrusting a small bowl at Disenk he smiled again and withdrew. Disenk carried it carefully to me as I swung my legs from under the sheets.

"What is it?" she asked, wrinkling her nose in bewilderment. I looked. Two shiny green leaves were floating in clear water. I stared at them, and gradually a tide of happiness swept over me. He must have put them in the water as soon as he came back from Kenna's funeral, I thought delightedly. One for her, one for me. A gesture of reassurance, a promise of forgiveness, permission to laugh again. Reaching into the bowl I fished out one leaf, shook the moisture from it, and handed it to Disenk. She backed away suspiciously and I took the bowl from her and set it on the table.

"Don't worry," I told her. "Put it in your mouth and chew it slowly. It is a kat leaf. Trust me!" I took the other leaf and laid it on my tongue. Hesitantly she imitated me, frowning at the bitter taste. For a moment we stood facing each other and chewing thoughtfully, but it was not long before we were giggling together over nothing.

We went down to the bath house arm in arm. I stood on the bathing stone with my eyes closed while I was washed and the fragrant warm water was trickled over me. Never had the feel of liquid on my skin been so insidiously sensuous, nor had the morning air been so full of delicious odours as I left the small room and went to lie on the bench for my massage. It will be all right, I thought deliberately, luxuriously, as the young man's hands began their daily chore. Time is moving me forward again. I laughed aloud on a tide of well-being and the capable fingers were temporarily stilled.

"My touch is not sure today?" came the query. I laughed again, knowing it was the kat but more than the kat. It was the breath in my nostrils, the strong, healthy beating of my heart, the tiny spot of burning on my heel where the sun had moved the shade away. Kenna was dead but I was alive.

"Your touch is wonderful, as always," I answered, and thought, it is over. I am free.

Hui greeted me as though nothing at all had happened. After his habitual keen glance over me to make sure my eyes were correctly kohled and my sheath spotless we proceeded with the day's duties. I had presumed that he would look strained, that there would be a certain aura of sadness about him at least for a while, but he showed no evidence of grief. I knew now in what esteem he had held his body servant but I supposed that the seventy days had leached out his sorrow. I had a moment of profound shock when halfway through the morning I heard someone enter the office behind me and Hui said absently, "Yes, it is permitted to clean now," but of course it was Neferhotep armed with rags and broom who busied himself around us. He did not call for beer.

The house returned quickly to its regular routine and so did I. Letters to my family were dictated, prescriptions noted and made up, the work went on in the herb room. Such rigidity served to make one day flow seamlessly into another with very little to distinguish them and soon Kenna's presence became nothing but an uncomfortable, fleeting memory.

Under the simple sheaths I wore every day my body slowly changed. My breasts grew more prominent, my hips gently rounded. I continued to exercise every morning with Nebnefer, to stand in the bath house and lie on the massage bench, to sit before Disenk's cosmetic table while she painted my face and dressed my hair.

I cannot remember the moment when I realized that Hui's establishment had truly become my home. I did not consider how the very restrictions placed on my life had forced an unnatural reliance upon its complete security, its unwavering predictability. I saw the same familiar faces from week to week, performed the same tasks, and except in my sleep I ceased to feel uneasy at the changelessness of it all. I was a prisoner unaware of her true state, a favoured child refused the challenges of unfolding maturity, so that although I became expert in the variety and application of all Hui's medicinal herbs and poisons, though my memory became faultless and my body perfect, my will remained dormant. I was not required to make a single decision regarding myself and I was content that it should be so.

Three months fled by. Then it was Payni, the middle of the season of Shemu again, three weeks before my naming day, and everything changed.

I had risen as usual and the morning had been entirely uneventful. There had perhaps been less to do during my afternoon hours in the office after the noon sleep and in spite of the absence of any real work Hui seemed tense and preoccupied, but I retired to my room pleased with my day. It lacked two hours to sunset. Walking through my door I came to an abrupt halt. Blue linen, the palest, most delicate colour I had ever seen, shimmered and cascaded over my couch, and the smooth contours of my bedcovering could be seen through it. On the table beside the couch a wig rested on a stand. Beside it was a tumble of jewels. Disenk turned from her cosmetics and smiled. Coming to me quickly she closed the door and ushered me forward.

"What is all this?" I wanted to know. She was already unfastening my sheath as she replied.

"Word has come from Harshira that you are to attend a small feast tonight with the Master and a few guests. They will be arriving at dusk. We must be busy."

"But who is arriving? Why am I invited too? What is going on, Disenk? Do you know?"

"Yes I know, but I have been instructed to give you no information," she said primly, and for a moment I was awash in the same anxiety and fear that used to plague me when I first arrived. I allowed her to seat me and remove my sandals. I was now completely naked but for the ribbon in my hair which she proceeded to gently slide away.

"Well, what is expected of me then?" I persisted. "Am I to go as a servant, or as the Master's apprentice? How am I to behave?" I was suddenly panic-stricken. Strangers entering the womb where I had learned to curl up safely. New eyes appraising me, judging me... Disenk was massaging my feet.

"You will behave as I have taught you, Thu," she said calmly. "You no longer belong to the fellahin. Perhaps you do not realize it, but you walk and talk and eat and converse now quite naturally like a lady. You have become accomplished."

"It is another test," I blurted. "After all this time, Hui is still testing me!"

"You are right," she admitted, "but I think that you will not be displeased when you know why. Now allow me to wash your hands and remove the old paint from your face. We must begin afresh."

"I have been a member of this household long enough that I can be trusted with its secrets!" I objected hotly, but I submitted to her soothing, efficient touch and gradually composed myself. It did no good to kick against the goad and besides, I was eyeing that river of almost translucent blue linen rippling over my couch with mounting interest. "Am I to wear that?" I asked Disenk, nodding in its direction.

"Of course. And the Master has said that if all goes well tonight you may keep it."

"If I behave myself and do not embarrass him, you mean," I muttered but my innate optimism was stirring, the long-buried need for adventure and challenge, and I decided quite deliberately to enjoy myself to the full. It was entirely possible that the invitation to dine would not be repeated. I had sensed Hui's deeply buried callous streak a long time ago.

Once washed, I sat before the little cosmetic table while Disenk worked her magic. Grey eye paint on my lids and thick black kohl drawn to my temples brought my glittering blue eyes into instant, alluring prominence. My eyebrows were also emphasized with the kohl. Carefully Disenk pried the lid from a tiny jar, and taking a fine brush she loaded it with the contents. "Tip your head back," she commanded and I did so, catching a sparkle out of the corner of my eye. Studiously she shook the fine grains over my lids and brushed them over my face. "It is gold dust," she told me, anticipating my question, and I was dumb with wonder. Gold dust! For me!

When I was allowed to raise my head Disenk handed me the copper mirror. The kohl around my eyes, sweeping my temples, caught all the light and sparked as I breathed. So did my skin. Magically I had become an exotic, seductive creature, a goddess in flesh. "Oh!" I gasped, hardly able to breathe, and Disenk firmly removed the mirror and began to place a dusting of red ochre on my cheeks and mouth. I could see her smile with satisfaction at her handiwork. When she had finished with my face she lifted my hair and pinned it to the top of my head, then she pulled a bowl towards her and knelt, lifting my foot into her lap. The orange liquid left her brush and went, cool and slick, onto my sole. My heart gave a great bound. "It is henna," I whispered, and once again she smiled.

"No noble woman would be seen at a feast without henna on her palms and feet," she said. "It is a sign of her position. It commands respect and obedience from her inferiors. The other foot please. Then I will paint your palms, and while the henna dries we will try on the wig."

It was a beautiful, heavy affair of many tightly woven braids falling beyond my shoulders. Gold discs swung at the end of each braid and were set to frame the face of the wearer, and a straight black fringe across the forehead completed the effect. It felt like a crown as Disenk settled it firmly on my head. It brushed my bare skin lightly, regally as I turned this way and that, admiring my reflection in the mirror once again. Oh Pa-ari, I thought with delight. If only you could see your little sister now!

The henna was dry. Wordlessly Disenk lifted the blue linen, helping me into it. Softly it draped itself around my ankles, its gold border glinting. Its skirt was loose but the bodice hugged my figure. My right breast jutted uncovered. Disenk picked up the henna and gently painted my nipple with it. My mother would hide herself in shame, knowing that her daughter was about to appear to strangers dressed like this, I thought, but I will teach myself not to care. Aswat is far behind me now. My hands and feet are hennaed. I am the Lady Thu.

All that remained was the jewellery, and I did not suppose that Hui would let me keep any of it once the dawn came stealing cold into my room. There was a gold circlet studded with blue turquoise for my head, a great gold pectoral that encircled my neck and lay halfway over my breasts, five rings of gold in the likeness of ankhs and scarabs for my trembling fingers, and a gold armband from which hung tiny flowers whose centres were drops of turquoise. The unaccustomed weight of the wig and the finery caused me to move with more deliberation than usual but it was not unpleasant. Disenk surveyed her creation critically and was satisfied. "You are ready," she pronounced, and I knew that she would be on display tonight as much as I. When the summons came I laid one reddened palm against her cheek and left her.

It was Harshira who stood outside the door, resplendent in gold-shot linen, a golden sash draped across his broad chest. I read no reaction to my transformation in his eyes but he bowed to me stiffly before leading the way along the passage. Dusk was filling the house and the stairs were dim but we descended into the sweet smell of scented lamp oil and soft yellow light. The servants were moving to and fro with tapers, driving back the impending darkness. They stopped and reverenced Harshira briefly as we passed them, and he nodded frostily, sailing on into a part of the building that had been forbidden to me until now.

We had turned right at the foot of the stairs. The passage here had widened into a stately hallway, blue-tiled, its ceiling sprinkled with painted stars. My glance fell from the Chief Steward's rolling buttocks to my own feet pacing the spotless floor. Light glinted on the tiny gems sewn into my new sandals, one between each toe, and my skin gleamed with oil. The hem of the gossamer blue sheath brushed my ankles like the merest breath of air, shimmering with my movement, and as I came to a halt behind Harshira a gush of saffron perfume from my body rose out of its folds to my nostrils.

Harshira knocked on the imposing cedar doors that confronted us and a slave opened them at once. Within there was a tide of male conversation, a gruff burst of laughter, a sudden gush of scented heat and full light. The tiny turquoise pendants of my armband tinkled as I consciously unclenched my hands and let them fall loosely to my sides. "The Lady Thu," Harshira intoned, and stood back for me to pass. I met his eyes. They said nothing. With a throat all at once gone dry I stepped into the room.

Hui was already rising, coming towards me, and for a moment he was all that I saw. He was smiling warmly, the moon god himself, all glimmering white and silver with his white braid threaded in silver hanging over one shoulder, the silver baboons, Thoth's sacred animals, clustered on the pectoral across his white chest, the thick silver bracelets gripping his muscular arms, the silver-shot folds of his floor-length linen. He was strange and beautiful and my Master, and pride swept me as he took my fingers and raised them to his hennaed mouth. "Thu, you are the loveliest woman in Pi-Ramses," he whispered, drawing me into the company, and it was then that I realized how silent the room had become. Six pairs of eyes were fixed on me, male eyes, appraising and curious. I lifted my chin and gazed back as haughtily as I could. Hui surreptitiously pressed my hand. "The Lady Thu," he announced quietly. "My assistant and friend. Thu, these men are also my friends, with the exception of General Paiis, my brother, of whom you have perhaps already heard."

He was uncurling from behind his small dining table, a tall, ridiculously handsome man with black eyes and a full, sardonic mouth. He was wearing a long yellow dress kilt instead of a red one but I recognized him immediately. It was all I could do, not to start forward and blurt out, "It's you! Did you ever succumb to the drunken princess's lust?" He bowed to me, grinning slowly.

"It is a pleasure to meet you at last," he drawled. "Hui has told me a great deal about the excessively beautiful and impossibly clever young woman he has kept sequestered in his house. He has guarded you so jealously that I despaired of ever setting eyes on you. But..." He held up a playfully mocking finger, "the wait has been worthwhile. Let me introduce you to yet another General, my comrade in arms, General Banemus. He commands Pharaoh's Bowmen in Cush."

Banemus was tall also, with the tight physique of the serving soldier. His movements, as he rose and bowed, were abrupt and assured, but his eyes, under a mop of curly brown hair anchored with a purple ribbon, were kind. A raised red scar cut across the corner of his mouth and he fingered it absently from time to time. It looked fresh. "There is not much commanding to do in Cush at the moment," he retorted, smiling. "The south is quiet and my men do nothing but patrol endlessly, gamble recklessly, and quarrel sporadically. It is to the east that Pharaoh looks with wary gaze."

"He would do better to gaze within his own land," another man broke in sharply, coming forward. He bowed to me shortly, officiously, his glance sweeping me non-committally from head to toe. He reminded me of a pigeon. "Forgive me, Thu," he said. "I am Mersura, Chancellor to the Mighty Bull and one of his advisers. When we here present get together we cannot resist the heated discussions that arise from the preoccupations of our several professions. I am happy to meet you." He strutted back to his cushions and I felt Hui's arm go around my shoulders.

"This is your table, between Paiis and myself," he said gently, guiding me to it. He snapped his fingers and a young slave appeared, placing wine and a bouquet of flowers in my hands. "Before you sit, some final introductions." The last three men were hovering behind him and I turned to them expectantly. "This is Paibekamun, High Steward to the Living Horus; Panauk, Royal Scribe of the Harem; and Pentu, Scribe of the Double House of Life." They made their silent greeting and I returned it, murmuring my delight at their acquaintance. They murmured back politely, and while I settled myself behind my table, laid the flowers beside me on the floor, took a sip of wine, they watched me intently. The High Steward in particular had a dark, brooding air about him that was more than the awesome dignity of his exalted position at court. His regard was steady and completely cool. At first I endured it meekly, cowed by the impressive company into which I had been so summarily thrust, but before long I became annoyed.

"Do I have a blemish on my nose, Lords of Egypt?" I enquired brightly, and the tension in the room broke up. Paiis grunted his laughter. Hui chortled. Paibekamun the High Steward bowed again to me, this time with a little more respect.

"Your pardon, Thu," he said with an icy smile. "I do not often succumb to such rudeness. Let us say that your beauty is somewhat startling. The palace is full of the loveliest women in the country but you are very unusual."

"Oh yes!" I replied as he retired to his table. "Do let us say that, Lord Paibekamun! And let me say in my turn that I am honoured to be allowed to dine in such illustrious company." I lifted my cup and drank to them and they toasted me back. Hui signalled, and at the end of the room his musicians began to play. Servants carrying steaming, laden trays poured through a door and began to serve us. Paiis leaned close to me.

"It wasn't just flattery you know, Thu," he assured me. "You really are exquisite. How do you come by your blue eyes?"

While my plate was heaped with delicacies and my cup refilled, I told him of my father's roots in Libu, then I asked him about his family. He spoke readily enough about Kawit, his and Hui's sister, and of his parents and forebears who had peopled the Delta for many hentis, but soon he brought the conversation around to me again, inviting me to talk about myself which I did with some hesitancy, aware of Hui eating quietly so close to me. I expected a rebuke from him but there was none.

The conversation sometimes flowed around me but more often was focused in my direction and I began to sense that I was being gently but expertly drained of information about myself. I was the polite centre of attention. I was the curiosity, the butterfly set free from its prison, and the experience was sweet. The food was wonderful, the wine heady, and the music wove with the warm virile voices, the darting men's eyes, the sheen of sweat on their arms and in the hollows of their throats that formed as the night deepened. I found myself joking and laughing with them, my temporary shyness gone.

Only Hui was quiet. He ate and drank desultorily, gave his orders absently, then sat back on his cushions and watched his guests. He did not speak to me once and I was anxious lest I had somehow offended him, but that anxiety was thrust away by my enjoyment. I had arrived. Arrived where, was a question I did not then ask myself. I was the Lady Thu, at ease among Egypt's greatest. It was a feast I would never forget.

Towards dawn the musicians retired and one by one the men rose amid a welter of soiled dishes and empty wine jugs, picking their way unsteadily through the wilted flowers and broken pastries to the door leading into the great reception hall and the porticoed entrance beyond. Hui took my hand and led me out with them. A scentless, warm wind met us, lifting the braids from my tired shoulders and pressing my crumpled linen against my thighs. The litters were waiting. Harshira stood in the shadows, ready to assist anyone too drunk to help himself. They took their farewells of me with wine-induced fondness, their voices loud in the blessedly cool air, and got into their litters and disappeared across the courtyard. But General Paiis lifted my fingers to his lips and then kissed me lightly on both cheeks. "Sleep well, little princess," he murmured in my ear. "You are a rare and exotic bloom and it has been a delight to get to know you." He swung away, springing into his litter and giving his bearers a curt command. He waved as the gloom swallowed him up and I thought deliriously—princess. He called me little princess and I am standing here in the same spot where he rejected that other princess, and I am the happiest woman alive.

Hui drew me back into the house, towards the familiar peace of his office. Once the door was closed behind us he invited me to sit but he perched on the desk, one long thigh crossed over the other, his legs the colour of milk under the still spotless, silvered kilt. I looked up into the red, kohl-rimmed eyes and as I did so he leaned down and lifted the heavy wig from my head, pulling out Disenk's pins and then pushing his fingers tenderly through my hair. "You are flushed," he remarked. "Are you tired now, Thu? Did the

evening exhaust you? What is your opinion of my friends?"
His touch was both soothing and arousing. Troubled, I bit
my lip and looked away and instantly his hands returned to
his lap.

"Your brother is charming," I replied. "I am not surprised
that the princess wanted to sleep with him. I heard an
exchange between him and a royal lady from my window
one night a long time ago." Hui blinked in surprise and then
laughed hoarsely.

"Paiis has a way with women. And do you want to sleep
with him?"

"No!" I said aloud, laughing back, but thought giddily to
myself, it is not the General who makes my breath come
faster, it is you, Hui. I want to sleep with you. I want you to
hold me in your arms, kiss me with those hennaed lips, I
want your red, red eyes aflame with desire as they travel my
naked body, your white hands sliding over my skin. You are
my Master, my teacher, the arbiter of my days. I wish that
you were my lover also. I shuddered.

"Good!" Hui retorted. "I think he would like to play with
you for a while because you are a novelty, neither pampered
noblewoman nor ignorant slave, but you will have the good
sense to avoid any sweet traps he may set, won't you? And
what of the others?" I considered carefully. The effects of the
wine I had drunk were wearing off, leaving my head heavy
and my limbs cold.

"General Banemus is an honest man, I think. If he ever
gave his word he would keep it. How did he get that scar?"

"Fighting the Meshwesh at Gautut, by the Great Green,
four years ago," Hui answered indifferently. "He acquitted
himself so well that Pharaoh gave him command of the
bowmen in the south. Pharaoh is not a man of sound judgement. He should have kept Banemus in the north."

"Gautut?" I was shocked. "But the District of Gautut is on
the left bank of the Nile, in the Delta, it is a part of Egypt!"

"Four years ago the Delta was occupied from Carbana to On by the Meshwesh," Hui pointed out. "Ramses and his army finally managed to repulse them. Their chief, Mesher, was captured. His father, Keper, pleaded for mercy for his son but Pharaoh would not listen. Mesher was executed. Did the peasants of Aswat know nothing of this, Thu? What age do they think they live in?"

"They are more concerned with how to pay their taxes and find their food!" I flashed back at him, stung. "What are events in the Delta to them? Merely the faint echoes of an Egypt that they cannot afford to care about!"

There was an awkward silence, during which Hui stared at me speculatively. Then he began to smile. "There is still a little peasant lurking behind that accomplished exterior," he said softly. "And her loyalties are primitive and unreflective. But it is all right, Thu. I like that tough little daughter of the earth. She knows how to survive." He stirred, uncrossed his legs, and began to unbraid his hair. "What do you think of Paibekamun, our aristocratic High Steward?" I watched the ropes of creamy hair fall free in a rippling wave.

"He is shrewd and cold," I suggested hesitantly, "and though he may smile and nod and converse, his true nature is well concealed." Hui tossed the silver threads that had been woven into his plait onto the desk behind him and slid to his feet.

"You are right," he declared flatly. "Paibekamun is an exemplary Steward, efficient and silent, and his King thinks very highly of him. So do I, but for very different reasons." He stifled a yawn. "You acquitted yourself well, Thu. I am pleased." I scrambled up.

"Then I may keep the blue sheath?"

"Little mercenary!" He tapped me lightly on the cheek. "I think you may, and the jewellery as well."

"Really?" I stood on tiptoe and kissed him. "Thank you, Master!" A look of sadness came over his face and he sighed.

"I have become very fond of you, my ruthless assistant," he said quietly. "Go to your couch now, and sleep the day away. Dawn is here."

I was halfway to the door when some devil stirred in me, a wicked yet pathetic impulse. I turned.

"Marry me, Hui," I blurted recklessly. "Take me for your wife. I already share your work. Let me share your bed also." He did not seem taken aback. His mouth quivered, whether from mirth or some other strong emotion, I did not know.

"Little girl," he said at last, "you have spent the years of your growing in this house, and I am the only man you have really known since you were obedient to your father and frolicked with your brother. You stand on the brink of a dazzling maturity. You have tasted true power once. You will do so again. There is a larger issue in Egypt than either your happiness or mine, and that is my true work. You do not share it yet. I am not the one to take your virginity, and though you imagine that I have taken your heart, it is not so. I do not wish to marry. Leave me now."

I opened my mouth to protest, to argue, even to beg, for ,I suddenly sensed a severing, but he gestured violently and I left him, pacing the empty, dawn-drowsy passages until I came to my own domain. Disenk rose from her pallet by the door and quickly undressed and washed me. I watched the water in the bowl become rust coloured as the henna dribbled from my palms. My head had begun to ache. So did my heart. Oh, Hui, I thought as I lay down and Disenk drew the covers over me. If you have not taken my heart, then where is the man who can possibly loom larger in my life than you?

The following morning I reported for work with some trepidation, not knowing how I might be received after my outburst of two nights ago, but my Master greeted me with a warm smile. "Do not become too comfortable, Thu," he said cheerfully. "Your naming day is less than three weeks away and I have decided to give you your gift early. Today you may come with me to the palace."

"Oh, Master!" I exclaimed. "Thank you! You have business there?"

"No," he grinned. "You do. An important man is complaining of abdominal pain and fever, and I have decided that you shall make the diagnosis while I stand by with my palette and take notes. You are perfectly capable of this," he assured me, seeing my expression. "Have I not trained you myself?"

"But how should I behave in the palace?" I asked in momentary panic, and he rolled his eyes.

"You will behave like a physician, briskly, kindly and competently. Put on your pretty blue linen and tell Disenk to henna your soles and palms. Wear the jewellery but not the wig. I will meet you in the courtyard presently and we will share a litter. Do not be long!"

I nodded vigorously and almost ran from the room. I was delighted and scared. My life had been a placid river for so long, with but one whirlpool, the death of Kenna. Now, in a breathlessly short time, it had become a torrent of stormy water, exhilarating and unpredictable in its surges. I was determined to weather each one.

Chapter 11

By the time I hurried through the main doors and out into the courtyard Hui was already waiting in the litter, bound in his linen like a sitting corpse. I climbed in beside him and at once he gave the order to move, leaning across me to pull the curtains closed as he did so. "Oh please, Master!" I protested as our conveyance rose onto the shoulders of the bearers. "Could we not leave them open? I have seen nothing outside your estate for more than two years!" He hesitated then grunted an assent and I lay back on the cushions, my eyes on the shrubbery of the garden gliding by. We were escorted by four household guards and I could hear their steady tread before and behind. The shadow of the entrance pylon slid over us and was gone.

We turned right, and there, just beyond Hui's watersteps, was the Lake of the Residence, its level low because of the season, sparkling dully in the bright sunlight. A small craft with one lone rower was passing, and behind it the bulk of a laden barge loomed majestically. On the farther bank three skiffs lay beached, their white lateen sails collapsed and flapping idly in the intermittent, hot breeze. Above them was a jumble of roofs and then the brazen blueness of the summer sky. My vision was suddenly obscured by a group of four or five servants hurrying in the opposite direction along the road which we were sharing. Their bare feet kicked up little clouds of dust. They were talking animatedly and hardly glanced into the litter as they went by. A contingent of soldiers swung out and marched past us. They were heavily bearded, with coarse kilts aproned in leather and horned bronze helmets. They ignored us. "Shardana mercenaries," Hui said tersely.

The sounds of the great city were more evident now, shouts and the creak of cart wheels, braying of donkeys, and other unidentifiable noises all blending into a hum of activity and industry that formed a faint, wind-shivered background to the gentle slap of water against the watersteps of the noble dwellings we moved slowly past. The road curved inward past these places, and huge walls reared up to our right, their tops hung with bristling palms and drooping tree branches whose shade dappled us. The watersteps were all guarded by men who watched the traffic carefully in spite of the fact that no one was allowed to use this road except those who lived or worked in the palace or the homes of the privileged that fronted the Lake.

My gaze remained on the water, and just as I had seen them so many months ago, Pharaoh's barges came into view, rocking at anchor at the foot of his dazzlingly white marble watersteps. Their gold and silver chasings flashed. The imperial blue-and-white flags rippled high on their prows. Guards stood solemnly motionless before them. Although I was no longer the spellbound country girl who had once gazed on these marvels open-mouthed, they still filled me with wonder.

We turned right again. The watersteps were now behind us, and a vast marble landing had opened out, ringed with soldiers. Our litter was gently lowered and we got out. "We must walk from here," Hui said. He reached back into the litter for his palette and box of medicines and I looked about.

Although the landing was surrounded on both sides by neatly trimmed trees and lush grass, it was so wide that we were standing in harsh heat where the shade could not touch us. Ahead, a granite pylon reared. Before its two sides, high standards lifted blue-and-white flags into the heavens and through its gateless centre I could see a paved path crowded with more trees. I am going to enter the palace, I thought, choked with elation. Somewhere beyond that pylon is the most powerful God in the whole world and I will be breathing the air he breathes, treading the floors his feet have rested upon. Each face I see has looked upon his face. Each ear has heard his voice. "Come," Hui ordered, and I gathered my wits and fell in beside him, walking under the pylon where the gate guards gave us a sharp glance and then bowed.

A short distance in, the path I had glimpsed divided, running to left and right as well as straight ahead. Hui gestured to the left. "That goes to the harem," he explained, "and to the right to the banqueting hall, the King's office, and the rear gardens. We go to neither." As he was speaking a man had materialized from the trees by the path and was approaching us. He bowed.

"Greetings, Noble Hui," he said. "I am the Herald Menna. You are expected." Hui gave him a curt nod and we set off, our four household guards behind us.

The pillars of the public reception area were easily visible long before we came up to them, four tall columns crowned in folded lotus buds and painted a spotless white. Soldiers stood at the foot of each one, eyes staring straight ahead, ignoring the people who came and went between them. Menna strode on. Beyond the pillars the coolness enveloped me like the embracing depths of the Nile itself and my footsteps echoed on the tiled floor, which was a dark blue shot through with sprinkles of darkly glittering gold. "What is it?" I whispered to Hui. His hooded face turned to me briefly and his red eyes gleamed at me in amusement. He was obviously not at all awed by his surroundings.

"The tiles are made of lapis lazuli," he said. "The flashes of gold are in fact pyrite. Only Pharaoh and those of royal blood are allowed to wear or use the lapis, for the hair of the gods is composed of it. It is a very sacred rock." The hair of the gods! I trod gingerly, marvelling like the child I had temporarily become, but I soon forgot my wonder, for we had threaded our way through the crowds in the reception hall and had entered the throne room.

Here the atmosphere of power and worship was almost palpable, and though many people came and went through the cavernous space they trod softly and spoke in subdued voices. Once again the floor was of lapis and the walls were too. I felt as though I was under a celestial ocean shot through with golden gleams. Mighty alabaster lamps stood on golden bases as tall as I. Incense perfumed the air from hanging censers. Servants in gold-fringed kilts and jewelled sandals, their hair imprisoned in ribbons of gold thread, stood at intervals around the walls, their kohled eyes watching the company. Every so often one of the throng would snap his fingers and a servant would detach himself from his place and glide forward swiftly to be sent on some errand or other.

At the far end, miles away as it seemed to me, was a raised dais that ran the width of the room. On it stood two thrones under a damask canopy. They were both of gold, with lion's feet and backs depicting the Aten with its life-giving rays ending in hands radiating out to embrace and invigorate the beings who would sit there. One of them was of course the Horus Throne. I had no eyes, then, for the crowd. We drew ever nearer to the thrones. The Herald went up three steps and bowed to them before slipping through a small door behind them, on the dais to their left, and Hui and I followed suit. I was dazed with the opulence and dignity of my surroundings, dwarfed and intimidated to feel myself suddenly no more than an insignificant insect crawling on the floor of a temple.

The place behind the throne room was small and full of shelves and chests. I thought perhaps it was a robing and retiring room. We were soon through it and crossing a larger space, still imposing but more human in its dimensions and furnishings. Elegant low tables and chairs were scattered about and several animal skins lay on the floor. At the far end the wall disappeared in a burst of exuberant shrubbery and I could hear the piping and rustling of birds outside. Of course a guard was there, his spear canting, his broad back to us, and just beyond him I caught one startling and tantalizing glimpse of a tiny, impossibly beautiful woman in transparent yellow robes bending to pick a flower that nestled amongst the greenery before I found myself in a modest glazed hallway with tall cedar doors to right and left. A perfumed humidity oozed towards me from my right but the Herald opened the left-hand door, intoned Hui's name, bowed to him, and retired. Hui strode forward and I followed.

This room seemed almost as vast as the throne room, a place of sombre shadows shot through by measured beams of brilliant sunlight from the clerestory windows cut high against the ceiling. I barely noticed the closed and guarded door on the left at the far end, the three or four blue-and-white clad servants standing like wooden statues on the periphery of my vision, the sumptuously elegant chairs with their glinting electrum legs and high silver backs, the gold embossed surfaces of the few low tables across which the dim light slid. For in the middle of it all was an enormous couch that dominated its surroundings, and rising from the stool beside it and coming swiftly towards us was the most beautiful man I had ever seen.

He carried himself with such innate grace and dignity that for a moment I was caught up in the sheer symmetry of his movements, but my eyes soon fastened on and then fled from one perfection to another. He was wearing a starched linen helmet of red and white stripes whose rim cut across his broad forehead and whose wings lightly brushed his squared shoulders. His face was wide, with a firm jaw, slim nose and mobile, well-formed mouth, all set on a short but lithe neck. The pectoral bumping gently on his muscular chest was very plain, a series of gold and silver links holding in the centre a black-and-white enamelled Eye of Horus with a jasper scarab hanging beneath it, and his one long earring, a pendant lotus, clicked softly against it as he strode. His calf-length kilt, secured by a thin jewelled belt, curved up over his tight hips and then dipped towards his private parts. Disenk had told me, during one of our interminable conversations, that this was the latest fashion for men but it did not suit those whose bellies had begun to sag. The belly approaching me above the whisper of the pleated cloth was so taut that its tantalizing striations were clearly visible. Wide silver bands encircled his upper arms with no suspicion of a fold in the flesh around them. He came quickly, moving in and out of the shafts of white light like a figure in a troubling dream or a god taking shape in a vision, luminously clear then indistinct, formed and unformed, until he came to a halt before us, his whole body bathed in dazzling sunlight, and smiled. The upward tilt of his hennaed lips did not dispel the air of easy authority he carried with him and his dark eyes remained politely watchful. The scent of myrrh invaded my nostrils, wafting to me from his healthy brown skin. So this was Pharaoh, the Son of the Sun, the Mighty Bull of Ma'at, Subduer of the Libu, Lord of the Two Lands. I wanted to clutch at Hui to prevent my trembling knees from giving way. He should have warned me, I thought furiously, unable to tear my gaze away from the glorious God himself. Pull yourself together, my girl, and concentrate on the moment, or you will have disgraced yourself for ever!

My Master had placed his palette and box on the floor and was bowing respectfully from the waist, arms extended. "So, Hui," Pharaoh said. "Your patient is ready. I do not think the malady is serious, but one must never take chances with so illustrious a body." His glance fell on me inquiringly and briefly our eyes met. I imitated Hui, hearing Disenk's voice as I did so. "The reverence to royalty must be done swiftly, with eyes downcast and the head between the arms. For Pharaoh himself one goes down on both knees and the forehead and the palms of the hands must meet the floor. One does not rise until bidden to do so." But Hui had only bowed from the waist and was even now straightening. Puzzled, I checked my deep obeisance.

"Highness, this is my aide and fellow physician, Thu," Hui was saying. "She will have the honour of examining the Great One today. She is eminently qualified to do so, having been under my auspices for the last two years. I shall of course observe her diagnosis carefully." He turned to me and I read pure humour in his blood-coloured eyes. "Thu, this is the Prince Ramses, eldest son of Pharaoh and Commander of the Infantry."

"Highness, I am your faithful servant," I choked, feeling a flush creep over my cheeks. You stupid idiot! I berated myself silently, furiously, my eyes on the floor between the two strongly boned, harmoniously muscled royal legs, but even in the midst of my embarrassment and confusion I felt his attraction and was conquered by it. The Prince put his hand under my chin and raised my face. The skin of his palm was rough, the texture of a man who was active with bow and spear, who moved from formal reception to barracks to bedroom with equal ease. The metal of his rings was cold against me.

"Banemus did parade-ground duty with me yesterday and he spoke of the blue-eyed enchantress in Hui's house," he said. "You seem too delicately lovely to be a physician. What is your lineage? Are you a citizen of Pi-Ramses?" I watched the movements of that very masculine but infinitely seductive mouth.

"No, Highness," I said. "I am from the south." His eyes lit up.

"From Thebes perhaps? Your family are minor nobles in that holy city?" I was saved from a reply by a voice from within the dimness.

"Ramses!" it called, echoing in the lofty ceiling. "Why do you pass the day with Hui when I am languishing here in pain and agony?" The words were petulant but the tone was cheerful, teasing. Ramses dropped his hand and laughed.

"The Mighty Bull is champing in his pen!" he said loudly. "I have business to attend to, Father. I will see you tonight." He swept by me. His footsteps echoed as he went to the door which swung open at his approach. Then he was gone, and the room seemed more gloomy than before.

"Well done," Hui whispered to me as we went to the couch. "I sensed your hesitation but you made a good recovery. Follow your instincts now, my little Thu. This is your moment." He had recovered the palette and he handed the box to me. The couch and its occupant were very close. Together Hui and I went down on our knees and pressed our faces to the cold tiles of the floor. This, at last, was Pharaoh.

"Rise," that happy voice commanded and we did so. Gathering up my courage I went forward. Hui took up his position a little behind me and uncapped his ink. I looked into the face of the ruler of Egypt.

Two small, alert eyes twinkled back at me from under the cloth cap prescribed by law, for from the time of his Appearing no pharaoh was allowed to be seen without a covering on his head. His face was full, the cheeks pendulous, the mouth resembling his son's but thicker, more sensual. He raised untidy eyebrows at Hui with a sharp, "Well?" and Hui introduced me. The royal gaze returned to me and I was bidden to begin my examination. I was terrified but determined not to disgrace myself or Hui. I began with some questions.

"What are your symptoms, Majesty?"

"I have a pain and grumbling in my bowels," he answered promptly. "I sweat with a mild fever. There is Ukhedu in my faeces." I bent to smell his breath as he spoke. It was hot and foul.

"What have you eaten in the last two days, Majesty?" His eyes slid mischievously to my one exposed breast as I straightened and his tongue came out to rest on his lower lip.

"This morning fruit, bread and beer," he told me solemnly, his glance shifting up my neck to my mouth. "Last night I feasted with my Vizier and his train and I rather think I partook of the sesame seed paste too excessively. I also drank copious amounts of Good Wine of the Western River. Perhaps it was tainted?"

"Perhaps." I was trying to ignore those lascivious eyes which had now wandered to my own. I saw them widen in surprise. "Have you suffered these discomforts before, Majesty?" He sighed.

"Sometimes, my pretty one. You have blue eyes, the bluest I have ever seen, like the Nile under winter sunlight. Surely you are too young to be playing at the stern craft of medicine!"

"Majesty," I retorted with mock severity, "I am here in a professional capacity to examine you and prescribe a treatment. If your Majesty wishes, you may flatter me later." I thought for a second that I had gone too far. His expression went blank and then became suffused with the same authority I had seen in his son. Then he relaxed and gave a high-pitched laugh.

"Little scorpion!" he chuckled. "I have not seen your tail but your tongue certainly has a sting in it! I like you! Proceed with your examination!"

Taking a secret, slow breath I pulled the sheet away from him, laying it discreetly over his hips, and began to palpate his abdomen. My fingers sank into his ample flesh, which had a doughy consistency. His skin was hot and dry, his lower stomach slightly distended. As I worked I felt his attention fixed fully on my face, my breast swinging free. I did not want to put into words my disappointment and disillusionment. This large, gluttonous, fat man with his bold gaze and foolish patter surely could not be the Lord of All Life. The God who sat upon Egypt's Horus Throne was tall and regal, sparing of word and graceful of action, a mysterious presence from whom must emanate the overwhelming power of the Godhead. The young man who had left, handsome and assured, charismatic and noble, he was really Pharaoh! They were playing a cruel trick on me, Hui and this flabby man whose penis was stirring under the sheet as I completed my probing. This could not be!

I kept my face impassive as my fingers explored the thick neck, then I stood back. "Your Majesty has a mild Ukhedu of the bowels, caused in all probability by rancid oil mixed with the sesame paste. Your Majesty's heart is strong and there is no swelling of Your Majesty's glands. I recommend a three-day fast of water only for Your Majesty, during which time Your Majesty will take the cleansing and restoring elixir I will prepare." I bowed, hearing the rustle of papyrus as Hui recorded my words. Pharaoh stared at me for a long time, then he broke into a wide smile that lit up his face. I could not help but respond.

"No wine, little scorpion?" I shook my head firmly.

"No wine, Majesty."

"How old are you?" The question was abrupt.

"I will be fifteen in two weeks, Majesty."

"Hmm." He pulled the sheet back up to his chin, holding it in both hands and peering at me over its edge like a naughty child. "And you are Hui's pupil?"

"I am the Master's assistant, Majesty."

"You are gorgeous." He closed his eyes. "I will sleep now. Send me the medicine. If it makes me sicker I will throw you in prison." I knew that he was joking but nevertheless I bit my lip. "Paibekamun!" For a moment the name he had shouted made no impression on me, then I turned. The High Steward was materializing out of the dimness, coming up to the couch and bowing. I smiled at him but apart from a sidelong glance he ignored me as he did my Master. Like the other servants in the palace he was dressed in gold-bordered linen, but a broad blue-and-white sash denoting his office was tied across his chest. "Have wine and honey cakes served to the Seer and his assistant in my private reception room," Pharaoh went on. Then as Paibekamun bowed again and backed away, the King's hand shot out from beneath the sheets and grasped my sheath, pulling me down towards him. "Tell me, Thu," he muttered breathily, "are you still a virgin?" I felt Hui stir behind me before I answered.

"Most certainly, Majesty," I replied. "My Master rules a very moral house." The cloud of rancid air enveloped me again.

"Are you courted? Is there no young man waiting impatiently for you to reach the age of betrothal?" I wanted to pluck his fingers from my linen but I did not dare. Instead I leaned a little closer until my nose brushed his. I do not know why I did so. Perhaps some dormant talent for coquetry was responding to his forthright questions, or a ruthless feminine need to see a man teased.

"No indeed, Mighty Bull," I murmured. "I have been entirely devoted to my Master and my work." He released me and I stood straight.

"Peculiar work for a woman," he said wryly, and heaved himself over on the couch. Hui tugged at my arm. The interview was over.

Back in the room with such pleasingly human proportions, with the sound of leaves quivering in the breeze and filtered sunlight splashing across the floor, I sank into a chair. I found myself shaking with reaction, and very angry. Hui sat also, and regarded me steadily. There was silence between us. Before long, a servant appeared, bowed, set a silver tray containing goblets and a dish of sweetmeats between us, and retired. Paibekamun did not come. I had no appetite but drank the wine greedily, and the rush of heat to my stomach served to calm me somewhat.

"You knew who my patient was to be yet you gave me no warning!" I finally burst out. Hui raised a finger to his lips.

"I did not want to frighten you," he explained. "If you had known, would you have behaved as you did? I do not think so."

"And how did I behave?" I asked acidly. Hui selected a cake and nibbled at it before answering. He did not seem disturbed by my obvious indignation.

"Like a good physician, like a curious child, like a seductive woman," he said. "In short, dear Thu, you were perfect. So was your diagnosis, and Ramses will not forget. Let us go home."

Outside the door the same Herald was waiting. Wordlessly he led us back through the ante-room, the throne room, the impossible expanse of the public reception hall and out into the blazing noon sun. On the landing, our litter bearers sprang out of the shade in which they had been lying. The household guards, left standing at the door to the throne room, were once more before and behind us. Hui had one more comment as we reclined on the cushions and waited to be lifted. "I did not know that Prince Ramses would be there," he said. I did not reply. Prince Ramses. I had eyed the crowds as we walked back through the palace, hoping for a glimpse of him, my heart racing at the mere prospect, but he was nowhere to be seen.

"Paibekamun is a cold man," I ventured later as we were turning into our own estate. Hui grunted.

"Paibekamun knows the etiquette of his position," he retorted. "He is not for you to judge." With that, we continued down the path towards the courtyard and soon alighted. Harshira was waiting, holding out one meaty hand to assist me, and as I grasped its reassuring firmness I thought how much more regal the bulk of Hui's Steward was than the same girth in our Pharaoh. "Thank you, Harshira," I said, and he smiled.

"I am your servant, Thu," he replied.

Under Hui's eagle eye I made up the medicine for Pharaoh—first a mixture of saffron to relieve his bowel cramps and garlic to slay the Ukhedu and then a restorative of kesso root, cinnamon and pepper. It had been a good naming day gift I reflected as I pounded my pestle into the herbs. I had rubbed shoulders with the privileged, I had actually touched Pharaoh himself, I had been in the palace. "It is not true that Pharaoh has no wealth," I remarked to my Master as he watched me. "Never in my life have I seen such splendour!" He laughed grimly.

"Pharaoh's Treasury is filled at the whim of the priests," he said. "You think you have seen wealth, Thu? Of course, compared to your family in their mud house at Aswat, our ruler is unimaginably rich. But the temples are richer. Did you learn nothing from your history lessons with Kaha? There was a time when the royal palace at Thebes was paved with gold and its doors were beaten silver. Do not turn the kesso into dust, foolish one." I laid the pestle aside at his reprimand and did not pursue the subject. When I had filled the two phials for the King and Ani had taken them away, Hui and I shared a simple afternoon repast and I went out into the drug of Ra's afternoon heat to swim.

Two weeks went by. I had regaled an envious Disenk with a highly coloured account of my brief visit to the halls of power, describing Prince Ramses of course but remaining silent regarding my reaction to him. That I hugged to myself. In the moments before I fell asleep at night, in the times when my hands were occupied but my mind could wander, and best of all, when I lay outside the bath house while the young masseur's hands moved over me, I day-dreamed about him. I was once again a servant girl, this time in the harem, seeing to the needs of Pharaoh's concubines. The Prince entered on some errand for his father.

Pain overtook him, he collapsed under my concerned eye. My box of medicines at the ready I ministered to him, my fingers moving over him to locate the source of the problem (and oh the sheer thrill of that fantasy!). He was imprisoned by his pain and my touch. He was able to inspect me closely as I worked. "We have met before," he said in surprise. "I now remember your blue eyes. Are you not a member of the minor nobility, from the south? Why are you in this menial position?" And he would take me to his own quarters. There would be a marriage contract in the end. I would be the Princess Thu, envied and idolized by the whole court, the whole country.

Disenk had listened to my excited story with nods of approval, as though she was responsible for my success. Of course, in many ways she was. "Perhaps you will go there with the Master again," she said rather wistfully, but Hui made no more mention of my small adventure and the days regained their former predictable shape.

The day after my naming day, however, I was summoned to the office. Hui was behind the desk, and on it lay a thin scroll. He had broken the seal and small pieces of blue wax littered the surface of his table. I thought at first that it must be a letter to him from my father and anxiety shook me as I bowed and perched on the edge of the chair my Master had indicated. My apprehension deepened as he said nothing. His thoughtful gaze travelled me slowly, from my neatly beribboned hair to my linen-draped knees, and I kept my eyes on his face. I do love him, I thought. Not with the fever I believed I felt, but with something more sane. As though he had read my mind he suddenly looked up and smiled warmly. "We have grown close to one another, you and I, have we not, my Thu?" he said. I nodded vigorously. "You were a sullen, impulsive, stubborn child when you hauled yourself aboard my barge that night in Aswat, so long ago. I knew when I first saw you that you would be important to me, but I did not know how attached to you I would become." He sighed. "There is a perverse pleasure in moulding the growth of another human being. One can quickly become as possessive as a master with a slave. Your fearsome native intelligence has saved me from that fate, I think. You have become a good physician in your own right, and in doing so you have ceased to be my toy. Yet you are very young." He pushed the scroll towards me. "This was inevitable. Give me your opinion."

I took the papyrus and unrolled it carefully. The hand was not Pa-ari's and I smiled in relief, but the grin soon left my face. The missive was written in very formal hieroglyphs, not the racing hieratic script of swift or casual correspondence, and was of a piercing beauty. This scribe was at the pinnacle of his trade. "To the Most Noble Seer and Physician Hui, greetings," I read aloud. "On the Feast Day of the Great God of War, Montu, we were pleased to receive and be attended to by your charming assistant, Thu. Her medicine has been most efficacious, and on allowing her to minister to us, we were disarmed by her beauty." I glanced up, shocked. "This is from Pharaoh!" I blurted. Hui waved at me to go on. "Having endured several sleepless nights injurious to our health and therefore to the health of blessed Egypt, we blame the intensity of her blue eyes and the pertness of her conversation. We have conceived a desire to alleviate our distress by a renewed and hopefully prolonged encounter with this female. We therefore petition you, as her guardian, to facilitate her removal to our harem as soon as the permission of her father, if he lives, may be obtained. We guarantee, of course, that all her reasonable needs will be met and that she will be treated with the care and respect accorded to every woman fortunate enough to belong to the Horus Throne. By the hand of my Chief Scribe, Tehuti, I am Ramses Heq On, Lord of Tanis, Mighty Bull, Great One of Kings..." I could not go on. The scroll rolled up with a rustle and I needed both hands to place it with exaggerated care on the desk. "Hui what is it?" I cried out. "What is it?"

"Pharaoh has conceived a passion for you," Hui said gently. "He wants you for his concubine. Do not be so distressed, my Thu. It is a great honour, one every daughter of our noble families would kill for. What do you think?"

Visions came tumbling through my mind: Pa-ari and me by the water's edge at home in Aswat and I watch with bated breath as he traces out my first writing lesson in the dirt; Pa-ari and I sitting together out on the desert while Ra sinks towards the horizon, and my restless ka finds a voice that goes shrieking across the wastes to the feet of the gods themselves; my mother and her friends sipping wine and gossiping while I sprawl beside them and dream of the merchant who will come to Aswat and need a scribe... The parade slowed. I saw myself on Hui's barge, wet and frightened and determined. I heard his mocking, arrogant voice. Hui the mysterious, Hui the Seer. The Seer...

My hands left the scroll and clenched. I felt my whole body tense, and I got out of the chair and stood rigid. "You knew it would come to this," I said softly, urgently. "You knew, didn't you, Hui? Because you planned it all. How stupid I have been! You bring me here, you keep me away from every contact outside this house, you alternately bully and coax me so that I become completely reliant upon your good wishes. You pamper and train me like an athlete for the wrestling, the wrestling, yes!" I was finding it difficult to catch my breath, so violent was my emotion. I thumped the desk with one angry fist. "What kind of wrestling, O my Master? The sweetest kind of all? You deliberately took me to treat Pharaoh, knowing his taste for young girls, gambling on his immediate interest. You have been using me all along! But why?" I burst into tears and could not go on.

Hui had risen, and now he came around the desk, and taking me in his arms he lowered himself into the chair I had left, cradling and rocking me as though I was a baby. I struggled to free myself, to no avail. He held me tightly until I gave up and curled into his breast. Then he began to stroke my hair soothingly.

"No, Thu," he said calmly. "I have not been using you all along. I have told you—I did indeed see your face in the Seeing Bowl before you stood in the darkness of my cabin at Aswat. I recognized you at once, and knew that you would be vitally important to me. To me alone! Are you listening?" I did not respond and his fingers did not pause, continuing to draw themselves tenderly down my scalp. "I did not know in what way you and I were linked," he went on. "It was only later that I began to see the possibilities latent in the situation. I cared for you. I care for you now. Do you believe me?"

"No," I said sulkily, my face pressed into his neck, and I felt his muscles move as he laughed shortly.

"That is better. Your tears never last long, my Thu, even when they are shed from self-pity. When I realized how useful you could be, I began to arrange your education accordingly. Do not be angry any more. Here." He lifted the hem of his kilt. "Dry your eyes and sit up and listen to me." I could not refuse him. Grudgingly I did as I was told, turning to look into his face, those pale, handsome features I had grown to love and fear. "You do indeed match Pharaoh's taste in female flesh," he said. "You are young and beautiful and your body is slim and firm. But those things alone would have meant nothing. Girls with those qualifications are numerous, and Pharaoh has bedded and discarded dozens of them over the years. Three things decided my course of action. Your blue eyes, so exotic and un-Egyptian, the intelligence that made you such an apt pupil, and your character. You are at heart a ruthless, scheming, selfish little thing with the ability to sink your teeth into what you want and hold on until it is utterly your own. Do not squirm! I speak only of your less endearing qualities. I too, dear Thu, and the men you met the other night who gathered here to look you over, we also are ruthless and scheming. But we are first and foremost loyal and worried sons of this mighty country." He had my attention now. I climbed from his knee and went rather unsteadily to sit in his chair behind the desk where I could see him better. Sobs still choked me but I had stopped crying.

"Explain to me," I hiccuped.

"We want you to accept a position as Pharaoh's concubine," he said bluntly. "We believe that you have the skill to hold yourself in his favour long after most of the other young concubines have ceased to distract him. You can intrigue him, entertain him, and as time goes by, influence him away from the disastrous policies he now endorses."

"That is ridiculous," I snapped. "How could I possibly make the Great One do anything other than make love to me? You would do better to suborn one of his advisers." I was still smarting from his earlier words and from the knowledge that I had been only a gaming piece. Yet I was flattered also. He naturally knew that I would be.

"His advisers know that their futures depend on showing the priests in a good light," Hui told me. "But his women have nothing to lose. Those who fall from grace simply retire to the luxury of the harem. And Ramses is very susceptible to the whims and wishes of women. He has a lascivious nature. He is a kind man, and honest in his way, but he is frightened. You are strong, Thu, and wily. You will get to know him and then manipulate his decisions." He leaned forward and spoke earnestly, without artifice. "Egypt needs you, Thu. Make Pharaoh your tool, for his own good and the good of Egypt. Help us to break the stranglehold the temples have on the Horus Throne and restore a true Ma'at to this holy country!"

"You are sure that I will accept, aren't you?" I said ruefully. "What if I refuse?"

"How could you?" he countered. "Is it not the culmination

of every dream you have ever had? Nay, is it not greater than your dreams? You are not one to turn away from such a challenge and besides, I will help you. So will Paibekamun and Panauk and the others." He came to his feet and held out a hand. "Talk it over with Disenk if you like. You can take her with you if you go. Think about it and give me your answer tomorrow. Then we will take a little trip to Aswat, to consult with your father." I walked to him but did not take his hand.

"You are talking again as if I will do what you wish," I said, my voice still muffled with the tears I had shed. "But it seems to me that you have used and betrayed me no matter how you may justify your actions, and I am wounded and sad. Why should I do anything to help you, Hui?"

"Because it will be Egypt you help, not me," he replied promptly, "and in spite of how you feel, did I not take you out of the bondage of the earth and give you a new life? Is that not worth a little gratitude?"

"Not if you did it for your own ends."

"I have already told you that it was not."

"So you did."

"Then swallow your pride and recognize that I love you even if I have used you. And Thu..." I had already moved to the door but I paused, one hand on the wood.

"Yes?"

"You need not have murdered Kenna after all. His hatred of you would have made no difference to me. You were always far more important than he." Were the words a reassurance, a threat or a warning? I did not know, and I had had enough. I did not look at him. I let myself out of the office and made my way almost blindly back to my own room, but as I went a thought struck me. I had met Pharaoh on the feast Day of Montu, the great Theban God of War. My totem, Wepwawet, was also a God of War. And did I not believe that I was born to be a fighter?

Chapter 12

Two weeks later, at the end of Epophi, we set sail for Aswat. The river was at its lowest, with very little current running to slow us down, and the prevailing summer wind out of the north took us inexorably south. Disenk and I travelled on Hui's barge, sleeping on cushions under the canopy that had been erected against his cabin, while his body servant, Neferhotep, shared his quarters. Behind us came the barge carrying our supplies and the numerous domestics who would care for us. Among them was Ani and his palette, on which he would write my father's agreement to allow me to enter Ramses' harem as a concubine.

I had embarked at Hui's watersteps with a feeling of pride, remembering how different my last journey on this boat had been. Somehow the word had passed among the household staff that I was to move into the palace, and I was treated with a new deference. On the servants' barge was my young masseur, my exercise instructor, the foods I liked and my favourite clothes. While Hui lay on his travelling cot hour after burning hour, a prisoner of his white skin, Disenk and I lolled under the canopy, sipping water or beer, and watched the country glide by.

Even at the height of the dead season, Egypt was beautiful. Scorched and parched, brown and dusty, there was still an ageless harmony in the lines of jagged palm groves and drooping tree branches, the clusters of whitewashed village huts giving way to the cracked earth of waiting fields, and behind it all the beige shimmer of the desert meeting the occasional cliffs sharp as knife edges against an unrelentingly blue sky.

The air began to change, growing purer and drier, and I pulled it into myself as though it was medicine for some sickness. I could be queen of all this some day, I thought as the panorama of Egypt slid past me. I will captivate Pharaoh. I will make myself indispensable to him in every way. I will climb from concubine to queen. Perhaps even Great Royal Wife, because I am so much younger than either Ast or Ast-Amasareth, his principal wives, and anything can happen. I will one day sit beside him in the throne room, and the noblest heads in Egypt will bend to me. It was a pleasant daydream as the hot wind lifted the hair from my sticky neck and sent rivulets of sweat down my spine.

Of the dark mysteries of the bedroom I did not think, nor did I dwell on the feel of the King's flabby flesh under my hands, the odour of his fever-laden breath. If I imagined those inevitable private moments at all it was Prince Ramses who received my caresses and who laid his mouth on mine. I knew the time would come when I had to conquer my initial distaste for Pharaoh's body, but the future still lay ahead. The present was everything.

Several times during the long, quiet days I sat with Hui in the foetid little cabin, talking to him while Neferhotep bathed and refreshed him. In the dark hours while we were tied up in some quiet bay, the servants' fire sparking into the blackness and their laughter and conversation drifting to us over the sullen water, we swam naked together, not speaking, glorying in the warm silken embrace of the Nile our father, and afterwards I would sit swathed in Disenk's linens, my knees under my chin, and watch my Master commune wordlessly with the moon, his brother. The experience should have brought us closer but it only served to remind me that my time with Hui was almost over, that an era was about to end and others would take his place of importance in my life.

For him there was sadness, I think. If I had been less self-involved, more attuned to the sensitivity that comes with maturity, I might have spoken to him of his feelings, but I did not want to consider them. If they began to intrude upon my selfish dreams I remembered how he had ruled me, used me, planned my days with no regard for who I was, and thus I regained the distance that had begun to grow between us. I did not think that I needed him any more, that the power in our relationship had passed to me because of what he wanted me to achieve with Ramses, but I was wrong. Hui still held all the dice. He always would.

We tied up in the canal of Wepwawet's temple one fiery noon and Disenk and I, surrounded by household guards, walked down the ramp and through the gaggle of excited villagers to be greeted by my totem's High Priest. Hui remained in his cabin, but I wanted to make my first act one of worship and thanksgiving to the god who had guided my path all my life.

They were all there, my old neighbours, in their coarse kilts and thick sheaths, their eyes inquisitive yet bashful as they took in the gold-tasselled canopy shielding me from the sun, the sheen of my black hair bound with a fillet of silver net, the flowing transparency of my ankle-length, pleated linen over white leather sandals on whose thongs tiny carnelians glowed reddish-orange. I smiled at them all, recognizing the girls who had feared and shunned me and suddenly pitying them for the harsh, deep colour of their skin, so damaged by the sun, the last evidences of fresh youth already giving way to an encroaching physical disso-lution. I would have looked like that if I had stayed here, I thought with an inward shudder as I greeted them. My feet would already be calloused beyond repair, small lines etched by the sun would be appearing on my face, and my hands would be rough and chafed from household chores. Poor things, they are not my enemies any more.

My guards pushed their way politely through the throng and I found myself before the High Priest. Beside him a shy little boy wielded a smoking censer. I bowed to the priest and he returned the reverence. "I remember you," I said with wonder. "You taught Pa-ari his letters but you would not teach me, and now you have been elevated to a much more exalted position!" He was younger than my memories had shown me, no longer a faceless adult but a youngish man with a cheerful expression and alert brown eyes.

"I should not have been so foolish, Thu," he answered gaily, "for we hear that you have become an accomplished scribe and a physician, moreover! Welcome home! Your god awaits you!" I smiled back at him and followed as he turned and walked into the outer court.

Wepwawet's temple was smaller than my childish memory had made it, still a jewel but compact, more rustic. In the outer court Disenk bent to remove my sandals and I held out my hand for the offering I had brought, the gem-studded pectoral Hui had given to me after my feast with his friends. It cost me dear to part with it, but I owed Wepwawet far more than I could ever repay and that feeling of indebtedness had grown a thousandfold as I had looked at the village girls. But for my god's indulgence I could have been one of them, standing gawking at the arrival of some painted and perfumed aristocrat come to pay her haughty respects to this minor deity. Not minor to me, I thought as I moved towards the inner court. I am your devoted slave, great Wepwawet.

The gritty floor of the court was hot and it hurt the tender soles of my feet. I paused in the thin shade of the inner pylon, the High Priest and his acolyte ahead of me and facing the closed doors of the sanctuary, and as I did so a figure detached itself from behind the stone and came forward. "Pa-ari!" I shouted, and a moment later I was in his arms. We clung to one another for a long while, then he put me away and looked me up and down.

"Gods you are a gorgeous creature!" he said, "and you smell wonderful. I have been allowed, allowed mind you, to accept your gift and place it before the doors. Apparently it is a great honour. The temple singers and dancers have been turned out on this momentous occasion. One of them is my betrothed. It is not every day that one of Pharaoh's concubines deigns to visit Aswat." He was smiling broadly but I could not read his eyes. He had grown into a handsome man, with a straight spine and broad chest, but his mouth was the same, ever ready to curve into a grin, and his gestures brought back vividly to me the joys and sorrows we had shared. I loved him desperately.

"I am not a concubine yet!" I hissed back as the singers and dancers of which he spoke began to file into the court behind him. "Not until Father gives his permission! Now let me perform my obeisances to Wepwawet in peace!" The music had begun, and a singer's lone voice rose in the verses of praise. The dancers lifted their systra. A drift of sweet incense enveloped me, and I knelt and prostrated myself before the sanctuary with a humility I showed to no other. This was Wepwawet's moment, not mine.

Afterwards, in the outer court, Disenk brushed down my sheath and briefly kneaded oil into my scratched knees and palms. As she did so, Pa-ari returned, his arm protectively around a dark, slim girl with the shy, darting eyes of a young doe. "Thu, this is Isis," he said simply, and I leaned forward to formally kiss her cheek, feeling all at once hentis older than she, and worldly-wise, and just a little jaded. Jealousy stabbed me and was gone. Isis had the lithe body of a dancer and my thought, as I straightened and summoned up a smile, was that as long as she continued to dance for the God she would not become plump and flabby. I could not imagine my brother coupling with a dumpy village girl.

"You are lovely, Isis," I said. "I am very happy to meet you.

You must be very special if my brother is in love with you."
Pa-ari beamed and the girl flashed me back a brilliant smile.

"He is a terrible tease," she told me. "According to him, I
may look forward to a life of constant childbearing and
unremitting household labour if I marry him."

"No," I rejoined. "You will be the village queen. May I
take him away from you for a while?" At once she pressed
his hand and left us. I wanted to say something complimen-
tary to Pa-ari about her, something politic, but the words
stuck in my throat. I still wanted him entirely to myself.
That much had not changed. He gave me a quizzical stare as
the shadow of the canopy fell over us both, and we made our
way out of the temple and across to the barge. The crowd
had thinned. Of course, I thought cynically as we strode up
the ramp and settled ourselves under the awning. They have
run home to tell their friends and neighbours what they
have seen.

Disenk, efficient and unobtrusive, handed us fly whisks
and cups of wine. She set refreshments before us and a bowl
of water and cloths with which to cool ourselves if we
wished. Then she went to sit in the shade of the mast, out of
earshot but ready if summoned. There was no sound from
inside the cabin.

"Father will receive the Seer tonight," Pa-ari said, sipping
his wine with relish. "After greeting you, naturally. He does
not say so, you know how Father is, but I think he will enjoy
having the great man come to him instead of being peremptorily summoned like the last time. He has not changed
much," he went on as if in answer to my unspoken question,
"and Mother not at all. She has been throwing one fit of
outrage after another since the Seer's scroll arrived with
Pharaoh's request, you know how narrow-minded the village
is, but she is secretly pleased. She never did understand you,
Thu."

"I know," I murmured, not taking my eyes from his dear

familiar face, the graceful, clever fingers curled around the stem of the cup, the brown hair fluttering against his bronzed neck. "Are you content to remain here, Pa-ari? Does your work in the temple satisfy you?" He nodded slowly.

"I am the priests' best scribe," he said simply, "and I take pride in that accomplishment. Father is resigned to the fact that I will never work the land, but he has the slave your mentor sent and the scandal surrounding his arrival and the deeding of the khatoarouras has long since died away. I am preparing to wed." He turned troubled eyes on me. "I know what that means to you, Thu, but you must also be aware that nothing will ever break the bond that unites us, not even my Isis. We have memories together that we made long before she danced into my dazzled vision!" He laughed. "You will make memories with Pharaoh but always we will have the secrets of our childhood to share." His words were a precious balm to my ka and I pulled him to me and hugged him. "I am building a home for Isis and me with my own hands," he said proudly. "It is beyond the temple, along the river path. And what of you, my sister? Are you happy? Are you sure that you want to be Pharaoh's plaything instead of some worthy merchant's wife?" His tone was light but I read true concern behind the humour.

Oh, Hui, I thought inwardly, jolted by Pa-ari's perception, how cunningly you have created your masterpiece! "At one time I would have been content to marry a merchant," I answered carefully, "but you see into my heart, Pa-ari. I can hide nothing from you. The daily round of life as mistress of a household would soon pall, and my restlessness would demand a new adventure. I intend to make the King my plaything, not the other way around!" Pa-ari hooted with mirth.

"Besides which, my princess, you are lamentably lazy and care nothing for the stern demands of duty! I love you, Thu!"

I wanted to tell him everything then. It hurt me that I

felt a caution with him, a reluctance to confide in him my inadvertent killing of Kenna, my guilty lust for Prince Ramses, the mission Hui and his friends had placed upon me. But a man in love can be indiscreet and I did not want little Isis to be privy to my secrets. Perhaps I did my brother an injustice, but I could not take the chance. So I laughed with him, and the conversation turned to more innocuous things.

In the violent blooding of a desert sunset, Hui and I left the barge and made our way along the path that led from the temple watersteps into the village. Ahead went two household guards. I followed on foot under my canopy, then came Ani, also on foot, and Hui in his closely curtained litter. Guards brought up the rear. For me it was a voyage back in time. There was the spot where I had waited for Pa-ari to be let out of school on the day he brought me the news of the Seer's coming. I fancied that I could still see the imprint of my bare feet in the dead grasses. The season had been the same, Shemu. Further on was the place, hidden by scrub, where Pa-ari and I had sat in the dirt under the sycamore by the river and he had begun my lessons by drawing the names of the gods. But under these memories that brought a lump of sadness and sweetness to my throat was the stronger, more potent remembrance of a walk at night under the ghostly palms, watched by the kas of the neglected dead, with moonlight splashing cold across my way and dread and determination in my heart. The uncouth little peasant girl had gone to meet her fate and now Pharaoh's concubine was retracing her steps in triumph. It was a heady moment.

At the edge of the village square I spoke and the guards halted. The expanse of beaten earth seemed disappointingly small to me now. It no longer stretched into infinity with a promise of escape. A few ragged children stood well back in a protective cluster and watched me silently. Several young men and women and a group of their parents took a few timid steps towards me before stopping and waving. I waved back, but already I could see my father's blond, tousled hair and solid bulk standing at the doorway of our house and forgetting my dignity I ran into his arms. He lifted me into the air before placing me gently down again and setting me away from him. His grave, thoughtful eyes smiled into mine. Pa-ari had been right. The lines of his face were perhaps etched a little deeper, his temples showed a suspicion of grey, but he was still my darling.

"Well, Thu," he said. "You look as out of place in Aswat, now, as a jewel on a pile of dung. But you remind me very much of your mother when I first saw her. You have risen in the world, my daughter. Come inside." He shared a few easy words with the guards, and putting a heavy arm across my shoulders, drew me into the house. He had completely ignored Ani, and Hui's litter which had been lowered to the scuffed dust of the square. My mother flew at me as I entered the tiny, dark reception room and smothered me against her bosom.

"Thu! My little princess! You are here, you are alive! I did not think to see you again! Have you been treated kindly? Have you been a good girl? Have you remembered to say your prayers regularly?" She smelled of sweat and herbs and cooking pots. I extricated myself with difficulty and kissed her brown cheek.

"I am very well, Mother," I answered her smilingly. "As you can see, I have been treated with more than kindness. It is wonderful to see you also." Her hands went to her hips.

"And what is this about the Great One inviting you to live in the palace? You would do better to come home and work with me, Thu. The harem is not a nice place, or so I've heard, and you will come to grief, an innocent country girl like you. Your father can find you a respectable husband right here! How did you come to the attention of the Great One anyway?" The question dripped with suspicion and I laughed aloud.

"Oh, Mother, I went to the palace with my Master to treat Pharaoh for a minor ailment. As for the harem, I'm sure that the House of Women is a perfectly safe and morally reproachless place to be!" I said. "After all, it is a serious thing, to be the wife of a God!"

"A wife maybe," she muttered darkly, "but what about a concubine?"

"That is enough!" my father said to her sharply. "Go and bring the wine and cakes!" She grimaced, muttered something under her breath, then gave me a brilliant smile before disappearing. I sank onto a mat on the floor and Father went down to face me, crossing his legs and fixing me with a speculative stare.

"None of it is quite as I remember," I said, glancing about the room to break the fleeting awkwardness that had overtaken me. I did not add that its clean poverty as well as its size appalled me. Had I really lived in such surroundings and been unaware of their poverty? My father raised his eyebrows.

"That is because you are so much older," he mocked me gently. "I have missed you, Thu, and I have often thought of the day you came stumbling across the field and clung to my thigh and begged to be allowed to go to school. I could not afford to send you, of course, but I made a mistake in thinking that it did not matter. I underestimated both your intelligence and your dissatisfaction. If I had been able to raise the necessary goods with which to pay for your education perhaps you would have been content to stay here with us in Aswat." Then he shook his head. "No, you would not!"

"Do not reproach yourself," I chided him. "You understand me, my father, and that is why you let me go north with my Master. I love you all, but I would have been desperately unhappy if I had stayed."

"And are you happy now? Will you be happy in Pharaoh's arms? Do you want to be a concubine, Thu? The decision is yours, not mine, and I will support you in whatever direction you wish to go." I looked into that calm, weather-beaten face and knew the sincerity of his love.

"I am happy now," I answered slowly, "and as for happiness in Pharaoh's arms, who knows? Perhaps he will be so happy in mine that he will make me one of his wives."

"That cannot be," my father said abruptly. "Rarely has a King married the daughter of a commoner, let alone a peasant, and then only for passionate love. Besides, what do you know about pleasing a man, Thu? There are women in the harem who have devoted their whole lives to that subject and yet are still discarded. Do not let your dreams of the future interfere with the realities of the present!" He was momentarily angry, why I did not know. And I was angry too, for his words had touched me on the tender quick of my secret fantasies.

"I do not see the end of my road," I said, "but I must walk it. I cannot stand in one place, no matter how delightful that may be. I want to look around the next bend, oh, my father!" He sighed.

"Then that is settled. Have you asked your Master if he will continue to house you if you change your mind? Will he find you a suitable husband, perhaps?" I could not disguise the slight shudder that took me.

"I do not want an ordinary husband. It is more glorious to belong to the Living God!"

My mother had returned and was quietly setting out the wine cups and a platter of her best sweetmeats. Several times she had drawn breath to break into my conversation with my father but thought better of it. Her dark eyes darted between us. I could see that she was bursting with comments but she sat down beside me and drank in a silence that must have been very difficult for her to maintain.

There was little more to say. The wine was strong and bitter and I drank it gladly. We spoke desultorily of this and that and my mother became animated as she described the latest antics of the long-suffering mayor's saucy daughters, but a constraint grew among the three of us. I tried to answer their few questions about my life with Hui but found myself unable to do so in language that did not emphasize the wide gulf that existed between his world and theirs, and they surely sensed that the village gossip did not interest me any more. Blood and family affection bound us, but little more. In the achingly uncomfortable silences we drank our wine and nibbled at the cakes my mother had so painstakingly prepared, and at length my father rose, indicating that I should rise also. "I will receive the Seer now," he said. "You can wait outside, Thu." His smile took the bite out of his command and I obeyed, walking into the deepening flush of the sunset. Father spoke to a guard, who went to the litter. The curtains twitched and Hui emerged, imprisoned in his linens. We looked at each other. Then with a nod for Ani to accompany him he approached my father who was once more standing in his doorway.

I wandered in the direction of the river, taking the way I had so often fled as a child. The villagers were still grouped in the square, staring at me like mindless sheep. I was unaccountably weary with the strain of this homecoming that was not a homecoming at all. Dimly I was aware of the guard who had fallen in behind me. My sandals had become clogged with grit and I stooped to remove them, and when I straightened Pa-ari was there. He was panting and his kilt had been tucked up around his hips.

"I ran from the temple," he explained, releasing his linen as he fell into step beside me and took my sandals from my hand. "There was some dictation that could not wait. I am sorry. What did Father say? Will he sign the contract? Where were you going?"

"To the river," I replied, and at the catch in my voice he grasped my fingers and together we found ourselves on the bank of the Nile, its muddy depths flowing just below. The gaunt trees behind us threw long shadows across the water as Ra lipped the horizon and we sat in their shelter and began to talk. The guard took up his station some way away and we forgot his presence. We shared our childhood and spoke of the years we had been apart. Pa-ari told me how he had fallen in love with Isis. I described Disenk and Hui and Harshira and General Paiis, but of Prince Ramses and Pharaoh himself I did not speak. Pa-ari wanted to know what the Delta was like, and the mighty city of Pi-Ramses, and I gave him my impressions as best I could.

The dusk turned into evening and the guard became politely restless until I turned to him and said, "I will be spending the night with my family but I will be back on board the barge for the dawn sailing. Please tell the Master, and ask him to send another soldier to stand by me." He bowed and left and Pa-ari chuckled.

"You give orders very confidently, my Libu princess," he teased, and I laughed with him. Our eyes turned to the gathering darkness on the farther bank and the gradually fading colours of the sky. The deep peace of the south was beginning to fall on this changeless backwater and I felt a corresponding loosening in my body. I leaned back against a tree. "Only here is there such a sense of the meaning of eternity," I half-whispered. "It is a clean, sane feeling, Pa-ari, and I miss it very much." He did not answer, but his fingers tightened on mine and I knew that he had understood.

By the time we walked back to the square, a new guard trailing behind us, full dark had fallen and the dull yellow glow of lamplight flickered from the doorway of the house. Hui and his entourage had gone. The welcoming smell of lentil and onion soup and the fragrance of freshly baked bread greeted me as I crossed the threshold. The meal had been set out on spotless linen on the floor of the reception room and I sank onto the mat before my dish as I had always done. Father said the evening prayers before the shrine, his naked, bent back, the sound of his deep voice and the rather rank odour of the lamp oil all serving to pull me back to a time long gone. The experience was bewildering. It was as though I had dreamed a childhood here while growing up in Hui's house, dreamed that I was a peasant girl in a small southern village with a soldiering father and a midwife for a mother and a brother who was studying to be a scribe.

As we were dipping our bread into the soup a man came in, grunted an absent greeting, and settled himself beside me, reaching for the food. My father did not introduce us. I presumed that this was the Maxyes slave, for he was heavily bearded and his thick black hair matched the matting on his chest. He ate quickly, and when he was finished he rose, murmured a good-night, drew a jug of beer from the flagon beside the soup, and went out into the night. No one remarked upon his behaviour.

After the meal was over I helped my mother remove and wash the empty bowls, then we all sat in the reception room and talked. The conversation was light. There was love in the smiles, in the old family jokes, but a restraint was on us that could not be broken. Before the oil in the single crude lamp was exhausted we stood by unspoken, common consent and I said goodbye to my parents, holding them to me tightly in a paroxysm of affection and guilt. I promised to send them regular scrolls from the harem and my father bade me be honest and trustworthy in all my dealings. Then they were gone and Pa-ari and I made our way to the room I had happily shared with him for so many years.

My mother had placed clean linen on my pallet, but its coarse texture irritated my skin as I curled up beneath it. The pallet itself seemed hard. I could feel the unyielding mud floor digging into my hipbones. My parents' voices came to me faintly, a reassuring susurration, and then became intermittent and died away. I could not see my brother in the pressing blackness, but as always I was able to feel his presence and I put out my hand to clasp his own. We lay there in a companionable silence for a while until he said, "I suppose I shall have to travel to Pi-Ramses if I want to see you again, Thu. What a nuisance! And will I be required to obtain permission from every petty harem official before I am allowed to at last prostrate myself before your august Highness?" I laughed and corrected him, and all at once the strangeness was gone and the night was close and warm and secret as it used to be when we emptied our hearts to each other. Words flowed easily, perhaps because we could not see one another and whispers are ageless. The hours passed unremarked while the invisible bond that held us together grew tight and firm again. Yet I did not speak of the reason for Kenna's death though the need to do so became almost irresistible. I did not want to be lessened in my brother's eyes and I knew that he would not understand.

He fell asleep just before dawn, and when I heard his steady breathing I rose, bent down to kiss him, and quietly let myself out of the house. The air was still stale with the night's heat and a promise of the scorching morning to come. A delicate, pale light was gradually flooding the deserted village square and the motionless ragged shrubbery that bordered the river. My guard detached himself from the thin shadow of the house wall and fell in behind me as I walked away quickly, my sandals dangling from my hand. I did not look back. They would wake soon, and yawn, and sleepily look out upon another day filled with their simple routines of work and rest, prayer and gossip, village affairs and neighbours' concerns. But by the time my mother had collected up her washing and gone to the river to stand knee-deep in the water and slap the linen against the stones, I would be resting under the awning of the barge, watching Egypt slide by while Disenk prepared the fruit for my first meal. I would have escaped.

She was sitting on the ramp waiting for me, and as I rounded the last bend in the path and came in sight of the watersteps she rose and hurried forward, her matchless little face lighting with pleasure. But at the sight of my soiled and rumpled sheath, my disordered hair and dusty limbs she stopped short, her tiny fingers fluttering in distress.

"Disenk!" I called out, suddenly wanting to embrace her with the relief of seeing the barge still at its mooring. "Am I late?" The helmsman was already mounting to his great steering oar in the stern and there was a flurry of purposeful activity around the ramp and the ropes that held us to the mooring poles.

"Your feet!" Disenk wailed. "Look at them! And the soil is so dry, it will ruin your skin and you are covered in it! Oh, Thu!"

"But you are a magician, Disenk," I retorted gaily as I ran up the ramp. "You will perform your spells and everything will be all right!" I left her hurrying aft and calling for water and I slipped into the cabin. As I did so I heard the captain give a short command, his voice echoing against the temple pylon ahead, and the barge lurched. We were underway.

The scent of jasmine, Hui's perfume, hung thick and sweet in the cabin as I let the curtain fall and stepped up to the travelling cot. Neferhotep was already busy. He nodded to me and then turned back to his preparations for Hui's morning ablutions. I lowered myself onto the sheets. Hui was not yet fully awake. He eyed me drowsily as I planted a swift kiss on his mouth, then he smiled slowly. "Well?" he said.

"I love you, Hui," I replied. "I am ready to go home."

Chapter 13

My arrival back at Hui's estate was the true homecoming. This time the sight of Harshira's regal figure before the entrance pylon filled me with joy and I ran down the ramp and hugged him. He detached himself with aplomb and smiled at me gravely.

"Welcome back, Thu," he said. "I trust that the gods have blessed your journey with peace and success."

"Thank you, Harshira," I answered happily. "I am so pleased to see you again!" I did not wait for Hui. Hurrying in under the pylon I almost skipped along the path to the house, mentally greeting each twisted tree branch, each manicured shrub, like an old friend. I turned aside on the way to say a swift prayer to Thoth, kissing the feet of the god in the garden shrine before hurrying on to the courtyard and the men who guarded the pillared doors of the house, and so inside and up to my own dear, familiar room.

It smelled faintly of saffron, and the intermittent puffs of hot air coming down the windcatcher carried the subtle odour of the fruit orchards, a fragrance I had ceased to notice while living here. Diving onto my couch I lay face down, my head buried in the cool freshness of clean linen, the softness of my cushions. I heard Disenk come in and behind her the servants carrying my travelling chest. After a long sigh of pure satisfaction I sat up. "Disenk," I said, "Do you think it is permitted for me to take a swim?" She had already opened the chest and was lifting out my sheaths and ribbons.

"Indeed, Thu, you are now permitted to go where you wish within the house and grounds," she said, "but please summon the canopy bearers. It will not be easy to repair the damage to your skin and hair done by the harshness of the south." I grinned at her as I slid from the couch and went to the door.

"You are a tactful servant," I remarked. "What you really mean is the damage I have done by my careless behaviour! But Disenk, it was good to walk barefooted by the river in Aswat, and sit in the dirt under the sycamores with my brother!" Her little nose turned up and she did not reply.

I swam many lengths of the pool, sat in the grass and watched the insects busy around me, submitted later to Disenk's oils and potions, and at sunset, painted and dressed, went down to eat a leisurely meal with Hui in the same exquisite room where I had been introduced to his friends. He told me, as we ate and drank to the music of his lute player and Harshira unobtrusively directed the servants who came and went with the heaped dishes and the wine, that the scroll my father had signed had already gone to the palace and a return message from the Keeper of the Door could be expected within a few days. I swallowed the broiled fish I had just placed in my mouth and stared at him, vaguely affronted.

"The Keeper of the Door? The official who administers the harem? Why will Pharaoh not send a scroll himself?"

"Because you are not yet very important to the Mighty Bull," Hui answered brutally. "You are a girl who caught his eye and you attracted and intrigued him with your knowledge of medicine, but you are far from burning in his thoughts." Seeing my outraged expression he waved impatiently. "I said, not yet," he went on. "Gods, Thu, what a high opinion of yourself you have! But that is good. Pharaoh will not be won by docility and meekness. Most of his dozens of concubines have those dubious qualities in abundance, and that is why they were nothing more than a passing fancy for our King. You may not be important to him now but you will be. It is up to you." I no longer had much appetite, and refused the honeyed dates held out to me. I picked up my wine.

"Tell me about him, Hui," I begged. My Master dabbled his fingers in the waterbowl and pushed his table away, leaning back on his cushions.

"Ra-messu-pa-Neter," he said slowly. "Ramses the God. Never make the mistake of underestimating him, Thu. For all his faults, he is not a stupid man. If Setnakht had lived to complete his desires for Egypt he would have placed a check on the priests once his arrangement with them had effected a suitable balance of Ma'at in the land," he went on, "but he died, and by the time his son was able to turn his attention from the threats of invasion that preoccupied him for the first eleven years of his reign it was too late. Egypt's economy was in the hands of the temples, and Ramses did not know what to do about it." I had been listening carefully to Hui's words but now I was watching his face. He seemed all at once very tired, the lids of his red eyes puffy, the lines of his pale face accentuated. "Egypt's stability hangs by a thread," he finished. "The yield of our gold mines in Nubia is lessening. Our administrators are people of foreign extraction who care more for their positions than they do for the good of the country. Amun reigns supreme in Thebes, unchallenged, for Pharaoh seldom goes there. This is what we face. This is what we want you to fight."

I felt very small and impotent at that moment. What could I, one young woman, do to halt such massive decay, to influence such a man? "What of Prince Ramses?" I asked diffidently and not altogether with a selfless interest. "Surely he can do something!" My voice must have betrayed me, for Hui fixed me with a calculating stare.

"So," he said softly. "You are becoming enamoured of our handsome princeling, are you Thu? Then beware! Ramses is a loner. He spends much time by himself, out on the desert, hunting or driving his chariot or communing with the gods—who knows? He keeps his thoughts hidden. Although he is twenty-eight years old he has but one wife and only a few concubines. As for his politics—no one has heard him make a statement for or against his father's methods of administration. Do not think to seduce him! From the moment your father signed that scroll you have belonged to Pharaoh and him alone, and if you give your body to another you condemn yourself to death."

This particular stricture had not occurred to me. I had not really considered fully the implications of the flattering offer from the palace. I had had some hazy idea that a concubine must be more free than a legal wife but of course it was not so. This was no village arrangement of convenience, this was a contract with the Living God, and any child produced must be known to be the offspring of the King beyond any doubt. I would be tied to that flabby flesh until death claimed one of us. Suddenly the prospect was horrifying. I left my table and crawled the short distance to Hui, laying my head in his lap, and my fingers went to his thighs, so firm, so sturdy. "I do not think that I can do this after all, Hui," I whispered against his warm, white skin. "I want to stay here with you." He pulled me away from him gently, then shook me.

"It is too late for that," he said. "And you can do it, Thu, I know you can. Make him dependent on you for his health. Make him dependent on you sexually as well. Be aggressive and forthright. Do not simper and approach him with downcast eyes as the others do, who imagine that is what he wants. It is what he wants, but not what he needs."

"I don't know how to behave with a man," I faltered. "I don't know what to do." He put one hand on the back of my head and drew me roughly towards him. His eyes had gone hard.

"Use your intuition, your instinct," he said harshly. "I

wish that I could teach you myself, but it is forbidden. You must go to him as a virgin."

Perhaps if I had not made an involuntary movement, swaying under the pressure of his hand, he would have retained his self-control. But as I stirred, his mouth opened and came down on mine with a force that instantly shocked and excited me and I responded, winding my arms about his neck, my fingers in his beautiful white hair. He tasted of wine and cinnamon. His probing tongue was warm, sending waves of excitement through me, and I pushed myself against him so that our bodies met. He grunted, his touch sliding down my spine, and then there came a discreet cough. We drew apart, panting. Harshira was standing close by, his expression inscrutable.

"General Paiis is here, Master," he said. Hui passed a trembling hand across his mouth.

"Show him in." He grabbed the wine and tossed back a long draught. He did not look at me.

Paiis came quickly towards us, smiling as he called a greeting and snapping his fingers at the servants who came running with refreshments. He sank onto the cushions I had so recently vacated, and glanced over both of us critically.

"Well, little princess, you look truly delectable tonight," he offered. "I am almost disposed to pity our King, for once he succumbs to such loveliness he will be your prisoner forever."

"You are very kind, General," I managed, preternaturally aware of Hui's knee so close to mine, the still rapid rise and fall of his chest, the General's astute assessment of the situation.

"He's not kind at all," Hui said drily. "He is speaking the truth. Have confidence, my Thu. Now run along to your couch like a good girl, and leave me to talk with my brother."

I obeyed at once, scrambling to my feet in relief and bowing to them both. I felt embarrassingly clumsy, all arms and legs, as I walked away.

"So, Hui," I heard the General say as I went through the
doorway. "Did her father agree? But of course he did. She
will cause a sensation in the harem. What a waste!" The
door was closed behind me and Hui's answer was lost.
Flushed, dishevelled and agitated, I made my way to the
sanctuary of my own room, Paiis's words echoing in my
mind. What a waste! A waste... But I fixed my inner attention on the vision of Prince Ramses, tall and glorious, and
by the time Disenk had undressed me I was calm again.

I went back to work with Hui during the days of peace I
had left, falling easily into our routine of dictation, consulta-
tion and the preparation of salves and potions for his few
patients. Of the wild kiss we had impulsively shared the
night we returned home we did not speak. Hui behaved as if
it had never happened, and therefore so did I. Yet it haunted
me. I did my best to replace Hui's hot mouth, the feel of his
hard flesh, the flare of lust in his fiery eyes, with an image of
Prince Ramses, and I was distressed to find that I could not
do so.

On more than one occasion, lying tossing on my couch as
the nights wore away, I considered forcing the issue with
Hui. I could drape myself in drifting linen, dowse myself
with perfumed oil, slip into his bedchamber, and seduce
him. The contract with Pharaoh could somehow be circum-
vented. Hui and I were nothing if not inventive. But a fear
of his rejection kept me from making the attempt. I was
beginning to realize the depth of his desire, not for me, but
for a return to a prosperous Egypt with a restored Ma'at at its
centre. He had decided to use me to foster his plan and I
knew that he would not be diverted.

As we busied ourselves together in his office he continued to instruct me in Pharaoh's character, his likes and dislikes, his prejudices and tolerances. He employed his old
method of making me repeat back to him what he had said,

and before long I felt that I knew the Horus of Gold better than his own wives. Hui also listed the King's ailments and the treatments that had been prescribed so that I should make no mistakes if called upon to examine him. Of life in the harem itself he said little although I pressed him. "It is better that you should form your own opinions, make your own way," he told me. "Living in the harem is not much different from living anywhere else. It can be as pleasurable or as horrific as you choose to make it." He had been grinding cassia seeds as he spoke, and their mild, refreshing aroma filled the room. Now he paused, and without looking at me said, "Remember to eat only the communal food you see the other women eating, or meals that Disenk herself has prepared. The more Pharaoh cleaves to you, the more jealousy you will stir up around you. Touch no wine or beer at all. It is too easily contaminated. I will keep you supplied with jars from my own vineyards."

The cassia was now little more than brown dust. Carefully Hui shook it into a phial and turned to face me. "Get to know the important women, Thu. Explore their characters, weigh their influence. Decide who your rivals will be. Choose your friends carefully, and trust no one but Disenk. General Banemus's sister Hunro is also a concubine. Seek her out, for I think that she will prove a worthwhile ally."

"You paint a dark picture of my future, Master," I said shakily, "and a lonely one. Shall I ever laugh in the House of Women?" My weak attempt at humour did not make him smile. He stared at me sombrely.

"I will see you regularly," he said. "I am often called to the palace or the harem. If you become ill, send for me at once. Do not submit to the ministrations of the women's physician. And be sure to continue with the exercises Nebnefer has taught you. Above all do not succumb to the dangerous lassitude that overtakes so many." He ran a hand through his thick hair and sighed. "You will do well, my unruly child," he said ruefully. "I have glimpsed something of your success in the Seeing Bowl." I was immediately alert.

"You have Seen for me, Hui? At last you have attempted to divine my fate?"

"I said glimpsed," he reproved me. "Your fate is not clear, greedy one, but I saw you afire with jewels on Pharaoh's arm and all his courtiers were doing you homage. You will not be lonely for long." Pleased and flattered as I was, I did not miss the note of uncharacteristic sadness in his voice.

"You are sorry to lose me," I said softly. "Hui, it is not too late…" He silenced me with an abrupt gesture.

"Your naming day is past," he broke in. "You are now fifteen, and have promised yourself to Pharaoh. Also I know you well enough to recognize that your innate ambitions would never be served by staying in this house. Pick up your palette." Hastily I did so, and he began to dictate. "One part cassia, three parts honey, three parts oil of the crushed olive…" The subject was closed.

Two weeks went by, and then it was New Year's Day, the parching Day of the Dog Star. All of Egypt was in festivity and no work was done in Hui's house. The Master himself had gone into Pi-Ramses to consult with the oracle of the temple of Thoth, whose month had just begun, on the predictions for the coming year. There was to be a great feast for all Hui's friends and their wives, and it was in a state of excitement and anticipation that I returned to my room from a walk in the garden that afternoon to find all my chests open and Disenk busy in the midst of a colourful chaos. My sheaths were piled on the couch, my sandals scattered on the floor, my hair ribbons and jewellery and other fripperies covered the table. I stopped short.

"Disenk, what is this?" She acknowledged my presence with a bow and a slight frown.

"Word has come from the palace," she replied absently.

"You are to appear before the Keeper of the Door tomorrow morning and I am packing your belongings but I cannot find the long woollen cloak the Master had made for you last Mekhir."

A faintness came over me and I went unsteadily to one of the chairs and lowered myself, trembling, into it. The reality of my situation had not been brought home to me until this moment, but watching my servant gather up an armful of pleated tunics and cross to a chest I was seized with terror. Tomorrow, she had said. And it was already late in the day. Soon the sun would set. Surely there should have been more warning! Didn't the Keeper know that I must have time to take my leave of this dear room, that I needed many hours to kneel at my window in the darkness and say farewell to the silhouette of the trees against the night sky, and the beam of lamplight that often lay across the courtyard from Harshira's office, and the sound of the wind as it left the windcatcher and came to flutter my sheets as I lay torpid in the heat of Shemu? Grimly I fought my panic.

"I have not seen the cloak since I snagged it on a branch and you took it away to mend," I said with desperate calm. "Do not pack the yellow sheath yet, Disenk. I want to wear it to the feast tonight." She shot me a sympathetic look and went on with her task.

"I am sorry, Thu," she said, "but the Master has given orders that you are not to attend after all."

"What?" I was dumbfounded, and the breath caught in my throat. "Why not?"

"You are to eat simply and go to bed early so that you may appear fresh and beautiful before the Keeper. The Master is sorry."

The Master is sorry! He would be down there in his banqueting room with its flowers and scented cones and rich wines, its graceful walls enclosing a crowd of laughing, feasting people, and he would be laughing and feasting too, without a thought for me who was to be torn from my home on the morrow. I knew better than to argue. I sat silently while Disenk moved to and fro, and gradually the chaos thinned and disappeared and the chests were shut. The light in the room was changing, growing sullenly red. It seemed ominous to me, and I embraced its message mutely. The end of a day. The end of my youth. The end of Hui and me.

He did not come to me at all through that long, miserable night. I heard the guests arrive, litter after litter disgorging excited revellers, but I did not get up to watch them. Paiis's voice, deep and distinctive, floated clearly to me, and I thought I recognized the Chancellor Mersura's light, fussy tones, but the others were anonymous visitors bent on pleasure. I tried to stay awake, thinking that when everyone had gone Hui might sit with me for a while, commiserate with me a little, give me more advice, even share some of the memories we had made together, but I dozed and then slept, and dawn came inexorably without him. Disenk entered, raised the window matting, placed fruit and water by the couch. "It is a fine morning," she said cheerfully. "The river is rising. Isis has cried." I did not respond. The Nile could go on rising and engulf us all, I did not care.

She dressed me in shining white linen, put a white ribbon in my hair and white sandals on my feet. She painted my face with great care and slipped silver bracelets onto my arms and a silver chain around my neck. One long silver earring, a lotus flower hanging from its slender stem, swung from my lobe. My lips, feet and palms were hennaed.

As I was sitting waiting for the stain to dry, the servants came and began to carry out my chests. One of them swept up the little cedar box my father had given me and I stopped him with a cry. "Not that! Put it here beside me on the table. I will carry it. Disenk, open it and lay my statue of Wepwawet inside!" I saw the man glance to Disenk for confirmation and was suddenly incensed. "Do as I tell you!" I shouted. "I am the mistress here, not Disenk!" He murmured an apology, bowing and raising his hands, palm up, in the gesture of submission. I was shaking with illogical rage. As he brought the box towards me Harshira's wide form loomed in the doorway.

"What is all this uproar?" he demanded. "Do not be difficult, Thu. The Master waits below. Are you ready?" I snatched up my precious box and stood.

"I am not being difficult, Harshira," I snapped, "and I would like to remind you that as I am now a royal concubine and you are not Pharaoh's Steward you have no authority over me any more." He did not seem perturbed by this outburst, indeed, he ignored it. Clicking his fingers at the servants to hurry he rocked back on his heels and planted huge fists on his hips. The last of the chests was manoeuvred into the passage, Disenk tripping after it, and Harshira raised his dark eyebrows at me. Summoning all my dignity I snatched up the box and glided past him, walking loftily behind the sum of all my months in this house, down the stairs and out through the entrance into the sparkling sunshine. My litter was there with Hui beside it under a protective canopy. The servants were disappearing with the chests in the direction of the river and I supposed that a barge would transport them quickly to the palace. At a word from Harshira, Disenk climbed into the litter and settled herself among the cushions. I stepped to Hui. He looked ravaged. His white face had a greyish tinge and his eyes were puffy.

"You did not come to me last night," I said with a lump in my throat, the words very different from the ones I had intended to say. Traces of my earlier anger gave them a bitter sharpness.

"I did not think it would be wise," he replied simply, almost humbly, and at his refusal to lull me with false excuses my defences dissolved. He nodded at the litter. "I have made up a selection of herbs for you, and included phials, mortar and pestle. If you need anything more, send for it. Take heart, little Thu. This is not farewell."

"Oh yes it is, dearest Hui," I whispered. "Nothing will ever be the same again." Reaching up, I stroked the ivory braid that lay over his shoulder, then I went to the litter and reclined beside Disenk. "Close the curtains!" I said sharply to Harshira and he obeyed. As his face loomed briefly near mine he smiled and said quietly, "May the gods prosper you, little one." Then Disenk and I were alone in the suffused glow of a filtered sun. Hui spoke and our conveyance jerked into the air. We were on our way.

I felt no urge to peer back at the house. I did not want to know whether Hui stood looking after me until I vanished. I did not want to watch the pretty facade of the house become slowly obscured by the verdant growth of the garden. Nor did I want to see the Lake and its traffic.

Disenk and I sat without speaking as we rocked under the shadow of the entrance pylon and turned onto the road. Glancing at her I saw a calm profile. Disenk accepted the twistings of fate, and I thought as I studied her strikingly aristocratic nose and the finely grained skin of her painted cheek that the suspicion of a smudge on my kohled temple would cause her more distress than any abrupt change in her fortunes. I admired her aplomb at that moment, and some of my despondency lifted. "Have you been inside the harem before, Disenk?" I asked her. She nodded.

"I have had occasion to visit the House of Women with the Lady Kawit when she called on her friend the Lady Hunro," she told me. "It is a marvellous place." Hui had also mentioned the Lady Hunro, Banemus's sister, but I had someone else on my mind.

"The Keeper of the Door," I inquired. "What is he like?" She made a little grimace.

"He is the most important person there," she told me. "If Pharaoh does not select a woman to sleep with, it is up to the Keeper to choose one for him. Therefore the women all vie with each other to bring themselves to his attention and placate him. He rules the harem with a firm hand. Even the Great Royal Wives must defer to him. Except the Lady of the Two Lands herself, of course. She is queen over all." I digested this information thoughtfully as we swayed along. The sounds of the road came to me dimly. I was hardly aware of them until they suddenly ceased and we swung right. A challenge rang out and was answered by one of our guards. "We are beside the royal watersteps," Disenk said. Turning to me she began a swift inspection of my person and then looked away, evidently satisfied. I feel like something being offered up in the market-place, I thought grimly, and I am supposed to be excited and grateful for the supreme compliment. Any other girl would be. I have too much pride, that is the trouble. But I vow that one day Pharaoh will be the one to be grateful.

We were challenged once more and then I felt the litter veer to the left. "Lift the curtain," I said to Disenk. At once she did so, looping it back and tying it, and I found myself looking at a small forest of sycamore and acacia trees. The water of a large pond glittered between the trunks. We were on a paved path lined at regular intervals with Shardana soldiers liveried in the imperial blue and white. The litter halted and was lowered. I eased myself out with as much grace as I could muster and Disenk followed.

I was facing a heavily guarded pylon set into a continuous wall, high and solid. I turned. A long way behind me the path met the edge of the vast landing before the watersteps, and through the trees I could see the way that led straight into the palace. Disenk and I were standing on the left-hand branch.

One of our guards had a scroll in his hand. He approached his compatriots under the pylon and presented it. I watched it pass from hand to burly hand and disappear.

Soon a word must have come back, for our guard bowed to me ceremoniously, jerked a thumb at our litter-bearers, and set off the way he had come, the others falling in behind him. The men in front of the pylon beckoned. Disenk and I went forward into the harem.

To our left there were more trees, a lush expanse of clearly well tended grass studded with bushes, and a large oval pool on whose surface lilies and lotuses rocked. There were of course no blooms on the lotuses but the lilies had opened pale, pink-tinged petals folding one into the other on their beds of dark green, flat leaves. Butterflies of an iridescent emerald hue flickered over them, and I could hear the croaking of young frogs newly resurrected from the mud of the Lake.

On the edge of the garden ahead was a mud brick wall with an outside staircase leading to a roof. It was a cool, sun-dappled prospect but I had no time to fully appreciate it. Clutching my cedar box I watched a man come stalking towards us, his blue kilt swirling against his ankles, his arms encircled with gold, his black wig falling in intricate waves over his shoulders. His heavily kohled dark eyes regarded me impassively. His age was impossible to determine. He was not young, but carried himself so easily and with such authority that he could have been any age. In his hand was the scroll our guard had relinquished. He bowed shortly, and the one square jasper set into the gold circlet that cut across his forehead shot a baleful red gleam at me as it caught the sun. "Greetings, Thu," he said coolly. "I am Amunnakht, the Keeper of the Door. The Horus of Gold has seen fit to bestow his favour upon you. You are indeed fortunate. Follow me." He did not wait for an acknowledgement but turned on his expensively shod heel and walked away. Disenk and I trotted after him, I hugging my box and Disenk cradling the medicines Hui had collected for me. I felt distressingly insignificant.

We were on a narrow path that ran between two very high walls, and at the farther end I could just discern another wall where the path appeared to terminate. Our footsteps echoed briefly, the sound mingling with other noises at first faint and then growing more distinct, the shouts and shrieks of children at play and the continuous splash of moving water. About halfway along the path a gate suddenly opened on our right and I glimpsed a dark passage, also walled on both sides, and the shadowy form of a guard at the farther end, standing stolidly before a huge, closed door. Amunnakht looked neither to right nor left but led us steadily on until he came to a halt before another gate on our left. He pushed it open and we followed him obediently.

I am not sure what I expected to see. I suppose I had imagined the harem to be much like Hui's house but larger, an elegant arrangement of sunny rooms and wide passages full of soft-footed servants and perfumed, quiet women. The sight that met my eyes was a shock. A very short passage led at once into a wide, grassy courtyard dotted with a few trees. In the centre was a stone basin into which a fountain spewed arcs of glistening water. Naked children paddled under the flow and scrambled in and out of the low-lipped reservoir, and all around, arranged under the trees or under gauze canopies, women sat or lay in pairs or small groups, watching the children and talking among themselves. Around the courtyard ran the cells, and above them, reached by a staircase in the corner to my left, was a second storey of roofed cells opening onto a narrow landing where one could stand and look down on the scene below. The courtyard was of course open to the sky.

Amunnakht moved on, along the right-hand side of the grassy area, and we passed several small doors, some open, some closed. Our progress caused little interest. A few of the women turned to look at us but soon turned back to whatever they were doing. The children, immersed in the sheer pleasure of cool water on bare skin, ignored us completely. At last the Keeper swung round and indicated a murky doorway.

"This is your room, Thu," he said indifferently. "The Seer has requested that you be placed with the Lady Hunro, and I have complied. Your servant will be quartered with the others of her station in the block at the far end of the path along which we have just come. If you need her, there are runners who ply between the cells and the rest of the buildings. She may of course choose to sleep on your floor." He snapped his fingers and a young girl came hurrying. She bowed and waited expectantly. "Take this body servant to her quarters," he commanded.

I stepped past him. The cell was small, almost cramped. There was no window. Two couches rested along opposite walls, flanked by two tables. One side of the room was obviously occupied, for chests took up the wall space the couch did not and there was a small, closed shrine and other personal belongings arranged in the available space. The furniture was simple and functional, the abundance of cushions and linens clean as far as I could see, but I was horrified. Disenk had disappeared. "Your servant will return once she has seen her room," Amunnakht was saying. "If you have any concerns or complaints you may approach Neferabu, the Steward in charge of this section of the House. There are two bath houses at the farther end of the courtyard." He made as if to withdraw but I seized his arm.

"This cell is not suitable," I said, indignation and fear making my voice shake. "I will not share it with another woman and besides, it is far too small. I am not accustomed to the constant noise this door will not shut out, and without a window there will be no light if the door is closed. I demand a room of my own, Amunnakht!" For the first time I saw emotion glint in his eyes. They filled with humour.

"I am sorry, Thu," he said without a trace of apology, "but

the single rooms are reserved for the Mighty Bull's favourite concubines. Some of them do not have windows either. When you have been elevated to that exalted position it will be my pleasure to escort you to more salubrious accommodation." I stared at him for a moment, wanting to cry, wanting to go home, very aware of the background of voices, laughter and playing children. Some of the closer women had abandoned their conversations and were watching us curiously. I gathered up my courage.

"Then I wish to register my first complaint," I said with dignity, "and not to Neferabu either. To you, Keeper of the Door. This cell is like a cattle stall but I am not a cow. I am not part of the herd. I do not intend to sit in there and chew on my cud forever. Remember that!" He bowed.

"I shall remember it," he said smoothly, "but let me give you a word of advice. It is my duty to see that the harem remains a place of calm and orderliness. The comfort of the women is my second concern—my first is that the Lord of the Two Lands is satisfied within his domain. Any woman who stirs up discontent is dealt with severely. There are no exceptions." Without warning he smiled, and the gesture transformed his face. "Do not make enemies here, Thu. Give yourself time to become used to the House. Discover its compensations. Look about you, and you will see that you have many advantages over the other women. Use them well, and keep your own counsel. For what is the sacrifice of a little luxury to you, O miraculous peasant from surprising Aswat, when you may capture the heart of the Living God? It is up to you." He turned on his heel and was gone, pausing on his progress to offer a word to this one, a smile to that one, and I watched him only slightly mollified. I was already lamentably homesick.

Disenk returned a short time later and behind her came several harem slaves wrestling with my chests which were then piled at the foot of my couch. I had been lying on it critically, testing it for firmness, and had reluctantly found that it was entirely agreeable. While Disenk dealt with the slaves I opened my cedar box and placed Wepwawet on the table where I could see him first thing in the morning and at the last at night, then I sat in one of the tiny chairs and sifted through my old treasures. The soft brush of the feathers, the cool resistance of the pretty stones that had caught my eye so many years ago, the dried spring flowers culled in their brief, startling fertility during some walk by the river, the clay scarabs Kaha had given me for each lesson successfully completed, fed reassurance into my fingers. You are still Thu, they told me mutely. You will not be lost in this maelstrom of uniform femininity.

I carefully extracted the golden snakeskin, now distressingly brittle with age, and laid it on my lap. You are like the snake that left this behind for you to find, I told myself. You shed one self when you took ship with Hui and you are in the process of shedding another, but you remain the Lady Thu, Libu princess, about to grow a shell even more glorious than the ones from which you have so painfully emerged. The sight and feel of the fragile thing served to soothe me even further and by the time I closed the lid of the box and placed it carefully under my table I was ready to explore my new surroundings.

They could have been much worse. At the far end of the courtyard, as Amunnakht had indicated, were two bath houses making up the lower corners of the building. They were larger than Hui's and contained benches for massage as well as a bewildering array of aromatic pots and jars that had Disenk clucking with pleasure. Each one had doorways that opened into the passages that ran between the identical harem buildings and at one end led into gardens and at the other, fed the wanderer back onto the pathway leading to the main gates.

There were four structures in all. Mine was the third from

the main entrance. The second was similar. The fourth, at the far end, was where the children lived with their nurses and servants and above them, on their second floor, were the schoolrooms and tutors' quarters. Each block had its grassed interior yard with pool and fountain.

The first building, however, was barred to Disenk and me when we tried to enter. Harem guards turned us away. We discovered later that it was the home of the Lady of the Two Lands, Ast. She had the whole of the ground floor to herself, and above her on the second floor lived the fabled Ast-Amasareth, the foreign woman who had become Ramses' powerful second Great Royal Wife. I could see little beyond the guards' protecting bodies but an empty and peaceful vista of grass, flower beds and shrubs. Disenk and I returned to my cell both hot and tired to discover that in our absence four flagons of wine had been delivered. Hui had kept his promise. It was now past noon and I was secretly grateful for my room's dim coolness. "Go to the kitchens and find me some food, Disenk," I asked her. "But first, break the seal on one of those jugs and pour me something to drink. Are there cups in the chests?" I could smell something delicious wafting across the courtyard and I was hungry.

As she was scraping away the wax with the imprint of Hui's vineyard stamped into it the doorway darkened and a man came in, bowing. He looked like a prosperous merchant with his air of contented importance. I presumed that this was our Steward.

"I am Neferabu," he introduced himself. "The Keeper has asked me to make sure that you lack for nothing, Thu, and to tell you that you will not be required to present yourself before the King until you yourself feel that you are ready. It is a significant honour," he went on confidentially. "The Keeper does not show such consideration to every new-comer. I am at your service. My room is beside the entrance." I thanked him with relief, unaware until that moment how anxious I had been regarding my first sexual encounter with Ramses. The Keeper had liked me, why I did not know. Or more probably, he had seen my potential as a favourite. That thought was definitely cheering.

Sitting in my chair I drank Hui's wine reflectively, enjoying its familiar tang. I was not quite prepared to sit out on the grass under the eyes of my fellow prisoners. By the time I had finished it Disenk was back, bearing a tray and lamenting, as she attempted to serve me, the lack of proper dining tables. "We might as well be camping on the desert," she complained. I was inclined to agree with her, but the food was beyond reproach and the mention of the desert reminded me of Hui's words about Prince Ramses. Where was he lodged? Surely somewhere very close, on the other side of the high, sheltering wall beyond the long pathway perhaps, where the sprawling complex of the main palace lay. Disenk removed the tray, slid the sandals from my feet and the sheath from my body, and invited me to rest. Outside the sounds of activity had all but ceased. The women were seeking their couches to dream away the hot afternoon hours and the children had been carried to their own quarters. I wondered where the Lady Hunro was.

When I woke towards late afternoon a woman was sitting on the edge of the other couch, swinging her legs and devouring what appeared to be a piece of cold duck. She was watching me, smiling. When she saw me open my eyes she shouted something through the doorway and a girl came in.

"Fetch this lady's servant," she ordered, then she pushed the last morsel of meat between her lips, brushed her fingers together, and came over to me. I was by then upright and fully conscious. "I am the Lady Hunro," she went on brightly, "and you, of course, are Thu. I have heard all about you from my brother Banemus. I am sorry I was not here to greet you earlier but I was busy dictating a letter to him. He is on his way back to Cush. When you have refreshed yourself I will introduce you to some of the other women if you like?" The statement was made as though it was a question and I nodded in agreement, rather bemused. She was not at all as I had imagined. Banemus's sister, I had presumed, would be an older woman of serious mien, beautiful, naturally, but carrying with her something of her brother's serenity. My expression must have betrayed my confusion for she laughed, throwing back her head to expose a long, well-muscled throat. Indeed, her whole body was muscular and well defined. I judged her to be about ten years older than I. Her hair was thick, short and very straight, her chin thrusting, her mouth prominent. Her likeness to the General lay in her eyes. They were brown and warm, and fixed me with a friendly regard. "I know what you are thinking," she said. "Can this woman come from the same family as sober old Banemus? But my brother can be very entertaining and witty when he chooses, and I love him dearly. I wish Pharaoh would have the intelligence to quarter him in the Delta." She shrugged. "But intelligence is not one of our King's major attributes."

At that moment Disenk hurried in and began to lay out my attire for the rest of the day. She had set up her cosmetic table against the rear wall between the two couches so as to catch the light from the door. Hunro greeted her effusively and for a moment they shared news of the Lady Kawit and the activities of the house where Disenk had once been employed. Then, as Disenk indicated that I should sit before the array of pots and jars to have my paint repaired and my hair done, Hunro turned her attention back to me. She settled on the head of my couch, pulling around her the thin linen cloak which barely covered her lithe body and watching Disenk's capable hands critically. "Now that you are here, Disenk," she said, "I hope you will do my paint sometimes. My servant is very good but she cannot compete with you. Every noblewoman in Pi-Ramses knows of your skill.

When are you to go into the palace, Thu? Tonight? Ramses is usually eager to sample the newest female fare. I had no sleep for the first three weeks I was here and I ended up prostrate before my Hathor shrine, begging the goddess of love and beauty to divert Pharaoh's attention to someone else. I no longer felt like the 'little Hathor' my parents named me." Her rich laugh rang out again. "Needless to say, my prayers were eventually answered. Now I am called to the royal bedchamber more to dance for His Majesty than to satiate his lust." She grimaced and dropped her voice. "He is a terrible lover, Thu. Full of heat and fire but it all fizzles out very quickly." I was shocked to hear the Lord of the Two Lands spoken of in this manner, for although I was already crushingly aware that his body did not in any way resemble the perfection of a god's, yet I still believed in the absolute sanctity of his divine person.

"How did you come to be here, Lady Hunro?" I asked. I could see her wry smile as a distorted image in the copper mirror I was holding up as she replied.

"Please just call me Hunro. I made much trouble for my poor father, who is one of Ramses' advisers, by refusing to marry the man of his choice and threatening to attach myself permanently to one of the temples as a dancer. I love dancing, Thu, and trained with the other noble girls from a young age to perform before the gods, but it is not considered proper for a noblewoman to make dancing a consuming career. My father gave me a choice. Marry or become a concubine. Ramses always liked me. Banemus would not let me run away south with him, so here I am. The life is good and I lack for nothing. I dance whenever I please. I administer my vineyards and cattle. I own a small portion of the faience works outside the city. And I do not have to defer to some demanding husband who insists that his house be run in a certain fashion." She shrugged. "Anyway," she finished, "you did not answer my question. Do you lose your virginity tonight?" Disenk had completed her work on my face and was kneading oil into my hands. I shook my head.

"No, not until I wish it to be so," I told Hunro. "And to be truthful, right now I would rather go home to Hui."

"And admit defeat? No, Thu," she responded thoughtfully. "You are not the sort to give up so easily. Not like the girl who slept on your couch before you." She slid from her perch and stretched, bending from side to side with hands clasped, and I soon learned that movement, for Hunro, was as natural as breathing and accompanied almost every conversation.

"What happened to her?"

"She killed herself. I had put up with her weeping and wailing for days. She was a pathetic little thing, delicate and pretty as a flower, but she had no spine." Hunro tossed back the hair from her flushed face and leaned down to place her palms on the floor. Her voice became muffled. "She managed to lift a dagger from one of the guards and she stabbed herself. It was the one brave act of her life. At least she did it out on the grass and spared me the sight of blood all over this room." I was momentarily speechless with horror.

"But why did she do such a thing?" I managed. Hunro pulled herself slowly upright.

"Because she fancied that she had fallen in love with some young butler in the palace and therefore could not bear to give herself to Ramses. If only she had waited Ramses would have soon tired of her bleating clumsiness and she herself would have recovered from her romantic fit. I have a lock of her hair around here somewhere. As a token from a suicide, it will bring me luck."

When I got to know her better I understood that behind Hunro's undeniable amiability there was a streak of callousness, something not deliberately cruel or insensitive but merely an indifference to those less strong than she. But at the time I was shocked. Her reaction might have been honest but it was not conventional.

"You say that your father is one of Pharaoh's advisers," I said, changing the subject hurriedly. I too was glad that the unfortunate girl had not killed herself anywhere near the couch on which I now had to sleep. "Do you also know Ramses well? And the Prince?"

"Which one?" she countered. "There are plenty of them, all named Ramses after our Pharaoh's true god, his ancestor Osiris Ramses the Second. Yes, I suppose I know Pharaoh quite well. I can help you to capture him if that is what you wish." Something in her expression, the way she formed the words, brought a moment of forceful revelation to me. Hunro knew. I had been quartered with her for a reason. She, as well as her brother and Hui and the others, believed that I could eventually exert such an influence on Pharaoh that the course of Egypt's history would be changed.

I knew another thing, also, at that moment. I did not care about their plans, not really. I loved Hui and wanted to please him, but I was willing to play their game for less idealistic reasons than the ones that obsessed the Master and his associates. A peasant with invisible mud between her toes and the taste of gritty black bread and lentils still in her mouth, I wanted to continue to enjoy jewellery and expensive linens, fine food and the best wines. I wanted luxury and power, respect and recognition, because in those things lay security and the realization of my childhood dreams. I would be a princess. I would be queen.

"Yes, it is what I wish," I agreed slowly, meeting her eye, "but it is what you wish also, isn't it, Hunro?" Her smile widened as we gazed at one another.

"Indeed it is, Thu," she purred. "Indeed it is."

Chapter 14

I did not feel ready to brave Pharaoh's bed until the middle of the following month, Paophi. Each morning I awoke thinking, I will do it today, I will send for the Keeper and tell him, but always something happened to divert me. My unacknowledged reluctance to do my duty was the true excuse, but there were many more. Within two weeks of my arrival in the harem it was known among the women that I was a physician. There were others, of course, men of high medical standing, but in coming to me the women knew that their ailments, and above all their most private requests, would not be relayed to the Keeper or worse, to the palace authorities. I would open my box of supplies and sit in a chair in a secluded corner of the courtyard, listening to the real or imagined needs of my compatriots, examining them and prescribing as best I could. Many of them were simply plagued with the vague distempers of boredom but it was not my business to recommend a more active life and in any case I knew that my words would fall on deaf ears.

I myself had embarked on a routine as similar to the one I had practised at Hui's as I could make it. Most of the women slept for as long as possible and would emerge from their cells, half-naked and yawning, to stumble into the shade and pick at their first meal of the day when the sun was already overhead. The temptation to follow their example was strong, but thanks to the rigid discipline I had endured under Hui's wise direction I was able to resist it.

In the morning Disenk roused me early and I would exercise, going through the rigorous movements Nebnefer had taught me, while the sun lifted higher, turning the pink and shadowed courtyard into a cup of golden light. Often I was joined by Hunro who would dance on the grass with a joyful abandon, her face an ecstatic mask as she lifted it to the glittering sky. Then, both of us panting and pouring sweat, we would run down the narrow path between the forbidding wall of the palace and the blocks of harem buildings until we came to the entrance of the compound. Of course we did not attempt to pass the guards. We veered right into the little-used harem garden that enclosed the whole huge complex on three sides, and plunged into the pool. Hunro was content to immerse herself and then get out, lying on the grass until she was dry, but I grimly swam the lengths I had been used to doing for a shouting, critical Nebnefer, up and down, up and down, until my arms and thighs trembled with exhaustion. I would collapse beside the woman who was fast becoming a friend, and until hunger overtook us we would talk aimlessly, with much giggling. We did not bother to take our servants with us. At these times we had no needs and besides, while we exercised, Disenk and Hunro's woman were in the kitchen preparing our food. When we were ready we would stroll back to our quarters and eat and drink like famished desert lions, self-righteously watching the first few sleepy denizens of the other cells stumble out and stand blinking in the strong sunlight. My appetite appeased, Disenk would escort me to the bath house where I was washed. This was followed by a body shave and massage from one of the resident masseurs.

Those morning hours became precious to me. They were a time of quiet and privacy before the courtyard filled with young children and gossip, before the few women I saw professionally each day began to drift in my direction.

At first the dozens of other concubines, a lovely, soft mass of big eyes and high voices and yielding flesh, were anonymous to me. Most of them remained that way, for I saw no reason to cultivate their acquaintance. After all, I would not be among them for long. But some stood out from the others. There was Hatia the drunkard who made her appearance in the late afternoon with swollen face and shaking hands and would sink gracelessly beneath her canopy to stare out upon the noisy crowd around the fountain. No one paid her any attention. She would sit thus, wine cup in hand and motionless servant behind, until sunset, at which time she would rise as silently as she had come, and disappear into her cell.

There were Nubhirma'at and Nebt-Iunu, a pair of nubile Egyptian girls from Abydos who had been raised on neighbouring estates and had been friends since their birth. Ramses, on a visit to Osiris's temple at Abydos, had been captivated by their singing and had contracted with both their fathers for their inclusion in the harem. They regularly went to Pharaoh's bed together and were summoned to him frequently, but it was hard for me to see them as my rivals. They were sweetly stupid, obligingly good-natured, and had eyes only for each other. One was never seen alone. They shared the same couch in the same cell and sometimes even ate with fingers intertwined. They consulted me together, coming into my cell with shy determination and asking for a contraceptive. "We know it is forbidden," Nebt-Iunu whispered breathily, hanging onto her lover's arm, "but although it is the greatest honour to bear a child to the Great God we really do not want to. Can you help us, Thu?" I did not want to help them. I did not want to be discredited, or worse, incur the anger of the God I myself had yet to encounter, but I was conquered by their pleading looks and transparent distress. I did as they asked, grinding up the acacia spikes with dates and honey and saturating the linen fibres with the mixture, thinking of my mother and the furtive consultations I had witnessed in her herb room. Perhaps we are not so dissimilar, I mused as I worked. Perhaps it is true that blood will out.

More often than not I had the cell to myself during the daylight hours. Hunro seemed to have much business to attend to, but she would slip onto her couch as Disenk was putting flame to the wick of my lamps and then we would lie watching the shadows gyrate on our walls and talking lazily. She spoke of Ramses and how to please him, her language unselfconsciously explicit as she described in graphic detail the mysteries of the royal bed, and I listened and stored away the information, bringing it out later to ponder and dissect while Hunro slept peacefully.

It came to me then that I could not expect any kind of fulfilment from my role as concubine. Not for me the antici-pation that brought a smile and a thudding heartbeat when a lover was close by. Not for me the moment of sheer joy when a beloved face appeared. There would be no tender-ness, no urgent yet gentle merging of body and ka. Such things would be forever beyond my reach, forever beyond my experience, and I was not yet sixteen years old. I was paying a high price for dreams that were not yet within my grasp, gambling with enormous stakes for a future that might never be mine. My sole purpose was to please Pharaoh. He had no obligation to please me. At least, not yet, my mind whispered back. Not yet... I tossed and turned restlessly. If I wanted love, if I wanted real passion and romance, I would have to come to the attention of the Prince, but even if I did, what then? I belonged to his father.

One early morning, when Hunro and I were speeding along the narrow path on our way to the pool with the air still cool on our naked bodies and the walls on either side of us still cutting out the new light, we almost collided with a small procession that was emerging from the Queen's domain. I was ahead, but at the sight of the cavalcade Hunro grabbed my shoulder and brought me to a sudden halt. We stood panting and exposed as first a Herald in blue-

and-white livery and then a Steward came towards us. The angle of a white canopy inched around the corner and then a dull flash of jewels, a wide, braided and coronetted wig, an expanse of flowing, gold-shot linen. The Herald stopped opposite us. "On your faces before the Lady of the Two Lands, concubines!" he snapped. Obediently we went down, kneeling in the cramped space with our foreheads against the gritty stone of the path, and the man moved away. I felt the tiny breeze of the Steward's passing and then the shuffle of the canopy bearers. Greatly daring, I lifted my head.

The miniature woman beneath the filmy gauze was as tiny and willowy as an artist's dream. The feet stepping delicately by were shod in sandals that could have fitted a child of ten and the transparent linen swirled around ankles I might have encircled with one hand. Yet as my rapid glance sped upward I realized with a shock that I was seeing an aging body. The Great Queen's belly sagged slightly and the vague outline of her small breasts beneath the pleats showed that they were not firm. Her high neck, draped in many gems, was ropy and in the second when I scrutinized her meticulously painted face I was aware of the clefts that ran beside her nostrils, the fan of lines about her eyes that the kohl could not disguise in the pitilessly revealing light of morning. Her bearing was haughty, her expression closed.

My forehead once more touched the ground. The footsteps receded and I had begun to pick myself up, one knee still resting on the stone, when I heard someone else coming quickly. Hunro was already on her feet. From the entrance to the Queen's quarters a man was striding towards us, arms swinging, head raised. My heart gave a leap. It was he, so handsome, so strong, so glorious with his square chin and flashing black eyes, the hennaed mouth I longed to kiss and the flexing thighs that begged to be caressed under the short kilt. Intent on catching up to his mother he merely glanced at us and I was grateful, for I was unpainted, drenched in sweat from the exertions of my exercises, and my sticky hair was plastered to my skull. Then all at once he checked himself and turned. Hunro and I extended our arms and bowed very low.

"Greetings, Hunro," the well-remembered voice said. "I trust you are well. And how is Banemus? We have received no message from him yet. Have you?"

"No, Highness," Hunro replied with her usual aplomb. "But you know my brother. He will be more concerned with the welfare of his contingent as they march to their fort in Cush than with dictating a scroll to the palace." The Prince smiled. His even teeth were dazzlingly white.

"And so he should be," he retorted. His attention turned to me. At first it was politely non-committal, then his gaze became keen. "It is the female physician, is it not?" he said. "The Seer's assistant? You are now one of my father's acquisitions?" I nodded dumbly and the smile returned. "He has made a good choice, I see." Without further comment he went on his way. I watched him hungrily until he was out of sight then I grimaced and fell into step with Hunro.

"Gods!" I groaned. "It is just my luck to be caught by him in this lamentable state! What will he be thinking of me?" Hunro shot me a sharp look.

"He will not be thinking of you at all," she said quietly. "Why should he? And for your own sake you must not let your mind dwell on him or you will come to grief."

I did not answer. When we came to the garden I attacked the water of the pool as though it was an enemy, slicing through it with ruthless power until the blood was pounding irregularly in my ears. It was time to make Pharaoh my slave.

That very afternoon I requested, through Neferabu, an interview with the Keeper. I had expected that he would come to my cell but I was sharply reminded of my true station when Neferabu returned to tell me that although the

Keeper was otherwise engaged he would be pleased to give me a few moments towards dusk in his office. Now that my decision was made I was impatient to put it into action. Irritably I accepted the message, sent for a harem scribe, and whiled away the intervening time in dictating a letter to my family and one to Hui. I said nothing of any great import in either of them, certain that all correspondence passed under the Keeper's eye before finding its way out into the world. I had hoped that Hui might have visited me or at least been called to treat someone in the palace and come to see how I was faring, but neither he nor word from him had arrived.

Just after sunset a runner came to escort me to Amunnakht. I went with ill grace, wrestling with my pride as we walked far to the rear of the compound, through a guarded gate, and out onto a wide yard of beaten earth. Against the far wall was a long series of many cells and beside them the kitchens. They were surely the harem servants' rooms. But we turned sharply right, brushed a short way along the inside wall, and then turned right again through a throng of soldiers who watched us carefully.

I found myself within a vast garden, on a path that soon veered left to run in front of a row of large cells whose doors were open. Inside I glimpsed men sitting behind desks, scribes taking dictation, scrolls piled everywhere, and presumed that these were the offices of administration for the palace. On my other side, indistinct through the trees, I could make out the solid wall of a huge building. After frantically trying to place my position I decided that I was actually inside the palace grounds and was looking at the seat of power itself. I was not particularly impressed. The little runner paused outside one of the offices, knocked on the open door, announced me to whoever was within, bowed, and hurried away. I did not wait to be invited, but walked forward.

The office was scrupulously neat, its desk cleared of all but a palette and a box of scribe's brushes, its walls lined with dozens of round, open-ended receptacles for scrolls. There was little else. I wondered briefly which niche held my contract and what other information about me was being amassed and recorded. It must have been a monumental task to document each woman in the harem. My inspection lasted only seconds, for Amunnakht was rising from his chair.

"Greetings, Thu," he said imperturbably. "May I offer you wine or a dish of figs? What do you require of me?" Mindful of Hui's warning I declined the refreshment. Amunnakht did not ask me to sit, in fact he regained his chair and crossed his legs, arranging his linen over his knees and looking up at me inquiringly. I wasted no time.

"I am ready to go to Pharaoh's bed," I declared without preamble. Amunnakht's perfectly plucked eyebrows rose. He nodded.

"Good. Ramses has been asking for you but I have told him that you are indisposed. He thought that was very funny, a sick physician. Nevertheless he will not be patient for much longer." I was secretly thrilled. Pharaoh had not forgotten about me, indeed, he had actually been asking for my presence! It was an excellent omen and my good humour was restored. "Do you need any advice, Thu?" Amunnakht was continuing. I blinked.

"Advice, Keeper?" For one idiotic moment I expected him to launch into a list of sexual instructions that would have seemed wildly indecent coming out of that urbane yet stern mouth.

"Are you aware of the etiquette of the situation? Do you know how to behave when you approach the God?"

"Oh!" I said with relief. "Oh yes, Amunnakht. I have been in the royal bedchamber before." Was that the suspicion of a smile on the Keeper's face? Did he sense that I intended to break most of the rules, that I had listened to Hunro, to Hui, to my own intuition, and had decided that the last thing I must do is behave like a shy, overawed virgin even though I probably would feel like one?

"So you have," Amunnakht replied gravely. "I had forgotten. Then I wish you the blessing of Hathor and the favour of our King. I had not yet selected someone to share the royal couch tomorrow night. You may have that privilege. A palace servant will come for you after sundown." Should I thank him? I thought not. Bowing, I retreated and found another runner waiting for me outside, doubtless to make sure that I returned the way I had come and did not go wandering where I should not.

The palace garden was still suffused with a peaceful bronze glow, and as I set off past the other offices I saw a cat jump from the lower branch of one of the trees, and reaching the ground, slither away through the flaming grasses with a boneless, fluid grace. I took the sight as a promising omen and said a quick prayer to Bast, cat goddess of sexual delights, asking her to prosper my endeavour.

That night I also prayed, long and earnestly, before my little statue of Wepwawet. I reminded him of my faithfulness, of the way he had answered my earlier plea and had taken me out of Aswat, and I begged him not to let his effort be in vain. I told Disenk that my moment had come and instructed her in what I wanted to wear. She became hesitant.

"But, Thu," she said, "with much respect, it is an untried virgin clothed simply in white linen that Pharaoh wants. If you go to him in gold and yellow with a wig on your head and fine jewels on your person he will dismiss you immediately."

"I do not think so," I smiled. "I will not be able to disguise my inexperience, Disenk, and I will not try. But I have a better idea. I will go as a person of authority, a virgin masquerading as a physician. Ramses will be intrigued."

"I hope you are right," she demurred unhappily and Hunro, who had been flexing one slim leg against the wall, touched her forehead to her knee and murmured, "It is very clever, Thu. You just might make it work." I shrugged, displaying more confidence than I really felt.

"If not, I will try something else," I said loftily. "I will rely on my instinct. I will be one concubine Ramses will not be able to discard."

I slept fitfully that night, waking several times to lie gazing into the darkness, once hearing the soft voices of the runners who kept a vigil in case any woman should need her servant and once being startled by the eerie scream of a desert hyena coming clearly and ghoulishly on the wind. The verdant Delta stretched a long way to both east and west before it met the intractability of the sand and I wondered if the sound was for me alone, a warning from the gods. But perhaps the animals crept into the city under cover of darkness to scavenge. That was just as likely.

Mentally shaking myself I turned over to slip once more into unconsciousness but the experience had started a flow of unrest in me that I had to deliberately subdue. I did not want to give my virginity to that man. Years ago I had been prepared to sacrifice it to Hui in exchange for a glimpse into my future, but I had been a child then, ignorant and reckless. It had been nothing more to me than a commodity, something to trade. Now it represented a great deal more. It was still a commodity but its worth had grown, become entangled in my mind with the value I placed upon myself as a whole, and in a moment of genuine insight I knew that Hui was more worthy to receive it than the Lord of the Two Lands. Yet for me it could never be a gift. I was at last using it to pay for the future I had wanted to see so long ago, and the revelation brought me both hope and shame.

I pursued my morning routine a little later than usual, wanting to be completely rested for the coming event. I checked the contents of my medicine box, and while I was doing so the fresh supplies I had requested from Hui arrived.

In the afternoon's heat I slept again, and until sunset I composed myself by playing dogs and jackals with Hunro. Then
it was time for the ceremony of dressing and painting. When
the palace servant appeared, I kissed Wepwawet's feet,
picked up my box, and followed him out into the fragrant
evening. I had chewed a kat leaf while I was waiting and my
anxiety had become nothing but a dim throb deep in my
belly. I was young, I was beautiful, I was wily and clever. I was
Thu, Libu princess, and I was going to conquer the world.

I had anticipated a long walk, time in which to collect
myself, but the silent servant led me out of my courtyard, a
few steps diagonally across the path that ran from end to
end of the harem, and straight through a gate in the palace
wall onto a short avenue. Almost at once we came to a door.
The man said a few words to the guards upon it and they
knocked. It was opened and we went in.

I blinked in momentary confusion. Without warning I
was in the royal bedchamber. I recognized the elegant chairs
with their glimmering electrum legs and tall silver backs,
the low tables exquisitely embossed in golden figures. My
eyes flew to the massive couch, bulking dimly in the soft
light of the many lamps on their cedar stands.

Someone was sitting on the stool beside it and I half-
expected to see the Prince rise briskly from it as he had on
the day Hui brought me here, but the linen-swathed form
bending to watch his sandals being removed was Pharaoh
himself. The servant who had escorted me was crossing the
floor to take up his station by the farther door. Ramses had
seen his movement, and looked up. Heart pounding I took a
step then went carefully to the lapis-inlaid floor, first my
knees and then my face and the palms of my hands as Disenk
had taught me. I had placed the box beside me. "Rise!" the
well-remembered voice commanded and I did so, pulling the
box back into my chest for the comfort of its familiar authority. I did not wait for permission to go forward. Squaring my

shoulders and taking a deep, quiet breath I stalked up to the stool.

Ramses had risen. I had not seen him on his feet before. He was taller than I but only just, so that as he looked me up and down with obvious disappointment our eyes met. His head was covered by a loose linen cap that served to make his cheeks seem more pendulous, his generous mouth more prominent than I remembered.

"The eyes are the same," he grumbled, "but that is all. I am tired, I have a headache. I was pleased when Amunnakht told me that you had recovered from your slight indisposition, for I was beginning to think that you were reluctant to gratify your Pharaoh. I was looking forward to a closer acquaintance with the sprite who called herself a physician. But what do I find?" He swung away petulantly. "A wigged and bejewelled creature who could be anonymous in any court gathering. I am not happy!" The last words were shouted. They echoed from the high, blue-tinged ceiling and thudded into me like blows. I was trembling inside but I followed him. As I did so, I noticed a motionless, blue-and-white sashed form in the shadows on the other side of the couch. With a shock I recognized Paibekamun. He was staring at me in puzzlement, his face a dusky oval in the gloom, and I met his gaze. Trust me, I tried to say to him mutely. Just trust me.

"Sit down, Majesty," I ordered in a firm voice. Ramses halted abruptly and I repeated myself. "Sit down. I am willing to wager that your Majesty did not follow my instructions last time regarding a fast of water only. Does your Majesty not remember his pain, his fever, from over-indulgence in the sesame paste? Your Majesty's head aches because the Metu to the head is clogged with too much wine, too much fine food. Is it not so?" I made myself busy as I was speaking, not looking at him, opening my box and lifting out my mortar and pestle. I began to unseal jars. Your

Majesty's person is sacred and precious to all Egyptians," I
went on reprovingly. "Your Majesty owes his subjects a little
self-discipline."

"Self-discipline?" Ramses roared, turning. "Who do you
think you are?" Then his tone changed. "What are you
doing?"

"I am preparing a mixture of setseft seeds, fruit-of-the-am-
tree, and honey to clear the Metu to your head. Your
Majesty will swallow it slowly, and while you do so I will
massage your feet."

This was the moment. My heart was now pounding so
violently that I thought it would burst out of my chest and I
was glad that the shaking of my fingers was hidden by the
action of grinding the potion. For what seemed like a henti
the King stared down at me, breathing noisily, then he
slumped back onto his stool with an exaggerated sigh like a
reprimanded child.

"Paibekamun!" he barked. "Fetch me a spoon!" The
shadow detached itself and glided away. "I wanted a few
hours of lovemaking," Pharaoh complained to my bent
head, "and I get a harangue from a harridan disguised as a
beautiful young girl. Already I rue the day I ever sued for
you, my little scorpion!" I did not answer. There was
humour in his voice. It was going to be all right.

By the time Paibekamun materialized with a golden
spoon the medicine was ready. Ramses took the stone mortar, and while he stirred the contents and dosed himself I
settled before him cross-legged, took one of his feet onto my
lap, and began to knead it. Occasionally he winced as my
probing fingers found a tender spot, but he continued to
swallow my concoction and when it was gone he handed
the empty mortar to the Butler and leaned back against the
side of the couch. His eyes slowly closed. This time his sigh
was one of pleasure, and I saw his penis stir with an
uncanny, independent life and grow hard. I stopped what I

was doing, and parting his filmy, voluminous linen cloak I took hold of his member, squeezing it tightly. It shrank, and Ramses' eyes flew open. "That hurt!" he said.

"No, Majesty, it did not," I contradicted him. "I am trying to treat your headache and fatigue. This is not the time for sex." I went on massaging, first one foot and then the other. Again he became aroused and again I deflated him. The third time he grew engorged he whispered to me, "Do it again, Thu," and I did. Then he reached forward and lifted the wig from my head. My hair tumbled about my face and he began to stroke it, running his fingers through it and pressing it against my face. I pushed him away, but before he could protest I knelt and tongued his toes, licking and sucking them slowly. He murmured something I could not catch. Carefully I extended my range, kissing his calves, the inside of his thighs, then abruptly I stood.

"Is your Majesty's head less painful?" I asked briskly. His sleepy gaze rolled over me and he struggled to his feet.

"Yes indeed," he said thickly, grasping at my sheath. "Come here." I evaded him, passing my hands provocatively over my clothing as if to smooth away the rumpling he had caused. It was time, I thought, to be what I truly was, an apprehensive virgin.

"I cannot," I said. He frowned and his eyes lost some of their glazing.

"Why?"

"Because in order to please your Majesty tonight I dressed in my best jewellery and prettiest sheath and I am afraid that in your Majesty's ardor, both will be ruined."

"What nonsense!" he snapped. "Do as you are told! Come here!" Meekly I obeyed, closing the space between us and inwardly tensing for the first touch of his chubby hands on my unsullied flesh. But he did not pull the sheath away from me as I had anticipated. He reached behind me, gently unclasping my necklet and laying it on the table by the couch. With the same studied care he lifted the earring from my lobe, slid the bracelets from my arms, undid the gem-studded belt that held the linen to my waist. As he did so he began to pant. His warm breath smelled of honey with a tang of the setseft seeds he had eaten. Easing the sheath down over my shoulders he let it slip to the floor. I was now naked before him. "There," he said huskily. "Is that better, little scorpion? May I now see whether or not there is a sting in your tail?" He pulled me against him sharply, his hands grabbing my buttocks, his face buried in my neck, and for a moment panic overcame me. I struggled, not able to draw air into my lungs, but he held me all the tighter. I knew that I must regain control of the situation, not just in order to set the tone for our future encounters but also for the sake of my own self-respect. No man would take me without my full consent, not even Pharaoh.

"Do you rape all your virgins?" I cried out. He went very still. His hold loosened, and as it did so I pushed him onto the couch. His knees buckled and he lay on his back, looking up at me with an astounded expression. I climbed up and knelt beside him. "I am afraid, Mighty Bull," I whispered, and it was the truth. "Can you not see that?" I brought my mouth down over his.

For one horrible moment I seemed to be outside myself, hovering somewhere close to the ceiling of the great room and peering down at the slight figure on the bed bending naked over the other sprawling, obese figure, with the Butler standing immobile against the wall and the body servants clustered like equally insubstantial ghosts at the far end of the room. I wanted to stay there and watch. I did not want to feel the King's mouth, his soft body, his questing hands, but I returned to myself as rapidly and painfully as I had left.

Ramses' lips were hot and quivering. His tongue poked at my teeth. Fiercely I tried to enter into the experience, to conjure up in my mind a vision of Hui's kiss, of Prince

Ramses' magnificent body, but the present was too immediate and my distaste too real. As Pharaoh twisted, rolling me onto my back, his mouth firmly clamped to mine as his hands sought my breasts, I became entirely cold. Again I fought that coldness, for I knew that beneath the thin armour of my virginity lay a nature both sensual and passionate and it should not matter what mouth, what hands, what body stirred it into life, but try as I might I could not drown myself in sensation alone. I hate you, I found myself thinking as the King parted my legs and thrust his fingers into me. I hate you for taking this away from me and I hate Hui for making me a whore and I hate the Prince for giving me a glimpse of what I can never have. I wish you all dead.

From that cold place my reason reasserted itself. As Ramses entered me at last with a crow of triumph and delight and I bit my lip so as not to recoil from the sudden pain, I vowed that he would pay, that somehow this would be made worthwhile. Grimly I waited, twining my arms about him, gripping his fat buttocks while he pumped. Then he ejaculated with another wild cry and collapsed upon me, his sweat oiling my skin. He lay quiescent for a moment then rolled away and propped himself on one elbow, smiling down into my face. "Now you are mine forever, little scorpion," he panted, and even as I smiled back I thought savagely, no. You are my captive though you do not know it yet. "Paibekamun!" Ramses called. "Bring wine!" I extricated myself from his embrace and sat up.

"I suggest that you do without the wine, Majesty," I said resolutely, "unless you want your headache to return. Have I not been enough stimulation for one night?" Kissing his forehead I left the couch. As I stepped into the circle of my discarded sheath and began to pull it back on I felt something hot running down my legs. I replaced my jewellery with calm deliberation, reached for my wig, put the mortar back in my box. "Will your Majesty dismiss me so that he may go to sleep?" He lay there staring at me, perplexed, then gradually his bright button eyes began to fill with a shrewd understanding. He started to chuckle and then to laugh, great full-bodied guffaws that rang to the roof.

"Oh, Thu!" he choked. "Well have I named you scorpion! But stay with me a little longer. We will have beer instead of wine, if you wish, and garlic steeped in juniper oil. Stay and talk to me." It was not a plea, of course. Kings did not plead. And yet in that moment I knew that one day the begging would come. I was tempted to comply, to jump back onto the couch like the girl I really was, and settle against the cushions, and we would prattle away to each other like old friends. But the liquid on my legs had trickled to my ankles, dark red and distasteful, making me shudder. I merely stood there, the box in my arms, and at last he grimaced. "Go then," he commanded, and I bowed and left him. The servant on the door by which I had entered opened it for me and went swiftly ahead, back along the short avenue now nothing more than a broad paleness beneath me, through the gate, across the dense darkness of the main path, and at last into the courtyard of my building. Here he bowed and vanished into the night.

The fountain gurgled and splashed silvery water into its grey basin. The stars' faint light made long shadows snake over the deserted grass. My footfalls seemed loud on the stone fronting the cells as I approached my own haven. One lamp was burning. Hunro was asleep. Disenk was there, waiting for me, her face drawn with weariness. She rose from the mat as I entered, and without a word began to quickly undress me. She did not comment on the sight of the blood. When I was naked she hesitated and I shook my head. "No, Disenk," I whispered. "I do not want to wash tonight. I am too tired." She nodded and held back the sheets for me. I fell between them, and she covered me and stole away.

I drew up my besmirched knees and put my hands over my face. I was cold and exhausted and utterly drained. I had succeeded. He would send for me the following evening, I knew it, but the knowledge was as ashes in my mouth. "I hate you," I murmured, no longer really meaning it, no longer caring about anything, and from that despair I toppled into a heavy sleep.

Nevertheless, I had instructed Disenk to rouse me at the usual time and sluggish and fatigued though I was, I forced myself through my routine of cleansing and exercise. Hunro joined me on the grass and afterwards in the pool. She began to question me closely, almost anxiously, about my night, but I was loath to discuss it then, and I put her off with abrupt answers. That it had gone well there was no doubt, but it had left me with an unexpected feeling of humiliation. The thought that I was now fully a woman brought me no pride, and before I could reassure Hunro, my shame had to fade.

In the afternoon Neferabu came and told me that Pharaoh demanded my company again that evening. I received the news calmly, dressed a small wound on one of the children who had cut himself when he had tripped on a stone, ate a light meal sitting in the shade outside my cell, and as the day faltered into sunset I submitted to Disenk's ministrations once more.

I had decided to go to Ramses this time as the white-clad girl he had expected before. Disenk wove ribbons into my loose hair, kohled my eyes very lightly, and dressed me in a modest sheath that covered me from unadorned neck to naked ankles. She did, however, rub yellow saffron oil into my skin so that at every move I exuded an aroma of sensual promise. I wanted to keep the King off guard. Last night I had been the autocratic physician melting into an inexperienced child. Tonight I would send a message of purity overlying a hint of knowing decadence. I left my box behind. I did not intend to exhaust the game of patient and physician. It had months of possibility in it.

The same palace servant came to escort me into the royal presence and I followed him without the trepidation of the night before. The same guards were on the gate into the gardens and on the doors of the bedchamber. Once again they graced me with keen glances as I passed between them. The doors were closed behind me.

This time the haze of recently burned incense hung in Pharaoh's room, bluish and sweet, and as I paused to perform my obeisance, a priest flanked by two little acolytes was just closing the ornate household shrine that stood in the far corner. They turned and bowed to Ramses, smoking censers still in their hands, and backed out of the main doors. Pharaoh acknowledged them then turned eagerly to me, bidding me rise.

"But where is our noble physician today?" he said jovially, taking my hand and leading me to the couch. "Is she perhaps ministering to some unfortunate and so had to send this charming substitute? I do not know whether to be insulted or gratified!" He was certainly gratified. His round face was flushed and his eyes sparkled in anticipation. I smiled back demurely, eyes lowered.

"She is indeed here, Great Horus," I answered, "but she has no interest in medicine this night. She has had a taste of other skills, and wishes to learn more." Do not flatter him, Hunro had warned. All the little girls flatter him, and he is astute enough to recognize their insincerity and be insulted by it. He is not a stupid man. He shot me a piercing glance.

"Hmm," he said. "Is that a mild sting from the scorpion's tail or a pat from a kitten whose claws are still inside? Come and sit by me, Thu. You look delicious without all the trappings. Will you take wine? Paibekamun, pour for us!" As the ever-present butler glided to obey, Ramses settled himself beside me on the couch, grinning impishly. "What?" he went on. "The physician will not protest when her God wishes to imbibe the fruit of his vineyards?"

I returned his smile. "The physician is not here," I answered softly, "and Thu, your lover, will take wine with you gladly."

"Drink then," he offered, handing me the brimming cup, and together we sipped the dark red liquid. "I dreamed of you last night," he said, his brown eyes tender over the rim of his goblet, "and when I awoke I wished that you were lying beside me. Is that not strange?" I answered carefully, aware that I was treading on dangerous ground.

"I am honoured that Your Majesty should consider me worth both desire and dream," I responded soberly. "I am Your Majesty's loyal servant." He must have expected more. He was obviously waiting for me to go on, his head cocked to one side, the smile holding on his face, and it came to me suddenly that I had answered cautiously and well, for his words had been some sort of a test. A fleeting throb of pity for him brushed me and was gone.

"You are wise far beyond your years, Thu," he said flatly, "and wisdom combined with beauty and extreme youth can be perilous." Impulsively I laid a hand against his full cheek.

"O Mighty Pharaoh," I whispered, "If those things are cemented together by an honest heart, how can there be any threat?"

He drew me to him then, nuzzling into my neck, kissing my chin, his hands deep in my hair, and I responded deliberately, pressing against him and winding my arms around him. This time his mouth on mine was familiar and I felt the faintest stirring of pleasure. Yet I would not succumb to it. The key to keeping this man on fire was simple. Put off the moment when his flame would be extinguished for as long as possible. Surely in all the dozens of women at his beck and call there had been a few who realized this! But such manipulation required courage and confidence, the ability to walk the rim of the cliff that fell away into royal anger and thus oblivion. It also required intuition coupled with careful instruction, and I had the advantage of both Hui and Hunro's cogent advice. I could not afford to enter into the hot, blind morass of Ramses' lust, be carried with him into that unreasoning void. Not for months to come.

Many times that night I pulled him back from the edge and many times I lured him towards it until at last we toppled over, he in an explosion of prolonged sexual release, and I in a sweat-drenched exhaustion. Both of us were trembling and limp when I crawled out from under him and reached for the wine, holding it to his lips with an unsteady hand and seeing him gulp it down before I drained the cup myself.

"You are not a girl, you are a demon," he croaked, the last words he said to me as I bowed to him, and clutching the limp folds of my linen around me, backed from the room. With my servant attendant I stumbled along the short passage, hurried past the gate guards, and sucked in great lungsful of the untainted pre-dawn air as I crossed to the harem.

Once my feet found the grass and I was alone I walked to the fountain and without pausing, knelt and plunged my face into the cool water, then I leaned on the basin's rim and watched the troubled surface grow calm again. As it did so the light was strengthening. Ra was approaching. His new birth was imminent, and the vanguard of his coming was turning the darkness around me into a sullen, shadowless grey.

My reflection became slowly visible in the rippling water, a blurred, ghostly shape with two black holes for eyes and a twisted, ever-moving slit of a mouth. "Not a girl, a demon," I whispered to it. "A demon." It leered back at me, its outline slowly heaving, its expression vacant. I pulled myself upright and made my way to my cell.

Disenk did not wake me and I slept as one dead until the daily bustle of the courtyard penetrated my dreams. Then I

forced myself to the bath house, reviving like a wilted flower
under the scented warm water Disenk poured over me and
the perfumed oils the masseur pounded into my skin. Both
the bath houses were full of chattering women at that time
of the day and the massage area was choked with them too,
slick naked bodies that gleamed like satin in the strong light
and gave off a confusion of overpowering aromas that
swirled around me and made me feel slightly ill. Some of the
women greeted me but I was still the newcomer, the peculiar
girl who dispensed medicine, and though I received many
smiles, they were either wary or politely preoccupied. I was
not sorry when, freshly washed and oiled, my wet hair coiled
on my head, I went back to my quarters.

As I approached my door I saw a familiar figure standing
outside, arms folded, eyes fixed with monumental indifference on the happy chaos before him. I began to run.

"Harshira!" I shouted as I came up to him. "It is so good
to see you! Is all well?" He turned to me gravely and bowed.

"All is well, Thu. The Master is within." I blinked.

"Here? Hui is here?" I burst over the threshold and threw
myself into the arms of the white-bundled figure who was
rising from the chair beside my couch. I hardly noticed
Hunro, who touched my shoulder as she went out. "Hui!" I
breathed, hugging him fiercely. "I have missed you so much!
What are you doing here? Why have you sent me no word
since I left home?" He returned my embrace and then set me
away firmly in true Hui fashion, taking my chin in one
gloved hand and turning my face to the light. He studied me
for a moment and then let me go.

"You are different," he said matter-of-factly. "You have
changed, my Thu. Disenk, bring us food. Thu, tell me
everything." Feeling completely revitalized I clambered up
onto my couch and found the words spilling out of me in a
flood. I could not take my eyes from him as he sat there
imperturbably and listened. Disenk returned with a tray of

something which we ate but I had no idea what I put into my mouth between my rapid sentences.

When I began to describe the last two nights, Hui came alive, questioning me sharply as to what Pharaoh said and did and how I had behaved. I answered unselfconsciously. It was as though I had become Hui's patient, telling him my symptoms for his diagnosis. "Good," he said. "Very good. You have done well, my Thu. But you must not drink Pharaoh's wine again. It is usual for Ramses to make exclusive use of a new concubine for a period of time, but if weeks go by and there is no sign that he is tiring of you, you will begin to attract much attention. Not all of it will be admiring. Be more careful!"

"I will. I am sorry. But tell me what has been happening at home. Do you have a new assistant? What have you done with my room?" He laughed.

"Nothing much so far. It has been reserved for guests. As for a new assistant, I have given no thought to the matter. Who could replace you, Thu?" I was secretly pleased. The niches I had carved in his house were still there, formed invisibly to my shape and empty. I asked him about Kaha and Nebnefer and Ani with wistfulness and he responded lightly, knowing my spurt of homesickness and doubtless not wanting to exacerbate it. Then he rose, gathering his swathings around him. I pulled at his hand.

"You are going? Oh, Master, stay a little longer. Walk the precincts with me. It has been weeks since I saw you!" He bent and kissed the top of my head.

"I would like to, Thu, but I have business to attend to in the palace. Pharaoh's mother needs my care and I must have words with Chancellor Mersura before I go. Have you been sending letters to your family? Is there anything you need?" I folded my arms.

"Yes, I have dictated to them and no, I don't need anything," I said sullenly, disappointed that he had not come into the harem just to see me. Tears pricked behind my eyelids, an indication of just how tense I had become. He nodded, satisfied, and went to the door.

"Just because I have delayed in visiting you until you were more at home here does not mean that I have not thought of you often," he said gently. "I will return soon, my dear." He was gone, his linen rustling, his body briefly shutting out the light.

I had a moment of overwhelming loneliness and discouragement. What if I progressed no farther in Ramses' favour? What if I was condemned to stay in this cell for the rest of my life? I would rather die than end my years like Hatia, drunk and ill, abandoned and forgotten by all. Fear swept me up in its dark wings and I laid my forehead on my knees.

Hunro's tentative hand on my shoulder brought me to myself. She studied me for a while then said, "It is not forbidden to leave the harem if we ask Amunnakht for permission and take guards with us. Such privileges are not usually granted so soon, and you have not been here long, but if you are with me I will guarantee to the Keeper that you will not run away. We will take a litter, and go into the city. Yes?"

"Oh yes!" I exclaimed, half-laughing, half-crying. "Oh, Hunro, what a wonderful idea!" She bade me get dressed and wait. She was gone for a long time, during which Disenk clothed and painted me, but when she returned she had two burly Shardana guards with her.

"The Keeper has allowed this," she said, "providing we return before sundown. The litter is waiting at the main gate. Are you ready?" Anticipation had edged out my fear. She reached for my hand and together we left the courtyard.

For several hours, in the close heat of the afternoon, our bearers carried us in a delightfully aimless manner through the maze of thoroughfares, crooked alleys, squares and markets of Pi-Ramses. We crossed vast avenues that led the eye to the pylons of temples and more modest paths thronged with barbarically clad foreigners, merchants and artisans, on their way to worship their own strange gods. With Disenk and Hunro's servant walking beside us and our guards shouldering a way ahead we negotiated roads choked with braying donkeys and barefooted citizens, creaking carts laden with earthen jars, mud bricks or precariously balanced tiles of brilliant hue from the glazing works. We halted by the markets, watching the dusty stall-keepers cry their wares to the passers-by. We even found our way to the docks where boats of every description rocked on the rising, brown surface of the Waters of Avaris to be loaded and unloaded by the sweating fellahin.

Once we happened upon a quiet corner where apple and pomegranate trees clustered together around a tiny shrine and a solitary pair of lovers sat in their shade, oblivious to us and the world around them. But such oases were rare. The city pulsed with vibrant, noisy life, with the heady, mixed odours of animal dung and dust and the faint but ever-present fragrance of the thousands of fruit trees, most of them hidden behind the orchard walls but whose essence pervaded the air around them.

Hunro and I stopped several times and sent the servants to buy rough cakes and greasy pastries from the street vendors, eating them with relish and licking our fingers as we lurched on, the sights and sounds of Pi-Ramses jostling by us while the guards called hoarsely, "Make way! Make way for the House of Women!" and Disenk's silver anklet with its little golden scarabs tinkled musically beside me, a sweet, delicate sound under the uproar around us.

We returned, exhausted and happy, to the haven of our cell just as Ra was westering. The harem was a peaceful sanctuary after the city's raw bluster. We lay out on the grass in the reddening light, drinking beer and gossiping, and I was able at last to tell Hunro of my nights with the King, for they had lost their power to shame me.

Chapter 15

The following night the royal summons came again and this time I did not try to control the King's lust. I did not enjoy the experience but neither was I repulsed by it, and afterwards I purposely made no attempt to leave. I could not hold him with sexual tricks alone, I knew. It was necessary to begin to reveal a little of myself, to give him another facet of my character. He had seen the physician, the virgin, the controlling seductress and in this I had followed the dictates of my mentor Hui and Hunro, my friend. Now I would embark upon other waters, alone. I would of course continue to enlarge upon the personalities I had constructed, or rather, that I had found within myself and enlarged, but I needed to begin to worm my way into his heart and mind, not just his loins. Therefore when we had finished making love I wrapped myself in a sheet and, refusing refreshment, sat cross-legged on the massive royal couch and talked to Ramses.

At first we chatted of small things—the continued rise of the river that would ensure a plentiful flood and a good harvest, my day in the city with Hunro, the faience factories that were attached to the rear of the palace and that brought merchants from all over the world to trade for Egyptian glass. I commented on the number of foreigners in Pi-Ramses, and Pharaoh, who had been settled comfortably in his chair and was picking over the food before him, said, "Your father is a foreigner, is he not? Some sort of foreign minor noble with an estate in the south somewhere?" I laughed.

"Majesty, my father fought in your father's wars and was rewarded with a veteran's portion of land in Aswat. He is Libu."

"Aswat?" Ramses echoed with a frown. His jewelled fingers paused, a sticky date halfway to his mouth. "Aswat? Where is that? Is it not a village buried on the edge of the desert somewhere?" Then his face cleared. "Wepwawet! Of course! But why would a nobleman, even a foreign one, require land? Had he none of his own?"

"None, Majesty." I hesitated, then decided to take the plunge. "My father is a peasant who works his own veteran's arouras. My mother is the village midwife."

"Really? Really!" The date was returned to the dish. Ramses gestured impatiently and a servant came forward noiselessly with a bowl of scented water and a cloth. The King dabbled his fingers and then held them out to be wiped. "You are a peasant, Thu? How extraordinary. I do have a few common concubines but they are all dancers or singers, I think. How did you come to be under Hui's care? But no." He left the chair and came to sit on the couch with me. Its frame groaned under his weight. "Tell me how my peasants live, Thu. Tell me what it was like to grow up in a village. I must say," he went on darkly, "that you do not resemble any coarse child of the earth that I have ever glimpsed. Still, I have many Libu administrators and servants in my employ and they are a handsome people. Have you sisters? Are they as striking to look at as you?"

So while he sipped intermittently at his wine and the night deepened I spoke of Aswat, of our modest home, of the mayor and his troublesome daughters, of the verges of the Nile where a dusty, half-naked child could find magic. I described the doughty, close-mouthed, pragmatic men who tilled their fields and worshipped their gods, made love to their wives and provided for their children. I spoke of Pa-ari, of my secret lessons, but I did not tell him of how Hui had come and how I had been prepared to trade my virginity for a chance to know my future. I touched on the villagers' reverence for the past, their fervent and innocent belief that the Living God could make all things right in the land, but I did not belabour the point.

While I was telling my stories with as much animation as I could, he kept his eyes on my face, nodding and grunting, occasionally smiling, once putting out a hand to caress my cheek. Then all at once he seemed to become aware of the guttering lamps, the smothered yawn of one of the anonymous servants, and raising a hand he halted my flow of words. I made as if to get off the couch and collect my sheath and sandals but he prevented me. Pulling away the sheet that had covered me he lay down, waving me peremptorily to lie beside him, and arranged the linen over both of us. "Paibekamun, dowse the lamps!" he commanded, then he dragged me close to him, curling around me. "Sleep, little Thu, my little desert waif," he murmured. "You are a wonder and a terror. There is no dishonesty in you, for you did not fear to reveal to me your baseborn origins. I am very pleased. Your skin still smells of saffron. I like that…" His voice died away and he began to breathe evenly. He had fallen asleep. Unbelievingly I realized that I was to stay for the night, that I would still be beside him in the morning. His body was warm and comforting. For a while I was uneasy in these still unfamiliar surroundings but gradually I succumbed to the animal contentment in which I lay and the dim room blurred and was gone. I slept.

The sounds of pipe and lute wafting muffled through the double doors woke me. At first I lay laxly in the dimness, thinking that Hui's feast had been going on for a long time, but then full consciousness returned and I sat up. A sweet young voice began to sing words of worship and adoration, "Hail Divine Incarnation, rising as Ra in the East! Hail Immortal One whose breath is the source of Egypt's life!"

and I realized with a jolt of awe and excitement that I was hearing the Hymn of Praise, the ancient chant that had roused each King every dawn since the beginning of history. I looked about me, at the man still snoring gently by my side, at the quiet shadows lying across the great room, at the still faint grey light pushing through the high, narrow windows and beginning to reveal the shapes of the elegant furniture standing arrogant and mute, and I relished the moment.

The Hymn ended. There was whispering and rustling beyond, and after a pause the doors were flung open. Hastily I pulled the sheet over my breasts. A small procession entered, servants bearing food and drink, warm water and cloths, and behind them a harp player took up his station in the corner and began to pluck his instrument. I stroked the Pharaoh's shoulder and kissed his ear. "It is morning, Majesty," I said. "I trust you rested well." He snorted, groaned, and his eyes flickered open. When he saw me there was surprise, but then he smiled quickly, broadly, like a delighted child, and pulling me down he blew into my neck before hoisting himself up and allowing his servant to wipe his face with the scented water.

"What a wonderful dream I had!" he exclaimed, watching expectantly as a tray was lowered onto his lap. "I was plunging into the Nile and it was good, cool and cleansing. You brought me a propitious omen, little scorpion, for such a dream means the absolution of all ills. Eat now. Eat!" I hesitated, but because I was ravenously hungry and thirsty, I decided to disregard the warnings I had been given. I began to tear at the fresh bread, washing it down with a draught of water. The servants had withdrawn to a polite distance, but when we had finished the meal they began to hover. Ramses eyed me mischievously. "I would like to make love to you again," he whispered, "but these donkeys are waiting to carry me off to my bath. I am going into the temple in person this morning to perform the sacred duties I usually leave to my substitute." He sighed loudly. "Now that the Amun-feast of Hapi is over Usermaarenakht will be returning to Thebes. He will of course wish to make sure that all is decently in order here before he goes. Usermaarenakht!" he said impatiently at my enquiring look. "The First Prophet of Amun! Gods, child, are all the denizens of Aswat as ignorant as you?" The thought of Amun's High Priest seemed to have upset him so I remained silent. When he did not speak again, but signalled for the dishes to be removed and held out his feet so that his sandals could be slipped on, I left the couch and shrugged into my cloak. My actions caught his attention. "Where are you going?" he asked sharply. I bowed.

"To my quarters, Majesty." He blinked rapidly several times and then that startlingly impish, merry smile beamed out.

"I like your company," he announced. "Go away and bathe and I will send for you so that you can come into the temple with me. Hurry up!" I bowed again and did as I was told, speeding through the dawn-drowsy gardens and across the path dividing the harem from the palace, and so into my own courtyard. I debated whether or not to exercise and decided against it. I must be ready when the summons came.

Disenk was not in my room and Hunro was still asleep, a motionless mound of rumpled sheets. I sent a runner for my body servant, and while I waited for her I paced the damp grass outside, alone in all that vast space, while the sky above the building turned from pale pink to a delicate blue and the air heated suddenly and became filled with the odour of unseen blossoms. At last I was to see Hui's enemy, Egypt's curse, Pharaoh's bane, the High Priest of Amun, yet my heartbeat was strong and steady and my mind calm. Lifting my arms and my face to the new day I smiled into the limitless expanse of blue. All was unfolding as Hui had said.

Bathed, perfumed, painted and clothed in transparent white linen embroidered with red flowers, I was ready for the palace servant who came to escort me to Ramses. My mouth gleamed with red ochre. My heavy wig of a hundred braids framed my kohled face and rested stiffly against my draped shoulders. Gold bands enamelled in crimson embraced my wrists and imprisoned my neck. I was beautiful, and I knew it. Proudly I swayed after the man who led me out the front entrance of the harem, Disenk behind me.

Several litters were assembled there, surrounded by a glittering, restless crowd of women and servants, all chattering in high-pitched voices as the morning breeze, not yet staled, plucked at their expensive linens and lifted the tresses of their elaborate wigs. Palace and harem guards waited on the perimeter, dappled in the tossing shade of the trees. I was taken aback. I had conceived the notion that Ramses and I would go to the temple together in a pleasant intimacy, but it seemed that half the harem had shared the invitation I had thought was extended to me alone. I looked for the Lady of the Two Lands but could not see her. "Where is Ast?" I muttered to Disenk.

"She will have left already," Disenk murmured back. "The Great Queen does not wait about with concubines."

"And who is that?" I pointed surreptitiously to a woman who was sitting on a stool on the verge and watching the confusion with lofty indifference. Several guards clustered near her and four servants were laden down with what appeared to be her cloak, cosmetic box, sweetmeat container and other things. It was difficult to judge her age or her nationality from where I was standing, but her skin was very sallow and I could tell that the thick, winged eyebrows had not been kohled. Their blackness was natural.

"That is the Great Wife Ast-Amasareth," Disenk answered softly. "I think you know of her. Pharaoh values her above all his other wives. She is very wise." Is she indeed? I thought cynically, looking her over. She must have sensed my scrutiny for her raven's eyes swivelled in my direction and fastened on me. Then one hand was regally lifted. One jewelled finger crooked at me. The gesture was imperious and unmistakeable. I threaded my way through the crowd, and coming up to her I bowed. She regarded me steadily for a moment, then she said, "You are the concubine Thu. You spent the night with Ramses. I am Great Wife Ast-Amasareth." Her tones were deep for a woman, imbued with a slight but musical accent that sounded familiar. My father's words had just such a twist but gentler, less obvious. I remembered that she had been a prisoner of war, brought back to Egypt from Libu.

Boldly I studied her. Only her eyes were beautiful, large and lustrous. Her skin was too olive, her nose too small, her mouth uneven. Yet the impression given by the whole was one of intelligence and magnetism. She met my gaze coolly until I felt suddenly impudent and lowered my eyes.

"News travels with amazing speed in this place, Great Wife," I answered her. "I was indeed honoured with a whole night on Ramses' couch." There was a pause before she spoke again.

"A night of lovemaking is one thing," she said smoothly. "A night of sleep with Pharaoh is quite another. Do you see the girl to your left, even now getting into her litter?" Surprised, I turned. A pretty young woman, far gone in pregnancy, was lowering herself with some difficulty onto the cushions and scolding the servant who was assisting her as she did so. "That is Eben, Pharaoh's favourite concubine," the husky voice went on. "Her star is fading and she knows it. The child will not save her, indeed, as a mother she will have lost all intrigue for the King. I reside above Queen Ast. Come and visit me." She waved me away and I saw that a litter had arrived beside her. I retreated. With supreme dignity she rose and settled herself gracefully inside it while her entourage sprang to surround her. She twitched the curtains closed without another glance at me. I rejoined Disenk. A procession of litters was forming and the group was thinning. I moved towards an empty one.

"Eben," I said to Disenk as we walked. "A foreign name." Disenk sniffed.

"Her mother is Maxyes or Peleset, I forget which," she commented disdainfully, "and her father is a palace guard. She is common and brainless." I scrambled onto the litter.

"You did not tell me about her." Disenk looked down on me with an expression of distaste.

"She is beneath your consideration."

I wondered, as I was lifted and we set off, whether Disenk regarded me secretly with the same contempt since my background was similar to the unfortunate Eben's. I hoped not, but then decided that I did not care. Much as I liked her, the opinion of a servant was becoming less and less important to me.

We were carried through the city, a cavalcade of colourful privilege, while the Herald called a warning and the guards cleared a way for us, and we alighted at the far end of the vast paved concourse that lay before Amun's mighty first pylon. The sphinx-lined square was black with people craning to catch a glimpse of Pharaoh. As I stood and looked about I saw him and drew in a quick breath.

Surrounded by his ministers and acolytes he was about to enter the temple. Ast was beside him, a tiny, glittering vision of blood and precedent, but my glance did not rest on her. It became fixed on Ramses. In the relative privacy of the royal bedchamber I was slowly becoming used to the mountain of distasteful flesh that encased him. Its weight and feel, though no longer repulsive, could not yet be disregarded as I hoped it would with the passage of time. But here, in the shimmering, merciless glare of light reflecting off the white surface of the concourse, it was transformed into the physical manifestation of kingly power. Regal and imposing, the huge body radiated the authority of a god. He was clad in a pleated knee-length kilt, its triangular starched apron encrusted with carnelian scarabs that glinted dully as he moved. From his belt hung the bull's tail, curving over his ample buttocks and brushing the ground, a reminder of his uniqueness as the Mighty Bull of Ma'at. His massive chest was almost invisible under a great pectoral of blue and green faience ankhs held towards his face by kneeling god-desses of gold. Gold gripped his arms, the wide bracelets mounding the skin, and jasper ankhs on spears of gold hung from his ears. On his head was the khepresh crown, the rich, dark blue of its lapis curves emphasized by the dozens of golden studs that covered it. Above his high-forehead the royal serpent Uraeus reared, Wazt, Lady of Spells, prepared to spit venom at any who approached with treason in their hearts. I saw his chubby hand, now transformed into a sym-bol of perfect pharaonic command, on fire with jewels as it rose and gestured imperiously. A horn blared. The divine pair moved in under the pylon and out of my sight.

I felt very small and insignificant as I joined the select crowd who followed after, passing my sandals to Disenk before the holy precinct enveloped me. The floor of the outer court was warm and gritty under the soles of my feet. My lover is a god, I thought distinctly, with surprise, as if the knowledge was coming to me for the first time. My lover is divine omnipotence. Who then am I, with my insulting, secret contempt for him, my sacrilegious, private belittling of his shortcomings? My presumptuous judge-ments were worth less than nothing, the tiny bleat of an anonymous mouse in the granaries of my lord. Humbled, I went through the customary obeisances and prayers while the doors to the roofed inner court were opened and Ramses and Ast approached the sanctuary. But my fervent reflec-tions ceased as a group of men came out from behind one of the vast pillars and joined the King.

The High Priest and First Prophet of Amun, Usermaarenakht, was easy to recognize, but not because he resembled the cunning embodiment of evil I had built up in my mind. In fact he was disappointingly ordinary to look at, just a middle-aged man of pleasant face and dignified bearing, a shaft of sunlight from one of the clerestory windows striking his shaven skull and making his spotless priestly linen glow. He wore the distinctive mark of Amun's Chief Prophet, the leopard skin, which clung to his back, its paws clutching his shoulders, its head lolling lifelessly on his right breast. To me it seemed as though the creature had him in its control. Its embrace was greedy, predatory. His companions were obviously the Second and Third Prophets, with their similarly closely shaved heads, their sashes of sacerdotal office and their white staffs. The High Priest bowed, somewhat perfunctorily I thought, to Ramses, and opened the sanctuary doors. A gush of fragrant incense poured out and I caught a brief glimpse of the God seated on his granite throne, his body encased in gold, his double plumes rising high above his noble brow, before Pharaoh and Usermaarenakht went in and the doors were quickly closed behind them. A chair was brought for Queen Ast. Chanting began, and dancers with systra tinkling in their hands filed into the inner court.

I looked about for Ast-Amasareth but saw Eben instead. The girl was leaning against a servant, her hands under her large belly, her expression strained. Sweat had beaded in her cleavage. I looked away with uncharacteristic pity, suddenly and fervently glad that our positions were not reversed. Ast-Amasareth's words came back to me and I vowed that I would do my best not to become pregnant with Ramses' child. Under no circumstances would I give the King an excuse to supplant me.

Whatever rites the King was performing took a very long

time and I was both bored and very thirsty by the time the horns barked again and he reappeared. As he paused for the Lady of the Two Lands to compose herself at his elbow, his kohled eyes travelled the company and came to rest on me. His hennaed lips curved in an unselfconscious smile. Ast had followed his gaze. I saw no recognition on her face but the dainty features settled into a mask of dislike. She whispered something to Ramses that wiped the smile from his face and together they processed out into the glare of the day and the roaring horde of expectant city-dwellers.

I had presumed to spend the rest of the day in my own quarters but a Herald accosted me as I left my litter and was walking under the leafy shade of the clustering trees to the entrance of the harem.

"Concubine Thu," he said without preamble. "Pharaoh has commanded your presence at his feast this evening to honour the departing High Priest of Amun. Prepare yourself accordingly. You will be summoned at sundown." He turned on his heel with the arrogance of all Heralds, who spend their lives conveying the orders of others, and I swung excitedly to Disenk.

"I must have something new to wear, something startling," I said as we passed the harem guards and paced the narrow, walled-in path to our courtyard. "I do not want to be elegant, Disenk, I want to be noticed!" Her tight little nostrils pinched.

"Elegance is to be preferred," she said firmly. "You do not want to cause the attention given to a common dancer or a superior whore. We may do something different with the cosmetics, Thu, but I strongly advise a decorous mode of dress." She was right of course. My plans did not include finding myself immobilized in the futureless mode of such women. Therefore at sunset I was waiting in my cell, garbed in a white, gold-bordered sheath with a high neckline and broad shoulder straps. One necklace lay against my collar-bone and

in its centre was one finely wrought likeness of the goddess
Hathor with her benignly smiling face and gentle cow's
horns curving towards my throat. One bracelet encircled my
wrist. One scarab ring sat on my right hand. The wig that
touched my shoulders was straight and very simple. The circlet cutting across my forehead held no adornment at all.
But above the thick black kohl around my eyes Disenk had
painted my eyelids with gold and sprinkled them with gold
dust. The lobes of my ears were also gold, and though my
palms and the soles of my feet were hennaed, my mouth felt
heavy with more gold. Gold dust clung to my arms, my feet,
the hollow of my throat, where the saffron-scented oil
gripped it, so that when I came at last to look myself up and
down in the copper mirror the effect was remarkable. My
clothing was as modest as could be, yet my face and body
glittered tauntingly with the promise of something exotic,
mysterious, subtly sexual.

I thanked my magician profusely, tasting the metallic
strangeness of the gold on my lips, and she smiled coolly and
nodded. She was to accompany me to taste my food and
drink and serve me, and for that I was relieved. I was feeling
once again the momentousness of an occasion I saw as yet
another test and I wondered whether the whole of my life
would be like this, one new experience to be conquered
after another. Inwardly I blessed Hui for providing me with
the accoutrements I needed and I wished for a fleeting
moment that I was going to enter Pharaoh's banqueting hall
on his firm, slightly daunting arm.

As it was, I went in alone but for Disenk, and was initially
unnoticed. When the summons came, we had followed the
servant back through the entrance to the harem in a sweet,
warm dusk, cutting across the soft grass to join the main
paved way to the palace entrance. It was swarming with
guards and guests and we were challenged then allowed to
pass. The mighty entrance hall had doors in its right-hand

wall and we drifted through them with the throng. The roar of excited voices rose to a din. I found myself in a room so vast that the ceiling was a mere suggestion, so wide that I could barely make out the row of pillars at the far end through which the night breeze was sending puffs of welcome freshness. Hundreds of people milled about, their gossamer linens brushing the garlands of dewy flowers lying on the low dining tables set ready for them. Young servants clad in loincloths slipped among them like sinuous eels, offering necklaces of woven flowers, cones of perfumed grease to be tied on top of their wigs, and cups of wine. One approached me and bowed. I allowed him to attach a cone above my head, and as I was reaching for wine a palace Herald interposed himself between us and nodded briefly. "Concubine Thu?" I returned his nod. "I will show you to your table. Follow please." To my surprise and delight I had been accorded a place right at the foot of the raised dais where the royal family would dine. "This is very good," Disenk said complacently as I tried to keep my balance in the crush of hot, anticipant bodies. "Very good indeed. You will be in Pharaoh's line of vision all night."

"Doubtless he did not plan it that way," I murmured back sarcastically, then gripped her hand as a blare of discordant horns sounded with sudden violence. At once a silence fell. The Chief Herald stepped out from the shadows to the left of the dais. His staff thudded against the floor three times and his chest swelled. "Ramses User-Ma'at-Ra Meri-Amun, Heq-On, Lord of Tanis, Great One of Kings, Mighty Bull, Stabiliser of the Lands, Lord of the Shrines of Nekhbet and Uarchet, the Horus of Gold, Victor over the Sati, Subduer of the Libu..." His sonorous voice boomed on, reeling out my lover's titles. I relinquished Disenk's palm, dry and cool, of course, although the banqueting hall was stuffy and breathlessly close, and wound my fingers together tensely.

Pharaoh strode across the dais. He had discarded the kilt

in favour of a long and flowing white tunic embroidered thickly in silver ankhs that swirled about his jewelled ankles. Behind him came Ast, tiny and doll-like, her many gems now glowing dully in the torch and candle light.

Then I felt the blood fill my face, for Ramses the Prince walked after his mother, kilted and bare-legged, his glorious face framed in a white linen helmet whose wings kissed the alluring curve of his collar-bones. His fine kohled eyes flickered dismissively over the crowded hall as he settled himself onto the cushions at his table but he glanced up and lifted a helping hand to the woman who was sinking beside him. I judged her to be in her late twenties, a slim, vigorous creature with the classical features of the goddess Hathor one saw on temple reliefs, and Hathor's warmly curving lips. "His wife, the Princess Neferu," Disenk whispered, seeing the direction of my gaze. Naturally, I thought with a surge of bitter jealousy. A classic Egyptian beauty with a classic Egyptian name. Pure, ancient blood. Nothing less for our Prince. Then I was ashamed, for she divined the intentness of my scrutiny and gave me a fleeting smile. The High Priest of Amun had brought up the rear of the small procession and the echoes of the Herald's voice were dying away, lost in the invisible gloom of the high ceiling. With a rustle the guests came to life and conversations broke out again.

I lowered myself onto my cushions, Disenk at my knee, and as I did so I realized that I had no interest in Usermaarenakht or his power or his pernicious influence on Pharaoh. I did not really care in what priestly snare my King struggled. Hui's all-consuming obsession, cold and crippling, held no fascination for me after all. Perhaps it never had. Perhaps I had been flattered by his insistence that only I could save my country, but the idea seemed idiotic now. I was a girl lost in the magnificence of a dream, afloat on an ocean of absorbing fantasy. With all my senses I inhaled my surroundings: the noisy confusion of voices and laughter;

the play of yellow light on a myriad of jewels that twinkled in a constant swirl of colours; the flutter and sway of rich linens; the soft glow of kohled eyes and hennaed mouths; the tantalizing odours emanating from the steaming, laden trays of food the servants were bringing, held high over their ribboned heads; and under and over and through it all, weaving mysteriously and quietly, the unremarked but seductive breath of Shu, god of the air, blowing from the night world beyond.

There were little loaves of bread shaped like frogs, and salty butter and brown, tangy goat cheese. There was quail stuffed with figs and smothered in cucumbers and onions. There were lotus seeds drenched in purple juniper oil and roots of wild sedge crusty with coriander and cumin. Delicate lettuce leaves curled around fronds of parsley and thin spears of celery. Honey and shat cakes abounded, and the wine was sweetened with dates. I had never eaten fare like this before. Disenk, unperturbed, ceremoniously tasted each dish before I placed anything on my tongue, and sipped judiciously at the wine before it slid, red and smooth, down my throat.

The cacophony in the hall increased as the evening progressed. When I had glutted myself and an unobtrusive servant had removed my table, I reclined on one elbow and watched the dais. Pharaoh was deep in conversation with the First Prophet, leaning across his wife who was daintily picking her teeth while her body servant replaced the cone on her head. The Prince's cone had also shrunk, the melting oil having trickled in a golden stream down his neck and between his hennaed nipples to disappear where the table shadowed his tight belly. His wife had placed a hand on his arm and was leaning close to him, saying something that made him smile and turn to her quickly.

I looked away, only to find Ast-Amasareth's eyes fixed on me expressionlessly. Her elbows were resting among the wilting flowers on her table and her ringed fingers were folded under her chin. There was nothing drunken in her steady regard, and after staring back at her I nodded. Coolly she returned the gesture.

I felt someone's hip slide down beside mine and swung round to find Hunro, cup in hand, grinning at me. "You look like an exotic foreign goddess," she said. "Are you enjoying yourself, Thu? Soon the dancers will appear and I shall join them. There is a troop of acrobats from Keftiu also, and a fire eater." She drank and then signalled for the cup to be refilled. "Everyone has noticed Ast-Amasareth's attention fixed on you tonight," she went on in a low, teasing voice. "Everyone has been taking a good look at you, including Paiis, but as he is here with someone else's wife and as you belong to Pharaoh he can only lust after you from afar." She threw back her head and laughed.

There was a crash of cymbals, a patter of light, bare feet, and six dancers ran onto the cleared space in front of the dais. The women were naked, with long black hair that almost brushed their heels. The men were clad in loincloths and had bells around their ankles. Hunro kissed my cheek and rose to greet them and there was a roar from the crowd as she was recognized. Pharaoh waved at her. Even Ast smiled faintly. Drums began to thud out an hypnotic beat and I saw Hunro's eyes slide lazily shut as her feet found the rhythm.

I too closed my eyes. I did not need to see the slow contortions of the dancers' bodies to be drawn into the sensuality of the moment. The reverberation of the drums, the wail of the pipes, the frenzied clapping that kept time to the music, surrounded and penetrated me with a completely physical exultation. For a long time I let it carry me, and then the music changed, the cymbals clashed again, and I opened my eyes to see the dancers disappear and the acrobats come tumbling out.

Prince Ramses had disappeared also, and it was as though the night had come to an abrupt end for me. Ast was yawning behind her hand. Pharaoh was still deep in conversation with the High Priest who had left his cushions and was seated in a huddle beside the King. The guests were screaming their appreciation of the entertainment, their faces flushed with wine, their linens dishevelled, and all at once I felt entirely sober and distanced from the happy stridency around me. I rose a little stiffly and Disenk immediately followed suit but I hardly noticed her as she tugged at my arm. "Thu, we may not leave before the King!" she admonished me. I ignored her and slipped through the swaying bodies, needing the coolness of fresh air on my face. Reaching the mighty pillars through which the night seeped, I passed between them and the guards did not stop me. Pausing on the path I reached up and removed the perfume cone from my head, and rubbing the remaining oil over my arms I let it fall, and looked about me.

The sky was black but ablaze with dustings of stars, and low on the horizon a pale crescent moon lay on its back above the dark bulk of a high wall a long way away. Between the wall and me the blurred masses of thickly clustering trees quivered restlessly, their trunks tall and indistinct, and I could hear the steady music of a fountain somewhere ahead.

Hot and tired I left the paving, and stepping onto the cool grass I began to move towards the sound. I knew that Disenk was following, but in the receding cacophony of the banqueting hall and the enveloping hush of the garden I could not discern her footfalls. Before long I came in sight of the fountain, a column of fluid crystal falling ceaselessly into its wide limestone basin. "Wait here," I ordered Disenk. "I need to drink." Going forward I approached the water, and leaning in and cupping my hands I interrupted the turbulent flow. I drank thirstily then dribbled the water down my neck and over my breasts.

I was just shaking the droplets from my fingers when I caught a movement out of the corner of my eye. Someone else was here, a dark shape on the other side of the glittering spout. It stirred, rose, and came towards me. Prince Ramses stepped out of the shadows. In momentary confusion I turned as if to flee, but it was too late. "It is the little physician, the latest harem acquisition, is it not?" he said. "What are you doing out here alone?" His tone was sharp, and as I performed a hurried obeisance and collected my thoughts I suddenly realized why. I straightened with a smile.

"No, Prince, I am not here for a clandestine assignation," I replied. "My servant waits over there. I am on my way back to my own quarters." He came closer, placing one foot on the rim of the basin and loosely linking his hands.

"It was hot in the hall, and the entertainment bores me," he went on. "I have seen it all before. Besides, I do not like to sit there and watch my father grovel before lesser men."

His words shocked me. Had he spoken them as if to himself, musing, because I was nothing more to him than the whispering trees or the shrouded flower beds that surrounded us? They contravened everything I had believed regarding the rigid code of loyalty by which the members of the immediate royal family lived. I stared at him, the last of the wine fumes dissipating. His kilt and linen helmet were smudges of grey in the dimness and his face was darkly indistinct. The oil that bedewed his body glistened dully in the starlight.

I did not want to speak up on behalf of Hui, not after the splendour-filled hours I had just dreamed through. I wanted to continue to float on a cloud of fantasy. But such an opportunity would not come again. Gathering up my native courage I said hesitantly, "I suppose that you are referring to the High Priest of Amun, Highness. I have heard that he commands while the Good God rules. It is a rumour that distresses many."

For the first time I felt his attention become abruptly, completely, fixed on me. With a tiny grinding sound his foot left the stone of the basin and he took two swift steps. Now I could see his eyes, dusky yet reflecting the silver of the stars as they scanned me keenly.

"Is that so?" he murmured. "Is it indeed? How many does it distress, I wonder? Are you one of them, my little concubine?" He put one finger under my chin, lifting my face towards what light there was. I wanted to turn and press my lips into his palm. I met his exploration without flinching, deliberately storing up the feel of his skin against mine, the warmth of his breath across my cheeks and mouth, the sight of his features so breathtakingly close. The constant ululation of the falling water was all at once very loud in the moment of stillness while he studied me. "You really are quite beautiful," he said at last. "And intelligent too, or so my father says. Such a combination is not always a good thing, Physician Thu, but then what does it matter when you are one woman among a thousand, eh?" He smiled, revealing his even white teeth, and bent his head lower. For one glorious second I thought he was going to kiss me, and panic, desire and prudence fought for control within me. But he only repeated his question. "Do such rumours distress you, Thu?" I was sure that he was aware of the tiny movement into him my body made, the lightning betrayal of my craving for his perfect body. Politely I pulled away from his grasp and bowed.

"The harem is always full of rumours, Highness," I answered. "Most of them do not merit serious consideration. But the Living God is Amun's incarnation here on earth and it is a distortion of Ma'at that a mere priest should have ascendancy over the Divine. If he does."

"Well said!" Ramses commented drily. "You should be elevated to Egypt's diplomatic corps, for your words are clever and yet tactful. Physician, talented concubine and now amateur official of the Double Crown. What next, I wonder?" His tone was sarcastic and my damnably fiery temper flared at it.

"I am a loyal Egyptian, Highness!" I snapped. "One among many who abhor the stranglehold the priesthood has on this country. And judging by your words a short time ago you are one of them, are you not?" I could have bitten off my tongue as soon as I heard what I had said but it was too late. Ramses was tugging at one of the wings of his helmet, eyes narrowed, seemingly unperturbed by my outburst. When he spoke it was with a smooth scorn.

"The fellahin in the fields are also loyal Egyptians," he said evenly, "but their opinions on the subtleties of government are about as sophisticated as the baying of desert dogs under the moon. Likewise the opinions of foolish young harem inmates. I strongly advise you to keep yours to yourself, Thu, and do your best to remember your station." Now a note of humour had crept into his voice. "If you can, of course, which is doubtful."

"But you started it!" I almost shouted at him in frustration, sounding very much like the baying desert dog of his analogy. My fists were clenched. "Change my opinion, Highness! Inform me on the subtleties of government!" He regarded me critically but another smile hovered around his mouth.

"I begin to see why my father is becoming besotted with you," he said. "Take my advice. Use your energies to become a good and loyal concubine, and leave weightier matters to your superiors. Love my father. He deserves this." I opened my mouth to answer but he raised an imperious hand. "You have gone far enough. Sleep well." Rounding on his heel he strode away and was soon lost in the gentle night before I could do him the customary reverence.

I sank onto the edge of the fountain and ground my teeth, maddened now by its stupid, interminable patter, lust and rage and admiration and humiliation churning inside me. Well, at least he will never again look through me, I told myself furiously. I can only hope that he does not take my foolish comments seriously.

But then, as I regained control of myself and began to walk back to where Disenk waited patiently, I knew that above all men I wanted Prince Ramses to think of me, to remember my words and how I said them, to ponder the sight of my face under the starlight and how my chin had felt under his hand. It does no harm to have a second arrow ready to fit to my bow if the first goes awry, I thought, as the path came into view and Disenk detached herself from the shadows. Perhaps I can gain the Prince's respect if Pharaoh tires of me. I was turning the matter over in my mind as Disenk and I crossed the vast concourse before the main entrance to the palace, now dotted with litters and guards and sleepy, grumbling guests, and veered towards the harem entrance.

Just before answering the harem guards' challenge I glanced back. Ast-Amasareth, a ghostly presence, was watching me from the murky grove of trees. Quickly I passed out of her vision but my spine was prickling as I came to the safety of my own courtyard. The power that the Great Royal Wife could project was considerable and I wondered fleetingly if she was a practitioner of magic. Probably. She was a mysterious and troubling woman.

Chapter 16

Ast-Amasareth sent for me the following noon. I had eaten some fruit and bread in the gloom of my cell with the door closed against the noise of the children outside, had Disenk apply my face paint, and was standing with my arms over my head so that she could pull a sheath down over my body when the Queen's emissary arrived. I emerged from the linen to see him staring at me curiously. "Concubine Thu?" he said. "The Chief Wife invites you to her quarters. I will escort you there." I nodded and Disenk, fastening a collar of enamelled flowers around my neck, took the opportunity to whisper, "Eat and drink nothing, Thu! Remember!" I touched her shoulder in response. She slipped on my sandals and I signalled to the man, following him across the child- and toy-littered grass.

We left the courtyard, turned right along the narrow path, and then right again at the entrance from which I had seen Ast, the Lady of the Two Lands, emerge with her son some time ago. A guard rose from his seat, saluted my guide, and we passed along a short passage open to the sky. Ahead were heavy cedar doors traced in silver, both firmly closed. Before we reached them we turned sharply left and I found myself bathed once more in sunshine. This courtyard was blessedly silent but for the slight rustle of a hot breeze in the spreading trees that surrounded a large central pond. The fountain here was smaller, more ornate than the one whose murmur filled my dreams, a shower of water not intended for the distraction of restless children but for the soothing of royal kas.

The wall surrounding the whole was carved in huge reliefs depicting Pharaoh seated in the Double Crown, receiving the symbol of life from Amun and dishes of delicacies from his adoring wives. The glyphs, those I could read as I passed under the dappled shade of the pomegranate and sycamore fig trees, wished His Majesty life, prosperity and happiness for millions of years. The servant led me up a flight of stairs that clung to the inner wall, across a short, girded landing, and straight into a large reception room through which a cool wind was blowing.

The Chief Wife was seated in a low chair before a table, one hand in the grasp of a servant girl who was kneading fragrant oil into the long fingers. At the far end of the room, a square opening gave me a glimpse into another room where a large couch stood, draped in fine linen and scattered with red cushions. Beside the Chief Wife's ebony chair reared a graceful lamp stand in the likeness of a young Nubian boy kneeling with the lamp itself fixed to his shoulders. A cosmetic table littered with pots and brushes took up a portion of the nearer wall. There were tiring chests, a scoured brazier, a small shrine, all the expected furnishings of a great lady's abode, yet the impression was one of austerity and restrained taste. A rectangle of brilliant white light cast from one of the high windows fell across a scarlet cloak flung over another chair. Its barbaric, lusty shimmer seemed at variance with the subdued atmosphere around it and made me slightly uneasy.

But the man was announcing me. "It is the concubine Thu, Majesty." Ast-Amasareth, withdrawing her hand from her servant's reverent clutches, waved me forward. Majesty, I thought as my arms went out and I lowered my head in respectful greeting. Of course she is. A legitimate wife and a Queen. Do not forget it, Thu my girl!

"Come and sit," the voice like slithering gravel mixed with honey commanded. "Take the stool. If a child like you can be said to look tired, then you look tired under your facepaint. Did you enjoy the festivities last night?" I lowered myself onto the rush weaving of the stool and swiftly studied her. No, she was not beautiful. Her nose really was too small and I noticed that her teeth, as she spoke, were as uneven as her oddly twisted mouth. The henna she used on her lips was a richer, deeper colour than usual, as though she had decided to brazenly emphasize one of her defects. Instead of repulsing it served to increase her strange attraction. I shifted my gaze to her undeniably gorgeous eyes and smiled politely.

"I enjoyed them very much, Majesty. Such occasions are new to me."

"Indeed." The servant was now pushing rings onto the graceful fingers. When she had finished she bowed and began to pour wine into two goblets. Ast-Amasareth made no move to pick up her cup. "I daresay that in time the novelty of Pharaoh's feasts will wear off and you will become as jaded with them as our handsome Prince." She was watching me carefully. "He can be counted upon to disappear at some point during the entertainments, only to be found by his guards communing with the moon in some secluded spot. By the fountain perhaps." She smiled faintly, her mouth distorting. Now it was my turn to say, "Indeed," and nod sagely, but everything in me was tensing. Hui had told me that the Chief Wife was wise. She was cunning also. Such a woman would not expect to cling to power only through her ability to mesmerize Pharaoh. It had not occurred to me before, but certainly she had a net of spies throughout the palace and the harem. I had come under her speculating eye. Someone had been set to watch me, had seen me with Ramses. It did not matter now, for I was no threat to a Queen, but perhaps in the future I might be forced to fight fire with fire. Whom, besides Disenk and Hunro, could I trust? I forced a laugh.

"That is exactly where I found him last night!" I exclaimed. "I was returning to my quarters and detoured to the fountain for a drink. He addressed me and favoured me with a few words. He is a gracious Prince and a fitting Heir to the Horus Throne." Ast-Amasareth's smile widened over the jumbled teeth.

"Oh, but he has not yet been designated Heir," she said. "Pharaoh has many sons and spends much time agonizing over the succession but he cannot decide who is most fitting. Besides, he fears a fatal challenge from whomever he ultimately chooses. Young blood runs hot and reckless in young men, dear Thu, as I am sure you must know, and our King does right to dread a knife in the back from an ungrateful son who feels that his father's usefulness is over." Languidly she pushed a cup towards me but I was only vaguely aware of the gesture.

"I cannot imagine Prince Ramses capable of such perfidy," I said slowly. "He is a good son, angry on his father's behalf at the deference the Living God is forced to pay to the High Priest of Amun. He told me so himself."

"Did he?" The Chief Wife's voice had become a sympathetic purr. "But perhaps the Prince is jealous of the attention his pious father pays to the servants of the God. Perhaps he is burning to be designated Egypt's Heir and they advise another. Perhaps his anger is not so pure." I saw the trap in time and managed to swallow the fiery retort that was already burning my throat.

"It may be so," I replied. "In any case, such matters are too high for me. My task is to please the King and mind my own business." At that she chuckled and flicked a hand impatiently at the wine.

"You are not the first female to have her head turned by the Prince's virile beauty," she said straightforwardly. "He does venture into amorous fields from time to time but he prefers his wife's bed and he would not, of course, risk his father's extreme displeasure by copulating with a royal concubine no matter how lovely." Her knowing eyes brushed mine, held, wandered away. "Drink, my dear, and appease your appetite with a morsel or two." I shook my head.

"Thank you, Majesty, but no. I rose late and have only just broken my fast." She looked at me shrewdly, picked up her cup, sipped, then set it back on the table.

"There!" she said. "The wine was poured in your sight from one jug. I have sampled it and am I not still smiling, foolish one?" Oh gods, I thought resignedly. There is no hiding from this woman.

"Majesty," I sighed, "at the risk of incurring your wrath I must say that I am a physician. I know full well that there are poisons which can be taken in tiny amounts and do no harm but when drained will kill. Such a poison might work slowly in your body and cause you a trifling discomfort hours from now when I am lying dead. Forgive me." Ast-Amasareth's lids lowered slowly over her dark eyes, then lifted again. She wet her lips reflectively and sat back, crossing one well-oiled leg over the other.

"My dear, my very dear Thu," she said wearily. "In the first place you greatly overestimate your importance. At the moment you are high in Pharaoh's favour but that favour does not extend beyond his bedchamber. In the corridors of state power you are nothing, and it is those corridors that I walk with His Majesty. Why, then, would I take the trouble to poison you? In the second place, I do not wish to spoil his pleasure or have you replaced with someone who will not keep him so amenable. A satisfied man is a happy man. Do we understand one another?" I swallowed. My throat was parched, burning with more than thirst. Her cool, veiled insult, her succinct, pitiless assessment of my position, had gone straight to the target of my pride.

"Perfectly, Majesty," I managed with laudable steadiness. "However, Your Majesty will forgive me if I still decline your offer of refreshment."

She inclined her head as if expecting such a reply, drank deeply, leaned forward to finger the sweetmeats on the plate before her, then said, "You come from the home of Hui the Seer I believe. He is a strange man. Tell me how you came to be under his roof." I relaxed a little then and recounted the story I had already told Pharaoh, omitting the things I felt might be used against me. The Chief Wife listened with interest, and when I had finished she regarded me silently for a long time during which I became aware of the complete hush in which we sat. No outside sound disturbed these quarters. After my small cell in the turbulent concubines' block it was a welcome quiet.

At last she said calmly, "There are rumours in the city that the Seer secretly pits his great powers against the priesthood of Amun and gathers about him those men who dream treason." My gaze flew to hers. Shock raced up and down my spine, and all at once the hush became a smothering blanket and I had to fight to breathe. Surely Ast-Amasareth was a witch! I forced my eyebrows upward.

"I know nothing of such a thing, Majesty," I responded with as much indignation as I could muster. "The Seer is a kind man who is dedicated to his medicines and his visions. Such rumours are surely the idle words of lesser men, for is my mentor not dedicated to Pharaoh's welfare and the welfare of his family?" Ast-Amasareth held up an impatient hand.

"Very well! Very well! Your own loyalty does you credit! Let us say no more on the matter." The hand made a brushing motion. "You may leave me now, Thu. You are more astute than your age and demeanour suggest, therefore I warn you to guard your tongue and let your ambitions extend no further than the warmth of Pharaoh's bed. You are dismissed." I rose at once, made my obeisance, and backed to the door, uncomfortably aware that she was watching my every move closely. It was with great relief that I was able to turn my back on her at last and follow the waiting servant down the stairs and across the still-deserted garden. I felt as though a giant had lifted me, shaken me, and set me down roughly so that everything in me rattled.

But one thing was clear. I would not allow Ast-Amasareth to get in my way. So far I had merely aroused her fleeting interest. I was safe for a while. But later, what then? What resources could I call upon that would come close to equalling the power she wielded? Only the protection of Pharaoh and the contents of my herb chest.

The courtyard was almost empty as I turned towards my cell. The women and children had dispersed for the afternoon sleep. Shedding my sheath at my door I ran onto the grass and began the exercises I had neglected of late, my body demanding to reflect the agitation of my mind, and soon the anger and fear oozed out of my pores with my sweat and were gone. I could not afford to dwell on either emotion, or I was lost.

I swam while the sun stood high and then began to tip towards the western horizon. At some moment I raised my head from the pool to see Disenk sitting cross-legged on the verge surrounded by the paraphernalia of my well-being— linen towels, oils, a canopy—but I did not join her until I felt all the effects of my late night and the disturbing meeting with the Chief Wife disappear. Then I hauled myself onto the grass and lay looking up into the heavily leafed branches of the trees above while my servant dried and oiled me. It seemed to me that I was no longer moving forward, that my life had slowed. Had I exhausted the impetus that had carried me so inexorably into the harem?

Draped in a linen towel I was making my way back to my cell, Disenk at my heels, when a royal Herald accosted me, hurrying from the direction of the palace. "The King requires your presence immediately, Concubine Thu," he gasped out. "Bring your medicines."

"Why?" I snapped. "What is the matter?" I was already brushing by him and Disenk was running ahead.

"It was an accident. His pet lion, Smam-khefti-f, clawed him. He has been carried to his bedchamber."

By the time I rushed into my cell Disenk had my clothes ready and my box sitting on the couch. She dressed me quickly. There was no time for paint or jewellery. I set off for the palace in nothing but my sheath and a pair of old and well-worn sandals, my box clutched under my arm. I was surprised at my own concern for the King. I took the shortest route that led directly from the harem into the royal bedroom and the guard on the doors admitted me at once.

Paibekamun met me. The room seemed full of anxious, whispering people whom I scarcely noticed but for the Prince, dusty and scantily clad, who stood by his father. Ramses was lying on his couch, covered by a sheet through which blood was oozing in a spreading dark stain.

"Is it bad?" I asked the Butler in a low voice. I was suddenly afraid and wished that Hui were here to take charge, to take responsibility. I felt very much alone.

"We do not know," the man replied quietly. "Pharaoh was reviewing his chariot troops with the lion beside him. It appears that the beast was stung on the nose by a bee, for he reared up and thrashed about. One of his paws raked Pharaoh's leg."

I approached the couch, signalling for a stool to be brought, and laid my box on the table. Ramses' head rolled towards me. He was pale, and beads of sweat had gathered on his forehead under the cloth covering of custom.

"So, my little scorpion," he wheezed. "Let us pray that you have come to soothe me today and not to sting. It seems that all my pets have barbs beneath their smiles." The words came from the testiness of pain. I took a moment to sink onto the stool and take his hand. It was hot and clammy.

"I do not sting today, Majesty," I smiled, "and I am sure that your lion intended you no harm either. May I inspect the wound?"

He managed a grin and the old sparkle briefly returned to his eyes. "How meek you are, Thu! How submissive! I know full well that you ask only out of politeness and in a moment you will rip off this sheet and poke into my leg with all the cold calculation of an embalmer. If you cause me discomfort you will pay for it at our next encounter between cleaner sheets than these!"

There was a movement on the other side of the couch and I glanced up. The Prince held my gaze. He still had a bow slung across his dirt-streaked shoulder and he was grasping it loosely with both hands. A single gold band had worked its way up his forearm and rested just below his elbow. These things were imprinted vividly upon my consciousness before I turned back to his father.

"You are incorrigible!" I scolded him. "And I am not one of your pets, Majesty. I am your physician. Hot water and virgin cloths!" I called to Paibekamun, and I rose and began to cautiously peel the sheet from the King's body.

The lion's claws had made two jagged, deep gashes in Ramses' fleshy upper thigh. Worse still, the animal's paw had been dirty. Dust and motes of unrecognizable refuse from the churned parade ground clung to it. After a close look I took out a phial and poured a few drops of the milky white poppy essence into a cup. "Majesty, I must wash and stitch you," I explained to him as I raised his head and held the container to his mouth. "It will hurt. Drink the poppy please, to dull the pain." He grimaced but did as he was told. The water had arrived, steaming in its bowl, and I was soon lost in my work as I arduously cleansed the mess and then settled down to pulling the edges of the rips closed. Ramses grunted occasionally but made no other sound. In spite of the poppy, the pain must have been excruciating but he bore it well and I was reminded that he had been a great soldier once, waging many battles with the foreigners to keep Egypt free. Indeed, it was as a soldier and strategist that he had felt most fulfilled. His campaign days were over, but he still had the inner discipline of the good fighting man.

I soon became completely absorbed in my work, oblivious of the comings and goings around me, but the unmoving presence of the Prince remained a shadow on the periphery of my mind. I began to sweat, and gentle, invisible hands wiped the moisture from my face.

At last I sat back with a sigh of satisfaction. Ramses would of course scar, but as I washed my bloody hands I knew that no further illness would result. Opening my box and taking out mortar and pestle I began to grind up a dressing. My back ached and my fingers shook. "Bring a large piece of fresh meat and linen strips," I ordered again, then I bent over my patient. His pupils were dilated and he regarded me drowsily. "The worst is over, Ramses," I said. "I am going to apply a mixture of ground rowan wood, byj soil and honey to the wound and over it I will tie a slab of meat to help you heal more quickly. Do you need more poppy?" He shook his head.

"Stay with me, Thu," he murmured. "They can set up a cot for you. Did I tell you that you look like a child with your hair in your face and no paint on your eyes?" He chuckled weakly at my expression and his eyelids drooped closed. Someone reached past me to drop a soiled rag into the now sullied water and I realized with a start that it had been the Prince's hand passing with such solicitude over my forehead and neck during my labours.

"Your work is impressive, Physician Thu," he said with a slight smile. "We are very grateful. When you have finished, go and bathe and refresh yourself. I will wait with him until you return." Ast-Amasareth's poisonous words returned to me then and I wondered fleetingly whether he was here out of a genuine concern for his father's welfare or a deliberate attempt to make himself seem the worried, loyal son. I had seen nothing of the other royal sons but passing glimpses at the feast and in the passages of the palace. They were but shadows to me, unreal figures of whom neither Hui nor his friends had spoken.

"Thank you, Highness," I responded. "You are very kind." I turned back at once to Pharaoh for the meat had arrived, borne with some dignity from the kitchens by Paibekamun himself, and I completed my tasks in a haze of relief.

Later, bathed and in a clean sheath, I went back to the palace and the Prince disappeared. Pharaoh still slept but his sleep was troubled by pain. He mumbled and tossed as I sat perched on the cot that had been provided, while outside the sun went down and night crept towards me. The servants brought me food and drink, which I refused, and lit the lamps. I dozed fitfully, waking occasionally to bend over the King and assure myself that all was well.

At some moment when full night smothered the palace, Ramses came to full consciousness. I was beside him at once, aware that the wound had leaked and his sheets were soiled. "Is that you, Thu?" he croaked. "My leg is stiff and fiery and I am very thirsty."

"I do not want to remove the meat until next evening, Majesty," I told him, pouring beer and helping him to sit up. "Drink now, and I will give you more poppy."

"It has made my head ache," he complained. "Where are my priests? The gods know that I do enough for the rascals! Where are they to say the spells?"

"I expect they are waiting for your summons," I replied. "But Ramses, you do not have a disease. There is no demon to be cast out, therefore no need for any chanting."

"Do not call me by my name," he rebuked me mildly. "For I have no equal in Egypt." He downed the beer in great gulps and I wiped his face when he had finished.

"Would you like to be washed, Majesty?" I enquired. "May the servants change your linen again?" Without waiting for his assent I signalled to them and stood at the King's head while they made him more comfortable, working with the ease of good training and long practice. Then I gave him more poppy, resisting the urge to inspect his leg. He was feverish but that was to be expected. I could only pray that no Ukhedu had spread.

He slept again, or rather, fell into a drug-induced stupor, and I followed suit, waking with a start towards morning to find Prince Ramses sitting on the foot of my cot, watching me. "How is he?" the Prince asked conversationally as I struggled to rise. "My mother will visit him later, and Ast-Amasareth has been anxiously waiting for news. The temples were crowded all night with panicked courtiers praying for him."

"But why?" I blurted, still stupid with sleep. "The clawing was nasty and the wound serious but not fatal." The Prince shrugged.

"Because if he died now there would be much trouble, perhaps even bloodshed. Some of my brothers would make a bid for power with the temples behind them. Some would promise the army anything for the support of the generals. Only my father tries to placate both temple and palace."

"But why placate?" I demanded. "He is King. He is God! Let him put the priests firmly in their place!" A soft laugh from the couch made us both swing round. Pharaoh was watching us from beneath swollen lids. His eyes were both wary and amused.

"The voice of injured innocence!" he said. "And how may your King put the servants of the gods in their places, dear Thu? Shall he waft them away with ostrich plumes? Shall he tap them into submission with the Crook or flick at them with the Flail? And what of the Scimitar? Ah, there is a possibility." He was trying to sit up and the Prince went to his aid. "He could approach the kingdoms of the foreigners. He could say, 'Send me men and arms to drive the priests of Egypt back to the confines of their temples and confiscate the land that belongs to the gods, and in return Egypt will reward you with her hearty thanks. Of course she cannot offer you more because her riches pass through one God's hands and straight into the arms of other gods.' And why?" He laughed again then groaned and clutched at his thigh. "Because my holy father Osiris Setnakht Glorified decreed that it should be so. He promised the gods land and gold if they would turn their faces to Egypt once more, if they would forgive her, if they would return her to her former might. Shall his son break the vow that was made, and bring down their wrath upon this country? We have had this out before." He was becoming flushed and agitated.

"It was not I who spoke, but your Physician," the Prince reminded him softly. "Yet her voice is the voice of many of your subjects, Father. The vow was made by my grandfather. If he knew that the yield of our gold mines in Nubia is falling, that trade with the countries of the Great Green is slowing down, that Thebes is growing as the centre of priestly power and influence and the High Priest of Amun lives in greater pomp than the Incarnation of the God, would he not absolve you of any guilt in moving to ruth-lessly reduce that threat?"

"The priests are no threat to the Horus Throne," Ramses interrupted testily. "They are rapacious and venal but they know that the people will not tolerate any danger to the true foundation of Egypt. What would you have me do? Call out the army and slaughter them? I do not trust the army. I do not trust anyone, even you, my mysterious son. Besides, the gods would have their revenge. Their servants are sacred."

"There is discontent among the tomb workers," the Prince said. "They no longer receive their rations regularly while the grain pours into Amun's Theban storehouses."

"Enough!" Ramses broke in loudly. "I do what I can. Did I not reopen the copper mines of Aathaka this year, and send officers to extract turquoise from Mafek? Have I not deployed thousands of mercenaries along the borders and set them to guarding the caravan routes? Do I not negotiate with Syria and Punt to bring wealth into Egypt?"

"Any gains we make go into the coffers of the gods!" his son retorted hotly and his father shouted, "Enough I said! Touch the gods and Egypt will fall! She will fall! I know the angry mutters of the malcontents who breathe treason behind their hands! They do not understand!"

I had been listening, bemused, to this increasingly incensed interchange but at the mention of treason I came to myself. It was the second time in so many days that the word had been spoken and a shudder of apprehension seized me. I went to Pharaoh. "Lie still, Majesty," I said. "Do not thrash about. You will destroy all my good work. See, the dawn is coming. I hear the priests at the door, preparing to sing the Hymn of Praise. Calm yourself." There was indeed movement beyond the double doors, and natural light was gradually seeping into the room, grey and dismal. We all fell silent while the stately music fell muffled on our ears, and when it ceased the doors were flung wide. The Prince got up.

"My soldiers require my attention today, Father, but I will return in the evening. Obey your Physician. I love you." He smiled vaguely in my direction and strode away through the gaggle of servants who bowed as he passed. The lamps were extinguished. A harpist took up his position in the corner and began to play. A tray appeared. I took it and was placing it on the table when there was a further flurry outside and a small entourage swept in. The servants went to the floor like scythed wheat and I too knelt and pressed my face to the cold lapis tiles. Queen Ast, Lady of the Two Lands, approached the couch briskly.

"Rise, all of you," she commanded. Her gaze passed uninterestedly over me and returned to her husband. Bending, she kissed his cheek. Once again I found myself marvelling at the exquisite delicacy of her face, the tiny perfection of her body, but this time I was able to discern something of her son's beauty in her even features. "You worry me, Ramses," she said. "I told you that you should have put that animal to death a long time ago. It was a pretty cub but it has become a formidable wild animal."

"Smam-khefti-f would never deliberately hurt me," Ramses bridled. "Even now I am sure he is regretting his loss of control. He was stung you know." Ast's expression revealed her supreme disbelief. She sighed pointedly.

"How is the wound?" she asked. "You! Physician, if that is what you are! Uncover it for me. I wish to see it." I swallowed and bowed.

"Forgive me, Majesty," I said, "but the dressing I have applied may not be disturbed until this evening." Her nostrils dilated. She turned to her husband.

"Really, Ramses," she said in a low voice, her words unintelligible to the servants but clear to me. "You must be losing your mind. Since when has a mere concubine been allowed to treat royalty? Are you so besotted?" Ramses rallied under this onslaught. Pain had grooved his pendulous cheeks and deepened the violet shadows under his bloodshot eyes but he spoke with an even authority.

"Thu is a physician in her own right, having been tutored by the Seer himself. Her ministrations are agreeable to me." Ast shot me a look of dislike.

"I know who she is. And what she is. I hope you do not live to regret your latest preoccupation. I am sorry that you are in pain. May I send you anything?" The ghost of a smile was hovering on Ramses' lips. I think at that moment I came close to really loving him as he shook his head and elaborately kissed her hand.

"Believe me, Ast, I have everything I need," he responded. "But come back later and keep me company. We see so little of each other except at feasts and official receptions." His wife nodded regally, looked me up and down once more with scorn, and sailed out, her attendants falling into place behind her. I watched her go with a surge of triumph. The Queen of Egypt, the most powerful woman in the land, was jealous of me. From the height of my conquest I pitied her.

Pharaoh and I ate together and I noted that he seemed much better. When we had finished, he dismissed me so that I could bathe and change my dress but he insisted that I return. For the rest of the day we talked companionably, played board games, and he occasionally fell into the light sleep of returning health. Three times we were interrupted by ministers requiring his Seal or his advice. The noisy courtyard of the harem seemed very far away.

At sunset I at last dared to remove the meat from his wounds and inspect their progress. Folding back the covering sheet and pushing away his sleeping kilt I carefully cut through the binding linen strips. The slab of beef came away easily and both of us stared at my neat stitches surrounded by uneven whorls of purple bruising. I breathed an interior prayer of thanks to my dear Wepwawet. There were no telltale signs of a spreading Ukhedu.

Calling for hot water I washed his thigh, and grinding up more rowan wood I mixed it with soothing honey and smeared the damaged flesh. As I worked I could not help but notice the gradual stiffening of his penis. Pharaoh was definitely feeling better. Laying a square of clean linen over the salve, I was about to close my medicine box when Ramses caught my hand and pressed it to his mouth with a great deal more fervour than he had shown to his wife.

"You do wonderful things with those little hands of yours," he said huskily. "I love you, little scorpion. You did not sting me much after all. Tell me, Thu, is there anything you want? What can I give you?" Savouring the moment I cupped his cheeks and kissed him slowly. What did I want? A dozen pictures flashed across my inner vision but I knew I must be careful. Now was not the time to press my advantage, to appear to be greedy.

"I love you also, Mighty Bull," I whispered. "You have been truly gracious to me. How, then, can I ask for more?"

"Easily," he said. "You simply open that pert mouth of yours, my concubine. Is it jewels? Fine linen? Sandals so light that they are as river foam on your feet? What?" I was thinking furiously. At last I rested my hands in my lap and lowered my gaze demurely.

"Since Your Majesty has been pleased to offer a gift, I may have the temerity to express a desire. Do not be angry, please." He grunted impatiently but he was smiling. I looked up, giving him the full benefit of my blue eyes. "I am the daughter of a peasant, as Your Majesty knows. I miss the land. Give me a field to be tilled, Great Pharaoh, an orchard or some small corner where I can pasture a few cows." He blinked and his heavy eyebrows rose to meet the rim of his cloth headcovering.

"You want land? But there is nothing easier, my dear. Where do you want it? Delta land is best. Its fertility will give you a good return if it is husbanded properly. Is there anything else?"

"Yes." I was buoyant with an incredulous happiness. I, Thu, was to be a landowner. This big, generous man could make it so with a stroke of the scribe's pen. "I would like your permission to visit the Seer whenever I wish. He is like a father to me and I miss him." Ramses nodded.

"Of course. Whenever you wish. And you can have your own skiff and litter to do so." He frowned mockingly. "But you must pay for such favours. At once. Take off your sheath, Physician, and do your duty as a good concubine, for your King is suddenly consumed with lust." I returned his frown and pulling the sheet over him I tucked it in firmly.

"Oh no, Divine One. I am endlessly grateful for your kindness and humbled by your love, but my duty as your Physician has not ended yet. No lust today, only healing. I order it." He burst into gales of uninhibited laughter, placing one stout finger between my eyebrows and erasing my frown. I could not resist his mirth and found myself laughing with him, and it was at that moment that a harem Herald was announced. I retired to the stool as Ramses beckoned the man forward.

"Speak." The Herald bowed.

"The Keeper of the Door has commanded me to bring you the news that the concubine Eben has just given birth to a royal girl, Your Majesty," he said. "Both baby and mother are well." Ramses smiled.

"A girl? That is wonderful. Send Eben my congratulations. Dismissed." The man backed out and Pharaoh barked, "Paibekamun!" The Butler glided forward.

"Majesty?"

"Choose some trinket from my treasury for Eben, a bracelet perhaps or a couple of rings. And tell the astrologers to consult together and decide on a propitious name." Paibekamun met my eye.

"At once, Majesty," he said. My gaze followed his tall figure as he moved silently away.

"Now if you insist on maintaining this ridiculous distance between us you can at least tell me a story which will bore me into slumber," Ramses was saying.

I wrenched my attention back to him. My fate must never be Eben's, I thought in terror. Be warned, Thu my girl. Eben got pregnant. Eben destroyed herself. Be careful, oh gods, be careful! My voice, when I began to recite, trembled, but Pharaoh did not seem to notice. He leaned back and closed his eyes.

Chapter 17

I made the short journey to Hui's house by water in my new skiff. It was a small gem of a boat built of good cedar, painted white, with prow and stern curving up gracefully to unfurl as two gilded lotus blossoms. It had a tiny cabin with blue damask curtains, many plump cushions, a low ebony table inlaid with silver, and a matching box for whatever supplies I might need on my travels. The litter folded neatly on the cramped deck was also of ebony, hung with blue damask. But best of all, my craft flew the blue-and-white pennant of royal possession on the crosspiece of its lateen sail and it was with great pride that I sat in my cabin with the curtains drawn back while the helmsman and two sailors in palace employ kept us slicing elegantly through the sparkling waters of the Lake. People on the bank paused to stare at me as I glided by and I smiled at them, full of contentment.

I had sent word that I was coming, and as my ramp was run out at the foot of Hui's watersteps, Harshira emerged from the shade of the entrance pylon and stood on the paving in all his commanding dignity, flanked by Ani and a Kaha who could not conceal his broad grin as he watched my litter being set up. I descended the ramp with Disenk behind me, my gold-sprinkled sheath swirling about my braceleted ankles, the breeze tugging at the silver and black braids of my wig. The helmsman offered me his hand and in a moment the firmness of stone was under my feet. Harshira bowed solemnly. Ani bowed also. Kaha sketched an obeisance and ran to me, taking my hand.

"Thu, you look wonderful! You are wonderful!" he cried. "Welcome home! Can you still recite the wars of Osiris Thothmes the Third Glorified?"

"Of course," I replied haughtily, then I threw my arms around him and held him tight. "Have you been elevated yet?" I asked. He rolled his eyes.

"I have been offered the position of Chief Scribe in the household of Nebtefau, Judge and Royal Councillor," he said as we walked towards the others. "It is a great honour, but Nebtefau sits on the council that governs Pi-Ramses and is a friend of the mayor. I do not relish the hours I would spend at his knee cramping my fingers to take notes on the boring problems of crime in the poor districts or making endless lists of supplies for the road menders. I prefer Hui's peaceful domain." He squeezed my fingers and released me. I greeted Ani and then looked up into Harshira's granite features. They broke into a brief but warm smile.

"Welcome back, Thu," he said gravely. "I trust that you are in good health. The Master awaits you anxiously. May I escort you?"

I slipped onto my litter. The sailors lifted me, and with Disenk on one side and Harshira pacing ponderously on the other we took the path through the bushy, gnarled trees and nodding flowers that I saw pass with a lump in my throat.

At last the litter was lowered. I stepped out.

He was standing just inside the shelter of the hallway, dressed in a short kilt, one strand of a plain silver necklet lying on his smooth white chest. His moon-coloured hair fell in a thick braid over one pale shoulder, tied with a yellow ribbon, and his glowing eyes were rimmed in black kohl. I could not speak. Halting, words struggling for birth, I drank him in. Seeing my hesitation he laughed, the odd, gruff sound flooding me with memories.

"Little Thu, my very dear Thu," he said. "You have changed yet again since I saw you last. You look delectable."

I wanted to fling myself upon him, inhale his perfume and the unique odour of his skin, press my lips to his colourless throat. I wanted to sit on his knee and be enfolded in his care. Instead I remained mute while he approached me and planted a kiss on the top of my head. "I know what you want to do," he went on, drawing my arm through his and walking me along the passage. "You want to go up and look at your old room, don't you?"

"You always could read my mind, Hui." I found my voice at last. "Why have you ignored me for so long? It has been three whole months since you came to my cell. Why have you not even sent me a letter? I have been lonely for you."

"I know." We had reached the foot of the stairs and he turned to me. "But I belong to your past, my Thu, and unless it was necessary I did not want the past intruding upon a difficult present until you were reasonably secure in your life as Ramses' possession." His mouth curved in a wry smile. "But I think that now it is safe for us to be together."

Oh, I do not think so, Master, I spoke to him in my mind, my heart tripping as I looked at him. No, it is not safe at all. For I am no longer a virgin yearning for your body in a pleasant fantasy. I am a seasoned woman. You may belong to the time of my growing and I may not adore you with the unfocused energies of extreme youth, but your body still calls to me and I want to respond. "Why do you call me Ramses' possession?" I asked sharply. "You chose those words on purpose, didn't you? I do not need to be reminded of my position, Hui, and do not think to humble me. I will never be wholly the chattel of any man."

"Still my fiery peasant," he observed. "That is very good. Run upstairs, dear one, and when you have relished your moment I will meet you in the office."

I made my way slowly up the steps, along the quiet passage, and paused outside the closed door to my room. At some point I had lost Disenk. I was entirely alone. Taking a deep breath I put out a hand and walked in.

It was as if I had left it not more than an hour ago. The window hanging was up and sunlight spilled over the polished floor and splashed up onto the simple couch with its pristine linen, its plain bedside table, the limpid beauty of the single alabaster lamp. The table where I had eaten and Disenk had laid out her sewing, grumbling at my stubbornness, sat waiting for me to draw up a chair and begin a laborious writing lesson.

Voices came to me from below and I walked to the window and looked out. The Head Gardener was in conversation with one of his assistants, a basket laden with bright green seedlings on the ground between them. Birds fluttered and quarrelled in the trees that crowded by the main gate. The sky was a shimmering blue.

I let the peace of the estate steal into me then I turned back into the room, going to perch on the edge of the couch. How small the room was in reality! How plain the furnishings, how modest the appointments, yet how tasteful and harmonious the whole. When I first saw this room I believed that I was in the heart of luxury. I should have stayed here, I thought. I could have made Hui marry me. This blessed tranquillity could have been mine for ever. But then I remembered my white-and-gold skiff rocking at anchor below the watersteps with the sun glinting on its golden lotus blossoms, and the rich ebony gleam of my litter, and I got up. With a last satisfying glance about my old quarters I went out and closed the door.

Hui was dictating to Ani when I knocked and was admitted to the office. Ani bowed out at once and Hui stood and stretched.

"Disenk brought in your medicine box," he said as he began to untie the complicated knots on the rings of the inner office door. "I presume it needs some replenishment after Pharaoh's unfortunate accident." The cord fell away and he waved me inside. I followed eagerly, dragging into my lungs the half-acrid, half-sweet aroma of the little room. Hui lit the lamps quickly. "Your procedure was excellent," he went on, opening my box and pulling down phials and jars from the shelves. "Although I would have added ground myrrh to the castor oil you applied after you removed the stitches, just to make sure that all Ukhedu was vanquished."

"There was no Ukhedu," I retorted, stung. "How do you know what treatment I applied, Hui?" He gave me a swift glance, his hands busy. I sighed. "Oh, of course. Paibekamun. And does the Butler also report to you on my sexual exploits with the King? Does he tell you how many times Ramses achieves satisfaction in one night?" Hui shook his head.

"No. Those things you will tell me yourself if all is not well in Pharaoh's bed and you need my advice. But you must not lose favour with Ramses, and therefore your behaviour as his physician is vitally important. Gods, Thu! Your supply of ground acacia spikes is completely gone! Are you concocting contraceptives for the entire harem?"

"No. For a few women only." I faltered briefly. "Most of the ground acacia I use myself." He made no comment as he refilled and stoppered the containers for my box.

"Do you continue to exercise regularly?" he enquired. "Take care what you eat and drink? Have Disenk prepare all your food and taste what she cannot control?" I thought of Ast-Amasareth and nodded, telling him of my uncomfortable visit with the Chief Wife. He listened carefully, and by the time I had finished speaking he had completed his task. We left the office, with regret on my part, and Hui poured wine for us in the outer office as we settled into chairs.

"If she cannot frighten you she will attempt to control your relationship with Ramses," he told me. "Let her think that she does so. How is our Divine Ruler? Desperately in love with you yet?" I felt a pang of guilty loyalty to the King at Hui's cynical tone, seeing Ramses' warm brown eyes as he clutched my hand and professed his love for me, but I pushed the emotion away and answered the question readily enough. Hui watched me, a smile spreading slowly over his face. "You are doing well," he praised me. "I am very proud of you, my Thu."

I was beginning to feel restless, why I was not sure. Hui's questions, his intense interest in my answers, made me both impatient and resentful. It all seemed rather petty, and I wanted to tell him that I did not much care any more what Egypt's fate might be but I dared not.

"It is ridiculous to believe that I can have any political influence on him even though he is besotted with me," I said cautiously. "I may be spending most of my time in his private quarters but I am not sufficiently important to be present at any formal receptions or foreign negotiations. I have only the vaguest idea of what is truly happening in the offices of the ministers. I have heard Ramses and his son argue over the King's internal policies and I am convinced that Pharaoh will never be swayed." I sat straight and put my cup back on the desk. "After all, Hui, if he will not listen to his own son, why would he listen to a concubine, no matter how fetching?"

"Because this concubine is different," Hui said firmly. "She is clever, she will last, and the longer she lasts the more tightly she may wind her cunning fingers around his heart and mind. It is not impossible, Thu." He folded his arms and leaned towards me. "Pharaoh's trading envoys will soon be returning from the far reaches of the Great Green. When their cargo has been tallied the Generals will approach the King to request an increase in the wages of their soldiers. Try to persuade Ramses to be generous. The priests will be clamouring for more than their share and bleating of a show of gratitude to the gods on the part of the Throne for a successful mission. Do what you can to keep the goods from them."

I met Hui's narrowed red gaze.

"You serve no god at all, do you, Hui?" I said softly. "You do not use your Seeing gift for any of them, do you, nor do you regard any god as the source of your mystery. Whom do you worship then? Yourself? Where does your heart really lie?" His eyes became slits.

"I do not answer such questions," he almost whispered. "I see that the crude child I picked out of the dirt of Aswat has become a complex woman. Join hands with me in this, Thu. The rewards will be enormous." I felt suddenly cold.

"For Egypt or for you?" I choked out. Abruptly he relaxed and the intensity went out of his stare.

"For both," he said briskly. "What monster have you suddenly taken me for, impudent one? Has the stifling air of the harem, rife with gossip and rumour, tainted your brain?"

"What does the Seeing tell you of the future, Hui?" I persisted. "Or does it show you merely dreams?" He sat breathing heavily for a moment, biting his hennaed lip, then his face cleared. He smiled.

"What it shows me for myself is mine alone. If I read for Pharaoh it is his alone. Do what you can, Thu. I do not ask for more. I certainly do not expect you to sacrifice yourself on the altar of Egypt's health. Enjoy the King. Enjoy what he offers. Why not?" He rose and poured more wine for me, turning his head to speak almost directly into my face. I was painfully aware of his closeness, his lips moving inches from mine. "And I hear that he has offered you land. Yes? A wise request, that. Good for you. My Land Surveyor, Adiroma, does much work for the harem women as well. When you have the deed in your hands, send for him. He is honest. If you wish it, my Overseer can take charge of whatever crop or herd you want to own. He will assure you of a profit."

"Thank you, Hui," was all I could manage. He withdrew and I gulped at the wine.

"Now," said my Master. "Let us take a walk in the garden,

and you can give me all the harem news. Tonight there will be a feast here in your honour. Meantime I have you all to myself." I took his proffered arm and we left the office. As we ambled along the passage towards the rear doors that stood open, I reflected fatalistically that there was probably very little harem news that he did not know already.

That evening I entered Hui's dining hall to find them all there, the men I remembered from a similar feast in the same place so long ago. They broke off their conversation under the muted twanging of the Master's harpist and saluted me: Paibekamun as taciturn as ever; Mersura the Chancellor with an arrogant lift of his smooth eyebrows; Panauk the Royal Scribe of the Harem, a man I had glimpsed once in Amunnakht's office and who had greeted me brightly but absently; Pentu, Scribe of the Double House of Life who doubtless spent his days closeted in the temple guarding and studying the precious tomes; and Hui's brother, General Paiis, who left his cushions to kiss first my hands, each one with deliberate passion, then my hennaed mouth with thorough expertise. "And that is the closest I will ever come to Paradise," he sighed, eyes twinkling, as he retired to his place. "How are you, my beauty?" I did not know whether to be offended or amused by the licence he took, answering him lightly as I sank down beside Hui. I was very aware of Paibekamun's dark gaze on me and found myself suddenly missing General Banemus's open, friendly face. Hui snapped his fingers and the first course was carried in. Conversation was desultory and general as the company ate and the wine was poured. I took my part with ease, no longer shy, smiling and chatting, humming sometimes to the harp music, but after the guests' hunger had been appeased, the tone of the gathering changed. It happened gradually, so that for a while I did not notice it. Polite questions became sharper, more pointed, the silences less congenial, and I realized that I was being examined.

The men began by asking for the details of Pharaoh's accident and my treatment, a natural curiosity tinged with what I presumed was the anxiety all courtiers had felt and of which Prince Ramses had spoken so bitterly. I answered readily enough, but then the questions veered into puzzling avenues. Was I happy in the harem? Had I made any friends there among the other women? Among the servants and guards? Were the other women content? What were their concerns? Prince Ramses was an admirable man, was he not? How well did I know him? Had I met his wife? The queries were not fired at me rudely. They came casually and I answered them lightly, but there was an underlying current of intensity to them that made me increasingly uncomfortable. I did my best to turn the conversation, but after a brief digression it always arrowed back to their strange preoccupation. I could not put my finger on just what that was, but the fact that they seemed to know made me all the more uneasy.

Hui remained silent, toying with his cup. I felt his attention on me, unobtrusive but constant, and all at once, for some reason, I was sickeningly reminded of Kenna. The memory of his death and the part I had played in it had faded until he had not come to my mind either waking or dreaming for months, yet now I seemed to feel his clammy flesh limp against me as he gasped out his life and I caught a phantom whiff of his polluted breath. My wine tasted sour and I put it down with a grimace of distaste. At once Hui stirred and Paiis spoke up.

"You must forgive us our rough male inquisitiveness," he said easily. "The harem is a mystery to us although Panauk works there. Hui! Tell your man to play something livelier! If we cannot have dancers we can at least sing!" It was a clumsy ploy that I dismissed. Those questions swirled in my head as the men burst into the song the harpist had obligingly begun. I noticed that Paibekamun did not join in. He reclined on his cushions, his features in shadow, his body motionless. I realized then that he made me afraid.

Soon afterwards the party broke up, and this time I was among the guests who stood beneath the entrance pillars, looking out over the shrouded courtyard while we waited for our litters. Harshira summoned them and then helped us, one by one, inside. Paiis offered, half-jokingly, to accompany me back to the palace, but I declined in the same mood, pride filling me as I told him of the skiff rocking at anchor, waiting for me. He bowed to me good-naturedly and scrambled inside his litter. The others took their leave of me cordially enough. Hui enveloped me in his strong embrace. "Stay well, little sister," he said, his alien eyes warm. "I shall be in the palace next week to attend the King's mother, and will see you then. Greet Hunro for me. Paiis has had a message from Banemus so you may tell her that he is well."

For some reason I did not want to remain in his arms. I extricated myself quickly, bid him a good night, thanked Harshira, and got into my litter with relief, inviting a sleepy Disenk to join me. The path was dark and secret, shadows and rustlings coming to me out of the moon shadows as the litter slowly passed the trees that seemed to lean together and whisper maliciously about me. I was not sorry to see the faint gleams of light from the lamp bobbing on the prow of my craft come fitfully through the branches and I hurried up the ramp. It was as though the ghost of Kenna had been watching my progress and was even now gliding after me balefully.

The short journey back to the palace confines on a peaceful, starlit Lake was uneventful and Disenk and I were carried to the entrance of my empty courtyard through a mildly scented, cool night. Our footfalls echoed on the strip of paving fronting the cells and I imagined Kenna hovering in the blackness of my doorway, waiting to spring at me as I walked in. I shook myself mentally, annoyed at the uncharacteristic fancy. The soft sounds within came from a sleeping

Hunro, and by the time Disenk had lit a candle and prepared me for bed I had forgotten my sudden and illogical
fear.

But that night I dreamed that I was kneeling in the
desert, under the burning heat of a sun that stood directly
overhead. My face was pressed into the sand, which stuck to
my lips and clung to my nostrils. Sweat was pouring from my
straining back, and my naked shoulders had begun to blister.
Fear was holding me down, mingling with the sun's implaca-
ble rays and pressing upon me, forcing its way into my skin
and flowing towards my heart, which was pounding errati-
cally. I tried to raise my head but the terror intensified, an
inexorable and brutal energy that kept me pinned to the
unforgiving earth.

I woke with a shriek and flung myself upright, one hand
flying to my chest where my heart was still leaping painfully.
My sheets were drenched with my perspiration and I was
shaking. The night was still. Hunro sighed and turned over
but did not wake. Outside an owl cried once. I was afraid to
close my eyes. "Come to me, come to me, my mother Isis," I
whispered into the dimness. "Behold, I am seeing what is far
from my city." The words of the old spell against evil omens
tumbled fresh from my tongue as though I had learned them
yesterday, for I knew the meaning of the dream and it was
horrifying.

The dead wanted something. The dead were speaking to
me. I had no bread, or beer with which to moisten the herbs
that should have accompanied my petition, but as I
breathed it over and over, it brought a slowly growing calm
until my heart regained its regular rhythm and my body
loosened. I had been thinking of Kenna, that was all, I told
myself as I prepared once more for sleep. The gods know I
did not mean to kill him, therefore he cannot want anything from me. I closed my eyes, but unconsciousness did
not return for a very long time.

In the morning I made my way to Ramses' private quarters without being invited, for I was still watching the progress of his wounds and went as his physician. The dream remained with me, an uneasiness that lingered even though the palace was alive with bustle and cheerfulness. I found Pharaoh dressed and shouting at Paibekamun who was trying to persuade him to accept a walking stick.

"I know perfectly well what it says!" he was yelling furiously as I prostrated myself and then approached. Neither man took any notice of me. "It is an inscription for the old and decrepit who hobble about mumbling to themselves! 'Come, my stick,'" he recited with biting scorn, "'So that I might lean on you and follow the Beautiful West, that my heart may wander in the Place of Truth.' Well I have no intention of following the Beautiful West just yet, Paibekamun, nor does my heart want to wander in the Place of Truth. Take it away!"

At the mention of a heart in the Place of Truth my own heart gave an unpleasant heave and my dream rushed upon me in all its horror, only to vanish. I walked forward. "Ah, Thu," Ramses exclaimed, his face clearing. "I do not need a walking stick, do I? I cannot be seen to stumble into the reception hall leaning on such a thing! The foreigners must not see the God of Egypt walking like a lame beggar!" He slumped into a chair while I knelt and gently probed his thigh.

"Must you receive delegations today, Majesty?" I asked. "You are healing very well but the leg must not be tested. A few more days of rest would be better." Indeed the ugly red gashes were less swollen and had closed satisfactorily. In spite of his bluster I could see that he was glad to be sitting, and he winced imperceptibly under my fingers. "If you will not use the stick then you must not walk any further than your own door."

"Nonsense!" he snapped, then his brilliant smile flashed

out. "Well perhaps you are right. Come, Thu. I will let my son see to the business of the day and I will recuperate still further in the peace of my own bedchamber. In fact I will lie on my couch. And so will you." He limped the short distance to the couch and settled upon it, gesturing me forward imperiously. "I missed your presence last night," he complained as I sat beside him and his arm went around me. "You were with Hui I hear, and he held a feast with his friends to entertain you. Were you entertained, little scorpion? Did you miss your King?" I smiled inwardly as I detected the note of jealousy in his speech. I nestled closer to him and held up my mouth to receive his kiss.

"It was a great delight to be back in Hui's house," I said innocently, "and I enjoyed his hospitality and the company of his friends. To tell you the truth, Majesty, I hardly missed you at all."

"Demon!" he shot back at me, but he was laughing. "Prove to me now how much you did not miss me."

I did as I was told. It took a very long time, and the proving was not as onerous as I had imagined. Pharaoh was becoming a better lover than the man Hunro had described to me, and the face of Prince Ramses rose only intermittently behind my closed lids as the morning burgeoned into the full, heavy heat of another afternoon and we whispered and thrashed among the disordered sheets.

I left him sleeping heavily, one arm outflung, the chubby fingers curled inward like a child's, and made my way back to my cell intending to exercise and bathe although the fire of the day had not yet moderated. But as I turned in at my own door I found the room in chaos. Disenk was standing with folded arms in the middle of the floor while two slaves were engaged in packing my boxes. Hunro was watching also, doing deep knee bends in her tiny dancer's kilt and humming to herself.

I paused, shocked and alarmed, my thoughts flying

through the many gloomy possibilities the scene might mean. Ramses was already tired of me and was too craven to tell me to my face. I had offended him with my forward speech and was about to be punished. I was not achieving the task Hui had set for me quickly enough and he had somehow been able to have me banished to some royal backwater where the truly ancient concubines dozed through the hours remaining to them.

The last stab of fear told me a great deal about how the deepest part of me truly regarded my mentor, and the degree of mistrust I felt shocked me even further. In spite of my rapid rise in the King's favour I was still tied to Hui's powerful hand, mind and body moving obediently to every twitch of his fingers. But I would consider it later. Hunro stretched and smiled at me.

"Do not look so distressed, Thu," she said. "You are to take up residence in larger quarters by the courtyard entrance, you know, one of the big corner apartments reserved for favourite concubines. You will not have to put up with my snoring any more!"

"You do not snore, Hunro," I replied absently, the explosion of chaotic fears gone. So I was to be elevated in importance. I had pleased the King after all, pleased him enough to have him lift me from the common ranks of the women. I had been doing the right thing. "Who inhabited it before me?" I wanted to know. Hunro arched her back, her hands buried in her hair.

"Eben did," she said matter-of-factly. "Eben has just been appointed Royal Nursemaid to the concubine children. You should have heard her wailing as they carried her possessions along to the nursery building." I shivered. Eben would spend the rest of her life feeding, washing, scolding and teaching manners to the dozens of Pharaoh's offspring who swarmed over the harem. I felt no sense of victory over her, no desire to gloat. Pity engulfed me.

With a series of thuds my boxes were being closed. Disenk gave an order and the slaves began to carry them out into the sunshine. My couch had already been stripped. I perched on its frame and watched Hunro tuck her head between her ankles. The courtyard was wide, but more than space separated the inmates of the corner apartments from the rest of the cells. I had not known that Eben had resided so close to me. The favourites did not mingle with the herd.

"Please visit me often, Hunro," I said. "I have no one else to gossip with." She unfolded and stood panting with her hands on her hips.

"Of course I will," she assured me. "I hope we shall continue to exercise together, Thu. Besides, we share the same hope for Egypt's future and we must decide how you are to handle Pharaoh now that you are so high in his favour. The trading fleet has been sighted, you know. It is on its way home." I stared at her. She was still smiling, looking at me with an expression of condescension on her pretty face.

"I think," I said slowly, "that I can handle Ramses quite well on my own, thank you, Hunro. I have been glad of your advice in the past but I no longer need to be told what to say or do, by you or by Hui." Her eyes widened briefly but then she shrugged.

"I hope you are right," she said crisply. "But be careful of your pride, Thu. Do not let it trip you up." I was about to make a hot response, for her words had cut me to the quick, when a shadow darkened the cell door. I swung round. Amunnakht was bowing imperturbably, a scroll in his hands.

"Your pardon, Concubine Thu," he said. "I am here to execute the order received from Pharaoh's Scribe." He tapped the scroll gently against the lintel. "Follow me." I did not look at Hunro again. Sliding off the now denuded couch I hurried after him.

The women gathered on the grass in the late afternoon sunlight watched us in what I took to be an envious silence as we crossed beside the pool and went on to the farther wall of cells, turning left along the paving. Amunnakht strode regally ahead. I felt rather than saw the mute Hatia turn her head to see us go. Nubhirma'at and Nebt-Iunu, the two young lovers, waved happily after me. Amunnakht stopped just beyond the foot of the stairs leading to the roofs and opened a door. He smiled non-committally, at me. "You are blessed indeed," he said. "And our King is generous." Bowing, he left me. I did not wait to see him go. I ran inside.

The first thing I noticed was the profusion of light streaming in wide shafts from the windows cut high in the walls and falling on my boxes, on the elegantly turned lion legs of the gilded couch, bringing Disenk's sheath to dazzling life as she dismissed the slaves and stepped forward. Bright mats covered the floor. There was another door in the left-hand wall. It stood open and gave out onto the passage that ran between my building and the palace. I knew that the queens lived in the next block. With a burst of excitement I told myself that before long I would cross that small divide.

The ceiling was painted with an expert likeness of Nut, goddess of the sky, arching her star-filled body over the space where I would sleep, and the interior walls were also vivid with scenes of palace life. In one corner an empty brazier stood ready to heat the cool winter nights. A shrine, likewise empty, waited with open doors to receive whatever god the lucky inhabitant of the quarters might worship. Lamp stands clustered at the foot of the couch. Two exquisitely carved tables gleamed dully. I sank into one of the chairs placed obligingly by the couch and heaved a sigh of pure satisfaction.

"Disenk," I said. "Bring out Wepwawet and stand him inside the shrine. Prepare incense. I will offer my thanks to my totem, for surely he has decreed a glorious future for his loyal subject!" My gaze followed her as she opened the crude little cedar box I had brought with me from Aswat, extracted the statue my father had carved, and set it on its stand within the shrine. I became aware all at once of the welcome quiet surrounding us. The splash of the fountain, the cries of the children, the laughter of the other women, could barely be heard. I closed my eyes. Oh gods, I breathed to myself. I will do anything to hold on to this. Anything at all. I will not allow Hui and his plans to endanger what I have achieved. I will speak to Ramses on the matter of the trading apportionment, but if my words incur his wrath I will abandon all future efforts to subvert his policies. The risk of loss to myself is too great. The odour of incense began to curl about my nostrils as Disenk lit the grains in the long holder. I rose and took it from her, making the ponderous motions of purification around the god's little silver house before I could go to the floor and begin my prayers. Wepwawet would stand by me, I knew. He had never failed me yet. Together the peasant girl and the God of War had weathered many battles. They were loyal to each other, Aswat's minor deity and the child of Aswat's earth, and there was great security in that thought. Inhaling the smoky air I started to pray.

Ramses sent for me in the evening. I found him seated beside his table in the mellow glow of a lamp, but his beaming smile eclipsed the light that bathed him. Well? his expression said. I knelt and kissed his feet, pressing my face against his warm flesh. "Many thanks, Mighty Bull, Great Horus," I said huskily. "Your kindness is unbounded. I do not know what to say." He patted the top of my head paternally, bade me rise, and reached behind him. Two scrolls were placed in his hand and I noticed for the first time that Tehuti, his Chief Scribe, stood by his shoulder. Ramses was still smiling, the unaffected expression of pure mischievous joy making him look like an excited child.

"That is not all," he said. He passed me one of the scrolls with the eagerness of anticipation. "Read it, my precious little scorpion!" I broke the seal and unrolled the papyrus, scanning the contents rapidly. The scribe's exquisitely turned hieroglyphs sprang out at me and I felt the colour of an instant exhilaration flush my cheeks as I understood what was under my eye.

"Oh Ramses," I managed. "This is too much. I do not deserve it." He laughed happily.

"I have deeded to you ten arouras in the Fayum oasis. Five contain an orchard. The rest is grass but you can have it seeded to grain if you wish. In fact," he leaned forward with mock solemnity, "you can do anything with it that you want. Why not have it flooded from the lake and wade about in the mud like a true peasant?" His expression was impish. "One more thing." He unrolled the second scroll himself, cleared his throat, and read sonorously aloud, "'In accord with the supreme authority I, Ramses Heq On, the Mighty One of Years, hold as God in Egypt I bestow upon the concubine Thu, beloved of My Majesty, the title of Lady and a place among the orders of minor nobility commensurate with the title, in recognition of her superior talent as My Majesty's personal physician.' The Heralds will call the news." He thrust that scroll at me also and sat back, hands on his knees. "Copies already lie in the chests of the Royal Archives. Are you pleased, Lady Thu?"

Lady Thu. Lady. A title, and enough arouras to support two large families for a year. I was a noble landowner. The delicious unreality of it stunned me, and all of a sudden I burst into tears.

"Come come," Ramses said anxiously. "Are you so disappointed? Do not cry, Thu. You will make your eyes swollen and besides, your King cannot bear the sight of a beautiful woman in distress."

"No!" I choked. "Not disappointed, Great One. Oh, not at all," and I collapsed into his arms. With my face against his warm neck I wept while he pulled me close and stroked my arm soothingly.

"There is much in you that is still a child," he said. "Paibekamun! Bring linen! Now blow your nose, my Lady Thu, and run along to your new playroom. I will send for you later and we will eat on the river and enjoy the night breezes. Yes?" I nodded, blew my nose, kissed him, and slid from his lap.

"Thank you, Ramses," I whispered. He made a face.

"How many times must I tell you that you may not use my name," he grumbled, but his mouth was quivering. He waved me away, and clutching my precious scrolls I performed my obeisance and left his presence, running in the late bronze light along the short passage between his bedchamber and the path that divided the palace from the harem and then through my own door.

Disenk rose obediently, her expression becoming startled at my tear-stained appearance. I babbled out my news, the scrolls still hugged to my chest. A smile of sheer satisfaction spread across her delicate features and I thought how much my title would please her snobbish little heart.

"Get me a harem scribe," I requested. "I want to dictate a letter to my family. Then clean me up, Disenk. I am to go boating with Pharaoh this evening." Her bow was profound and she glided out with alacrity.

I have had much time lately to reflect upon my life. I do so with anger, with great bitterness, with hot shame when I consider my naïvety, but I do not think that I fear the censure of the gods any more. For in that moment when Ramses read to me from the scroll bestowing a nobility upon me that I in truth did not deserve, the emotions of gratitude and humility that welled up in me and spilled over into tears were entirely genuine. I have been cold and calculating. I have been selfish, deceitful and unscrupulous. But on that occasion my heart was touched and opened naturally, revealing a blossom long hidden in darkness. Surely the gods will forgive me all else because of that brief blooming! It was

Panauk who answered my summons. I greeted him with surprise for although I knew he was a scribe of the harem I had identified him more closely with Hui's house than with the maelstrom of the women's quarters. He congratulated me politely on my elevation, sank onto the mat, and set his palette across his bare knees.

I dictated quickly, telling my mother and father of my good fortune and wishing them well, those two insubstantial shades from my past. I ended with a message for Pa-ari. "Dearest friend and brother," I said. "Now that I am to have charge of my own land I need a reliable scribe. I beseech you to come to Pi-Ramses with Isis your betrothed. I will find good quarters for you both and see that you lack for nothing. Think well before you refuse me! I love and miss you. By the hand of Panauk, Scribe of the Harem, for the Lady Thu." I watched Panauk inscribe the last words. Then he looked up.

"It would be a good thing to have your brother as your personal scribe," he said. "His loyalty would be above reproach. The scribes assigned to the harem are on the whole discreet men, but a brother could be trusted to keep every secret safe." I turned on him furiously.

"A scribe may not comment on the contents of the dictation!" I snapped. "You know that, Panauk! Please have the scroll sent as soon as possible. You are dismissed." He gathered up his tools and bowed himself out, but his lack of respect had caused an ache in me and I was glad to listen to Disenk's admiring chatter as she dressed me for my outing on the Nile.

Late in the following afternoon I sent for Hui's Land Surveyor, Adiroma, requesting that he bring maps of the Fayum. He was a small, brisk man with a seamed face and hands clawed by disease. I watched as one of his deformed fingers traced the outline of my land on the papyrus he had spread out on my table.

"It is a munificent gift, Lady Thu," he said. "It embraces

good soil right on the edge of the lake. I see that it abuts temple property. I advise you to allow me to travel there with my assistants and ascertain the borders correctly, though perhaps the god's men will not wish to contest the boundaries considering who has deeded it to you." I thrilled to his easy use of my new title. The novelty of it would never wear off, I was sure.

"Thank you, Adiroma, that would be excellent," I replied. "How long before you can report back to me?"

"With favourable winds I can be there in a day and a half," he told me. "The survey will take two or three days. Before I go I will search the archives to make sure that the history of the land is pure. I am sure it will be."

"So you will bring me word in about a week." I straightened after casting one last proprietary look at the wandering trace on the map that enclosed a piece of Egypt belonging solely, completely, to me. Passing him a cup of beer, which he had said he preferred to wine, I said, "Take someone with you who can judge the fertility of the soil and make recommendations to me on its use. I intend to have it farmed, Adiroma." He took the cup carefully in his gnarled hand.

"That is good, Lady. But if you make it yield you must have it handled by an honest Overseer. Too many harem women who own land only wish to add to their store of trinkets and baubles, and their servants grow fat on the remainder. Besides, if the land is not loved it will not produce well." I felt myself warming to this capable little Surveyor.

"My father used to say the same thing," I smiled. "Can you recommend such a person?"

"Of course. I will take one of the Master's Overseers with me. My charge for the work will come out of your first crops."

"Agreed."

We drank our beer in leisurely fashion and when his cup was empty he rose, bowed, and went away, taking his maps with him.

Chapter 18

In the following months I scarcely saw my new quarters. Every day I was summoned to walk with Pharaoh, whose leg had completed its healing, or to tell him the stories about Aswat of which he never seemed to tire, or to massage away the tensions and worries that often stiffened his massive body. Every evening there was a feast or a boating party. Often there were temple ceremonies, for in addition to the seven days of holiday each month established by ancient custom there were the feast days of Amun every third day that Ramses had added to the sacerdotal calendar. Sometimes we took skiffs into the Delta marshes, and while Ramses and I reclined lazily on cushions his courtiers would stand poised on the prows of their crafts, ivory throwing sticks in their hands, waiting to bring down the ducks that lived in profusion amongst the high reed fronds.

Adiroma returned. He entered my quarters in the company of a tall, bronzed woman with a pleasant, well-painted face, and a direct gaze. They bowed, and Adiroma indicated her.

"Greetings, Lady Thu. May I present Wia, Overseer of Land and Cattle to the Master." I blinked, hiding my surprise. I had never seen a female overseer before. I looked her over surreptitiously. There was nothing masculine about her, although she carried herself with confidence and I could imagine her striding purposefully over the fields. She returned my smile cautiously, sliding into the chair I offered and placing the scroll she was holding in her lap. I noticed that the nails of her blunt hands were cut very short.

"You are both welcome," I said as Disenk poured beer in a glowing dark stream that caught one of the shafts of white light from my high windows. "What do you have to tell me, Adiroma?" He cleared his throat.

"The land is indeed beautiful," he said. "The irrigation canals that bisect it are lined with healthy palm trees. There is a small date grove, and just within the desert boundary there is a house, very dilapidated but surrounded by pomegranate and sycamore trees. It has a tiny but neglected garden."

"And the boundaries?"

"There is no problem." He shuffled his notes. "To the north your land abuts that of the temple of Sebek and beyond his domain is his town. To the south is also a temple, that of Herishef. The west is desert and to the east, of course, is the waterway that feeds the lake. I have searched the records and the boundaries are secure and correct. They will not be disputed."

Sebek the crocodile and Herishef the ram-headed. My precious land stood between two powerful gods of fertility. In fact Sebek was he-who-causes-to-be-pregnant, and many barren women made the pilgrimage to the lake to offer food to the god's sacred manifestation who lived in the water. If the beast, whose ears and forelegs dripped with the gold and jewels with which the priests festooned him. accepted the food it was a sign of his benevolence. I would have to be very careful. I certainly did not want Sebek's form of approval. I turned to Wia.

"Overseer," I addressed her formally. "What of the soil? What do you recommend for my arouras?" Wia unrolled her scroll. One thick silver band encircled her brawny wrist.

"The soil is black and of excellent quality," she said. "It has been abused by being allowed to revert to grass with the yearly flooding, and livestock has been pastured on it, but in my opinion it will yield much grain if the stubble is turned under after each harvest and the irrigation canals are kept clear." She glanced at me. "The details are in my report, Lady Thu, which I will leave with you. The date grove has likewise been neglected but if pruned the trees will give a good return. The garden of the house will naturally provide vegetables and pomegranates, but not enough for barter." I was impressed with her thoroughness.

"What do you suggest?" She let the scroll roll closed.

"Have the arouras dug over and seeded to barley. Prune and tend the dates. For the moment, have a portion of the house garden planted with chickpeas and garlic. Both can be sold. If you do this I can promise you a healthy profit."

I sat thinking. I wanted the house repaired for my own use. Naturally I would have to visit my arouras from time to time to see to the work done there and besides, the idea of my very own dwelling thrilled me. A house would have to be built for my Overseer. Fellahin would have to be hired, seed purchased, and until the first harvest I would be carrying it all.

"Are there outbuildings?" I wanted to know. Adiroma nodded.

"The house kitchen, outdoor shrine and servants' quarters survive but in very poor condition. However, as all of it is built of mud bricks the repairs can be swift and cheap." Not cheap enough for me, I thought. Aloud I said, "Thank you both for your assessments. If you will submit your account to me I will promise to pay you from my first crop." Wia smiled thinly. Adiroma coughed politely.

"As it happens," he said hesitantly, "the Master has already paid us. He did not wish you to begin your farming venture under any debt, Lady Thu."

For a moment I could not fill the silence that had fallen. I stared at the Surveyor blankly while a tide of dismay, apprehension and disappointment washed over me. I am still a child to Hui, I thought resignedly. He is still the benevolent

father doling out favours. I can only break the bond by severing the threads that anchor me to him one at a time, yet
how can I begin with this one? How can I pay for everything? I rose and immediately they followed suit. Wia placed
her scroll on the table.

"Please thank the Master for me," I said dully, "and tell
him how much I appreciate his kind gesture. I will dictate a
letter to him at once." They bowed and left, and I regained
my chair and sat forward, chin in hand, brooding. I would
indeed thank Hui myself but I did not feel grateful. I felt suffocated, and suddenly remembering my last feast at his
house, the odd, eager questions of the men, their inquisitive
sharp eyes, I also felt threatened; why, I did not know. Hui
loved me. Hui wanted only to help. Then why did it seem to
me as though I was putting my hand into the gaping jaws of
Smam-khefti-f? Ashamed and yet uneasy I spoke to Disenk.
"Bring me my jewellery box."

I sat with the pretty ebony and ivory box on my knees
and sifted through the contents, mostly the various earrings
and bracelets, anklets and hair ornaments Ramses had
tossed my way in his careless, generous manner. I selected a
silver necklace studded with jasper suns and a silver bracelet
engraved with a series of Eyes of Horus and hung with the
god's golden tears. Reluctantly I handed them to my servant. What were they worth? A deben at least. Enough to
buy food for how many workmen for a year? Two to repair
the house and outbuildings. One Overseer. Three for the
field work and care of the trees. A deben would buy grain,
vegetables, fish and beer for them if I and they were careful.
"Take these to Amunnakht," I said to Disenk. "Tell him that
I want the equivalent in edible goods over the next year,
beginning at once." Seeing her expression I explained. "I
need to pay my workmen. Amunnakht will not cheat me."

"Neither will the Master," Disenk protested. "Go to him,
Lady. He will take your silver and you will not lie awake at

night worrying about his honesty."

"No." I laid the baubles gently on her tiny palm. "No, Disenk. I want to do this my own way. Obtain a receipt from the Keeper of the Door."

But where would I find my staff? I wondered anxiously when she had gone. I was determined not to ask Hui for help. I did not want to be more obligated to him than I already was, for the more I owed him the more guilty I would feel about my increasing reluctance to further his ambitions with regard to Pharaoh, yet I had no other resource. I did not want to rely on Ramses either. The land was mine alone, a proof of my passage into adulthood, its soil a symbol of my success, and I wanted to nurse its rebirth as carefully as though it had emerged from my own body. That image, springing vividly into my mind, was not as pleasant as it should have been and I poured myself a cup of the rich barley beer and drank it quickly.

In the end it was Hunro who found a reliable overseer for me, a man who was working on her brother Banemus's estate as an assistant to Banemus's Chief Overseer and who was worthy of promotion. I met with him, was satisfied with his answers to my questions, and hired him, requisitioning my first goods from Amunnakht and sending my new servant south. I did so with great pride, and with even greater pride I received his letter a month later, a detailed account of all that had been done and a list of his disbursements. I was on my way to the secure wealth I had always craved.

Two months later I had not heard from Pa-ari. Aswat had answered my letter with a heavy silence and though I was becoming anxious I did not write again. The Chief Royal Herald of the House of Women assured me that my scroll had been delivered safely, and I refused to beg Pa-ari to come. However, my Overseer's letters arrived regularly and I read with delight how he and his charges had repaired the servants' quarters for their immediate use and were making good progress on the house. The date palms were being pruned and the fields cleared of debris. I longed to see it but I wanted to wait until it was entirely restored.

I did not mention the work being done there to Ramses and he did not ask how I was enjoying my responsibilities as a landowner. He had received word that his trading vessels were about to dock at Pi-Ramses. The mission had been completely successful, and Pharaoh was preoccupied with planning the ceremonies of welcome and the distribution of the goods the ships contained. He and his Chief Minister of Protocol were closeted together for many hours, and I was informed by Disenk that the High Priest of Amun was on his way from Thebes.

I was with the King when the scrolls containing the extent of the bounty were brought to him by Tehuti. Wrapped loosely in a sheet, I sat on his couch, fruit and wine at my hand, while the sweet aroma of burning olive wood drifted through the room from the brazier in the corner and the lamps gave out a steady glow. The evening was cool, and Ramses himself had flung a woollen cape over his short kilt when he had gone to sit in his chair at the announcement of his scribe's entrance.

The man bowed, tumbling his lists onto the table, and at Pharaoh's nod he selected one and opened it. Behind him two other scribes went to the floor, settling their palettes across their knees. One I recognized. He was Tehuti's assistant. The other wore a golden armband with the likeness of Amun imprinted upon it. The god's twin plumes rose tall and graceful from his crown and his benign face seemed to radiate a contented complacency. This scribe came from Thebes, from the Temple of Amun. Ramses sighed and smiled, and only I detected the resignation behind the inviting expression on his face. "Begin," he ordered. With a glance at me, Tehuti took a breath.

"Two thousand ingots of copper, three thousand of lead

and seven hundred sacks of incense." He waited. Ramses' corpulent fingers were tapping out an irregular rhythm on the table.

"One thousand ingots for the Royal Treasury," he said at last. "Three hundred for Ptah, two hundred for Ra at On, and five hundred for Amun. Of the lead, two thousand for the army and the remainder to Ptah. Two hundred sacks of incense for the palace and its personal shrines, one hundred for the army, and the remaining four hundred to be distributed among the temples." Again there was a tiny sigh, and although his glance did not slide to the priestly scribe he seemed to be waiting for an interruption. The scribe laid down his pen.

"Your pardon, Great Pharaoh," he said softly, "but Amun has need of more copper than Your Majesty is prepared to allot. Amun has contributed gold and men to this expedition. Moreover, Amun's workmen are engaged in making many chests of copper to hold an increase in gifts to the God, and his temple at Takompso has been lacking copper doors for a long time."

"Amun already has the disbursement of twenty-one times more copper than all other temples in Egypt combined," Ramses answered. "I do not see why I should provide more. Perhaps Amun's overseers are careless in their apportionment of the metal."

"Your pardon, Mighty Bull, but Your Majesty did not think so when Your Majesty requested copper for the manufacture of new dress accoutrements for the army last year," the scribe objected stubbornly. "If Your Majesty will not increase this portion, Amun may very well be unable to meet any new demands Your Majesty might make in the future. Amun supports eighty-seven thousand people throughout Egypt. Copper is a vital medium of payment, quite apart from its other uses. We are happy with our allotment of lead and incense, however."

"I'm so glad," Ramses murmured, "seeing that lead is used primarily in the faience factories and Amun grows many of his own incense-bearing trees. Very well. Take an extra two hundred ingots of copper from the Royal Treasury." Both scribes' heads went down and the soft shushing of their pens could be heard. "What next?" Ramses asked.

"One hundred sacks of incense from Your Majesty's private grove at Pwene arrived at the same time as the goods from the expedition. That need not concern us now," Tehuti said loudly. "Of gold in grains, sixty thousand. Of bars of silver, twenty-five thousand. Of blue stones of Tafrer, six pyramids. Of green stones of Roshatha, five pyramids." He paused. Ramses closed and opened his eyes very slowly. He looked not so much tired as supremely patient, even uncaring. My presence had been forgotten and I was listening avidly.

"Seeing that Amun obtains twenty-six thousand grains of gold from his own lands every year, I see no reason to apportion him any," Ramses said. "I will take thirty thousand grains, and the rest can be distributed evenly among Ptah, Ra and Set."

"Majesty!" the temple scribe interrupted hotly, "I beg you to consider that it takes twelve kite of gold to pay for the grain allotted to one tombworker for a year. You yourself have placed the construction of all royal tombs at Thebes in the hands of the servants of Amun. If the gold apportionment to Amun is not increased, there is a danger that your workmen will not be paid, and what will result? Unrest, perhaps even bloodshed. Amun cannot afford to pay these men out of his own coffers. He has his own servants whose bellies must be filled. Your workmen often receive their pay from Amun's storehouses as it is. Majesty, your ruling is not just! Is not Amun the God of Victories? Has he not caused Egypt to triumph over her enemies time and again? Does he not deserve a portion, however small, of the good fortune the trading ships have had?" Ramses' hand now lay flaccid on the surface of the littered table. He was looking at the lapis-tiled floor that gleamed darkly blue between his sandalled feet. By the sheer immobility of his features I knew he was angry and I expected an explosion of divine rage at any moment but it did not come. As the scribe's indignant diatribe ceased, Ramses looked up.

"In spite of the gold I continually pour into Amun's store-houses it seems that his servants find it difficult to procure enough grain to pay my workmen more than the minimum amount set by the Overseer of Buildings," he said mildly. "Why is that, I wonder? And if Amun is indeed the God of Victories, why are his servants so often miserly in their donations to Egypt's fighting men? I do not need you to remind me of the obligations my father shouldered, upstart. Nor do I intend to go back on my word to the God whom I love and revere. It is the sound of his servants' voices, not the tones of the God himself, that tires and saddens me." The scribe flushed but his eyes glittered and I knew that he was not going to give way.

Ramses was speaking again, giving in, allowing Amun this much of the gold, that much of the precious blue and green stones, and I sat hunched under my tent of sheets, hands clutching my ankles, teeth clenched. Who do you think you are anyway? I asked the temple scribe furiously and silently. You are nothing but a minion. Where is the High Priest? He is the one who should be honouring the Horus Throne by his presence, but he is showing his contempt by sending this puny little under-scribe. Usermaarenakht knows that this is not a negotiation. So does Ramses. This is a worn and famil-iar formula in which the temple gets what it wants and the King may keep a semblance of his pride.

I no longer listened to the details of the discussion that was nothing more than a waste of words, time and papyrus. Tomorrow, in the great outer court of Amun's Pi-Ramses home, the treasure and the trinkets, the riches and the oddities, would already have been divided into appropriate piles over which the delegates from the several temples would hover protectively through the long, elaborate ceremonies of rejoicing. There would be a great feast in the palace. The priests, temple guards, temple scribes, would eat Ramses' food and drink his fine wines. They would applaud his expensive entertainments and ogle his beautiful women. Then they would have their booty, for such it was, loaded onto barges and they would disappear like rats, like locusts exhausted after their rape. Words slipped vaguely into my ears... Turquoise, chests, vases, images of exotic animals, foreigners who had come to Egypt with the trading fleet to do homage to the most powerful God in the world... Which God? I wondered cynically. Ah Ramses, dear King, with your childlike enthusiasms, your careless generosity, your eager fumblings, why do you allow yourself to be humiliated in this way?

When I came to myself the scribes had gone and Ramses was rising stiffly from his chair. Paibekamun was offering him mulled wine and its steam wafted fragrantly, mingling with the olive wood smoke. Ramses took the cup, shed his cloak, and stretching until I heard his spine crack he came over to the couch. His pendulous cheeks looked doughy and his eyes were bloodshot. "I could have dismissed you hours ago, Thu," he said wearily as I made room for him and he collapsed upon the mattress. He leaned back against the pillows, took a mouthful of wine, and held it before swallowing noisily. "I had forgotten that you were here. You should have made your presence known. I would like to make love to you immediately but I am just too tired. I must be in the temple at dawn tomorrow to perform the sacred duties in person and then I must sit in the forecourt to distribute the bounty the ships brought home." I watched as one of his body servants unloosed his sandals and another came with hot water to wash him. He lay unmoving, like a misshapen cloth doll stuffed with straw, as they reverently lifted his feet, his arms.

"The bounty has already been distributed," I said. "All you have to do, Majesty, is watch it disappear." My tone must have been more acerbic than I had intended, for he suddenly waved the servants away and sat up, glancing at me keenly.

"My little concubine has the temerity to disapprove of her King's judgements?" he said sharply. "Perhaps she would like to don the Double Crown and attempt to exhibit more discretion than her Lord?"

I knew that he was exhausted and on edge, that he had been forced to control his temper all evening and that effort alone had taken its toll, but for the sake of the loyalty I felt I still owed to Hui I decided to speak up. My position had never been so secure. I was high in Ramses' favour. He would listen to me. He was watching me over the rim of his gold cup, frowning, his bloodshot eyes attentive. I shook back my tousled hair in a gesture I knew he liked, and gave him the full force of my blue eyes from under lowered lids. "Majesty," I began softly, "it distresses me to see you seemingly cornered by such lesser men as the under-scribe, to see you give away the fruits of your labour and your worry. The whole of Egypt belongs to you by right of your Divine Incarnation. Why then do you allow the priests to abuse your generosity and carry away your gain like an army of ants descending on a ripe date? Are their treasuries not already greater than those of the Great House? Forgive me, Horus, but I am angered by their rapacity. I do not understand."

He gazed at me for a long time, and his steady scrutiny gradually deepened into an expression of cool conjecture that I had never seen before. It made me uneasy. He drank again, still regarding me, then he heaved himself further upright and left the couch, taking a chair that placed him opposite me. He crossed his legs, jerked his cup at Paibekamun, waited while it was refilled, and not once did his eyes leave my face. The pouches under them seemed to darken, the light from the lamp on the table beside him making a series of bars of shadow over his features, giving them a stony cast. When he did speak, his voice was hoarse.

"You have angered me, Thu. By what right do you, a mere concubine, question the wisdom of your God? Yet because I love you, because you have given me great pleasure and have shown some intelligence in the treatment of my ailments, I will now stoop to acquaint you with the true state of internal affairs that exists in Egypt. You are honoured. I discuss these things only with a few of my ministers and with Chief Wife Ast-Amasareth. Listen well, and then do not insult me with the ignorance of your shallow concern again." His naked foot, broad and blue-veined, began to swing to and fro, its shadow expanding and contracting across the tiled floor. I wanted to fix my gaze on it rather than on his face, for his words had humiliated me and I felt like a reprimanded child, but I made myself meet his eyes. They were like hard, black raisins. "First of all," he continued curtly, "you must understand that by long and holy tradition, all temples are exempt from taxation by the Horus Throne. This is as it should be. The gods pour out their blessings upon Egypt. Why then should they be forced to channel the gifts they give so freely? Their servants administer for them the sacrifices that come into their precincts from worshippers and petitioners and the yield from their fields, herds and vineyards. And why not? To attempt to steal from the gods would be a grave blasphemy. One might say," he said, anticipating my mute objection, "that the one who sits upon the Horus Throne, being the Incarnation of Amun himself, has the right to command what goods he wishes from wherever he wishes, but the Incarnation rules beneath the God. The spirit of the God is in him but he is not the God. No Pharaoh would dare to change the way of ancient Ma'at. Certainly not myself." He paused to sip the wine from which fragrant coils of steam rose, but his foot still swayed its signal of irritation. "So," he rasped, "that avenue of income is closed to the Double Crown. Secondly, because of the promises made to the priests by my father in exchange for their support during the time of trouble, I am bound to conciliate Amun. I know full well what political and economic power his priests hold. My father had no ministers that he could trust, and indeed, long before the time of trouble the secular positions had gone to the priests and become hereditary so that a man might be Treasurer and also High Priest, and pass both stations to his son. The noble families of Thebes and Pi-Ramses control both temple and palace administration. Why do I allow this?" He smiled faintly, humourlessly. "Because I have no choice. Theirs is the power. Its roots are deep in Egyptian soil. My power resides in less stable earth. I have inherited an army made up of largely foreign mercenaries hired by my father to subdue the native nomarchs who rose up when the strength of the central authority failed. Each town, each nome, preyed upon the other, Egyptian against Egyptian. Libu and Syrian adventurers were hired to bring peace. They and the foreign slaves I captured and brought home from my wars remain my only weapon. They must be paid, for their loyalty is to gold, not to the Throne. How are they paid?" He shifted in the chair, one ample hip heaving under his thin linen, and his features changed as the lamplight threw new shadows over it. "By taxes, of course. And what may Pharaoh tax? He may have one-tenth of all crops and animals from all land and people not belonging to the gods. And that is not much, my Lady Thu. He may collect dues, he may tax monopolies held by his nobles, he may make requisitions. He has his gold mines, of course, but their yield is lessening. You did not know that, did you? Every year brings fewer grains to swell a Treasury on which the demands grow. He has his trading vessels. But trade is also dwindling. Amun has his fleets on the Great Green and on the Red Sea, trading with Phoenicia, Syria and Punt, and Amun can offer more in trade than Pharaoh can. Amun is richer. Ptah and Ra also have their ships, but the temple records of those gods reside at Amun's temple in Thebes. The priests of Amun supervise the administration of all other temples. They also supervise my secular administration because they are also my overseers and ministers. This too I inherited from my ancestors. So Thebes grows in strength and Pi-Ramses declines. And I allow it to happen."

There was a long silence. Ramses' cheek slid into his palm but his attention remained fixed on me. I dared not move. I could feel his anger, still curdling at my effrontery, and I was terrified that I had incurred his permanent displeasure. I heard and understood his words but their impact was dissipated by my own inner turmoil. "I allow it to happen," he repeated at last. "And why? Because I do not trust my Generals, I do not trust the members of my administration and I do not trust my sons. If I move to shake off the weight I carry I could plunge Egypt into yet another henti of anarchy and bloodshed. Whom can I trust? The majority of my high state and court officials who do not belong to families of priests are foreigners. Of my eleven Butlers, five are Syrian or Libu. Not him," he jerked his head at Paibekamun, motionless in the dimness beyond the circle of the light. "He is Egyptian born and bred. But to announce an upheaval would be to put them all to the test and they would fail. Amun rules Egypt, not me." I managed to clear my throat. It was dry and burning yet I felt choked.

"What of your son, Majesty?" I whispered. "Surely Prince Ramses with the men he commands..." He laughed harshly.

"My sons, you mean," he said. "Ah yes, my little Horus-Fledglings. All with their military toys, their quarrelling and foolish jealousies. Do you know how many sons I have, Thu? Pa-Ra-her-unami-f, Montu-her-khepesh-f, Meri-Tem, Khaemwaset, Amun-her-khepesh-f, Ramses-meri-Amun, all of them legitimate, all of them eager and hot-blooded, all of them panting to be declared my Heir. And the eldest, of course. Prince Ramses. He of the mysterious air and godlike beauty. Trust him? Trust any of them? No! For they are fawned upon and flattered and bribed and courted by every faction at court and in the temples with any pretensions to power in Egypt, and if I make a move to declare any one of them the Horus-in-the-Nest the rest will scream their disappointed outrage and the power mongers will swiftly take sides. No. I am content to let the gaming pieces fall where they may. When I feel the touch of the God upon my shoulder, and my days in Egypt are numbered, then I will declare a successor who can untangle the maze Egypt has become if he has the strength and the wit. I have done my part. I have kept the foreign wolves from the borders. Let him deal with the rats within. As for you…" He struggled out of the chair, pulled away the sheet I had been clutching to my neck, and pointed to my sandals. "Leave my presence, and do not insult me again with your foolish and arrogant ideas of what should be. You are like a suckling babe trying to read the Admonitions of Imhotep." He had become a powerful and cold stranger, this man with whom I had wrestled and laughed, who had stroked my head when I sat at his feet during the feasts and beamed with an indulgent delight while he showered me with gifts. I did not dare to look at him. Quickly I slid from the couch, put on my sandals, and prostrated myself before him, conscious all the time of his rancour, his contempt for me. Head down I backed to the door, but as I reached it I risked a glance at him. He had already turned away and was talking to Paibekamun. Crushed, I slunk into the darkness.

Chapter 19

I was not invited to the formal distribution of the treasure the ships had brought home. After a night of restless sleep and lurid dreams I sat just within my door where my shame could not be seen, and watched and listened to the furore as the other women prepared to enjoy the great day. The harem was emptying. Even the drunken Hatia, swathed in red linen, her pallid face garishly painted, paced unsteadily in and out of my vision, her body servant behind her, as she waited for the summons to the litters. The occasion seemed to infect the precincts with a kind of hysteria. Children cried, harried servants exchanged sharp words as they rushed to and fro, and the high, shrill voices of the inmates filled the air like the senseless gibberish of a flock of agitated birds.

Disenk hovered at my rear, silently passing me water that did not seem to quench my thirst and fruit that stuck in my throat. I was not particularly disappointed at missing the festivities. I would have had to stand under the tenuous shade of my gauze canopy for hours, my feet aching, the sweat gathering under my fine sheath, the metal of my jewellery burning against my skin. No, it was the public nature of my disgrace that ate at my vitals. The whole court, the entire harem, would notice my absence, comment upon it, whisper about it with unfeeling glee. She rose too fast, they would say with mock concern, their eyes alight at the delicious tit-bit of gossip. She was arrogant and aloof, and now she is paying. Poor Lady Thu. Poor trumped-up little commoner.

I both dreaded and longed for a visit from Hunro, but no

one darkened my door, and at last the vast courtyard emptied and I dared to emerge and walk alone upon the dry grass. Sitting beside the pool with its busy fountain I gave way to rage and a mounting trepidation. Would Ramses forgive me? Was his affection deep enough to overcome my indiscretion?

Later, kneeling before the pool with my folded arms upon the rim and my eyes fixed unseeingly on the play of sunlight infusing the surface, I heard the bray of horns and faintly the roar of the crowd gathered around the temple forecourt. Palace and temple guards in leather-scaled armoured tunics, their bronze helmets flashing, would be holding back the thousands of city dwellers pressing to catch a glimpse of Pharaoh and the mounds of gold, silver and precious stones with which he would be surrounded. The Queen, tiny and regal, would be at Ramses' right hand, Ast-Amasareth with her red, red mouth over jumbled teeth at his left.

And who would be standing in my place, behind the God, with her hand resting lightly on his shoulder? Did I have a rival already, or was the space vacant? I did not want to think about such things. I did not want to consider any of it. There was a griping pain in my belly and my head was beginning to ache.

Disenk persuaded me to submit to a massage, and I lay in the coolness of my room while her hands passed soothingly over me. Was it my imagination, or was she treating me with less esteem today than yesterday? I closed my eyes and willed myself to become calm. I was building a pyramid out of a small stone, driving myself deeper into nothing but a foolish fantasy. Damn you, Hui, I thought as I felt my body gradually relax. You and your insane ideas. For what, in the end, can Ramses do but struggle to compromise with and conciliate the priests? I dozed in the intensifying heat of noon.

I knew that the women would not return until the following dawn, for the celebrations would fill every room of the palace with music and dancing, drinking and revelry, so I spent the remaining hours of the day in reading, swimming, and talking to Disenk. But at sunset, when I was sitting quietly by the pool as the solid shade of the building behind me crept over the grass and Disenk was about to serve me my evening meal, a royal Herald approached, bowed, and handed me a scroll. "A communication from Aswat, Lady Thu," he said politely. I thanked him, my mood lifting immediately, and tore the missive open. It had to be from Pa-ari, telling me when he would arrive. I must talk with Amunnakht, I thought happily as I unrolled the papyrus. Quarters must be prepared with the other harem scribes, and furnishings provided. My food forgotten, I began to read. The sight of the script written in his own meticulous, neat hand gave me a rush of reassuring warmth.

"My dearest sister," I read. "Forgive the length of time that has passed since I received your letter. And forgive, also, the words I must reply. I cannot come to Pi-Ramses. I am now fully employed in a position of trust by the priests of Wepwawet, and Isis and I signed our marriage contract last month. We have a house behind the temple, with a small garden and fish pond, and we are expecting our first child towards the end of the year. Please understand, dear Thu. I love you but I would not be happy in Pi-Ramses, and surely the harem does not need yet another able scribe as much as Wepwawet, and my wife, need me here. Write to me soon and tell me that I am forgiven, for until then I will live in the utmost fear that I have lost your affection."

But I do need you, Pa-ari, I thought in anguish as I let the scroll fall from my hand and curl in upon itself. I need you desperately. I have no friends here, no one who will give me a rock of unselfish love on which to plant my feet! Oh my brother, will you desert me also?

I was shaken by a fierce jealousy, seeing in my mind's eye the little mud brick house in the shadow of my totem's temple, the slow-moving orange fish undulating placidly in the depths of the modest pool. Pa-ari would come home to the adoring dark eyes of his Isis and together they would eat their simple meal in the peace of an Aswat evening while the sunset glowed red in their tidy little garden and the palm trees stood in a dignified stillness, outlined against the copper-coloured sky.

"Disenk," I called gruffly, "bring me my medicine box. I will lie here in the grass and chew kat leaves. I do not wish to exist in the glare of this reality any more." Picking up Pa-ari's scroll I held it to my face, trying vainly to catch from it a whiff of his comforting smell, but the papyrus was dry and odourless. I tore it in two and dropped it into the water.

My punishment lasted three days, during which Pharaoh's silence was like a wall of adamant around me. The women eyed me warily. Their servants, when I chanced to meet them, were respectful but distant. Hatia shocked me by giving me a smile of such malevolent complicity as I passed her on the second day on my way to the bath house that my scalp prickled. I hated them all, the silly, shallow females, the ridiculously snobbish underlings, the spoiled, pouting children always underfoot. I wanted to scream at them, strike out in some way, but I moved from my privileged quarters to my bath, from the pool where I swam to the grassy spot where I blatantly exercised under their avid eyes, with my chin high. "Never mind," Hunro said on the one occasion when she came to my rooms. "It cannot last, Thu. Ramses is not used to hearing intelligent argument from the women he sleeps with, only from the Queen and the Chief Wife who do not challenge his virility any more when they open their mouths to engage him on some point of political strategy. You madden him but you also fascinate him. He will send word soon." She grinned at me, the picture of vigorous good health and beauty, making me feel pale and thin. "If not, you can always choose a lover from among the rest of us. There is satiation in a woman's arms as well as a man's, you know." I answered her sourly, curtly, but she was right, for on the evening of the third day I was summoned to the royal bedchamber. I went apprehensively, feeling as though I would have to conquer Pharaoh all over again.

But he greeted me effusively, enfolding me in an embrace even before I had fully risen from my obeisance and leading me to the table where sweetmeats and wine had been set out. Still holding my hand he urged me to sit and then bent over me, searching my face, his smile one of unaffected joy. "Dearest Thu!" he said. "I have missed you so much! My nights have been miserable without your warm body beneath the sheets and I have not slept well. How are you? A trifle wan, I see. Can it be that you have missed me also?" He spoke as though we had been apart for months rather than three tortuous days and I thought resentfully that if he had missed me so acutely it was his own fault, yet I could not help but respond to the note of insecurity in his voice.

"My King," I responded, "of course I have missed you! And I have been prostrate with the fear that I had seriously offended you and you had banished me from your presence for ever." He wagged a finger at me, took the chair opposite, and raised his eyebrows.

"You did offend me. And I have chastised you, my Lady. Let us speak of it no more. Tell me of Adiroma's report on your land. I hear he took a female Overseer with him to the Fayum. Most intriguing!"

I looked into those dark brown, lively eyes and thought how grossly Hui had underestimated this man who knew with pitiless omniscience the exact limits of his position and who obviously kept his stubby finger on the pulse of his domain. For the first time it struck me as puzzling that Hui, powerful and intelligent in his own right, a privileged physician with access to every member of the royal family, should have a weaker grasp of Ramses' true character and the issues confronting him than I did. But perhaps Hui had never faced his King in the way I had, nor heard his clear, succinct exposition.

I described my dealings with Adiroma and Wia as vividly as I could. It was not difficult. At the thought of my property I was filled with delight and did not need to feign animation. Ramses listened with a smug smile. "I am happy to have been able to bring you such pleasure, my little scorpion," he said at length. "Your words have kindled an interest in me. How would you like to take a trip to the Fayum, you and I, so that together we may inspect this piece of Egypt's dirt you have imbued with such sacred virtues?"

"Oh Ramses!" I cried out, leaving my chair and climbing onto his knee. "You are a good man and I love you! I would like it more than anything else in the world!"

"I am not a man, I am a God," he returned, amused as always at my enthusiasm, his arm encircling my waist. "And I hope there is something else in the world you like better, otherwise your King will be bitterly disappointed." He heaved himself upright, carrying me with him, stalked to the couch, and threw me upon it. Both of us were laughing. Falling beside me, he pulled me to him and began to kiss me avidly and I found, to my great surprise, that I had missed the scent of his skin and the taste of his mouth. Lust rose in me, and with a grunt I surrendered to its mindless insistence.

He had not directly commanded me to stay for the night. When he fell at last into an exhausted sleep I dressed, and Paibekamun let me out into the cooler air of the passage. As he held the door for me he said in a low voice, "The Master wishes to see you as soon as possible." I turned sharply. The face so close to mine was indistinct in the dimness. It told me nothing. Yet the impression of aloof superiority Paibekamun always gave was as strong as ever as our breath mingled. It came to me then that Paibekamun did not like me at all.

"If that is so, why does he not come to me?" I inquired, tired and annoyed. Behind us, on the great couch, Pharaoh stirred and groaned but did not wake. Paibekamun shrugged, a supremely indifferent gesture.

"I do not know. Perhaps he is too busy." Deliberately he withdrew and closed the door and I was left to make my way towards the harem. The guards at the meeting of passage and path greeted me quietly and I answered them absently. What did Hui want? Was something wrong? Had there been bad news from Aswat about my mother, my father? I sighed audibly as Disenk heard me coming and opened for me. Why had Hui not sent a message to my quarters? I did not worry about it overmuch. I was too relieved to be back in Pharaoh's bed.

Early in the morning I received word that Ramses was too occupied to travel at present but I was to be ready to sail to the Fayum at dawn the following day. At once I ordered out my skiff, hoping irritably that news of my visit to the Master would not reach Pharaoh and make him wonder why I had fled to my old home as soon as I was restored to favour. His jealousy was seldom expressed but very real and I did not want to prompt it so soon. As unobtrusively as possible I slipped out my private door, along the path, through the main entrance of the harem, with Disenk behind me, but of course I passed several guards on the way and Hunro, swimming her lengths in the pool just within the boundary of the House of Women, waved to me as I left.

However, once on the Lake I regained my equilibrium. The morning was fresh, with a strong breeze blowing off the water that tugged at the hangings of my cabin and pulled at my hair. My helmsman was singing softly as he guided us. My two rowers were working in unison. I could see their naked backs gleaming in the sun. The road on the bank was almost empty.

I could have reclined on my cushions for ever, savouring the feeling of freedom the scent of the orchards brought to me, but all too soon Hui's watersteps came into sight and we berthed, the helmsman scrambling from his perch to run out the ramp for me. This time no delegation waited to welcome me home. Disenk and I walked under the pylon. Hui's porter rose from his stool and at my terse order let us proceed. The only sounds came from the birds who whistled and piped above us.

The courtyard glared white and deserted but beyond the entrance pillars there were the subdued murmurings of household industry. A servant padded by at the far end of the long passage, catching the shaft of light from the open rear doors as he went. There was a clatter of dishes upstairs and an abrupt, nasal laugh. We waited. Presently the imposing form of Harshira emerged from the gloom in which we stood, and coming towards us with his usual unhurried dignity he bowed.

"I see that I am not expected, Harshira," I said.

"You are indeed expected, Lady Thu," the Steward replied calmly, "but we did not know at what time. Please forgive me this lapse. Disenk, you may wait in the servants' quarters. The Master is in his office, Lady." I nodded and brushed by him.

I knocked on the office door, and at the invitation to enter I went in. The inner office was open and as I approached it Hui came out. He looked tired but his smile was generous as he saw who it was. Taking my hands he pulled me forward. "Thu!" he exclaimed. "So my message reached you. Sit down." I arranged myself in the familiar chair that had received me so many times before.

"I cannot stay for long, Hui," I said. "Tomorrow Pharaoh and I are sailing to the Fayum to inspect my land. Why did you not come to see me yourself?" He had perched on the edge of his desk and was looking down on me.

"So you are back in the King's favour," he said thoughtfully. "Good. I am sorry for the summons, Thu, but there is an outbreak of fever in the city and many noble families have required my attention. Tell me what happened between Ramses and you."

"I am surprised that Paibekamun has not acquainted you with every word!" I responded hotly. "I resent that man, Hui. He has a secret contempt for me. There is no human warmth in him!" Hui leaned down and stroked my cheek and as always at his touch I felt my indignation begin to evaporate.

"Tell me, little one," he repeated gently.

"It was your fault," I said sulkily. "The scribes were there and Ramses was making decisions about the apportionment of the goods the trading vessels brought home. I listened, and afterwards I remonstrated with him. Too much was going to Amun and not enough into the royal coffers. He was very angry. He gave me a precise lesson in royal policy and sent me away." I swallowed. "I was in disgrace for three whole days, Hui! For three days I was scorned by all and I did not know if Pharaoh would ever invite me into his presence again!"

"But he did." Hui folded his arms. "He is your prisoner, Thu. He may appear to discipline you but he cannot live without you. After a decent interval you can bring up the subject again. Eventually he will submit." I stiffened.

"No, I don't think he will," I said deliberately. "I trusted your judgement, Master, but in this instance I believe it to be flawed. I have come to know Ramses better than you. He is perfectly aware of his situation, its causes and its dangers. He will not act to free himself because he cannot. I will never be able to change his mind, and I have no intention of trying any more." I rose and faced him. It took an act of courage to meet his eyes, this man who had been friend and mentor, father, judge and arbiter of my fate since I was little more than a child. I felt as though I was standing against a god. "I owe you everything, Hui," I went on with difficulty.

"All my dreams have come true because of you, and I can never repay you for all you have done. But I can no longer risk losing all I have gained. You and your friends—they think that Egypt can be righted, that Ma'at can be restored, but I have come to the conclusion that under Ramses it is impossible. Besides, which Ma'at, Hui? The Ma'at of an Egypt long gone? I will not plead the cause you follow with Pharaoh any more. I beg you to forgive me."

He did not move. His whole body went very still, apart from his eyes which travelled my face, sliding over each feature and back again. His own face was curiously blank. For a long time I stood tensely under his examination, outwardly calm but inwardly trembling. Then he sighed, nodded, and slid from the desk.

"Very well, Thu," he said equably. "You have been an obedient girl. You have done your best for me. Of course I forgive you. Now." He walked to the open door of the inner office. "You are in a hurry. What do you need to refurbish your medicine box?"

"I forgot to bring the box, Master," I said humbly. "But I need more acacia spikes. They are very important to me. And castor oil, and grey antimony for my salves. Cinnamon and fresh natron…" He held up a finger.

"I will make them up for you. Meanwhile, drink some wine." He pulled the door closed behind him, and miserably I poured wine and stared into its scarlet depths. I had let him down. I had failed him, and no matter how strong my resolve to avoid the subject of policy with Pharaoh in the future, I wished things could be different.

Hui emerged with a small chest which he placed in my hands. "The acacia spikes may appear to have a slightly blackish tinge," he said. "But do not worry. They are still efficacious even though they were harvested some time ago." Brushing the hair from my forehead he placed a lingering kiss between my eyes, sighed again, and pushed me kindly towards the passage. "Be happy, little Thu," he said. "I wish you well." A stab of alarm went through me. His words sounded like a farewell. I swung round to speak but his door was closing, and even as I stepped forward it was firmly shut.

Lifting my hand to knock I paused and lay my fingers flat against the fragrant cedar wood. No. I had made a decision. I had cut one more thread that bound the child I no longer was to the Seer who must not control my destiny any more. Nevertheless I was troubled as I sent for Disenk and we walked back to where my skiff rocked, and I saw the ramp run in and the ropes cast off with a sense of foreboding. Behind lay the roots I had sunk day by day, month by month, during my long sojourn in Hui's house. Ahead was the palace, where I was not yet anchored by any but the most delicate tendrils. I felt uncomfortably defenceless.

But just after dawn the next day I made my way proudly to the palace watersteps where the royal barge floated, waiting for me. The morning still held a fleeting coolness and the fragile pink in the eastern sky had not yet turned to blue. Although the distance to the Fayum was not great, little more than a day's swift sailing, a whole flotilla of craft jostled behind Pharaoh's boat and the steps were crowded with servants weaving their dance of preparation and calling to each other. All movement ceased as I came into view, Disenk behind me carrying the box containing my needs for the journey, and every head was lowered. I had placed a foot on the ramp of the barge when there was a further commotion. Ramses was coming, surrounded by his servants and guards. He strode purposefully towards me, smiling, looking refreshed, his jewelled sandals briskly slapping the stone. I, along with everyone else, prostrated myself. "Up!" Ramses barked, and I felt his heavy hand on my neck. "A fine morning, a beautiful morning," he almost sang. As I rose he flung an arm around my shoulders and ushered me onto the deck where chairs and cushions had been arranged.

In a flurry of activity the ramp was pulled in, the helmsman scrambled up to his post, the guards deployed themselves around the edges of the deck, and we cast off. The imperial flags of blue and white began to flap as they caught the breeze, and the captain's voice echoed as he set the pace for the rowers.

Ramses sank into a chair, lifted his feet onto a cushion, and folded his hands across his abdomen. He was wearing a long, pleated skirt fringed in gold tassels and topped by a filmy tunic. The royal Uraeus glinted above his wide forehead, and his gold-worked linen helmet moved stiffly against the gems lying across his collar-bones as he turned to beam at me. "A brief respite from the demands of the court," he said happily, "and my scorpion will once more be transformed into something less venomous. A dove, perhaps? A lamb? I feel expansive today, my Lady Thu, so we will sit here under the shade of the awning and allow my subjects to catch a glimpse of my holy person. Is not the season of Peret still glorious, though Shemu is almost upon us? Once past the city we will delight in the greenness of the orchards, and the crops springing thick in the fields." He leaned sideways and his kohled eyes twinkled into mine. "You see," he went on. "For your sake I am turning myself into a farmer today. Would I make a good farmer, Thu? It is a pity that you received your land too late to be sown this year, but we can stand in the mud together and take a rustic satisfaction in the future!" He was teasing me and I answered him in the same vein as the jumbled might of Pi-Ramses drifted past, its filth and noise interspersed with scented fruit trees and the flower-bedecked gardens and white watersteps of the rich.

At noon we ate and then retired to the sumptuous cabin where we made love and slept, and when we emerged into the bronze glow of the late afternoon the barge was still gliding on, seeking the canal that would turn us west towards the Fayum oasis.

As evening fell all the lamps were lit and we floated on, a string of bright stars resting on the bosom of the river. Often, during that magical day, the people on the bank would look up, stare, and then cry out to one another, "It is the King! The God is passing!" and I would hold tight to Ramses' hand as they bowed and called blessings to us that rang in my ears like precious music.

Not long into the dark hours we entered the cabin once more, talking quietly before our bodies curled together in peace and sleep, and when we woke, the barge had already docked at the Fayum.

The Fayum, with its vast lake surrounded by thousands of lush green fields and abundant groves of trees, is a jewel of beauty and fertility set in the midst of the desert, but I remember little of the things I saw. For one small sliver of it was mine and mine alone, and the emotion that seized me as Ramses and I stepped from the barge onto that soil cannot be described. Wordlessly I trod my ten arouras, and the image of myself toiling across the broken clods of my father's field to wrap my arms around his solid thigh and beg to go to school came vividly into my mind. Already I could see the results of the work that had been done. The irrigation ditches lined with palms had been partially cleared. Fresh, dark and earthy-smelling, the sod which had been grass for grazing was turned under and would be broken up so that my seed could be sown at the beginning of the next season of Peret.

Ramses did not walk with me. After taking one look at the sun-soaked, rough ground he ordered a chair and sat beside his litter, watching me as I paced to and fro. But when I had taken my fill he picked his way with me up the shattered stone path to my door, through the ravaged garden and beside the scummed pool, and received with me the obeisances of my servants. The Overseer apologized for the state of the garden. "I thought it necessary to begin work immediately in the fields and to rebuild the house and servants' quarters," he explained anxiously. "I hope I am following your instructions faithfully, Lady Thu. The garden and the pool will be restored when more important tasks have been accomplished." I agreed with him of course. Ramses grunted rather disparagingly as we made the short tour of the house itself. It was unfurnished, the rooms small, but I loved it. Excitedly I planned what I would do with every corner, and I pleaded with Ramses to allow me to spend one night in it alone.

"But it smells musty and is probably full of noxious insects," he grumbled. "Scorpions lurk in cool places." Then he grinned. "But you have an affinity to scorpions, don't you, Thu? Very well. You may rest here tonight providing you are guarded." I thanked him effusively, he went on smiling benevolently, and at sunset Disenk set up a cot in one of the rooms and palace guards took up their station outside.

I did not sleep much. I lay in the dark, listening to the tranquil silence, hugging my joy tightly to myself as the hours flowed away. Twice I got up and wandered into the moon-drenched, tangled garden, not minding the rank odour that rose from the black water of the pool or the patches of brittle weeds over which I sometimes stumbled. It was mine. All of it belonged to me.

Peasantlike I had formed an immediate bond with the earth. It would not betray me. It would not reward my care and diligence with the ingratitude of selfishness. It would recognize the melody I would play through my honest Overseer and his staff and would respond by weaving a harmony of fecundity. It would give in response to my love. I did not want to leave it, and in the morning I prostrated myself on the threshold of my house, and incense in my hands I prayed that Bes, bringer of happiness to all homes, would infuse every room with his presence and drive from them all evil.

The remainder of that day I would rather forget. It haunts me still in spite of all I have done to wipe it from my memory. There was a harem in the Fayum, the Mi-Wer, a place where the very old, discarded concubines of royalty were sent, and Ramses decided to pay it a perfunctory visit. He was unannounced, and a flustered Keeper of the Door greeted him with many awkward prostrations and apologies, casting sidelong glances at me as I stood uncomfortably by.

We toured the precinct quickly, Ramses pausing to speak to this one or that one, and we had not been there longer than a few moments when I was in a fever to be gone. The building was old, the cells small and dark. Although the gardens were as verdant as the rest of the Fayum, they were melancholy and full of a kind of silence that weighed heavily on the ka and made the body tired.

Several hundred women inhabited the place, women with wrinkled, desiccated skin and rheumy eyes, women with the twisted limbs and grey, lifeless hair of impending death. Their voices were croaks or whispers, their movements slow and difficult. Some sat motionless under the trees, staring into space hour after hour. Some lay on their couches, misshapen shadows in the dimness of the open cells we walked past. Sadness, resignation and the patience of a slow dying saturated the air in spite of the attendance of many servants, and by the time the gates closed behind us I was in a state of near hysteria. To end like that. Like that! The prospect was insupportable.

Ramses brushed me as we got onto our litter. "Thu, your skin is utterly cold!" he exclaimed. "And you are shaking! Come. You need to eat. We will satisfy our hunger and then go into the temples to make our sacrifices. You will like that much better, for Sebek and Herishef are worshipped by women in the prime of life and their Houses will be full of younger flesh." It was the only reference he ever made to our visit to the Mi-Wer and I was glad. I could only have sobbed out my impressions of that tomb for the living if he had asked me for them.

But in the temples of Sebek and Herishef, where indeed the courts were crowded with younger female petitioners, I refused with a panicked desperation to perform any sacrifice, and Ramses, doubtless to avoid making a scene, did not force me. Later, when his priests had enticed the gem-encrusted Sebek to the edge of the lake and his grinning snout with its rows of pointed teeth opened to receive the gift of food Ramses had placed in my hands, my nerve again failed me. I stood shaking, the bread and fruit and morsels of meat slipping piece by piece onto the paving, while the crocodile god snapped his jaws impatiently and the priests watched me from under lowered lids.

In the end the King thrust a plate under my fingers and I let the offering slide onto it. He passed it to one of the priests, took my elbow, and led me away. "You are not a scorpion today, you are a frightened hare," he remarked not unkindly, as embarrassed and near to tears I paced beside him. "So you fear the gift of fertility Sebek and Herishef bestow? Why is that, I wonder? Can it be that you do not wish to bear your King a royal child?"

I wanted to stop and turn to him, grasp his hands and hold them to my breast. Remember Eben? I wanted to cry. Where is she now, Great Horus? Do you spare one thought for the woman you once doted on, or send to enquire after the baby you fathered on her? May the gods have pity on me if I should ever fall into that black pit! The women of the Fayum harem seemed to peer at me dismally out of the thin shade of the surrounding trees. I shook my head.

"Forgive me, Mighty Bull," I managed. "Perhaps it is as you say. Perhaps not. Your pardon." He did not reply, and we reached the litter and were carried back to the barge in silence.

It was a relief to return to the bustle and vitality of the

palace harem. Thoughts of that other harem buried in the depths of the Fayum came often to trouble me in the days that followed, but I was able to balance the uneasiness they caused me by bringing to mind my precious fields. They represented life and vigour and hope. They would provide the only fertility I had ever wanted.

I was constantly in Pharaoh's company. My own quarters became a place to hurriedly change my attire between one delightful interlude and another as I moved from banqueting hall to the royal bedchamber, from pleasant ambles in the palace gardens, trailed by guards, servants, heralds and ministers, to temple precincts thick with incense smoke and ringing with the sweet voices of the holy singers. If I was not called to assuage Ramses' lusts, I was summoned to treat him for some minor ailment or other, usually his indigestion or indisposition after he had eaten and drunk too recklessly, for he loved the pleasures of the table almost as much as the dark delights of the couch.

My star shone day and night. I was beautiful and adored. All bowed to me. The courtiers gave way to me. Servants spread the bounty of Egypt before me with the anxious looks of those who feared to offend, and I revelled in it all.

My secret terror I kept to myself. As night after night I sat at my table before going to Pharaoh and ground the acacia spikes into dust before mixing the powder with the mashed dates and honey I prayed with a sober fervour to my totem Wepwawet, and to Hathor, goddess of love, that the contraceptive would remain efficacious and no life would be conjured in my womb.

It is unworthy of me, I know, to record that my finest moment came one scorching morning on a formal progress to the Amun temple where Pharaoh was to officiate at the dedication of a new altar of silver. He had appointed special sacrifices to be made, and everyone who was anyone gathered in their finery under the brilliant sunshine and jostled

for position in Amun's outer court. I had been carried
through the city on my pretty litter, Disenk at my side.

Once having stepped onto the hot pavement beyond the
towering entrance pylons of the temple, I was surrounded by
guards and escorted into the pool of quiet and order that
encircled the royal family. Ramses, in full regalia, dominated
the little group, the Double Crown rising on his head, the
pharaonic beard jutting from his wide chin. His hands
already gripped the crook, flail and scimitar that symbolized
his omnipotence but he smiled at me as I approached and
bowed. Queen Ast on his right gazed past me steadily, her
painted eyes narrowed in the feeble shade of the canopy
under which we stood, and her son, dressed in a flowing
pleated skirt and soft linen shirt that only served to accentuate his masculinity, greeted me politely.

I had arrived just before Ast-Amasareth, who now swept
up to the King, executed the abbreviated obeisance that was
her right as a Queen herself, and engaging him in conversation, moved to take up her position on his left. But Ramses
waved her back, the gold and lapis flail glinting at his broad
gesture. "You may walk behind me today, Ast-Amasareth,"
he said. "But do not fret. You have not incurred my wrath in
any way. Come, Lady Thu. Be pleased to grace your lord
with your presence under the protection of the Fanbearer on
the Left Hand. It will be good to inhale your perfume as it
mingles with the holy myrrh of the God today." A soft
sound, half shock half indignation, came from Queen Ast as
Ast-Amasareth halted, momentarily nonplussed, and I slid
between her and Pharaoh.

"Thank you, Majesty," I murmured. "I am uniquely honoured." I shot a glance at the woman whose place I had
usurped. She was backing away and bowing, a tight smile on
her face, but her eyes were cold as they met mine.

To my credit I did not allow my triumph to show. I lowered my gaze discreetly to my feet, lined up now with

Ramses' own. Our shadows were short and faint on the blinding stone. The King took no further notice of me. Irritably he was calling to his Chief Herald to sort out the chaos to the rear. But I did not need his attention to reinforce the meaning of the demonstration. Neither did anyone else. Nothing and no one now stood between Ramses' affections and myself.

Nothing, that is, but the tiny niggle of apprehension that nestled within me. My monthly flow was very late. Carelessly, busy as I was with the concerns of the court, I had lost count of the days, and when I had taken the time to sit down and reckon them my blood had run cold.

Pharaoh barked an order. Horns brayed from the temple walls. We began to walk slowly, and above my head the white plumes of the ceremonial ostrich fan trembled. From within the inner court a column of incense rose almost invisibly into the deep blue of the sky, and the tuneless yet compelling tinkle of a thousand finger cymbals filled the air. Behind me I heard Ast-Amasareth's light breath and fancied that I could feel it, hot and venomous, on my neck. With stubborn deliberation I turned my attention from my belly to the victory I had achieved today, and my worries were forgotten.

Yet the following morning I was brutally reminded of the precariousness of my situation. After the interminable temple rituals and a feast to honour both Amun's men and the silversmiths who had created the altar, Ramses had been interested in little more than sleep and I had managed to steal a few peaceful hours on my own couch. I woke feeling sluggish and heavy towards the middle of the morning, rising only to sit in the shade before my door and stare dazedly out upon the crowded courtyard while Disenk went to prepare my first meal.

By the time she returned I was more alert, and I picked over the contents of the tray she set beside me. There was a dish of sesame seed paste, sticks of celery, fresh lettuce leaves, a pomegranate, five figs steeped in purple juniper oil, and a cup of grape juice from which arose the bracing aroma of mint. I had dipped a stalk of celery in the paste and was biting into it and reaching for the juice when Disenk grabbed my wrist. "Wait, Thu," she said urgently. "Something is wrong. Wait."

I put the celery back on the tray and watched her. My heart began to pound as the moments slipped away. She sank cross-legged to the floor beside my chair and her eyes were fixed on the tray. A frown of concentration creased her smooth forehead. Otherwise she did not stir. A cloud of birds swooped by high overhead. A loud argument between two of the women by the pool broke out and ended in a burst of laughter. A ray of sun began to warm my foot as the shadow in which I sat shifted imperceptibly. Finally I took a deep breath.

"Disenk," I ventured a little hesitantly, for she was still staring fiercely at the food. "What is the matter?" She blinked rapidly and chewed her lip.

"I prepare your food with my own hands," she said in a low voice. "I take everything from the communal supplies and my choices cannot be predicted. They are arbitrary. This celery, Thu. Great bowls of it filled the kitchens this morning. I selected stalks from different bowls. I cut each stalk and ate a little before setting the remainder on your tray. I do this with everything, every time you wish to eat. And your wine and beer come directly from the Master and are well sealed." She glanced up at me. "Yet something is not right in these dishes, something I cannot quite place. All is as I laid it out, and yet it is not." Her small hands moved over the food, touching the cup and the edges of the dishes as though they could give her the answer she sought, then she froze. "The figs," she whispered.

"Disenk..."

She swung towards me. "There are five figs," she said deliberately. "Five. I set out only four! Someone slipped another fig onto this plate." Our eyes met, and in spite of the warmth of the morning a shiver of cool air seemed to flutter against my skin.

Disenk scrambled up. Gingerly she lifted the dish of figs and stepped out onto the sunny grass. There were always a few puppies rolling and tumbling about with the children and this morning was no exception. I watched as Disenk unobtrusively made her way into the sunshine and set the dish down. She retreated to my side and together, tense and immobile, we waited.

For some time the offering went unnoticed, but then one fat, furry body became aware of the sweet odour of the figs and detached itself from the general mêlée. It approached the dish and sniffed the food cautiously, looked back at its plump companions, then its pink tongue came out. I heard Disenk draw in a quick rush of breath. With gluttonous speed the puppy wolfed down the figs, put a brown paw on the plate, and thoroughly licked up the juices before losing interest and beginning to wander away. I realized that Disenk's nails were biting into my shoulder. The little animal did not get far. Suddenly his gait changed. He began to totter, then he stood retching. Limbs jerking, he fell onto his side, and then he went limp. I sat still. Disenk went forward, moving uncertainly, her normally graceful body clumsy as she used a corner of her sheath to recover the dish and paused to examine the puppy. She was all eyes as she returned, set the dish on the tray, and gazed out upon the rollicking children and their gossiping mothers.

"The creature is dead," she said at last. "I will take the rest of the food away." Mechanically she lifted the tray and set off towards the courtyard entrance, and as she went my gaze was distracted by Hatia. The woman was in her accustomed place, buried in red linen and unmoving under her canopy, her servant equally motionless behind her. Both of them were watching me steadily.

As casually as I could I rose, stretched, and withdrew into the safety of my chambers. Safety? I thought. Reaction was beginning to set in. My heart had gone from pounding to a nervous flutter and I was flushing hot. Someone had tried to kill me. Someone had attempted to sweep me away without compunction. My mind flew to the events of yesterday, to the cold glitter in Ast-Amasareth's eyes as she was forced to give way to me. Had I at last become a serious threat to that ugly witch? I had always suspected that she practised an evil magic, for how else was she able to retain her powerful hold on Ramses?

Or was it Hatia? Oh surely not! Hatia was sodden with wine. She lived for the jug that never left her side. Or did she? Hatia had been in the harem for a very long time. Silently, inconspicuously, she inhabited her place on the grass day after day, year after year. Nothing that happened escaped her notice. Forgotten yet always present, she would make the perfect spy. And I did not think that she was as indifferent as she seemed. I remembered with an unpleasant jolt the glance of pure malice she had given me once during the three terrible days of my disgrace. Was she Ast-Amasareth's tool? Did the wine she imbibed with such singleminded, chilling purpose come from the Chief Wife's vineyards?

It was useless to speculate. Ast-Amasareth, Hatia, the murderous intent could have originated in the jealous mind of any of the hundreds of women who envied me my exclusive place at court and who believed that with me in my tomb they might have a chance at that same privilege.

As the shock of the moment faded I became restless, and with folded arms and head down I paced in and out of the shafts of white light falling from my clerestory windows. I had not taken the warnings of Hui and Hunro and Disenk seriously enough. I had imagined myself to be invulnerable, but now I would have to consider every morsel I put into my mouth, suspect every hand held out to me. I was indeed alone, and it came to me then that I was learning how everything gained in life has a price. I wanted to run to Pharaoh, pour out to him my indignation, demand that his police turn the harem upside down so that I might be vindicated, be secure, but as my feet measured out the bounds of my luxurious prison I knew that such a response would only increase my danger. Pharaoh could not protect me at every moment, even if he was willing to try. And suppose that the culprit was found to be the Chief Wife? Doted upon and spoiled as I was, I knew that a concubine, even a titled one, would not emerge triumphant against one of the most influential women in Egypt.

Should I plot to remove her? The prospect gave me a delicious thrill. To think of that twisted mouth disfigured even further by pain, that thin body contorted as my poison coursed through it, quietened my heart and lifted my head. But what if Ast-Amasareth was innocent? I sighed. No. There was nothing to be done.

When Disenk came back with her customary self-possession restored we discussed the matter briefly and I wrote in my own hand a message for Hui, telling him what had happened. Disenk vowed to control the preparation of my food more tightly. I asked her about the behaviour of the other harem servants. Had she seen or heard anything that might now be considered suspicious? She shook her head. The servants gossiped as fervently as their mistresses but nothing had alerted Disenk. In the end we dropped the subject but it remained in my mind, an amorphous threat that clouded my waking hours and followed me into my dreams. For I knew that poison in the hands of an expert could be administered in a dozen different ways and I could only hope that Hui and I were the only adepts in Pi-Ramses.

Chapter 20

A week later I received a summons from Prince Ramses. During the preceding days the incident of the poisoned figs had begun to shrink in my mind to the proportions of a necessary hazard. Harem life for the privileged favourites had always been fraught with danger. It was a risk that accompanied the prize of Pharaoh's approbation, something to be included in the calculations of one who was bent on climbing the treacherous cliff of royal influence, and I should not have been surprised at my brush with its reality.

It was disconcerting to know that I was hated and even more unsettling to have to choose not to retaliate. Revenge was in my nature. However, I had become resigned to my position by the time the Prince's Chief Herald appeared at my door, greeted me respectfully, and requested my presence in the Prince's private quarters. Disenk was slipping bracelets onto my wrists and had just laid aside my perfumed oil.

"But I cannot answer the Prince's summons immediately," I told the man. "I am on my way to Pharaoh. Would His Highness wait until tomorrow?" I was secretly surprised to hear from the Prince. I had seen little of him for a long time and had done my best to put a stop to my disloyal daydreams.

"His Highness knows that your time is not your own, Lady Thu," the Herald responded. "Therefore His Highness beseeches you to attend him tonight on your way back to the harem."

"But that will be in the middle of the night," I reminded him, puzzled. "I do not wish to wake His Highness."

"The Prince will be fishing after sundown," I was told, "and then he intends to entertain some friends. He will not sleep." I nodded.

"Then I will come."

When we were alone again Disenk spoke up. "It may be a trap, Thu," she said. "You will be returning in the hour when the palace is deserted." I considered, then shrugged.

"The Prince's Chief Herald is no shifty-eyed mercenary," I pointed out. "Unless the Prince himself wants me dead, I think I am safe. I will ask one of the door guards to escort me, Disenk. After all, I cannot begin to restrict myself to the confines of my rooms or the King's. I will go mad!"

"I think the Prince does not wish to have it known that he has sent for you," Disenk suggested. "Otherwise he would have you brought to him during the day or he would approach you at some feast. I will accompany you tonight, Thu, and wait outside the royal bedchamber. I will walk with you to the Prince's quarters." I thanked her and we hurried out. The sun was still free of the horizon but had already set behind the harem building and the shadows were long on the grass. I shuddered as I passed the spot where the unfortunate dog had lain. One of the servants had carried the carcass away but I imagined that I could still see the crushed place where it had died.

The King was in high spirits, teasing me and recounting jokes as he nibbled on honey cakes and downed a quantity of wine which did nothing to dampen his ardour. Before he collapsed into the deep slumber of the satiated we had made love several times. When I was sure that my movements would not wake him I straightened the pillow beneath his head, smoothed the sheets over his limp body, and let myself quietly out. Disenk uncurled from the dark corner where she had been dozing. Without a word we turned sharply left, following the high wall of the palace, past the bedchamber in which the Mighty Bull lay snoring gently, past his private

reception area and its ante-room. The portion of the palace
garden that lay between building and sheltering wall was
drowned in night. The moon was setting, and only weak
starlight dribbled fitfully over the ground and faintly tinged
the darkness between the branches of the trees. Ra lay
buried in the womb of Nut the sky goddess, waiting to be
born anew, and without him the world's senses were
dimmed.

At the foot of the stairs that clung to the outside of the
palace and led to the Prince's quarters two guards were talking softly. At our approach their hands went to the swords at
their waists but I called my name to them and turned to
Disenk. "Well?" I whispered. She ran a hand through my
hair and rubbed at a smudge of kohl on my temple. Her lips
looked black in the uncertain light.

"Do not eat or drink," she reminded me, and I nodded
once and mounted the stairs behind the patient soldier. The
gloomy garden slowly receded below, but at last the stairs
became a landing and a tall double door appeared, set in the
wall. The soldier knocked, and a familiar voice immediately
bade him enter. I waited, hearing myself announced, then
the man bowed me inside and, as I stepped past him, closed
the door behind me.

I was not in a room, I was standing at one end of a passage
that ran away into dimness on my left. But directly ahead
were more doors, open wide, and pale light splashed the
floor at my feet. I went forward. At once a servant repeated
the guard's action, closing himself outside, and I found
myself alone with the Prince.

His reception room was surprisingly bare. The walls were
painted in desert scenes of beige and blue and a large repre-
sentation of the Prince himself, standing astride in his chariot with a whip raised over the heads of his straining horses,
dominated the far wall and gyrated spasmodically as the
lamps flickered.

The Prince's desk, on which lay a few scrolls, a broken arrowhead and a white leather belt to which an empty scabbard was attached, was a simple affair of oiled wood and so were the plain chairs with their woven flax seats and the one low table where a lamp stood. Another burned in the far corner on a stand carved in the likeness of a bundle of tall papyrus stems.

The impression I received in the swift moment before the Prince left his chair and came towards me was one of economy and a solitary comfort. But there was also an unsettling suggestion of impermanence about my surroundings, as though he lived on the stage of a palace play while his true domicile was elsewhere, hidden.

He was wearing nothing but a linen loincloth, and as he strode across the floor the subdued light slid over the long, flexing muscles of his brown legs, the tight ridges of his stomach, the two dun nubs of his nipples on the dizzying planes of his chest. Glossy black hair framed his features. He had obviously been painted much earlier in the day, and enough kohl remained to accentuate the clarity of his eyes. A trace of henna reddened his mouth, now widening in a smile. I sank into my obeisance with an inward cry of submission.

"Greetings, royal concubine Lady Thu," he said. "You may rise. I beg you to forgive my attire, but I have been night fishing and then swimming with my companions. There is nothing more exhilarating than slipping beneath the dark waters of the Nile while the surface gleams with streaks of moonlight. Unless it is sitting in the desert sand while Ra spreads his dying blood across the horizon. You may sit if you wish." I did so gladly, for I did not want him to see the sudden feebleness of my knees, and answered his smile with one of my own. He came close and regarded me reflectively. "We have seen little of each other these past few months," he went on conversationally. "But I have heard much about you. When all other subjects are exhausted, the talk around me always turns to the young concubine with the extraordinary blue eyes and the sharp tongue, who has transformed the King into a panting lap dog." I looked up at him quickly but there was no malice in his expression. His smile radiated warmth and approval. "No other concubine has held his interest for this long," he said. "My congratulations, Lady Thu. You are indeed an amazing woman." Now something in his tone rang a warning. I rose so that I would feel less vulnerable.

"Thank you, Highness," I replied, "but I can take no credit for either my beauty or the facility of my tongue. I am as the gods have made me."

"Oh, I do not think so," he said. "No. I think that you are a very clever, very resourceful child of the earth. I am not sure whether I envy my father or pity him."

"Highness, you are unfair!" I protested indignantly. "I have done Great Horus nothing but good! I have healed his wounds, I have attended to his every need, I have made him happy!"

"No doubt." He had come to a halt in front of me, still smiling, and his eyes searched mine. "But so have many other women before you. To remain in my father's favour takes more than the ability to please and you know it. It takes calculation, purpose. Do not mistake me, Thu. I am not condemning you. Far from it. I admire your tenacity. I have a proposition for you."

Warily I studied him. The smile had gone but he had stepped closer so that now I could smell his body. My fingers spasmed with the sudden desire to touch the hard silkiness of his skin. "Beyond that wall," he said, jerking his thumb into the gloom, "lie the quarters of my brother Prince Ramses Amunhirkhepshef. He is one year younger than I. He is not in his rooms. In fact, he is never in his rooms. Most of his time is spent north of the Delta, lying on the

beaches of the Great Green and playing with his concubines. Across the gardens lie the quarters of my other brothers. One of them is so stupid he cannot count the number of
ears he has. One of them stays in Thebes where he serves
the Amun temple. He wishes to remain a priest all his life.
One of them has a vicious temper and delights in whipping
his horses, his servants and his women. None of them care
much for our father and even less for Egypt. Father, however, places each of us before him equally, and agonizes over
which of us is worthy to be declared his Heir. Meanwhile
Amun's stranglehold on this country tightens." His voice
had not risen but all at once I felt my shoulders imprisoned
in his powerful hands. "I believe I am the only chance for
salvation that Egypt has," he said steadily. "But my words are
not heeded. Father will not see how disastrous it would be if
his choice should fall on any other royal son. I know his
fears, of course. He trusts none of us, even though he sees
my love for him, my devotion to my country, and that
hurts." The fine feathery brows were drawn together in a
frown. "But he trusts you, my Lady. He loves you, he will listen to you. Help me as I plead my cause before him. Add
your voice to mine as I try to persuade him to declare me his
Horus-Fledgling."

I felt his hands begin to move, to slide down my arms and
up again, raising ripples of sensation on my skin. I swallowed
and stared at him, fighting against the honeyed lassitude
invading my body, my mind. Honesty had coloured his
speech, yet his eyes remained shrewd as he measured my
reaction to what he was saying.

"You are mistaken, Prince," I managed. "Once before I
attempted to influence the Mighty Bull, and I suffered his
extreme displeasure for three of the worst days of my life. He
loves me but it is the Chief Wife who has his ear on matters
of policy." It had been difficult to put that thought together.
I was sure I had mouthed nonsense but his smile opened

again, revealing all his perfect teeth. His hands enfolded mine briefly then he withdrew. I began to suspect that I was being manipulated and I tried to care but I could not.

"That cold foreigner," he said scornfully. "She will not help me. She refuses to ally herself with any one of us for fear she may have gambled on a loser if the wrong son inherits the Horus Throne. But I am determined to win. I am Commander of the Infantry, I have the army behind me, yet it is vital that I achieve Divinity with the blessing of my father, not with force after he is dead. Egypt must not suffer civil war." He came close to me again, too close for politeness, so that even though he was not touching me I felt overwhelmed by his power. "I do not make this request lightly," he went on in a low voice. "I understand that unless you approach my father with the utmost delicacy your words could be misconstrued. Yet I trust both your tact and the fascination you hold for him."

"Highness, you overestimate both," I managed weakly, my eyes fixed on the movement of his mouth. "I would be risking more than three days of banishment if I anger him a second time."

"I will make it worth your while to try," he urged. "The Heir inherits his father's harem when he becomes Pharaoh, you know that don't you? He may discard or use the women as he pleases. You are very young, my Lady Thu. I would choose to keep very few of my father's hundreds of concubines, and you would be one of them. The rest would of course be dispersed to the various harems of retirement. You would be safe from such a terrible fate when the Double Crown sat on my head, indeed, I would pile riches and preferments at your feet. Is that not worthy of a few words in my father's ear from time to time?"

He had leaned even closer to me with the intensity of his words, and I could contain myself no longer. With a fierce, despairing inner wrench of surrender I closed the tiny gap between us. Now at last my fingers met the glorious resistance of his body and my mouth opened under his. His lips were as assured, as enticing, as I had always imagined they would be. I felt him grasp my waist and ease my body against his. So young, so firm, I thought giddily. Fire and heat. Solidity, not the yielding flabbiness of Pharaoh's flesh. Pharaoh's flesh...

Gasping I pulled myself out of the Prince's embrace.

"What a fool you must think me, Highness!" I cried out, half-mad with the desire and the rage battling inside so that I felt deathly ill for a moment. "I hazard my very existence for your sake, and what have you promised me in return? Nothing. Nothing! Suppose your father, by some remote possibility, listens to me and designates you his Heir? He goes to sail in the Heavenly Barque and you don the Double Crown and inherit the harem. Then you are free to forget your fine promises of this night, to ignore me or banish me as well as to take me to your bed and then discard me! No. It is not enough." He was breathing heavily, and as I watched, a thin trickle of sweat coursed down his neck and onto his chest.

"Well, what do you want then?" he asked in exasperation. "Gold? Land?" I pressed both hands to my forehead. I was shaking all over as though I had a fever.

"No, Highness," I said, dropping my arms and striving to be calm. "I want you to dictate a scroll making me a queen of Egypt in the event that you become King. I want the scroll witnessed by a priest and any scribe you trust, and then given into my care. And do not forget that I can read very well." He stared at me in astonishment, then his handsome face broke into lines of amusement and he began to chuckle.

"By Amun I do pity my father," he grinned, "for surely I see the wiles that have ensnared him. You are an impudent little witch, my Lady Thu. Very well. I will consider your proposal if you will consider my request." Suddenly I felt well again, and strong.

"You will?"

"Yes."

"I thank you, Highness!" Bowing elaborately I walked to the door.

"Where are you going?" he demanded. "I have not dismissed you yet." I halted but I did not turn around. I was afraid that if I did so I would fly into his arms, onto his couch, and thus wreak my own destruction.

"Dismiss me then I beseech you, Prince," I said quietly. "For the respect I bear to your father." There was a silence which was not broken, and after a time I opened the door and went resolutely away.

That night I had the dream again. I was kneeling in the desert as before, my mouth and nostrils choked with sand, my naked back blistering with the heat of the sun. Fear was all around me, but this time a voice muttered and whispered within it, the words, if words they were, rapid and unintelligible. Nor could I determine whether the voice had a sex. It droned on chillingly, rising and falling without taking breath, and in the midst of my terror I strained to hear what it was saying, for I knew that if I could catch its meaning I would be free. I woke entangled in sweat-soaked sheets with nausea churning in my bowels, and arms flailing I struggled to sit up. Through the open door of my bedchamber I could see Disenk in the faint first light of dawn, curled up peacefully on her mat, but this inner room was still sunk in darkness.

I tried not to peer into those dense shadows in case the power that had held me doubled over in my dream should be lurking there, mute now but still full of malevolence. Earlier I had not wanted to consider my confrontation with the Prince. I had hurried back to my comfortable womb, Disenk at my side, both of us very tired, and fallen between my sheets where sleep had claimed me. But now I sat limply, staring at the barely discernable outline of my legs under their covering of linen, and remembered all he had said.

Gradually it came to me, with a sadness I had never felt before, that my cherished vision of Pharaoh's beautiful son had been an illusion. His apparent kindness was a sham, a ploy to ensure his own comfort. Every smile, every act of selflessness, increased his value in the eyes of the court and served to swell his popularity. I did not doubt that his mystery, his reputation for remoteness and the solitary pursuits that took him, alone, onto the desert and into the Nile in the dark hours, was a carefully calculated act to remove him from an association with any one faction in the minds of those circling the arena of power in Egypt. Above it all he could be seen as full of new possibilities, a fledgling god of honesty and lofty impartiality who could only compare favourably with his useless brothers.

But he was as ambitious, as venal and greedy, as any. He wanted Godhead. He wanted the divinity the Double Crown would bestow, and all the authority that accompanied it. He was jealous of his father also. Whether he loved the King or not was unclear, but he had not been able to hide his lust to appropriate all that belonged to the elder Ramses, and that included me. I should have been flattered but I was not.

It also came to me, like a savage blow from a friend I had trusted, that the Prince only wanted to use me. It was not I, Thu, being invited to aid in Egypt's salvation, it was the concubine who held Pharaoh in the palm of her painted hand and who could thus be fitted into the Prince's larger schemes and then forgotten.

They all want to use me, I thought miserably. Hui, the Prince, even Pharaoh himself. There is no one who truly cares for my welfare. Pa-ari has grown away from me. Disenk may hold some affection for me but she would give the same loyalty to whoever employed her. Only my land will not betray my care. No matter what, it will receive me with love.

I could no longer ignore the sickness curdling up into my throat. Sitting on the edge of the couch I folded my arms tight against my breast and began to rock to and fro. Hopelessly, grimly, I tried to cling to my exploration of the Prince's character but it was impossible. A more disturbing reality was intruding, and at last I could not hold it back. "Oh gods," I whispered. "Oh, please, no," and the sound went scuttering and scrabbling around the room like claws on rock, like the malicious voice of my dream. My doom had fallen. I knew that I was pregnant.

Then I let the anger come. It was a guard, a defence against the anguish of a great defeat. Rising, I paced the floor and cursed Hui who had brought me to this place, cursed Pharaoh who would now abandon me, cursed the gods of the Fayum whom I had offended and who had taken this pitiless revenge on me. My words hissed out like venom, and still I could not exhaust the well of poison burning my tongue and scoring my heart.

I did not come to myself until I felt a touch on my arm. Disenk stood anxiously beside me, wrapped in a sheet, and I realized that I could see her clearly in the strengthening light. "Thu, whatever is the matter?" she asked. I came to a halt, chest heaving, fists clenched. Very well, I thought. Very well. I can fight this. I can still win.

"Disenk, bring me my physic box," I ordered. She opened her mouth to speak again but closed it when she saw my expression, and went into the other room. I sat in my chair and waited. Presently she laid the box on my lap.

"I will bring you food?" she said, but I shook my head.

"No. Leave me."

When I was alone I lifted the lid and began to go through my medicaments. I was looking for my phial of savin oil but I could not find it. Frowning, I emptied the box, setting out on the table each container. The savin oil had gone. I paused, thinking. It was a dangerous drug, too dangerous to prescribe in any but the tiniest doses, and I was sure that my box had held a good supply. Where was it? I had not broken the seal on it since my arrival in the harem, for aiding in the abortion of a royal child was the gravest of offences. Had I taken it out to make room for something else? Given it back to Hui? In my agitation I could not remember doing either.

Then what of the physic nut? I shook the clay pot holding the deadly things. They were usually ground up and mixed with palm oil to kill rats in the granaries but the seeds of the small tree made an efficient purge. Too efficient. Their potency was uncertain and the same dose could either empty the patient or kill her. Kill me. Quickly I tossed the phials and jars back into the box and slammed the lid shut. "Disenk!" She came running, still obviously bewildered, but she had put on her sheath and combed her hair. "I am going to Hui's house," I told her. "I will go on foot. I do not want guards or litter bearers to gossip about my movements today and you must keep this a secret. If I am summoned, tell the messenger I am drunk or in the bath house or visiting the other women—anything. I don't care what you say, but do not let it be known that I have left the harem. Lend me one of your sheaths and your plain sandals. Get me a basket I can carry, and that thick linen cloak of yours with a hood that you wear sometimes when the nights are cool. I know we are now at the beginning of Shemu but no one will notice, I think. Hurry up!" She stared at me, her eyes round.

"Thu, tell me what is wrong," she begged. I considered, then relented. She was my body servant. She would know sooner or later anyway, particularly if my efforts to rid myself of my fatal burden proved useless.

"I am pregnant," I said shortly, and turned away so that I could not see her expression. "Bring me the things I have asked for."

While I waited for her a thought struck me, and leaning against the table I began to giggle and then to laugh hysterically. The month of Pakhons had begun. It was three months to my Naming Day. In three months I would be all of sixteen years old.

An hour later, wrapped in a cloak and clad in a servant's sturdy sheath, my feet laced in Disenk's unadorned sandals, I answered the desultory challenge of the guards on the harem gate and set off along the river road. The rush basket on my arm held my box of medicines covered by a cloth. The sun had now risen fully and the morning was already breathlessly hot. I had not walked any distance for a long time, and soon my ankles and calves were aching in spite of the regular exercises I did. The path was busy with the traffic of servants, hawkers and donkeys who kicked the dust into a fine pall that had me coughing as they elbowed past.

The distance to Hui's house was not great by water, but on foot it seemed to take an eternity of heat, grit and noise. Blisters formed and broke on the sides of my feet where Disenk's ill-fitting sandals rubbed, but at least the discomfort served to take my mind off the enormity of my trouble and I reflected grimly, as yet another donkey loaded with produce forced me to step aside, that I probably would not last a week in Aswat, so soft had I become.

But finally Hui's pylon came into sight. Before walking under it I descended his white watersteps, and sitting in the shade of his tethered barge I sank my feet, sandals and all, into the river. The bliss of such coolness was indescribable and for a while I gazed out upon the sparkling water, the palms on the opposite bank tossing in the breeze, the skiffs breaking the surface into foam as they glided past, with a lightening heart. But the mood fled. I rose and entered Hui's domain.

The porter beside the pylon challenged me. I could not have avoided him, but he seemed completely disinterested in my strange appearance and let me go on with a curt bow. The garden was deserted, imbued with the heavy, pleasant silence that always blanketed the Master's estate, and so was the courtyard as I broke through the trees and opened the gate, treading the hot, blinding pavement and pausing between the imposing pillars.

No one was there, and I could see right to the end of the long passage. The rear door was open onto sunny greenery. The tiled floor gleamed. Removing Disenk's smothering cloak and her caked, dusty sandals I brushed off my feet and walked resolutely straight to Hui's office. The door was closed but I could hear his voice within, the steady drone of a dictation. Love and a strange kind of grief welled up in me as once more I wanted to crawl onto his knee like a child and curl against his warm chest. I knocked and the voice rose irritably.

"Enter!" I did so. Hui was behind the desk with Ani on the floor at his side, palette under his hand. At the sight of me he scrambled up and bowed. Hui rose. "Thu! Gods, I hardly recognized you! Whatever has gone wrong?" I moved forward and sank into a chair.

"Hui, Ani," I acknowledged them wearily. "I am very thirsty. Is there any beer?" At a nod from Hui the scribe bowed again, smiled at me uncertainly, and went out. Hui crossed to a jug on one of the shelves, poured for me, and handed me a cup. I drank gratefully. "I have walked from the harem," I said, wiping my mouth and setting the empty cup on the desk. "No one but Disenk knows that I am here and I cannot stay long. I need your help, Hui. I am pregnant."

There was a long silence. Hui, in the act of regaining his seat, paused. All expression gradually left his white face until only the wide, red eyes seemed alive. Then he lowered himself fully into the chair.

"Are you sure?"

"Yes."

There was another uncomfortable hesitation during which he made a pyramid with his slim fingers and rubbed them thoughtfully against his chin. I found myself near to tears as I waited for his reaction. Oh, Hui, be kind, I begged him mutely. Commiserate with me, come around the desk and hold me, tell me that you will make everything all right because you love me! But those carefully manicured fingers continued their slow movement and he went on staring at me dispassionately. At last he sighed and his hands flew apart in a gesture of bafflement.

"I had such high hopes of you, Thu," he said flatly. "I am very disappointed. How could you let this happen?" I swallowed, crushed at his words.

"I did my best to prevent it, Master," I replied. "I did not forget to use the acacia spikes. But the gods of the Fayum are powerful and in my fear I slighted them. What precautions can stand against such might?"

"What are you babbling about?" he cut in sharply. "You were careless, that is all. Now you must take the consequences." His tone was cold, and I felt an anger rise with the misery in me.

"I am not at fault," I said hotly. "Do you think I wanted to put my position at court in jeopardy? I do not need your recriminations, Hui, I need your assistance. Help me!"

"And how am I supposed to do that?" His formality, his aloofness, cut me to the quick.

"Pretend that I am your patient," I said. "I opened my box this morning, Hui, looking for the savin oil. I could not find it. If you will not prescribe to rid me of this baby, at least give me more oil!"

"You returned the savin to me unused some time ago," he retorted in the same vein. "It seems you are making a mess of your life, Thu. No, I will not give you more oil." I sprang to my feet.

"Hui! You are serious? For the sake of the gods, give me

the oil or treat me with something else! I will not have this baby! I would rather die!" He was around the desk in a flash, his strong hands gripping my shoulders, his face thrust close to mine. His eyes blazed.

"You stupid child!" he spat. "Savin oil is a poison! You know that! The amount needed to abort the child would probably kill you! You say you would rather die anyway but those are just foolish words!" I wrenched myself free and slapped the desk furiously.

"Why are you being so cruel? If I have no savin I will try something else. Extract of oleander! Physic seeds! Castor oil! Anything! I will not lose all I have gained just because you are afraid!" We faced each other furiously, both panting, then he pushed me back into the chair and squatted beside me. He took my hands. I tried to pull them free but his grip tightened.

"Listen to me, foolish one," he said more calmly. "I am indeed afraid. Afraid to prescribe for you in case my physic kills you. Afraid that in your own fear you inadvertently kill yourself. You must not behave impulsively, Thu. How do you imagine I would feel if Egypt was no longer bright with your presence? Stand back from the situation and think."

"I have been thinking," I replied sulkily. "What difference will it make whether I make an effort to salvage my future now and die in the attempt, or fall from Pharaoh's favour and die gradually year by year until I am removed to the ghastly harem in the Fayum?" My voice shook. "Hui, tell me what to do!" He began to stroke my hair, and as always, his touch was like a soothing oil sliding over my skin. The tenseness began to flow out of me.

"Do nothing," he said quietly. "Just because Ramses has lost interest in his concubines before when they have born him a child does not mean that he will lose interest in you. How many times must I tell you that no one like you has ever entered the harem before? Only Ast-Amasareth comes close to exerting the influence over him that you do. A different influence, I know, but just as powerful in its way. Have faith in your ability to weather this storm, my Thu. It is indeed an upheaval but it need not be disastrous." I leaned my head against him and closed my eyes.

"I do not want this baby, Hui," I whispered. "But I will do as you say. You are probably right. Ramses loves me, and the gods know that I really do not want to die. When my time comes, will you be with me to deliver the child?" His hand went on moving reassuringly over my skull.

"Of course I will," he said. "I do love you, my recalcitrant little concubine. Now tell me how it feels to own a piece of Egypt. I hear from Adiroma that your land is very fertile and will make you rich in time. And what was that nonsense about the gods of the Fayum?" So, relaxed against him, I began to speak of Pharaoh's gift and my disgrace before Herishef and Sebek, and when I had finished he kissed me gently and sent for food which we shared in an amicable silence. Then he escorted me to the door and kissed me again.

"Keep me informed of your physical progress," he admonished. "I am always here when you need me, Thu. And leave the poisons alone! Promise me!" I promised, but as I walked back to the harem in the stupefying heat I felt my despair return. Whatever happened, nothing would ever be the same again and I wished that I had not given Hui my word. I did not think that it would be easy to hold on to the King's affections with a child tugging at my sheath. And deep down in my ka I knew that Hui could have helped me if he had wished.

I was able to re-enter my quarters without detection. Although the courtyard was now alive with women and children no one gave me a second look, wrapped in the cloak and soiled as I was. As I crossed the threshold, drained and footsore, and placed the basket on the floor, Disenk hurried out of the bedchamber to meet me. I sank into a chair and she thrust a scroll into my hands. "This came for you a short while ago," she said. "It was delivered by a royal Herald I had never seen before. It carries the Prince's imprint, Thu!" My fingers made dirty smudges on the pristine papyrus as I cracked the wax seal, and my aches were forgotten. Rapidly I scanned the contents.

"In the event of my accession to the Horus Throne I, Prince Ramses, Commander of the Infantry of Pharaoh and eldest son of the Protector of Egypt, promise to raise the Lady Thu, concubine, to the rank of Queen of Egypt, with all the privileges and rights attending such an exalted position. Signed by my own hand this second day of the month of Pakhons in the season Shemu, year sixteen of the King." Sure enough, the Prince's signature was scrawled across the bottom of the scroll, together with the witnesses I had asked for, Nanai, Overseer of the Sakht and priest of Set, and Pentu, Scribe of the Double House of Life.

I let the scroll roll up and lifted it to my breast. So soon! Only last night I had made my impudent demand and already it had been met! The speed, the inferred ruthlessness of the Prince's decision, almost took my breath away. "Disenk," I said, my voice shaking, "bring me wax and fire." She did so, and when I had resealed the precious letter I pressed one of my rings into the soft wax. "This is my guarantee of a queen's crown," I told her. "Hide it. I suppose it is too difficult to lift the tiles and place it under the floor. You had better sew it into one of the cushions. Do it today, but please wash me and rub salve into my feet first. They are very tender." Her meticulously plucked eyebrows had almost disappeared into the short, dark fringe of her hair and she took the scroll gingerly, her whole body a question.

For a moment I debated whether or not to keep her in ignorance, then decided that such secrecy would be fruitless. She already knew of my condition. In fact, Disenk knew all about me. So I spoke of my unnerving encounter with the Prince and how I had fared with Hui. When I had finished she turned to me, the scroll in one hand.

"The Master is right, Lady," she said. "Why take the chance of ending your life so soon, when the results of your pregnancy are far from being sure? Such an act would be madness. And now you have the Prince's assurance. In the unlikely event of Pharaoh's rejection, the Prince will still elevate you."

"You forget that if I am rejected by the father I cannot plead the cause of the son," I reminded her drily. She shrugged delicately.

"It is a strong possibility that the Prince will seize power in any case upon his father's death," she pointed out. "He is after all the Commander of the Infantry, with complete authority over the majority of soldiers in the army. Of course he would rather achieve his aims peacefully, but he seems determined to see the Double Crown placed on his head however it may be done. You will be a queen in either event, Thu."

"But Disenk, the King is still only forty-seven years old," I murmured. "Suppose that he lives as long as Osiris Ramses the Second Glorified? I could be in my dotage before a queen's crown is placed on my grey head." Disenk shot me an odd look.

"Perhaps," she said softly, "but perhaps not. Heed the Master's advice, Thu. Do nothing foolish."

She left me then, to fetch water and oils, and I slumped back in my chair. The fact of the King's age had not occurred to me before, but now I considered the dismal possibility I had posed to my servant. I was indeed an idiot. Even if I remained in favour, even if my lover received my petition on behalf of his son and designated him Heir, I would still have to wait until Pharaoh died to become a queen.

My eyes came to rest on the little statue of Wepwawet my father had carved for me with such loving care so long ago, and I smiled at it grimly. "Well, my totem?" I whispered to him. "Divine ear and arbiter of my fate? Am I to receive the crown in the full vigour and beauty of my youth, a royal gem set upon a dazzling career, or will it be a consolation tossed to the aging tool of a Prince no longer enticed by lust and ambition? Sweet God of War, how shall this battle be fought?" Wepwawet went on smiling his enigmatic wolf's smile and I leaned back and closed my eyes. I had always been a gambler. The gaming pieces had been rearranged, that was all. Success was still possible.

Chapter 21

Nevertheless, I did not want to lose Pharaoh's love. The promise of a queen's crown in the future was little more than the silhouette of an oasis on the far horizon. Far better to hold onto the benefits of the present. I hid the evidence of my pregnancy for as long as I could. Troubled with nausea in the mornings I was sometimes able to excuse myself from spending the whole night with the King, but there were many occasions when I lay beside him as dawn crept into the room and prayed that he would not wake to see my pallor or the cold sweat that broke over my skin as I struggled to control the urge to vomit.

I thought of Eben in those desperate moments. Had she endured the same secret torments? Or had she paraded her condition proudly before Ramses in the deluded belief that her hold on him was unbreakable? The latter, probably. I had never spoken with the favourite whose place I had usurped but she had seemed sullen and arrogant on the few occasions I had seen her. Surely she would have left a greater mark on both harem and palace if she had been a more intelligent woman!

The round of feasts, boating parties and ceremonies went on, but though I tried to throw myself into them, their allure began to pall. Each day I stood before my copper mirror, angling it and fingering my stomach, demanding of Disenk whether or not my shape was changing. I performed my exercises with the single-minded fanaticism of a temple visionary, hoping feverishly that my womb might open prematurely, but to no avail.

Day inexorably followed day, week flowing too quickly into week. Shemu marched forward, the months of Payni and Epophi slipped away and I turned sixteen. Mesore, the last month of Shemu, seemed to fly by with hostile speed and the New Year began with the frenetic celebration of the first day of Thoth. Then the population, sated and exhausted, settled down to wait for the rising of the Nile that would herald another season of flooding and sowing.

I too was anxious that Isis should cry copiously, for I was depending on a generous flood to raise a good crop on my land, but a greater worry was consuming me. My waist had thickened and I began to watch Pharaoh for any signs that he had noticed, but he was as loving and affable as ever. I did not raise the matter of the succession. I did not dare. There would be time enough for that subject later, if my royal benefactor remained my royal lover.

In the first week of Thoth Ramses discovered the truth. We were lying side by side one night with all the lamps but one extinguished because of the heat. The darkness had an almost palpable quality, smothering and breathless, and we had made love with the mindless abandon that extreme heat sometimes brings. I had broken my rule afterwards and drunk copious amounts of beer, and Ramses had gone so far as to remove the cap that was supposed to cover his skull at all times, testily ordering Paibekamun to have cool water brought. When it arrived I took over the task of washing him myself, knowing that he liked my touch and appreciated the implied homage involved.

When I had finished he surprised me by taking the cloth out of my hands and passing it gently down my arms, my back, my legs. "Majesty, you must not," I protested. "It is the duty of a body servant." I was standing by the couch and he glanced up at me, one of his beatific smiles lighting his chubby face. A fresh linen cap sat on his head, but wisps of greying hair stuck out around it, making him look like an amiable baboon. Once again I felt a flood of genuine love for this unassuming man, this unlikely god. He squatted there, the dripping cloth clutched in one meaty hand, and pursed his lips genially.

"But I am your servant, Lady Thu," he said. "A servant of love, a slave. Only you and Paibekamun will know that Pharaoh has debased himself thus, and Paibekamun will not tell!" He twinkled up at me. "Will you?" I opened my mouth to make a witty rejoinder but the cloth, followed by his fingers, was passing over my now undeniably distended abdomen. I stiffened. All at once he rose, and sitting on the edge of the couch, drew me towards him. I met his eyes. "Either my Lady is eating too much honey or there is a royal bud inside her, preparing to flower," he said. "Yet it cannot be the honey, for she only bulges in one place. You are pregnant, aren't you, Thu?" My impulse was to push him away and grab a sheet with which to cover myself. Instead, I forced an answering smile.

"Yes, it is true," I admitted. "I did not want to give your Majesty the happy news until I was certain."

"Hmm." His glance became shrewd. "It seems that you have waited a very long time to assure yourself. Well, I am pleased. Your old lover's seed is still potent and his little scorpion will become his little fruit tree. It is the way of things, is it not?" He planted a soft kiss on my cheek. "I have exhausted you tonight," he said. "Go now, and if there is anything you need you must ask for it from Amunnakht." I began to gather up my clothes.

"Does your Majesty still desire my presence tomorrow to go duck hunting in the north?" I asked diffidently as I pulled on my sheath. Ramses looked shocked.

"But of course, why not?" he declared. He patted my abdomen, kissed me again, and turned away, heaving himself onto his couch with a groan. "Sleep well, Thu," he called as I moved to the door. "A mother must get plenty of rest. Guard the royal life within you." I did not answer, making my final obeisance and letting myself out in silence.

As I walked back to my quarters, absently acknowledging the greeting of the guards at the palace wall and facing the welcome draught of air that always blew along the narrow path between palace and harem, I dissected every word, expression and gesture of the last few moments, searching for a withdrawal, a new coolness on Ramses' part, but I could find nothing. Give him time to absorb the news, I told myself as I entered my own door and Disenk rose from her mat to prepare me for bed. Perhaps everything will be all right. Perhaps I will be the exception to Pharaoh's well-known, cruel rule. Perhaps his love for me will triumph. Perhaps. Who knows?

I got onto my couch and composed myself for sleep and my gaze fell on the large cushion in the depths of which nestled the vital scroll. I tried to tell myself that ultimately the King's reaction would not matter, that even if he did cast me adrift I would still become a queen in the fullness of time. But the vision of him crouched at my feet and grinning up at me, cloth in hand, came back vividly, and I knew that it did matter. It mattered a great deal. I wanted more than anything else in the world to be able to trust him.

The following day we went duck hunting in the lush northern marshes. Ramses was his attentive, cheerful self, and on the next evening I took my accustomed place on the dais at his feet, jewelled, wigged and painted, while he feted a delegation from Alashia. I accompanied him back to his chambers afterwards, and in the hour before dawn we made love and fell asleep together, but he had gone when I woke, and Paibekamun hustled me away with a speed that bordered on contempt.

Anxiously I waited for another summons, for I knew that the court was about to decamp to the desert, less in search of game than to briefly enjoy the pretence of a simpler life, but it did not come. I spent four sleepless nights and tense days before the aristocrats and ministers returned and Ramses sent for me. He greeted me as though he had not seen me for a year, and I was forcibly and unpleasantly reminded of the occasion when I had offended him and been temporarily banished, but when I asked him somewhat hesitantly why I had been excluded from the mass exodus he looked shocked. "The desert is no place for a pregnant woman, particularly one who is to bear a royal child," he explained. "I would do nothing to endanger your health, my Thu. What did you think? That I was about to abandon you? Come. Smile for me, and let me feel the baby kick in your womb. Then we will walk in the garden and have a picnic by the pool, just you and I." I had indeed been afraid that he was about to abandon me, but I was reassured by his manner, and further reassured by the summons to more feasts and entertainments when it seemed that nothing had changed.

I was able to cling to my illusion for another two months. By then it was Athyr, the weather cool and the river almost at its peak and running swift and strong. I was in my eighth month. I had given up my exercises, for they caused me discomfort, and I found myself enveloped in a pervasive somnolence that had me sleeping late and spending much time sitting outside my door on the grass, my thoughts drifting.

Ramses was sending for me less often and his lovemaking had become cursory in spite of my redoubled efforts to be inventive between his sheets. His conversation was still affectionate but often vague, as though his thoughts were elsewhere, and though I did my best to please him my all too obvious desperation made him wary. Still I held rashly to the belief that even though his desire for me was waning it had not been kindled by another woman, and once my baby was born and I had regained my slim figure, I could easily recapture the Mighty Bull.

But one day I saw a girl striding past the fountain. She

paused to dabble her fingers in its crystal flow before straightening and moving on, a supple, slender form with all the sinuous grace of the desert lion. Her black hair swung against the small of her back as she went, and she held her head high. I called to Disenk. "That girl," I said, pointing. "Find out who she is, Disenk, and how long she has been in the harem. I do not recall having seen her before." A premonition of disaster had gripped me at the sight of her, and the baby had set up a flurry of painful kicks against my belly.

Soon my servant returned, and I could tell from her demeanour as she approached me that the information I sought was not good. The sense of an impending storm intensified and my head suddenly began to ache. Disenk bowed. "Her name is Hentmira," she said. "Her father is Overseer of the Faience Factories in the city. The family is very rich. Pharaoh saw her in the crowd at the New Year's Day celebrations and sent Amunnakht to invite her into the harem." The New Year's Day celebrations! And I had been on Ramses' arm, smugly oblivious, while his eye was already roving! A revulsion for the King and rage at my own blindness shook me.

"Is that all?" I asked tightly, seeing her hesitation. She shook her head.

"Hentmira has taken possession of your old cell," she went on. "She and Hunro have known each other for years. Their parents live on adjoining estates. I am sorry, Thu." The condescending pity in her voice enraged me further, and with a savage gesture I ordered her away.

So I am an outsider once more, I thought furiously, miserably. The old order closes ranks, and in spite of my title, my land, I am still nothing but a nonentity from Aswat. Jealousy poured, hot and acrid, through my veins. Hunro and that arrogant little upstart sharing the room where Hunro and I had talked together. Doubtless Hunro was far more comfortable exchanging frivolous memories and private family jokes with a fellow noblewoman than she had ever been trying to find a common ground with me. Hunro, flexing and swaying as she spoke, would tell Hentmira about me. "The woman who shared this cell before you, my dear, became Pharaoh's favourite in spite of the fact that she is a mud-wader from some tiny backwater down south. But she hasn't lasted, you know. She's pregnant. These peasants can be indecently fertile..." And Hentmira would curl her aristocratic lips in a superior smile and agree. I squeezed my eyes shut and clenched my fists in agony. No, I told myself fiercely. No, it is not that. Hunro was my friend, and I have no idea what virtues this Hentmira possesses. My hurt belongs to Ramses, Ramses, King and lover, who grows ever colder. Oh gods, what is to become of me? I am deathly afraid.

Three weeks passed, and it was the month of Khoiak. The Nile overflowed its banks, spilling its water and the vital silt onto the earth, and a scroll arrived from my Overseer to report that the flood had reached a height of fourteen cubits, and all my land was covered. The news was a flicker of joy in an otherwise dismal month but my mood soon darkened again. I tried to avoid any sight of Hentmira, for the King was silent and his messengers no longer knocked on my door, but sometimes I saw her treading the grass on her way to the bath house, her magnificent hair tousled and her eyes swollen with sleep, or sitting under the white gauze of her canopy in the company of the other women with whom she had quickly developed an easy familiarity. Her unaffected grace accentuated my bloated size and clumsiness. Her unspoiled youth made me feel old, jaded and used.

Khoiak also brought the great annual feasts of Osiris, when his death, burial and resurrection were celebrated with many rituals all over Egypt but primarily at Abydos. The harem emptied at this season as the women took part in the festivities, many of them journeying to the holy city, but because of my condition, and because Pharaoh had not invited me to participate in the rejoicing with him, I worshipped in Osiris's shrine at Pi-Ramses.

It was as I was struggling to lower myself onto my litter outside the harem gates, surrounded by a loud confusion of women, servants, guards and litter-bearers all shouting and jostling for position, that I noticed Hentmira. Clad in a transparent yellow sheath that stirred against her shapely ankles and set off her tiny waist, a plain gold circlet imprisoning her gleaming hair, she was deep in conversation with the Chief Wife. Both were standing in the shade of the trees, well apart from the uproar, but their eyes were on me. Ast-Amasareth caught my gaze and smiled thinly, then deliberately turned back to the younger woman, but Hentmira continued to look my way inquisitively. What are you staring at? I wanted to shout at her rudely, stung both by her open interest and by Ast-Amasareth's snub. Can you not see your own destruction in my misshapen body? Sebek will capture you too, proud concubine!

But suddenly it was I standing before the Chief Wife, watching with a prurient interest as poor Eben cursed fretfully at her bearers. I looked away, sick at heart. With a last heave I managed to settle myself on my cushions. "Close the curtains, Disenk," I ordered, my voice thick, and once she had done so I turned on my side and lay in the softly filtered light with my hands covering my face. I could not shut out those faultless, aristocratic features, or the Chief Wife's twisted, cold smile.

Yet on the evening following the conclusion of the cycle of Osiris Feasts I was summoned to Pharaoh's chambers. Unprepared, I was lying naked on my couch while Disenk read to me, but all lassitude fled as the Herald bowed himself out. I came to my feet with renewed vigour, pouring out a stream of commands to my servant. My best sheath, the one with the golden flowers embroidered all over it, my wig of a hundred braids, my gold and carnelian necklet, the faience earrings... Disenk rushed to obey and within the hour, resplendent in my finery and carefully painted, I was rapping on Pharaoh's door.

Paibekamun admitted me, sketching a bow. I pushed past him eagerly. Ramses was lying on his couch, his knees drawn up, his features twisted. My confidence began to drain away as I approached him. I could not perform a full obeisance but I did my best as he watched me, then he waved me closer. "Thu, I have missed you terribly," he said. "Did you bring your herb box?" So that was the reason for the summons. Pharaoh was ill. Swallowing my bitter disappointment I nodded.

"I carry it always, Majesty," I told him. "And if you have missed me so much, why have you not sent for me? I have been no further away than a short walk." He looked abashed.

"I have been much occupied with state matters," he muttered. "Besides, you have been in no condition for lovemaking." I bit back the retort that had risen to my tongue, and placing my box on the table I opened it.

"What is wrong?" I asked.

"I have pains in my belly," he complained, "and an excess of wind. The cramps come and go." In spite of my discouragement I could not repress a smile as I removed the sheet covering him and gently felt his abdomen.

"The festivals of Osiris are only just concluded," I said. "Your Majesty knows perfectly well what the matter is. Your Majesty has eaten and drunk too often and too freely, as usual." I flipped the sheet back over him briskly. "I prescribe a large dose of castor oil, and when that has achieved the desired result, two days of nothing but honey mixed with saffron. Your Majesty must of course fast during the treatment."

"Nasty little scorpion," he said under his breath. I busied myself with extracting the castor oil from my box, and measuring out my supply of saffron.

"There!" I said crisply. "Have your servant bring you honey and add to it one ro of saffron twice a day. Is there anything else, Majesty? May I be dismissed?" He looked miserable. His eyes met mine, slid away, came back to me as I stood waiting. Then he waved at me irritably.

"Oh sit down, Thu! Talk to me! Tell me of your own health. Tell me what you have been doing. In spite of what you may think, I have indeed missed you."

"Just what have you missed, my King?" I said softly as I took the chair. "Have you missed the delights of my body perhaps? It is the same body you loved to handle, indeed, it is surely even more desirable seeing that it shelters your child, conceived of the love you say you bear me." His round face flushed and he fought free of his bedclothes and sat up, wincing.

"You should be my minister of foreign affairs," he said wryly. "Such a talent for polite manipulation and subtle insult should not be wasted. I have given you a title, importunate one. I have given you land. Why can you not be content with that? What else can you possibly want?"

His words were an admission that my nights in his bed were over. A weight settled slowly about my heart. I felt it, heavy and cold, in my breast, and with it came a despairing recklessness. I no longer had anything to lose. Others would caress him, make him laugh, whisper to him in the darkness. Others would bask in the munificence of his royal smile, walk beside him, sit at his feet, be warmed with the reflected glory of his Godhead. My tiny nemesis stirred in my womb and I placed a hand over it.

"Did you see my sheath move?" I said quietly. "That was your child, Ramses. You will say that the harem is full of your children, but surely there is no child running about under the sun that was conceived in such passion and adoration as the one I carry. You said you loved me. Did Pharaoh lie? Or did he exaggerate? My love for you has not died because I carry your burden. Was yours so shallow as to be killed by a swollen belly?" I knew now that he no longer loved me and I was trying to goad him into admitting his insincerity. My eyes never left his face. I saw the colour slowly drain from it, to be replaced by a blankness I recognized as his rising anger. I did not care. I would say what I liked. Let him punish me if he wanted. "I still love you, Mighty Bull," I went on, my voice breaking. "And I love this child of our happiness enough to fervently desire his legitimization. Make him legitimate, Ramses. If you love me, then marry me."

He had been listening intently and now he blinked and jerked forward. "Marry you? Are you insane? No matter what I feel for you, Thu, I cannot marry a commoner!"

"But I am no longer a commoner," I pointed out calmly. "I am a noblewoman. You made me one yourself." He glared at me, vexed.

"That was to please you," he said hotly. "Gifts of jewellery, land, a title—it was all to keep you happy. Your blood is still common!"

I came to my feet, my own temper rising on a dark tide of shame, the familiar taste of a long defeat acrid in my mouth. I had thought that in leaving the dust and dirt of Aswat behind all those years ago I had also shed my lineage, but it was not so, it would never be so. Like the brittle snakeskin I had picked up on the desert and put in my cedar box, I would carry it with me wherever I went, whatever I did. Desperately I tried to cling to reason.

"You married Ast-Amasareth," I countered, a damnable quaver in my voice betraying my distress, "and she is not even Egyptian!"

"That may be so, but the Chief Wife comes from ancient Libu royal blood and is therefore completely acceptable," he said loftily. I stepped to the couch and leaned on it, thrusting my face close to his, my control gone.

"So do I!" I cried out. "My father is a Libu prince, exiled from his land, forced to soldier in Egypt! One day he will be sent for and we will all go back to his tribe and he will rule and everyone will recognize the royal blood in my veins! I am a Libu princess, Pharaoh! Hear me!" I no longer knew what I was saying. There was a stirring in the room behind me but I was scarcely aware of it. Ramses lifted a hand to whoever was preparing to move in his defence, and turned his attention back to me. An expression of pity filled his face.

"No, my poor little Thu," he said kindly. "It is a pleasant fantasy. Your father is a peasant. We have had some fine times together, you and I, and you are a brilliant physician. Do not ask for more than I, your King, have given." I fell to my knees, fingers gripping his sheets convulsively, all pride dissolved.

"What of the Empress Tiye, she who so bewitched Osiris Amunhotep the Third Glorified that he adored her for as long as he lived?" I choked. My mouth was trembling and my words were slurred. "She was a commoner. I know it from my history lessons. Oh, Great Horus, I could be to you as she was to her royal husband! Marry me! Make me a queen, I beg you! I am still your little scorpion! I love you!" Ramses nodded, and I felt decisive hands lift me, thrust my box into my fumbling grasp, propel me to the door. Before I knew it I was outside, sobbing, and the mighty cedar panels had closed firmly in my face.

For a moment I steadied myself against the wall, then blinded by my tears I began to stumble along the passage. I heard the guard at the far end speak and I thought he was addressing me, but when I looked up I saw Hentmira, a vision of seductive beauty, emerging from the dimness. She halted and bowed. "Good evening, Lady Thu," she murmured respectfully, and waited. Mumbling a reply I hurried past her, head down, and I heard her continue to Pharaoh's door and knock. The door was opened, greetings exchanged, and the light behind me was cut off. In my humiliation and anguish I crept away.

Ramses did not send for me again, and I was left to spend the remaining time of my pregnancy in an increasing isolation. I heard that one of the palace physicians had been called to attend him, and Hentmira was seen draped over him at several of his feasts. I went from raging at his perfidy to castigating myself for losing control during our last ignominious encounter, but in the end my mood became one of sullen acceptance. The baby would soon be born, and then I intended to stretch every nerve, tap every resource, to recapture the King.

I wrote a letter to Pa-ari, pouring out my unhappiness, and I wrote also to Hui, begging him to visit me. I had heard nothing from him since he had refused me his help despite his assurances that I would have his support. No reply came from either of them, and those final days dragged to their inevitable conclusion.

I considered approaching Prince Ramses, who was also maintaining an ominous silence, but decided that such a meeting would be fruitless. Even if he had wanted to extend a hand to me, which I doubted, what could he do? Take his father to task because Pharaoh had cast me off, and risk the King's displeasure falling on his own head? The Prince, ambitious and quietly ruthless as he was, would do nothing to endanger his chances to mount the Horus Throne. I did not want those chances put in jeopardy either. If another son was named Heir, the scroll he had dictated would become worthless.

Hunro visited me once, bringing a gift of exotic sweet-meats made by the natives of Cush and sent to her by her brother Banemus. She questioned me sympathetically and tactfully about my fall from favour, and both of us scrupulously avoided any mention of her cellmate Hentmira. Her manner was polite, even warm, but somehow distant, and I derived no comfort from her. Indeed, I felt drained when she at last went away. So ended the month of Khoiak.

I was brought to the birthing stool on the third day of Tybi. The first day of the month was the Feast of the Coronation of Horus. It also served as the day our Pharaoh celebrated his Naming Day, and my first pains coincided with the greatest palace festivity of the year. As I paced out the confines of my quarters, restless and afraid, I could hear the tumult of rejoicing going on all around me, a dim but constant cacophony of horns, cymbals and song. Every citizen of Egypt was drinking and dancing. The Nile would be choked with torch-lit boats crammed with people throwing flowers onto its placid surface, splashing in its shallows, building friendly fires and roasting ducks and geese on its sandy banks.

The harem was empty, but beyond its high walls the palace precincts throbbed with light and noise. Between my still brief contractions I wandered to my door, looking past the vast courtyard drowned in peaceful shadow to the shifting glow against the night sky caused by the thousands of lamps and torches crowding the palace gardens. Shrieks and laughter came to my ears, yet I was as severed from the revelry as though I stood on the bluish moon overhead. Disenk saw to my needs, feeding me sips of water and bathing my brow and spine where the sweat of my increasing effort kept gathering, but Disenk seemed faceless to me, a stranger. I wanted my mother, the sound of her voice coming back to me clearly and startlingly as the pain worsened. I wanted Hui. I had sent for him. He had promised to attend my confinement, but the hours went by and he did not come.

I was able to sleep fitfully now and then. The second day of Tybi dawned and the merrymaking went on. For a while the pains ceased and I was suddenly hungry, but towards afternoon on that long, bright day my belly began to tighten again, this time with an ominous inevitability that terrified me, and I took to my couch where I lay groaning and tossing. Where was Hui? I called to him vainly.

Towards evening one of the harem midwives arrived, and she and Disenk coaxed me onto the litter that waited outside my door. I knew that I was being taken to the birthing room in the children's quarters, but the knowledge, and the short journey between courtyards, was ephemeral in my mind. I had turned inward to the grim work my body was trying to accomplish, and the rocking of the litter, the hands that helped me to alight and walk the short distance into the stark room, the lamplight, the waiting nursery servants, flickered and wavered without substance on the edge of my consciousness.

I endured another seven hours of torment before I was brought at last to squat on the birthing stool, and shivering and crying, expelled my son. I heard him wail, a high, strident sound, and in a daze of exhaustion and relief I watched while the midwife washed him, cut off the navel cord, and laid him on the bed of mud bricks required by custom. It was only then that I noticed the huge statue of Ta-urt, goddess of childbirth, standing fatly and benevolently in one corner. She smiled down at me complacently while my baby's cries subsided and I summoned up the energy to smile back. It was done. It was over.

Disenk raised me and together we went out to the litter. The night was still deep, and this unfamiliar courtyard lay like a mysterious and unexplored country. I was sleepy as I curled up on the cushions but I did not have time to settle into their softness. A moment later the litter was put down and Disenk reached in to me. "These are not my quarters," I said, puzzled, and she shook her head.

"No, Thu. It is customary for the new mothers to remain in the children's courtyard for some time so that they may care for their babies and be tended better." I withdrew the hand I had extended to her.

"But I do not want to stay here," I protested. "I want to sleep on my own couch, Disenk. Set up a basket for my baby in my own bedchamber!" Her face, in the dim light, was drawn.

"I am sorry, Thu, but it is not allowed. You must follow the custom."

"To Set with the custom!" I cried, struggling to get out of the litter, desperate to flee to my own safe little room. "I want to be away from here, Disenk! Lead me back to our courtyard!" But I was weak, and the hands, kind but firm, that detained me were not.

I found myself ushered into a small cell and laid on a narrow couch. A lamp burned beside it. Disenk went away but quickly returned and placed a snuffling bundle in my arms. The tiny face turned towards my body, seeking comfort.

"A wet-nurse has been appointed for him," Disenk said. "I will bind your breasts presently, Thu, but now take pleasure in him. He is a beautiful little boy." I looked down into features so like Pharaoh's that the breath stopped in my throat. I wanted to hate this scrap of life, this creature who had destroyed my dreams, but I could not. I stroked the wisp of black hair atop his funny little head and sighed.

"Bring me beer, Disenk," I ordered shortly. "I am very thirsty. And if I am to be incarcerated in this miserable cell, go and fetch my cosmetics and perfume. I may be a mother but I am not dead yet."

I was watching the wet-nurse suckle my son the following morning when a scroll arrived for me. It was from Hui. "My dearest Thu," it said. "If I had known that the birth of your child was to be so soon I would not have been unavailable to your messenger. Can you ever forgive me? I am giving considerable thought to a suitable gift for you on this momentous occasion and I am praying that the King's astrologers choose a lucky name for such a privileged baby. I will visit you as soon as possible." That was all. He had not told me where he had been, but I could guess. On the other side of the wall, lost to my urgent summons in the maelstrom of celebration.

Hard on the heels of Hui's unsatisfactory letter came a Herald in palace livery. My baby had fed and was sleeping in my arms when the man came up to the couch, bowed profoundly, and placed a leather pouch on the sheet by my hip. "I bring greetings and congratulations from the Mighty Bull to his beloved concubine, the Lady Thu," he said formally. "His Majesty thanks you for giving him a royal son, and wishes to show his appreciation with this gift." He had turned to go when I stopped him.

"Wait!" I ordered, then I gently put the baby beside me and pulled open the pouch. It contained a thick gold anklet studded with buttons of moonstone over which the one band of sunlight falling into the room slid like pale green oil. I could have purchased four years' worth of seeds for my land in the Fayum with it, or hired an assassin to stick a knife into Ramses' flabby back. I hefted its weight then dropped it back into the pouch. "Here," I said peremptorily, holding it out to the astonished Herald. "Return it to Pharaoh, and tell him that his gift is not acceptable unless he brings it himself. You may go." He backed out hastily, the pouch clutched in one unbelieving fist, and I bent over my boy. His eyelashes quivered. One chubby arm flailed, he burped politely, then sank once more into a deep slumber. I could imagine the King's anger and embarrassment when he heard my words from his Herald's lips but I did not care.

Outside my door other babies wailed and children ran to and fro, the voices of their nurses raised in admonition or caution. Somewhere close by a woman was crying. Above me I could hear the droning, incessant chorus of a class chanting its lesson. This harem block seethed with almost unceasing noise and activity and I loathed it. I had fallen as low as I intended to go.

A gift from Hui did arrive in due time, a phial of the purest crystal in whose facets I could see my distorted reflection multiplied a dozen times. Its base and stopper were crafted of filigreed gold and it appeared to be full of dark grey grains which gave off a sweet but peculiar odour when I opened it. "Again I beseech your mercy for neglecting you," the accompanying scroll said. "I obtained this curious phial and its contents from the Sabaens with whom I trade for medicines. I do not know its country of origin. The grains are Arabian frankincense, the best and costliest incense of all. Inhaling its smoke will cleanse the body and clear the mind. Use it sparingly, Thu, and in good health." I was distressed that he had not brought the precious thing to me himself and I turned it over in my fingers, marvelling at its uniqueness and trying to decide whether to return it or not. In the end my greed won the contest. No Egyptian craftsman had the knowledge to manipulate crystal in this way and I was sure it was very valuable.

In due time an official scroll arrived, announcing that my son should bear the name Pentauru. I did not know whether to laugh or be enraged, for Pentauru meant "excellent scribe" or "great writer." It was not a name for a royal prince. Princes did not become scribes. But then I reminded myself that my baby's royal blood was mingled with my own, that my mysterious grandmother had loved to tell stories, my brother was a respected scribe, and I myself had longed to unlock the wonderful door of written knowledge. A fascination with words ran in my family. Pentauru was sleeping in his basket beside my couch and I bent over him, stroking his smooth little cheek and calling his new name to him softly. By the time I became a queen he might indeed be a great scribe, and with my elevation he would become a prince as well.

Disenk had brought all my belongings into the children's

428

quarters including the cushion with its secret burden, and I often found my eyes drawn to it as I grew stronger. The Prince's promise had acquired an added importance now that my arms were full of a new responsibility. My son must grow up to claim his proper birthright. Two futures were now inscribed on that piece of papyrus, and if it were mislaid I knew that the Prince would repudiate his word to me. I was no longer in any position to influence the King.

But in spite of everything I still hoped to recover his affections, and by the end of Mekhir I felt strong enough to move back to my own rooms. A message from my Overseer had come, telling me that the sowing had begun on my fertile arouras and was proceeding well.

A letter had also come from Pa-ari, full of love and concern, apologizing once again for being unable to answer my invitation and acquainting me with the fact that Isis, his wife, would give birth sometime in the season Shemu. I wanted to see him, to sit with him in the peace of the garden I had imagined as his and drink wine and reminisce. Perhaps another journey to Aswat could be arranged later, but for the present, I must work to re-establish myself at court.

Accordingly one day I summoned the Overseer of the Children's Quarters and sent him to Amunnakht the Keeper of the Door with a request that I return to my previous place. Two hours later the Keeper himself stood in my doorway and bowed. I was delighted to see him.

"Greetings, Amunnakht!" I said. "It is a long time since we met. Come and see my son. He is beautiful, is he not?" The man returned my welcome with the grave dignity I remembered so well, and entering the dim cell he bent obligingly over the basket. Pentauru was awake and looked up at him drowsily, both tiny fists curled under his chin.

"He is indeed a fine boy," the Keeper agreed, straightening, "and you are now as slim and youthful as ever, Lady

Thu. My congratulations." I indicated the table and Disenk hastily poured wine and passed a cup to him. He shook his head. I faced him resolutely. For all his quiet urbanity he was a formidable man whose word was law all through the harem.

"You know that I wish to return to my old quarters," I began as confidently as I could. "I am fully recovered from the birth and ready to resume my former life. I do not find this cell congenial and there is no longer any need to keep me here." Amunnakht spread his hennaed palms.

"I am sorry, Lady Thu, but that is not possible. Pharaoh has decreed that you must take up residence permanently in this block." I stared at him, the heat draining from my body.

"But why? Is he punishing me for refusing his gift? He must know that I was hurt because he did not come to me in person! I longed to see him! Is that any reason for condemning me, Amunnakht?" I stepped forward. "But perhaps my old quarters are occupied and there are no other rooms ready for me at present. Is that it? Is it?" I was grasping for any shred of hope, but the Keeper shook his head.

"No, my Lady. Your old quarters are still empty, and so are the similar rooms on the other side of the courtyard. The Lord of All Life has spoken. You are to remain here." I thought I caught a flicker of sympathy in his dark, carefully kohled eyes and I grabbed for his arm.

"But what am I to do here, surrounded by fractious women and wailing infants?" I cried out. "I will not be reduced to the title of Royal Nurse, Amunnakht, I will not! Plead with the King for me, I pray!" He shook himself free of my grip.

"I may advise the Mighty Bull, Lady Thu, but it is not my place to try and alter his decrees," he replied kindly. "You have enjoyed his blessing for much longer than your predecessors. It is time to retire with as much grace as you can conjure."

"And do what?"

He shrugged. "You are free to visit your friends within the harem. You may request permission to spend time in the house of the Seer or go about the city with the guards. You have your land to nurture. Many women find great satisfaction in such things."

"Well, I will not!" I spat at him, fear spawning this mounting rage. "I am not a sheep, Amunnakht, I am not a milk cow to go wherever I am led and stand meekly when I am tethered! I will die if I am imprisoned here!"

"No, my Lady, you will not," he rejoined calmly, undaunted by my outburst. "You will see to the care and later the education of your son. You will seek compensations in places other than Pharaoh's bed. If you do not, you may find yourself banished to the Fayum." My rage was snuffed out at his words and the fear rose up behind it like a cloud of black ashes.

"For the sake of the gods, Amunnakht, speak to him for me, help me," I whispered. "I can get him back if he will give me the chance. What woman can fascinate him the way I did? He will soon grow tired of the others, and then he will remember me." Amunnakht bowed and walked to the doorway.

"That may indeed happen," he said, turning with one hand on the lintel, "and if it does I will be the first to bring you his summons. But until then you must learn patience and I warn you, Lady Thu, that Pharaoh has never reinstated a concubine who has borne a child. He regards such an act as a betrayal, for he fears his many sons. You knew that, though, didn't you? I wish you continued good health." Then he was gone, his shadow following him out into the bright day.

I sank, trembling, into a chair. Disenk remained motionless by the table, watching me. Pentauru stirred in his reed basket. I saw a young girl go by outside, a cat draped across

her arms, and presently a servant ran after her calling frantically. A naked child tottered past, thumb in his mouth.
Three women paused briefly by my door and called to
unseen friends before they wandered on.

Suddenly my surroundings began to close in on me. The
plaster walls of my cell leaned inward. The ceiling dipped
drunkenly over my head. I felt the back of my chair become
fluid and begin to encircle my chest and I could not breathe.
Clenching my fists and squeezing my eyes shut I forced my
lungs to expand. "Disenk!" I gasped. "Give me a drink!" I
felt a cup nudge my stiff fingers, and without opening my
eyes I took it and gulped at the bitter wine. The moment of
mindless panic slowly dissolved, leaving a composure that
was nevertheless still tainted with terror. "He cannot do this
to me," I muttered. "Hentmira will have her day and then
Ramses will want me back. It must be so. Otherwise,
Disenk," I finished, looking up at her, "I shall kill myself."
Disenk made no reply, and I drained my cup in a brooding
silence.

It seemed to me, in the following weeks, that the
Children's Quarter was a happier place than the courtyard I
had left. The women here were no longer competing with
each other for Pharaoh's favour, agonizing over what mode
of dress or exotic style of facepaint might catch his eye on
public occasions, or watching their friends and enemies
alike for any sign of a threat. The gossip circulating had
more to do with the progress of the barter and commerce in
which most of the inmates were engaged than with who was
sharing Pharaoh's bed and the nature of her status measured
by what gifts she had been given. The fountain and its wide
basin served as a gathering point for innumerable Overseers,
Stewards, Scribes and Surveyors consulting with their
employers under the billowing white gauze canopies. There
was no doubt that many of the women had become very rich
in the pursuit of their business interests. They were far more

approachable and friendly than my previous neighbours. There was, after all, no sexual jealousy to colour their relationships, but in my eyes they were still prisoners compensating for their incarceration, even as Amunnakht had advised me to do.

Though I began to adjust to new routines I fiercely rejected my fate. I began to exercise regularly once more, usually watched by a crowd of curious children. I bathed, cossetted and played with Pentauru, taking much comfort from the feel of his plump, warm body. I entered into a voluminous correspondence with my Overseer in the Fayum and pored over every detail of the progress being made on my estate.

Deep in my heart a flame of hope continued to burn. Pharaoh would get over his rancour. He would begin to miss me. Hentmira would eventually bore him and his thoughts would turn to the intimacy we had shared. All I had to do was wait.

Chapter 22

But the months of Mekhir and Phamenat came and went with no word from the palace. On my arouras the crops grew green and thick. My garden there was cleared and tamed. The house was repaired. Gods' feasts marked the passage of time. Pentauru began to smile sunnily and drunkenly at me when I bent over him, and he was soon able to sit up without support. Every afternoon when the heat had started to abate, I took him onto the grass of the courtyard and laid him on a sheet, watching him kick and flail his sturdy limbs under the shade of my canopy and crow at the flowers I picked to dangle before his eyes and place in his fist. He was a placid child, easily pleased, and in spite of the chaos he had brought into my life I grew to love him.

When Pharmuti arrived, I had to face the probability that I no longer occupied a place of affection in Pharaoh's mind, indeed, it was likely that he did not think of me at all. Somehow I would have to save myself. I still believed that if I could just see him, create an opportunity to meet him face to face, his memories of me would return and with them his desire. In the precious hours of night silence I pondered my problem. It was no use trying to gain entrance to his bedchamber. The guards would turn me back. Nor could I walk through the main doors of the palace. Leaving the harem was easy, but the soldiers thronging the public reception area of the palace knew very well who had permission to approach the inner sanctuaries and who had not. I could perhaps linger by the watersteps and hope to catch Ramses coming or going, but again, he was protected by many servants and guards wherever he went and I did not imagine that I would be smilingly bowed into his presence. Nor could I spend hours by the water without attracting attention.

Should I dictate a petition and have it placed in his hands? It was worth a try. But I did not want any harem scribe knowing the shame of my efforts. Accordingly I sent for papyrus, and on the exquisite palette Hui had given me so many months ago I wrote a carefully worded letter to my King, respectfully requesting an audience. As the black hieroglyphs took shape under my reed pen I missed my brother with a sudden jolt of homesickness. I could have dictated this missive to him. I could have discussed my plight with him, sure of his understanding and support even though I knew he had not approved of the course I had steered for my life ever since Hui had docked at Wepwawet's temple watersteps. When I had finished I sealed the scroll and summoned a harem Herald to deliver it.

My answer came within three days. Pharaoh was much occupied with state matters. He had no time to devote to the concerns of a concubine. He advised me to take any problem I might have to the Keeper of the Door. The message was delivered verbally and I found myself flushing with mortification as the callous words filled the air. So Ramses did not want to see me. Well I would give him no choice. There must be a way to avoid his guards and reach him in person. I would not admit defeat.

In the end the solution was simple. Oiled and perfumed, painted and wigged, I wrapped myself once more in Disenk's old woollen cloak and walked out of the courtyard, along the path in the opposite direction to the harem entrance, and through the gate into the servants' compound. The guards stationed where the path opened out onto the dusty stretch of ground before the cells barely glanced at me, a harem servant on an errand for her mistress, and unnoticed I turned right and then right again, through another gate and onto the paving that fronted the Ministers' Offices. I had not been challenged, for although soldiers clustered to either side of the entrance, the avenue was busy with other servants coming and going.

I had been this way once before, a long time ago when I had come to tell Amunnakht that I was ready to brave Pharaoh's bed, and in spite of my nervousness I smiled to myself as I remembered how determined and yet anxious I had been then. My body may have softened under the harem's insidious influence but my will was as indomitable as ever. I drew the hood of the cloak more closely around my face as I passed the Keeper's office, careful not to risk a glance within. I heard his measured voice and presumed that he was dictating to his scribe.

The path took a sharp angle, and all at once I was facing an even wider thoroughfare lined on my side with palm trees. On the other side a row of great columns reared, holding up the massive stone roof of Pharaoh's office. Shadows moved beyond them and a fully armed soldier stood guard at each of their feet. As I hesitated, hidden by shrubbery, a scribe laden with scrolls hurried out and disappeared in the direction of the banqueting hall.

Quickly I shed the cloak, folding it and laying it down at the foot of one of the palms. Smoothing my silver-plaited wig and pausing to slip on the sandals that I had carried for fear their white leather and gem-studded thongs would attract attention, I stepped boldly out. If Ramses was not attending to administrative business today I was doomed, but I prayed fervently as I approached the soldiers that he was following his usual daily routine and would be seated behind his desk, holding audience with his ministers. Deliberately I looked straight ahead, moving with a self-confidence I did not feel. One of the guards made as if to detain me. His spear wavered. Nonchalantly I smiled at him, spoke a greeting, and sailed between the columns and into the welcome coolness of the room beyond.

It was full of men. Four scribes sat cross-legged on the floor, knee to knee, pens poised over their palettes. A white-clad minister leaned against the wall, arms folded, and another stood beside him. Two more flanked the desk, and before it, blocking my view, I recognized the imposing figure of the Overseer of the City, the Vizier To. The gossamer linen that hugged his body from armpits to ankles was hemmed and fringed in gold, and gold gripped his upper arms and encircled his shoulder-length wig. As I approached he was speaking earnestly, one hennaed palm extended.

"...and he is at least proving to be honest, Majesty. I would not have recommended him otherwise. We must look elsewhere for the reasons. I suspect embezzlement of grain, not careless accounting, but I cannot be sure until..." His voice trailed away as he sensed that he no longer held the attention of the others. Turning, he saw me, and his action brought the King into view.

Ramses was slumped loosely in his chair, his helmeted head resting against one hand. I could tell immediately by the glazed look in his kohled eyes and the set of his jaw that he was bored. His other hand was engaged in playing with the heavy pectoral resting on his chest. Somewhat uncertainly, the men bowed to me. Vizier To moved away from the desk and I came to a halt before Ramses, lowering myself into a deep obeisance.

It was some time before I heard a strangled, "Rise!" and I came to my feet. His eyes were no longer glazed and he had stiffened, sitting forward. The look he gave me was furious. "I have already refused you an audience, Lady Thu," he snapped. "How you managed to find your way in here without being accosted is beyond my comprehension and I will speak to the Captain of the Palace Guard about the laxness of his men. I am far too busy to hear your complaint. Take it to Amunnakht. Begone!" I stood my ground, heart pounding, and strove to meet his eyes, painfully aware of the ministers frozen on the periphery of my vision. I had assumed that the moment he saw me Ramses would dismiss all others from the room and angry or not, would hear me out. Then I could have freely had my say, wheedled and coaxed, pouted and cried, moved close to put my hands on him in the ways I knew he could not resist, but what could I do with such an audience? He could not soften in the presence of his ministers and I could not seduce him. As I searched his face I realized that he would not dismiss them because he needed their silent authority to buttress his, and to prevent me from making him appear at fault. Very well, I thought. I cannot shed my clothes and wrap myself around him, but I have nothing to lose by speaking my mind, and that I will do.

"You did not come to see your son, Great Horus," I said. "You did not come to visit me, the woman you professed to love. I hurt. I am sad, and lonely for you. You severed the link between us without warning and you refused to grant me a moment in your august presence. I am bereft." He puffed out his hennaed lips.

"If I went into the harem every time one of my concubines gave birth or desired my body I would be too busy to see to more important matters," he replied testily. "You forget your place, Lady Thu. You are not a wife. Your rights are the limited prerogatives of a harem inmate. According to the clauses of the contract your father signed, I owe you shelter, food, clothing and such other creature comforts as you need. Nothing else. You have been treated with exemplary affection by your King and I fear it has gone to your head. I understand your distress, and therefore I will not have you disciplined. You are dismissed."

I stared at him reflectively. If I tried to goad him with the secrets of his bed in front of his nobles he would have me dragged away at once. I was finding it difficult to equate this brisk, impersonal man with the Pharaoh who had sat me on his knee and tickled me, fitted himself around my back and buried his hand in my hair as we fell asleep together, murmured feverish words of lust in my ear as the lamps guttered. You old hypocrite, I thought with distaste. How did it happen that I almost loved you? It is over. Everything is gone. I can see now that you will never take me back. I have already receded into the murky history of the harem, one star that streaked across your sky and then faded, unremarked.

"I think that I have fulfilled the duties of a concubine with wholly laudable skill," I retorted coolly, and was rewarded by the sudden flush that stained his cheeks. "After all, that was the other side of the bargain the contract represented, was it not, Mighty Bull? And you recognized the uniquely satisfying quality of my services by bestowing a title and a small estate on me." Careful, I told myself. Do not go too far. "It is clear that Your Majesty wishes nothing more to do with me now that I have done you the supreme honour of producing a royal son," I went on, "but I do feel that my achievement deserves greater acknowledgement than a golden bauble studded with moonstones. Don't you?" He was sitting upright now, breathing heavily, his spine rigid, both clenched fists jammed against the surface of his desk.

"I can have you whipped for that!" he shouted. "How dare you address me in this fashion? Who do you think you are?" I stepped right to the desk until I felt my thighs press against its edge.

"I am your little scorpion, Ramses," I said in a low voice. "Did you expect me to scuttle under the nearest rock when you tried to crush me? I have loved you, I have tended your wounds, I have shared your innermost thoughts. Now you kick me aside like so much rubbish. You know me, Pharaoh. How can I help but sting?"

It was a good speech, I thought, and it was having its impact. The King's mouth was pursed and he was glaring at me, but one hand had relaxed and was trembling slightly. I was not sure, in the moment before he responded, how much of what I had said was the true anguish of lost trust and affection and how much a calculated effort to force guilt upon him. I did not want to know. I waited tensely, my eyes locked with his, and in the end it was he who lowered his gaze.

"What do you want?" he asked quietly. I leaned towards him.

"I want to return to your bed," I said urgently. "I want to be again the companion for whom you pine!"

"That is not possible." He folded his arms. "I no longer desire you in my bed. If you love me as you say you do, then tend to my child. He is, after all, the proof that your King once chose you above all others in whom to plant his divine seed, and such a great honour should afford you much dignity among the other women."

"Dignity!" I rejoined indignantly. "There are dozens of harem women who have borne you sons and daughters! Such dignity is as common as dirt!"

Behind me in the room there was a murmur of consternation. I bit my lip. In the heat of our argument I had forgotten the men listening avidly to my denunciations and so, I think, had Pharaoh. Bowing, I lifted my hands in the universal gesture of apology and supplication. "My King," I pleaded softly, "forgive my angry words. They spring from an aching heart. If Your Majesty no longer requires my services as your concubine, then give me leave to retire to my estate in the Fayum. Let me go and see to my land and my crops, so that I may try to replace the satisfactions of your bed with the peaceful embrace of a less intoxicating lover." He looked startled, then he frowned.

"You would run away from your son? No!"

"I could take him with me," I said eagerly. "You would not need to worry about his education, Majesty. I would hire a tutor for him. And as for my fidelity to you, you could send as many guards with me as you wished, to make certain that I did not behave indecorously." I clasped my hands. "You do not need me any more. I am of no use to anyone but my child. Let me go! The Fayum is not far. You could recall me at any time. Please, Majesty!"

He looked at me speculatively for a long time, his expression closed, while I tried not to betray my deep agitation, then he pushed himself away from the desk and rose.

"You are a prideful and bitter child, Thu," he said at last, "and your fantasies are indeed those of the desert scorpion, venomous and unfathomable. You have stung me many times, and sometimes the pain was a delight, sometimes an adventure. But now you have been foolish enough to wield your barb in the presence of my ministers. That is unforgivable. Therefore you will be held to the terms of your contract with the Double Crown, and you may count yourself fortunate that I do not have you beaten and imprisoned for your supreme insolence. Your request is denied." Suddenly I needed the desk to keep myself upright. I clung to it desperately.

"Please, Ramses," I choked. "Please. You do not know what it is like to be surrounded by women and children every day, to be unable to escape that noisy chaos, to have lost any purpose in life, to dress and paint for no one but yourself! I am afraid of the harem. It will pull me into its suffocating embrace and I will disappear. Forgive me if I have offended you, and show your mercy, I beg! Do not condemn me to such a fate! Let me go, Ramses! Let me go!" His face was now a mask of disapproval, and even before I had finished speaking he was looking past me and snapping his fingers. I whirled about. A burly guard was approaching purposefully. "Oh, Ramses, no!" I cried out in despair. "For the love you once bore me, have pity!" But he had already seated himself again and was signalling curtly to the Vizier.

"Continue, To," he said brusquely. The men in the room loosened and turned their attention back to the business I had so abruptly interrupted. To cleared his throat. The scribes picked up their reed pens. No one was looking at me as the guard firmly grasped my arm and I was marched between the columns and out into the sunshine. Once on the path I shook myself free.

"I know my way back to my quarters without an escort," I said haughtily. "Unless of course you were ordered to take me to my door and lock me in." He hesitated then bowed and turned on his heel and I recrossed the paving, found Disenk's cloak where I had left it, and arranging it over my arm I began to walk back the way I had come.

I was in a state of shock. The scene in Pharaoh's office was still a confusion of jumbled words and feelings in my mind but I knew that before long the whole nasty exchange would arrange itself into a memory that would burn and haunt me for ever. I found myself on grass and realized that I had been lurching along the path like a drunkard. I was light-headed and weak. Carefully I kept my eyes on my sandalled feet, the leather glaringly white against the beige flagstones, the pretty gems sparkling as I moved.

A shadow formed ahead of me, and glancing up I saw that I was now level with Amunnakht's office and the Keeper himself stood outside it in conversation with a scribe. They broke off and bowed as I approached, and Amunnakht shot me a puzzled glance. I went right up to him.

"I would like to visit my mentor, the Seer," I said, amazed that my voice could be so even and natural. "Have I your permission, Keeper?" The request had been unpremeditated, an instinctive need to run to the one place where I could re-establish my wholeness. Amunnakht looked along the path the way I had come, then back to me. "Yes, I have been in the palace without your leave," I said impatiently, "and Pharaoh has reprimanded me severely. I promise I will not do it again, and I hope that my rash action will not bring a similar tongue-lashing to you, Amunnakht, for not keeping a closer watch on your charges. I expect you will want to consult with him about my request but I doubt if he will object. He will see visiting Hui as a lesser evil." I managed a wry smile. The Keeper looked mystified.

"You have my permission subject to that of the King, Lady Thu," he answered. "I will approach him with the matter as soon as he has finished the ministerial business of the day." I did not wait for more but nodded and immediately went on my way. The interview with Ramses was beginning to coalesce into a progression of knife-sharp images and I did not want to feel their cuts until I was able to cry in the privacy of my own cell.

I spent the afternoon on my couch with my baby cradled fiercely in my arms, sobbing out my humiliation, but towards sunset Amunnakht sent word that the King would allow me to visit Hui if I was escorted by a harem guard. To make sure I do not run away, I thought grimly as I laid Pentauru in the basket that was rapidly becoming too small for him, and ordered Disenk to repair my face paint.

While she valiantly attempted to disguise my swollen eyes and reddened nose I stared at my unprepossessing reflection in the copper mirror and picked at the cold goose and raw celery on the table beside me. The fate to which the King had so spitefully condemned me was utterly unacceptable and something must be done, but what? Hui would know. Hui cared about me, even if Pharaoh did not. He would suggest something clever. Surely there was no problem without a solution.

So I tried to cheer and strengthen myself as Disenk's cool hands moved over my skin, but my brave thoughts were no more than the shreds of a cold comfort and I had to struggle to stop my tears from flowing once more as I bent to kiss my sleeping son and went out alone into the warm red evening.

I had no taste for the calm beauty of the sinking sun as it tinted the Lake of the Residence on its journey westward. I sat tensely in the cabin of my skiff, jaw clenched and hands pressed between my knees, blind to the pink glitter of my craft's wake and the gentle slap of the wind-worried sail. Hui's watersteps came into view like the vision of something for which I had yearned over many weary years.

Leaving my helmsman and his rowers to tether the boat and wait for me under the trees beside the water, I walked under the pylon, past the porter's cubicle where I exchanged a few immediately forgotten words with the old man, and along the path to the house. As I went, the sun finally disappeared below the horizon, falling into the mouth of Nut, and twilight crept about me.

I stepped through the garden gate and onto the paving of the courtyard, and as I did so Hui came striding round the corner of the house. We saw each other at the same time and halted. The gloom of the coming night began to gather between us, and all at once it seemed to me that we had become participants in a mysterious ritual or performers in a play whose origins were anonymous and threatening. I had imagined flinging myself into his sheltering arms, crying out my pain against his soothing chest, but as I looked at him he seemed so strangely separate from everything around me, everything familiar in my daily life that I took for granted, that I could only stare at him with a kind of helpless ache in my heart. "Hui," I said, "I am in trouble. I am afraid."

He did not speak. Inclining his head he came silently across the courtyard, a sliver of paleness in the soft dusk, only a loincloth breaking the clean lines of his body. He had obviously been about to go swimming. Planting a kiss on my forehead he brushed by me and I followed him back into a garden already pregnant with shadows.

He led me away from the path and through the shrubbery. We skirted the lotus pond, plunging deeper into the tangled growth beneath the trees, until we came to the foot of the wall that divided his estate from his neighbour's. There he turned and nodded. "Tell me," he said. It was as though his words had breached a dam in me. Fists clenched, eyes on the dark mud bricks of the structure behind him, I told him how I had been forbidden to return to my quarters, how my request for an audience had been denied, how in stubborn desperation I had gone to Pharaoh's office and begged to return to his bed, begged to return to my land in the Fayum. "He has no right to cast me off like this!" I cried out in the end. "I have done my best to be everything to him, to please him in every way, and how am I rewarded, Hui? He has thrown me away like so much rubbish, tossed me from him as though I was a soiled kilt he no longer wishes to wear! He humiliated me before his ministers. He spoke to me coldly, as though he did not know who I am! I hate him!"

Suddenly I closed my mouth, for with those words came the shock of a great relief. It was true. I hated him. Under the innumerable stings of wounded pride, disillusionment, rejection and crushed hopes was a sea of loathing for the man on whom I had bestowed my virginity, my affection and my loyalty, and who had rewarded me for these gifts with a fickle indifference.

"I hate him," I repeated in a whisper. "I wish he was dead. I could kill him for what he has done to me."

There was a long silence. Hui had not stirred throughout my tirade. He was watching me carefully, his arms loose at his sides. Around us the night was deepening. Colour had bled from the trees leaving them as dim ghosts trembling and murmuring above our heads. Darkness was seeping from the ground to envelop us in secrecy and Hui's white body was becoming grey and insubstantial. I could hear his breath, a calm, measured sound, but his intense gaze belied the serenity of its rhythm.

At last he spoke, and it was as though I had been waiting

for his words to expose and confirm the black thing already fully formed in my heart. "Could you?" he said quietly. "Could you indeed? Then why don't you? He has treated you despicably. He has condemned you to a life of insupportable boredom and utter predictability. He has shamed and belittled you. None of it is your fault. You have done your best for him and it has availed you nothing." He stepped closer to me and the shadows slid over his pale face and settled in the hollows of his unearthly red eyes. "He treats Egypt with the same uncaring callousness," his voice went on hypnotically. "He would not be missed. You have tried to help this country and you have failed through no fault of your own. Killing Pharaoh would be an act of kindness."

As I watched his sensuous lips close over the strong teeth, all passion left me and I went very still inside. An act of kindness, I thought deliberately. Oh no, my Master. An act of thwarted ambition on my part and an act of treason on yours. But whatever the motives, we are cast from the same mould, you and I, attracted to each other like lust to young flesh, like thirst to heady wine, like rage to revenge...

"You always knew it would come to this, didn't you, Hui?" I said slowly. "Even if I had been able to complete the impossible task of swaying the King's policies, a task you knew was probably beyond any human capability, you still saw his murder as ultimately necessary. That is why you have never really tried to influence Ramses through your gift of Seeing, isn't it? You might have been able to sway him to less damaging political decisions but you did not bother, for you wanted him dead. All these years you have waited for the right time." He did not reply. He went on staring at me expressionlessly, breathing easily, but I thought I sensed the glimmer of a smile on that well-formed mouth. "And your friends," I continued, feeling my way cautiously through a maze that was suddenly becoming clear in my mind. "That arrogant snob Paibekamun, your brother Paiis,

General Banemus, Panauk, Pentu, Mersura, they want him dead too, don't they? Will the army take over Egypt then, Hui, with the Prince settling comfortably on the Horus Throne? How long have you all been meeting and plotting, dreaming your treasonous dreams? Is the Prince a part of it all?"

I should have felt used, betrayed. After all, they had seen in me a chance to bring their aim a little closer to fruition and I had meant less to them than the cups from which they had carelessly drunk their wine. But I did not. I shared their desire to rid Egypt of its ruler. I had my own reasons now. I was one of them. I belonged. Was that something Hui, in his devious wisdom, had known would happen?

"You are an astute young woman," Hui said, and the smile I had glimpsed broke out. It contained no warmth. "What you say is true, and I have told you many times the reasons for our actions. But the Prince is not yet involved. We believe that once his father is removed he will be amenable to our suggestions for re-establishing Ma'at in Egypt, for there will no longer be a barrier of loyalty between himself and his own good sense. But we will approach the Prince when the time comes. Are you with us?" His hands came out, grey moths in the dimness, and I felt them cup my cheeks. "You have killed before," he whispered, his breath mingling with a hint of his perfume, jasmine, "and for a much less laudable reason. I know you, Thu. Sooner or later, with or without my help, you would have come to the same decision, for you are too proud and too unscrupulous to spend the rest of your life imprisoned in the harem." His fingers moved against my skin. "Wouldn't you rather take the chance of becoming queen to a vigorous young king when he comes to the throne and chooses his women than wither away as the cast-off of a fat old man?" I pulled away from his caress.

"Why should I do it?" I asked sharply. "Why risk myself?

Let Paibekamun rid you of your bane!"

"Paibekamun would be immediately suspect, along with all those who are in constant attendance on the King," Hui retorted. "But you are merely one among hundreds of women and moreover, you are no longer admitted to the royal presence. No hint of guilt would brush you."

"If I am no longer admitted into Ramses' presence," I snapped back, "then how am I to get close enough to...to kill him?" The words tumbled from my tongue, their taste darkly exotic and yet familiar. "It is no use trying to poison his food or drink. He has his Butlers taste everything." My heart had begun to beat more rapidly and one thought after another flashed across my mind.

I turned from Hui and began to pace, vaguely aware of the new coolness of the grass beneath my sandals, the faint pricking of the first stars above my head. "I suppose I could contrive to feed his lion something that would inflame the beast, but it might attack someone blameless. An accident by water or out on the desert is too difficult to plan. Help me, Hui!" But I did not look at him and he made no move as I went to and fro before him.

For a while I pondered feverishly, a fire like the intoxication of wine creeping slowly through my veins and making me giddy. Then all at once an idea so diabolical, so delicious struck me that I grunted and came to a halt. Of course, of course. I ran to Hui. "You must give me arsenic," I blurted. "I cannot feed it to him directly, but I will put it into the precious oil with which I used to massage him. I will make sure that the new favourite, Hentmira, slathers it all over him with her loving hands. No one will suspect the oil, and if they do, it will be Hentmira who takes the blame."

"You would like that, wouldn't you?" he said. His voice was husky, vibrant with the same excitement I felt. "But what if she then accuses you?" I grasped both his arms and shook him.

"Only Hunro will be able to connect me with the oil, and she will deny my involvement. She is one of us, isn't she?" He nodded. "It is perfect, Hui. Nothing can go wrong!"

"A word of caution," Hui said. "I know exactly what the arsenic will do if it is placed in food or drink but if it is applied to the skin I am not sure how quickly it will react. I have performed no experiments to determine such a thing. I think it will depend on how large an area is covered, whether the body is sweating or not, how high a concentration of poison is in the oil, but I am not sure. It will certainly destroy Hentmira as well as Ramses if the dose is high enough to achieve your aim."

"Then give me so much that the outcome will be certain," I retorted. "Why should I care about Hentmira? Let her succumb to the dangers of the harem if she is stupid enough to believe that Pharaoh's favour renders her invulnerable." The image of myself, heavily pregnant and dishevelled, tear-stained and distressed, flashed across my inner vision. Hentmira had bowed to me in the narrow passage and had murmured a respectful greeting but the door of Pharaoh's bedchamber had closed behind her while I had been left, distraught and shamed, to creep back to my cell in the darkness. Recklessness seized me, a delirious surge of madness, and it seemed to affect Hui too for he pulled me against him, lifted my chin, and lowered his mouth onto mine.

I closed my eyes, and as I did so all the old yearnings that had plagued me during my stay in his house came back to me. My hands found his hair, that thick, silver mane, and I slid my fingers into its silkiness. He tasted of jasmine. I did not know which sense to plunge into first, so powerful were the messages from all of them, but it did not matter, I could let them all engulf me, for this man was Hui my friend, Hui my mentor, Hui the phantom lover of my girlish imagination, and in his arms I would find the fulfilment I had always sought. I whispered his name as my knees refused to hold me up any longer and his arms encircled me, lowering me to the ground.

There was no tenderness in our lovemaking. Both of us were on fire with the frenzy of the plot that linked us, and as it consumed us we devoured each other. But there was no crude fumbling, no dislocating awkwardness as we fought to possess the essence of the mood and one another. That night remains one of my saddest memories, for it was not the unexpressed love between us that drove us together as it should have been. The harmony of our bodies, the complete satiation of our lust, came from a source of corruption and thus did not heal as it might have done. Yet I tasted him, felt and touched him, kissed and fondled the foreign, moon-tainted flesh I had craved, I think, since I first saw it, and received at last from him the capitulation of his will.

Afterwards we lay panting in the grass, his head slumped across my breasts, until our breath slowed and I began to doze. Then he stirred and rose, sighing. "Wait here," he ordered, and sweeping up his rumpled loincloth he walked away in the direction of the house. Propping myself on one elbow I watched him go, a column of moving paleness soon lost in the gloom. By the time he returned and placed a phial of white powder in my hand I had tidied myself and was becoming anxious. "Use it well," he murmured, and bent to kiss me. "I love you, Thu."

"I love you also, Master," I whispered back, but he was already leaving me, flitting between the palm trunks until the night swallowed him up. When I could no longer see him I glanced into the sky. There was no moon.

The Children's Quarters were quiet and I was able to cross the courtyard to my cell unremarked. Disenk was asleep on her mat before the cell door and I stepped over her carefully, not wanting to wake her. She had left one lamp burning on the table by my couch. After a swift glance into

Pentauru's basket where he lay naked and spread-eagled in unconsciousness I got my box of medicines, and carrying it into the pool of light I opened it and extracted the pretty honey alabaster jar which contained the blend of oils I used for my massages. I removed the stopper and looked about quickly. All was still. I did not hesitate, did not give myself time to think, unless it was a fleeting moment of reassurance as my eye passed over the cushion containing the Prince's scroll. Gingerly I eased the wax from the phial Hui had given me, and careful not to spill any of the contents on my skin I tapped the powder into the jar. As I watched it form a small pyramid on the surface of the oil I found that I was sweating.

All at once a tiny sound made me turn around. Disenk was standing just inside the door, one hand running through her tousled hair, her face flushed with sleep but her eyes alert. "What are you doing, Lady?" she asked in a low voice, and as I continued to stand there, the empty phial in one hand and the jar in the other, I saw her suddenly understand. "Is that not your massage oil?" she persisted. "And what is in the phial? Is it something the Master gave you? Oh, Thu! You are going to kill him, aren't you, you and the Master." The words were a statement and I could do nothing but nod. Her eyebrows lifted. "Good," she went on. "With your permission I shall fetch you a soothing drink and by then you will be ready to be undressed and washed." Her eyes swivelled to my motionless hands. "Be careful," she added, and was gone without waiting for my dismissal.

As I replaced the stopper on the jar I reflected with a cold shiver that such knowledge had put us back on an equal footing. I had not missed the tone of new familiarity when she spoke to me. Nor had she seemed surprised or shocked when she realized with her usual astuteness just what I was doing. Could it be that she also had been one of Hui's plotters long before I pulled myself out of the Nile and up onto the Master's barge all those years ago? After all, had she not been in the service of Hui's sister? Gods, I thought to myself, slumping into a chair. Am I losing my sanity? Or am I as much a victim as Ramses?

A curious suspicion began to grow in my mind and I got up and reopened my medicine chest, pawing through it to find the container that had held my supply of acacia spikes. I had ceased to use them when I had become pregnant with Pentauru and I could not remember whether there had been any left. I found the container, but only a puff of darkish dust remained.

Frowning, I stared down at it. Hui had told me that the darker colour of the spikes was due to their age since harvesting. He had assured me of their potency, but what if he had been lying? What if they had already been too stale when he gave them to me and he knew it and no longer cared because my usefulness to him was over? Oh surely not! Hui would not do such a terrible thing to me, would he? I remembered the feel of his hands on me this night, the words he had groaned in his passion as we wrestled together. Once more I closed my box firmly. No he would not. The idea was ridiculous. Hui was ruthless but not cruel. I heard Disenk's sandals patting on the paving outside the door and was suddenly very tired. I would consider nothing more until the morning.

Chapter 23

I woke in the morning with my intention as steadfast as ever. I ate and drank on my couch, watching the wet-nurse suckle Pentauru, and when she had gone I cuddled and played with him before placing him on the floor to kick and gurgle while I went to be bathed and then had Disenk attend to my dressing and painting. Holding the mirror to my face I studied my reflection and marvelled that my eyes, so blue and clear, gave back to me nothing more than an innocent health. My skin glowed. My hair, glossy and shining, framed a beauty that I knew was a match for any woman in the harem. Ramses was a fool. Sighing inwardly I deliberately diverted the tumultuous and wounding emotions that followed that thought to a contemplation of Hui and me locked in passion, and the piquancy of that memory drove the bitterness away.

When Disenk had finished her ministrations, I took a small basket, laid a piece of pretty linen in it, and filled it with various cosmetic creams and potions. Among the pots and phials I placed the jar of deadly massage oil. Then I sent Disenk out to pick some flowers and to unobtrusively make sure that Hunro and Hentmira were alone together in their quarters. While I waited for her to return, I knelt beside my son and talked to him softly, delighting in the response of his foolish, unstinting smile and the clutch of his chubby fingers, so trustingly curled around mine. "Little prince," I murmured to him. "My royal scribe. I love you," and he crowed and chirped back at me ecstatically.

The flowers were still dewy from the water the harem

gardeners had poured onto them at dawn and I shook the droplets onto my arms to feel their coolness before laying them in the basket and setting out on the short walk through my courtyard and along the path to my old building.

As I neared my old door I felt someone's gaze fixed on me and I turned. Hatia was staring my way, her living corpse's eyes boring into me across the sunny grass. On impulse I raised a hand and saluted her but she did not stir. Shrugging, I walked on.

Both women looked up as my shadow darkened their door, then Hentmira scrambled out of the chair in which she had been sitting and bowed. "Lady Thu!" she exclaimed in obvious confusion. "We are honoured!" Once before, she had made me feel ancient and jaded. I forced a smile.

"My greetings to you, Hentmira," I replied smoothly. "Hunro, how are you?" The dancer had been leaning against the wall. Now she straightened, twirled her fingers, and grimaced.

"Bored and anxious, Thu," she said. "I have pulled a muscle in my leg, and I hear from my Overseer of Cattle that a blight is working its way through my herd in the Western Delta. It is wonderful to see you." Stepping forward she embraced me. "Forgive me for not coming to visit you," she went on ruefully. "The harem is a strange place. Nothing but a short path separates the buildings from each other and yet there might as well be a desert between them." Going to the door she leaned out and shouted for a runner to bring sweetmeats and wine, then she took my arm and pulled me to her couch, settling herself on it beside me. "How is your son?"

I watched Hentmira's face and did not miss the slight withdrawing as I answered. I knew the source of it well. It was the spectre that loomed behind every moment spent as one of Pharaoh's concubines. Answering Hunro quickly and lightly, I turned to the younger girl, retrieving the flowers from the basket and passing them to her.

"I know that the gardens abound with lovely blooms," I said apologetically, "and you may order your servant to bring you bouquets whenever you wish, but I wanted to remind you that you are like the flowers, Hentmira, fresh and delicate, and you must do your best to stay that way." I smiled at her as she pressed the petals to her face, blushed prettily, and lifted her dark eyes to meet mine.

"Thank you, Lady Thu," she said. "You are gracious indeed. I am told by the other women that I have supplanted you in the King's affections and that I must beware of you, but I think that you are kind and generous, and though I may satisfy the God's physical needs it is not possible for someone like me to fill the privileged place you held in his heart." I glanced at Hunro. Her face was expressionless. Pharaoh's heart is like a cracked pot I thought scornfully. Its contents leak away as rapidly as it is filled. Reaching into the basket I drew out a small container.

"This is also for you," I said. "It is a mixture of natron and alabaster meal with sea salt. Add a little to honey and anoint your face with it. It is very efficacious for softening the complexion." She thanked me profusely again and I looked at her with frank curiosity.

My first impression of her as proud and haughty was fading. I had mistaken shyness and the easy grace of her body for arrogance, and with that realization came a twinge of pity and genuine liking for the girl. She fulfilled Pharaoh's sexual fantasies perfectly, a biddable, docile virgin, and because she did so she was already placing the knife of rejection against her thin ribs. She must be like a soothing balm to Ramses after months with a scorpion, I thought ruefully. Poor Mighty Bull! Poor sweet Hentmira...

"The other things in the basket are for you, Hunro," I said, "and if I had known you had pulled a muscle I would have included a liniment. As it is, you will find the herbs I promised you hentis ago for strengthening all the muscles, and dried myrrh and elderberries to burn. The smoke will sweeten all your linens. There is cinnamon to chew for energy and uadu-plant to add to oil and smear on your sweaty feet after you have been dancing all night!" We all laughed at that, Hentmira giggling most fetchingly. A servant entered and set out cups and wine and a dish of date-and-honey cakes and we settled down to eat, drink and gossip.

I learned more about Hentmira during that hour than I wished. She was indeed infuriatingly modest, speaking of her family and when pressed, her own accomplishments, with a winning self-effacement. She seemed entirely unaware of the impact of her beauty, which of course enhanced it greatly, and I was reminded uncomfortably of my own fall from a similarly blissful pinnacle of ignorance. She was a lamb ripe for slaughter, an innocent waiting blindly for the film to be stripped from her eyes.

Suddenly I did not want her to die. Watching the purity of her profile as she moved, the bashful glow of her almond-shaped eyes, the vulnerability of her slender shoulder bones, she gradually became a responsibility, someone to be protected and sheltered. I tried to shake off the increasing compassion I felt, reminding myself that my future was at stake, that in accepting a position in the harem she surely knew that she was also accepting its dangers, but as she leaned to touch my forearm with hesitant fingers or smiled at me with unaffected warmth I grew more uneasy. Was her engaging diffidence a mask designed to win the loyalty of those around her or was it part of a uniquely honourable character? I could not tell, and as the wine jug emptied and the last of the cakes was shared, I became ever more painfully aware of the jar of massage oil still nestling in the bottom of my basket. I did not know what to do.

But then, as Hunro yawned sleepily and we fell silent in the increasing afternoon heat, it came to me that it did not matter. Even if Hentmira survived the application of the poison she would be accused of murder and condemned to some terrible fate, probably death. I could find some reason for urging her to wear gloves when she used it, or visit Hui yet again and beg an antidote from him if such a thing existed, but then Hentmira would immediately suspect the truth and I could not change my plan. No other way of penetrating the defences that surrounded Pharaoh was open to me. I wished it was. I wished with all my heart that some other concubine, some greedy, grasping woman with no scruples, could suffer instead of Hentmira, but Ramses had eyes for no one else and I could not wait for his ardour to wane.

Perhaps she would fall ill and survive, while Pharaoh died. Perhaps her very health and youth would offer some protection, and when she recovered, her sentence would be exile. So I struggled within myself, justifying the decision that I had momentarily doubted, and in the end, with fingers that shook only a little, I withdrew the jar. I will give it to her directly, I thought. I will place it straight into her hands, my fate to hers. Will her innocence condemn her, or will a germ of suspicion cause her to ponder my motives and pour the oil away? In my distress I did not know what to hope for.

"I will leave you both to your afternoon sleep," I said, sliding off Hunro's couch and holding out the jar to Hentmira. "It has been a very pleasant morning and I have been happy to get to know you, Hentmira. This is for you to use when Pharaoh asks for a massage." I gave her a smile of complicity. "He likes one after he has made love, as of course you know. I have used this blend of oils on him before and he has often remarked on its relaxing effect. There is not much here. Use it all, and if he still appreciates it I will make up some more for you." She took it gingerly, her eyes wide.

"Thank you, Lady Thu!" she exclaimed. "You have been so kind to me, so good. I did not expect..." She faltered, dropped her gaze, then stepped to me impulsively and threw her arms around my neck. "They told me you were cold and malicious and would hate me but they were wrong. Thank you!" Through the curtain of her soft black hair draped across my face I looked at Hunro. She was no longer yawning. All drowsiness had left her and there was a lively speculation in the eyes that met mine.

"I will walk to the courtyard entrance with you, Thu," she said, and I nodded, disengaged myself from Hentmira's grateful arms, and picked up my basket.

"Please come and visit me, Hentmira," I said as I left, and was rewarded with a brilliant smile that even now haunts me in the night hours when such turmoil rages in me that I cannot rest. Then Hunro linked arms with me and we made our way out onto the sun-drenched grass.

"What is in it?" Hunro asked in a low voice as we cut past the splashing fountain. I waited until the few women who had not retreated to their couches to escape the worst of the heat were out of earshot before I answered. I noticed that Hatia's customary spot was empty though her canopy still billowed in the dry breeze.

"The Master gave it to me," I said. "Whatever happens, Hunro, do not touch it. When Hentmira uses it Pharaoh will die." She was quiet for a time and we approached the entrance to the path that ran beside all the harem buildings. Then she said, "And Hentmira?"

"I do not know. Neither did the Master. But I believe that at the least she will be very sick."

"So Banemus might be coming home soon." She withdrew her arm and pulled me around. "The Master approves this?"

"Yes. Do not worry, Hunro. Pharaoh's food and drink will be investigated first, and by the time it has been proved harmless Paibekamun will have removed the jar and all trace of the oil. But if Hentmira is able to bring the jar back to your cell I rely on you to make it disappear."

"You can depend on me. But it is a pity about Hentmira. She is a very estimable person. What if she survives and accuses you?" I shrugged.

"There will be no evidence left, and Egyptian justice is not summary. No one is convicted on hearsay alone. Besides, are there not other women in the harem to whom poison is an occasional tool? Will it matter once Ramses is dead?" She raised her eyebrows, smiled faintly, and turned back towards her cell.

I walked on, a lump forming in my throat. I too am an estimable person, Hunro, I thought fiercely, tears pricking behind my eyelids. I am not really cold or malicious. I am a desperate woman caught in a grim trap, forced by circumstances not of my making into detestable solutions. I can be kind. I can be selfless and generous. I can be a good friend if I am given the chance. Ask my brother. Loyal Pa-ari! He would climb onto the harem roof and shout the words for all those jealous, spiteful women to hear! Thu is a true follower of Ma'at! Thu's heart will not judge her harshly! Thu is capable of unstinting love!

When I entered my cell Disenk regarded me anxiously. "Thu! You are crying!" she exclaimed. I went straight to my couch and flung myself upon it.

"Open my medicine box and bring me the tincture of poppy and a cup of water," I ordered her. "I must sleep, Disenk. If I do not sleep I shall go mad!" She pursed her lips but did as she was told, and I drank the poppy and water in one draught then lay back and closed my eyes. As the drug began to take effect and my mind quietened I was assailed by a violent but momentary vision of Kenna, grey-faced and dying, his eyes full of torment. Then the poppy claimed me and with it, a blessed peace.

I needed it to sleep again that night, for an anxiety greater than I had ever known seized me with the coming of darkness and I started and cried out at every moving shadow, every sound. Even Pentauru with his winning baby ways could not soothe my terror, indeed it seemed to infect him for he became fractious and irritable in my arms. I dosed both of us. He responded to the poppy at once but I lay for an eternity before I succumbed, shivering at the way the spear of dancing lamplight created vague shapes that loomed threateningly over me and performed a sinister dance on my walls. The drug produced incoherent dreams and I woke late and thickheaded to another hot, bright day of almost insupportable tension.

I spent it sitting on cushions outside my door, Pentauru on a sheet beside me. Fear and anticipation arrowed through me every time someone approached, and sweat washed my limbs as he or she passed me by. I could not eat, but drank beer steadily to unloose the knot in my stomach that would not be moved.

Once a servant did halt before me, and a great wave of nausea rolled up my throat as he bowed and extended a scroll, but it was only a communication from the Overseer of my estate. The crops had sprung up strong and free of disease and he wished to begin the harvest at the end of Pakhons. Did I wish to travel to the Fayum to witness the gathering? I thanked the man and sent him away, then I sat with the papyrus gripped in my lap, staring unseeingly out at the noisy, populated courtyard. In my mind's eye the curved sickles sliced cleanly through the proud stalks of my grain and the golden bounty quivered and fell, quivered and fell as the harvesters advanced across the field. Yet, though I eagerly sought diversion in the vision, it began to acquire the ponderous and chilling inevitability of a killing rite. My hand held the sickle, raised it, swept it through the burning air, and over and over again Ramses toppled to the earth, blood gushing from his mouth and staining my feet. Powerless to control the vivid inner mirage I was forced to endure it until it finally faded. I longed for oblivion but did not dare to swallow more poppy. The life of the Children's Quarters went on cheerfully and prosaically around me and I knew that my insane vigil would continue for another day. The prospect was almost insupportable.

In the early afternoon the courtyard emptied of women and filled with the heavy, hot silence of sleep. I went to my couch but lay staring at my ceiling until I heard life begin again outside. Then I resumed my place. Disenk brought out the sennet board and tried to persuade me to play, but though I fingered the cones and spools, I was afraid to commit myself to a game that engaged cosmic forces as well as the intelligence of the participants. If I lost, if I ended on the square that denoted a plunge into deep waters, I would know for certain that the gods had abandoned me. It was better not to know.

I succumbed to the need for more poppy that night, but the amount I drank did not produce full unconsciousness and I wandered in a twilight world of half-sleep where Pharaoh and I laughed and talked in his bedchamber, loving and carefree. But the colour and animation of that fantasy drained away, leaving me sitting bolt upright and wide awake in the hour when night's dark hand has a choking hold on man and beast alike and even sounds are muffled. With heart thumping I strained into the dimness. Something had woken me, some shapeless threat of evil that lurked within the shadows. I tried to call out to Disenk but my voice would not obey.

As the moments passed the presentiment of horror grew, but nothing sprang at me from the invisible corners of my cell and slowly I began to realize that the source of the menace was inside me, that it had crept from me across the courtyard, along the path and into the palace where even now Hentmira's innocent hands were smeared with death.

Reaching out, I lifted the statue of Wepwawet, and cradling him against my breast I rocked to and fro, whispering incoherent prayers to him, to my father, to Hui my Master, until the first faint hint of dawn began to thin the darkness around me and I was able to slip into a brief, troubled sleep.

The morning brought no lessening of the vise which I had created. I struggled in its relentless grip. Woodenly I allowed Disenk to swathe me in linen and precede me to the bath house, and for the first time the gentle flow of the scented water against my skin was not soothing. It seemed to intensify my inner agitation, and the hands of the young man who had massaged me almost every day since I had entered the harem made me bite back a scream. Other women passed in and out of the bathing quarter in various stages of undress, wafting a dozen different perfumes on the humid air and commenting desultorily to one another in their soft, high voices. Their presence, their feminine, sensuous movements, was stifling, and with an incoherent word I left them, trying to walk casually back to my cell though every nerve in my body demanded that I flee.

Disenk began to paint my face and I clenched my fists as her expert fingers went to work. I was able to contain myself until the brush laden with red ochre swept over my lips, but suddenly I found my mouth full of the metallic taste of blood and with a curse I groped for a piece of linen and scrubbed the offensive colour away. My servant made no remark and I did not explain my action.

I was able to eat sparingly and drink a little water, and by the time I was ready to hold Pentauru I felt calmer, but as I bent over his basket he looked up at me with an unblinking, reproachful stare. My arms went out to lift him but his face puckered and he began to howl. I withdrew hastily, angrily. "I cannot bear his crying, not now!" I blurted to Disenk.

"Take him to his wet-nurse for a while. And then go into our old courtyard. Try to find out what is happening, if anything, before I decide to take to my couch and drown myself in the oblivion of the wine jar. Hurry up!"

She was gone for some time, and long before she returned I slowly became aware that the mood of the quarter had changed. The low background susurration of voices that accompanied every activity in the building had ceased. The women who usually arranged themselves comfortably on the grass for a morning of dallying with their children and sharing conversation had fallen silent, and when the new quiet had penetrated my self-absorption and I looked out my door, I saw them ushering their charges away while their servants dismantled the canopies and picked up the cushions and board games and toys. None of them looked happy. An atmosphere of ominous expectancy had pervaded the precinct but I did not dare to go and ask why.

The courtyard emptied but the doors of the cells remained open. From my vantage point I could see the shapes of the inmates hovering just beyond the lintels. A word of doom had spread and I believed that I knew what it was. Shaking in every limb I withdrew to my chair, sat down with exaggerated care, and waited. And as the moments went by a curious composure fell over me. My body ceased to tremble. My mind stopped its frenetic racing and came under my control once more. I could think coherently and coolly. At this, the climax of suspense, I was sane again, and it was Disenk who betrayed distress as she hurried into my presence, panting and agitated.

"Hentmira is very ill," she said without preamble. "I did not dare to go inside her cell for fear of drawing attention to myself and thus to you, but there is much coming and going of servants and priests. The Lady Hunro saw me and drew me aside briefly."

"Priests?" I exclaimed. "Who is attending her?"

"The palace physician. He has called in the priests to contend with the demons of sickness. The Lady Hunro thinks that she is dying, Thu." I could feel nothing at her words. I was encased in an armour of stone.

"What are her symptoms?"

"A rash has broken out all over her body. She vomits continually and her limbs convulse. I could hear her crying most piteously as I stood with others outside the cell." I did not want to think of that.

"And what of Pharaoh?" I almost whispered. "If the palace physician is attending Hentmira, does this mean that Ramses is already dead?"

"No." Disenk shook her head. With a gesture I gave her permission to sit and she sank onto the stool beside my couch and laced her fingers together tightly. "The rumour is that the Master has been summoned to treat him. They say he is not as ill as his concubine. That is why he released the palace physician to care for Hentmira." Our eyes met. "Will he recover, Thu?"

"I do not know." Panic was struggling to break through the defence that encircled me but I refused it entry. "I will not know for several hours. Did Hui answer the summons?"

"The Lady Hunro could not tell me."

"And what of the jar of oil?"

"Hentmira did not bring it back to the cell with her. The Lady Hunro said that Hentmira returned from the palace in the early hours of this morning and went straight to bed. But she began to fret and moan an hour later and by dawn the Lady Hunro was sufficiently alarmed to send for Amunnakht. The Keeper summoned the harem physician who sent for permission to consult with the palace physician. At that time Pharaoh was sleeping and so the palace physician came to examine Hentmira. He is still there."

Silence fell between us, but it was loud and uneasy with our unspoken thoughts. At last I rose.

"Go to Hunro's cell," I ordered Disenk. "Offer my services to the palace physician. Everyone knows that I was the Master's apprentice and have treated many of the harem women. It would be strange if I ignored Hentmira's plight. While you are there, try to discover Pharaoh's symptoms, and whether Hui has come or not." She looked uncomfortable for a moment but left the stool, sketched a bow, and went out.

I poured myself wine, and going to my doorway I leaned against the jamb and sipped the rich red liquid with deliberate attention to its taste. The jar had not come back to the cell with Hentmira. I would have to presume that Paibekamun, having been alerted to the plot, had retrieved it once she had left and I could only hope that he had discarded what remained of the contents and smashed it. I did not like having to trust that he had done this. It gave me a tremor of apprehension. Nor did I like the fact that from what I had heard, Hentmira's plight was the more desperate. Perhaps the poison was taking longer to travel through the metu of Pharaoh's larger body. All I could do was wait.

When Disenk returned it was with disturbing news. "The palace physician has gone to attend Pharaoh," she told me quickly, "but he has left his assistant with Hentmira and he thanks you for your offer. You are to go to the girl at once." She hesitated and dropped her gaze. "The Master cannot answer the royal summons, Thu. Harshira sent word that he has gone to Abydos to consult with the priests of Osiris and to See for them. He goes there every year." I was mystified.

"But he did not tell me that he was going away," I said. "When did he leave?"

"Apparently he has been gone for a week and is due back in Pi-Ramses the day after tomorrow, according to the message Harshira sent to the palace."

"That is impossible! I was with him three days ago, in his garden! He gave me the poison then! You remember,

Disenk?" She did not answer but I saw her lick her lips nervously. "It is a lie," I went on slowly. "Harshira is lying. I have no doubt that Hui has gone to Abydos but he did not leave a week ago, he left immediately after I saw him that evening. He is protecting himself in case something goes wrong. How did he intend to protect me, Disenk, if something did go wrong? How could he come to my aid if he was in Abydos?"

The answer, of course, was that he would not come to my aid. He might love me, he might desire me, but he spoke the truth when he said that he and I were cast from the same mould. Self-preservation came first. Still, I was hurt and angry. Hui remained the Master. He was more devious than I. I could prove that you were in your house three days ago, I thought mutinously. My sailors took me there. The palace guard waited for me by your entrance. I spoke to your porter and he let me pass.

But neither sailors nor guard saw you, my mind ran on, and all your servants, from lowly porter to imposing Steward, would naturally lie for you. Harshira has done so already. No one could prove that I did not go to your house and steal the poison, knowing you were away. The building is familiar to me, and so are the movements of all your servants. Curse you, Hui! You have outmanoeuvred me once again. Would you really throw me to the jackals if our plot was discovered?

My plot. I shivered, suddenly chilled, as Disenk made no response to my outburst but stood there with a question on her flawless face. It was my plot. I had poured my venom against Pharaoh into Hui's ears. I had expressed a fervent desire to kill the King, and all Hui had said was "Then why don't you?" I was the one who had paced in the dimness until the means presented themselves to me. My hand had mixed the arsenic into the oil, carried it to Hentmira, placed it in her own warm fingers, and arsenic was not a rare poison. It was easily obtainable everywhere. I swallowed and closed my eyes. "Get my medicine box," I ordered Disenk. "I will go to Hentmira now."

There was still a crowd outside the cell the doomed girl shared with Hunro but the women were keeping a silent vigil, sitting on the ground, some with their backs against the wall. The monotonous rise and fall of chanting came out to meet me as I threaded my way through them. The cell door was open. I gathered up my courage and went in. Hunro glanced up at me as my shadow fell across the threshold. She was perched cross-legged on her couch, outside the circle of concern around the other bed. I went over to her.

"What news of Pharaoh?" I asked under the cover of the priests' loud singing.

"The physician's assistant has been commanded to join his master at Pharaoh's bedside as soon as you have taken charge here," she told me. "Hui cannot come, as you must know by now. There is talk of rotten food. Pharaoh's symptoms are the same as Hentmira's and they shared a dish of candied figs last night. Or so it is said."

"How ill is he?" She cast a sidelong glance at the group around Hentmira's couch.

"I do not know." I turned away then and joined the palace physician's assistant, touching his shoulder gently. He made way for me, and I approached Hentmira.

She was close to death. Already she was deep in the coma that would lead her ultimately to the gates of the Judgement Hall, and as I bent over her I had a moment of inexpressible relief that I would not have to look into eyes brimming with anguish or hear her soft, hesitant voice distorted as she fought to take breath and speak. Her skin was cold and clammy under my hands, her parted lips blue, and I noticed as I surreptitiously inspected her palms that they and her forearms were angry with a thick, raised rash. Her eyes were only half-closed. They glittered dully. Her face was streaked with the tears of her torment. The sheets were foul with her bloody excretions. I stood back.

"There is nothing to be done," the assistant said. "Thank the gods the convulsions are over. The Keeper has sent for her family, but what can we tell them? She will die before they arrive."

"Were you able to give her anything?" I managed to ask. I wanted to fly at the priests who were filling the room with their choking incense and their senseless drone, but the words they sang were no longer for healing. They were for an easy separation of ka from body and Hentmira needed them.

"I tried to dose her with poppy but she could not keep it down," he said. "If this was caused by rotten food then I must begin my apprenticeship all over again. It seems more like the work of a poison to me." He began to put away his phials and instruments. "I must now attend Pharaoh, and I fervently hope that he has been spared the ravages that overtook this poor young woman. I leave her to you, my Lady."

I hardly noticed him go. Pulling up a stool I sat beside Hentmira. I knew better than anyone that there was nothing left to do but wait for the inevitable. I ordered her linen to be changed and a bowl of warm water to be brought, and I forced myself to carefully wash the flaccid limbs, the thin trunk, even the ashen face of the girl who had prompted such jealousy in me. The action was a self-imposed penance, a gesture of guilt and sadness, but I did not know if it was an evidence of regret. I did not think so.

Laying my hand over her ribs I felt the irregular, faint flutterings of a heart that could not go on beating for much longer. Oh, Hentmira, forgive me, I pleaded mutely. Your heart struggles valiantly for life and it will lose, but at its weighing in the Judgement Hall, under the eyes of Anubis and Thoth, it will be victorious, whereas mine will accuse me when my time comes, and will the gods understand? Do you? And will you plead for me before the Divine Ones, out of your mercy and generosity of spirit? As though she had heard me, she sighed. Her breath hitched, hitched again, and I withdrew. My punishment is to watch you die, I thought. I could have sat by Ramses' couch to view his death throes without a qualm, but you tear me to the quick.

Some time later I became vaguely aware that the light in the room had changed. The day was advancing. People entered the room, a short, grey-haired man, an older woman with such a disturbing likeness to Hentmira that it seemed as though the body on the couch was suddenly a mistake.

I spoke to them, watched them touch their daughter with distressed, uncertain hands, and heard their cries when at last, towards sunset, the last breath left Hentmira as modestly and quietly as the girl herself had been. Signalling to the priests to cease their chanting I rose stiffly from my stool and slipped away, sending a harem runner to tell the Keeper that the sem-priests must be summoned. I wondered, as I crossed the crushed grass and narrowed my tired eyes against the red onslaught of the sunset, whether a tomb for Hentmira had even been begun, and whether any funerary equipment lay stored for her. Probably not, for who would have thought that someone so young could die so soon?

As I turned out of the courtyard towards my own quarters I saw Hunro coming from the direction of the front gardens. She had been swimming. Her hair was plastered to her head and hung in wet ropes below her naked shoulders, and she had tied a piece of linen carelessly around her waist. "She's dead," I said without preamble as my friend came up to me. "I am sorry for that, Hunro." Hunro made a face.

"I am sorry too," she said. "Hentmira was a most agreeable room-mate." Something in her manner, a coolness, a small distance, alerted me.

"You have word of Pharaoh," I said.

"Yes." She bent her head, and gathering up her thick hair she squeezed it vigorously. A trickle of water pattered into the dust of the path and formed a tiny puddle. "They are saying that he is vomiting and weak, and complaining of a bad headache, but there is no sign of convulsions and his condition does not worsen." She would not look at me. "I think he will live."

And who are you to be the judge of that? I wanted to shout at her. Are you a physician, Hunro? I have taken all the risks for you, for you and Hui and your brother and all the others! I have endangered myself, I have imperilled the fate of my soul, while you all sat back and watched! Even if I have failed I do not deserve the disdain I see in your averted face! "Perhaps he will," I said coldly to the cheek and shell-like ear presented to my view, "and then again, perhaps he will not. We must wait and see."

I was the first to walk away. I did so with squared shoulders and a brisk gait that hid the resentment and uncertainty I felt, and as I went it came to me that I could keep going. I could stride past the entrance to the Children's Quarters, go through into the servants' compound, and thus into the palace grounds. I could present myself at the door of the Keeper's office. I could tell Amunnakht that the King and Hentmira had been poisoned, that Hui and Paiis, Banemus and Paibekamun and the rest of them had hatched a plot to murder Ramses and Hunro had agreed to make Hentmira the unwitting tool. They had approached me but I had refused. I had, of course, taken the oil and various other preparations to Hunro and Hentmira, but my action had been innocent. It was only now, with Hentmira dead and Pharaoh ailing, that I realized what had probably happened. As a physician, I recognized the symptoms. Hunro had obtained poison from the Seer. Hunro had put it in the massage oil. They were traitors, all of them, plotters against the God and against Egypt herself.

At the doorway to my own courtyard I paused. But what if Pharaoh died? Then we would all be safe. Then I would hold the Prince to his promise and I would be elevated to royal status. I would be free. It did not matter that Hui had taken steps to protect himself. I would have done the same thing. Better to wait just a little longer, and see what transpired. I turned towards my door.

Since Hui was not available to attend Pharaoh, I wondered if I would be summoned to add my ministrations to those of the palace physician. Ramses had been impressed with my healing skills and not once in all the time I shared his couch did he consult another doctor. In the week that followed I sent Disenk to Amunnakht, offering my services, because it would have seemed strange had I not done so and because I burned to know in what state the Lord of All Life lay, but my submission was politely declined and indeed I heard a few days after Hentmira's death that the Master had returned and had gone immediately to examine the King and consult with his personal physician. He made no move to visit me and sent me no message. I began to be afraid.

Hentmira was taken to the House of the Dead, but no wails of mourning for her filled the harem, although for a few days a sober quiet infected every building. I tried not to imagine the shock and grief her family must be enduring, or the necessary but horrifying indignities being perpetrated on her beautiful young body as the embalmers prepared her for her burial. No official decree to observe the formal seventy days of mourning came from the palace, either because Pharaoh was too ill to think about it, as I hoped, or because it was not the custom.

I began to have curious dreams in which I left my cell and instead of walking over the grass my feet left the ground and I flew, sailing over the wall of the harem and swooping high above the palace complex. The mirage was extremely vivid. I saw the whole royal estate laid out below me in an oasis of tossing green trees, and then the dust and cacophony of the city trailing along the Waters of Avaris. I saw Hui's house. Drifting west I found the Nile, a wide rope of silver that wandered away south in a haze of searing heat, but then the true nature of my position would come to me and the exaltation would fade to be replaced by a fear that sent me plummeting and screaming back towards my courtyard, and I would land on the grass from whence I left with such force that my ankles would break and the pain would wake me, sweating and crying.

I had to fight a desire to camp outside the door of Pharaoh's bedchamber. I did not want to eat or drink or sleep, attend to my son, be dressed or painted. I did not want to do anything until I knew what was happening behind those forbidding cedar panels through which I had so often gone in light-hearted anticipation.

Time after time I went over the events of the past few days in my mind. Had Hui given me enough arsenic? Why was it that Hentmira had died with only her hands polluted while the King, who had doubtless been slathered in the oil, was surviving? Had his divinity saved him? Had the gods, recognizing one of their own, stepped in to lessen the effect of the poison?

But after pondering the problem in the feverish, obsessive way I was beginning to think about everything, I decided that of the two, Hentmira had received the larger dose. Her hands had been repeatedly covered in oil whereas the parts of Pharaoh's body that she massaged would have the arsenic ground into them but once. I should have thought of that. So should Hui. I cursed myself for my crass stupidity, but as no word came from the palace I still believed that the King would ultimately die.

The mood in the harem was solemn. The women spoke of nothing but the precarious state of Pharaoh's health. Wisps of incense smoke wafted from the doors of the cells as the inmates prayed before their private shrines. Groups still gathered on the lawn but the conversation was hushed and earnest. I ordered Disenk to spend as much time as possible with the King's personal staff. They were of course a close-mouthed group of servants, tactful and well-trained, but they surely talked among themselves and besides, was not Paibekamun one of them?

For three days Disenk returned with only the vaguest news. Hui and the physician had consulted. The King was still vomiting and clutching his head. Prayers were being said for him in every temple. But on the fourth day she was able to tell me something more definite.

"I managed to converse with the Butler who was commanded to examine all the food and drink served to the One on the day he fell ill," she informed me as she deftly set out my evening meal. "A slave was summoned to taste every dish and sample every jar from which the King's wine was poured. He showed no symptoms of any kind." She cast a sidelong glance at me. "Poison is now suspected, and the movements of everyone who came into Ramses' presence are being examined. His clothes, utensils and cosmetics are also being scrutinized." I stared down at the plates being laid before me with their burden of lettuce and celery, the steaming delight of leeks and freshly grilled fish, the oily gleam of dates steeped in honey. A pink lotus flower was floating delicately in the scented water of the fingerbowl and its fragrance came to me faintly. I could not imagine putting any of the food into my mouth.

"Suspicion cannot fall on Hentmira," I half-whispered. "She is dead. Therefore I am safe."

"Perhaps." Disenk bowed and retreated behind my chair, the position she always took as she prepared to serve me. "But Pharaoh is recovering, Thu. He slept soundly this afternoon and was able to drink some milk." I sat there numbly, unable to lift a hand to the salad that lay quivering before me.

"Speak to Paibekamun," I said, my voice thin and insub-stantial in my ears. "Ask him what he has done with the jar of oil."

"I would have done so," she answered, "but I cannot find him." I was unable to see her face.

For two more days I suffered through a weight of impend-ing dread that only grew heavier as the hours dragged by. Disenk and I wove our pattern of routine around each other with the precision of long familiarity, and perhaps I only imagined that she spoke to me less than she used to do.

Word of Pharaoh's continued recovery was announced publicly by the Heralds who called the news in every court-yard of the harem, and the women went back to their idle gossiping with obvious relief. I also tried to return to the small pursuits that had filled my time before but I found them numinous with a kind of horror. Each word, each action, acquired an aura of profound but unintelligible meaning, as though they did not belong to me at all. Even Pentauru, as I held him in my arms, and kissed and cuddled his plump warmth, seemed to be the possession of another woman, in another time, and the more I pressed him to my body in an increasing panic the more intangible I felt myself become.

I knew, in some sane corner of my mind, that every moment passing placed me further away from the threat of discovery, knew that I should be relaxing into a progressive safety, but instead the terror grew, and with it the odd cer-tainty that a doom had already overtaken me, that each hour was borrowed from a life of peace and promise I had known hentis ago.

Often, sitting tensely by my couch or pacing just inside the shelter of my doorway, I was seized by a mad urge to flee, to walk out of the harem and lose myself in the orchards and fields beyond the city. Ramses, Hentmira, Kenna, Hui, Disenk, even my son, I would shed them all as I went, until naked, innocent and free my feet would find the searing cleanliness of the Western Desert and I would be a child again with all my life before me.

But it was a dream, a fantasy of absolution and healing when in reality neither guilt nor the sickness of my ka could be expunged, and when the soldiers came to arrest me it died.

Chapter 24

I had been waiting for Disenk to bring my morning meal when the two guards darkened my door. The wet-nurse had just finished giving Pentauru his milk and was preparing to leave, and I was playing with him on my couch, tickling his swollen belly while he laughed infectiously. The men neither knocked nor hesitated. By the time I had sensed their approach and looked up, they were standing beside the couch, swords drawn, faces impassive under their helmets. Their threatening presence filled the little room. The Herald accompanying them stepped forward. Pentauru began to cry and I grabbed up the sheet to cover myself.

"Lady Thu," he said. "You are under arrest for the attempted murder of the King. Get dressed." The wet-nurse began to shriek and the Herald turned to her impatiently. "Be quiet, woman! Take the child to the nursery. Hurry up!" I did not move.

"This is ridiculous," I said haughtily, gathering Pentauru to my breast where he looked up at me with frightened eyes. "You have the wrong cell. The King suffers from rotten food I am told." My legs felt like lumps of wood but I forced them to obey me. I slid from the couch and backed away, Pentauru still in my arms. "I do not believe that the King has ordered this intrusion. Show me the proof! And you!" I snapped at one of the soldiers who was eyeing me up and down appreciatively. "Keep your gaze on the floor! I am a royal concubine." But he behaved as though he had not heard and the Herald withdrew a thin papyrus scroll and handed it to me.

I shook it open, one arm still protectively around my son. It was a command to the Captain of the Palace Guard to have me placed in custody on the charge of extreme blasphemy, being, of course, the attempted murder of a god, and it was signed by Ramses himself. His name and titles had been written in a shaking hand but were entirely recognizable. I threw it back at the Herald. "Where is the evidence?" I demanded. For answer he nodded at the guard who had been staring at me. The man took hold of Pentauru, and tearing him from me, almost tossed him to the wet-nurse. The woman glanced at me, all frightened eyes, then scurried out. The last I saw of my son was a tuft of unruly black hair sticking up above the wet-nurse's brawny elbow, but his howls echoed for a long time.

"Get dressed," the Herald repeated impassively. I shook my head.

"I do not dress myself," I retorted. "I will wait for my body servant."

"No, Lady, you will not." The Herald looked about, and seeing one of my sheaths on a chair, crumpled and discarded from the night before, he snatched it up and held it out. "Put this on. You will be attended later."

I could do nothing more but obey. Insolently, though my pulse was racing and I was assailed by a wave of faintness, I let the sheet fall to the floor and coolly pulled the proffered sheath over my head, smoothing it past my hips with a slow gesture. Then I looked at the Herald inquiringly. He swallowed, gave me a sudden and shocking smile of disarming sweetness, and bowed. I followed him out of the cell.

The courtyard was already busy and the women and children fell silent and watched me as I walked bare-footed and dishevelled but with head high through their midst, the Herald before me and the two burly guards to either side. We turned left, passed through into the servants' compound, angled across the packed dirt in front of their quarters, and out through a rear gate.

I had never been this way and I looked about me with interest. I was on the edge of a vast open space, obviously a parade ground, for a dais stood at one end. At the other were the barracks. Soldiers lounged in front of their doors, polishing armour and repairing weapons. A group of them were playing some game with a large ball and much raucous shouting. They ignored me and my escort as we passed, rounded a corner, and came to a row of tiny cells that fronted an untidy expanse of sand and soil. Far to my left I caught a glimpse of stables. Beside them the chariots were ranked, row upon row of gleaming vehicles. The unremitting sun beat down upon the empty, dismal prospect but I did not have much time to study it. The guards pushed me into one of the cells. "Food will be brought to you," the Herald said, "and a servant will bring you such things as you need." I opened my mouth to voice one of the many questions beginning to churn about in my mind but the door had already slammed shut and I was alone.

As my eyes became adjusted to the dimness I looked about. The walls and floor of my prison were of undressed mud brick, crude and dark. There was an ancient cot, a plain table, and that was all. A little light came from one tiny square cut in the door and I rushed to it, only to see the two guards who had flanked me taking up their watch one on either side.

I retreated to the cot and sat. I had been arrested. I was a prisoner of a different kind than the harem inmate I had been. Yet my mood was not despairing, indeed the terrible grip of anxiety in which I had lived lately was gradually lessening. This was a temporary discomfort. No matter what suspicions might fall on me, there was no direct evidence to connect me with the attempted assassination of the King. Providing, of course, that Paibekamun had kept his wits about him and destroyed the oil jar...

That thought gave me a moment of unease and I ran my fingers through my uncombed hair and deliberately turned to more pleasant daydreams. I would be acquitted. Ramses would be sorry. He would send for me to apologize. He would shed tears of love. Contrite, he would draw me into his arms and the past would be forgotten. The cell smelled of urine and garlic. It smelled of desperation and misery and oblivion. I pressed my hands between my knees and waited.

After a very long time, during which the heat inside the room intensified and my head began to ache, the door swung open and a servant girl appeared, balancing a tray. She put it on the table then stood staring at me stupidly. I left the cot and went to see what she had brought. There was a bowl of soup, fresh bread, some fruit and a jug of beer. "Where is your obeisance?" I asked her sharply and she immediately bowed.

"I am sorry, Lady Thu," she stammered. "Is there anything else I may bring you?"

"Yes. You can bring me my very own Disenk." She flushed and her hands found each other awkwardly.

"Your pardon, Lady Thu, but Disenk has not been seen in the servants' quarters today and in any case, I have been assigned by the Keeper to take care of you." I stared at her, appalled.

"Disenk is not to attend me? But why?"

"I do not know, Lady." Her eyes fled mine, making her seem deceitful, although she was probably just a simple and honest girl, not yet fully trained.

"In that case," I said caustically, "you can go to my cell and bring me my clothes and cosmetics. Also my jewellery and the two boxes you will find in the chest against the inside wall. One holds my medicines and the other some keepsakes from my childhood. Bring my cushions and a covering for this floor. Particularly the cushions, do you understand? I must have some comfort in this abominable place.

Visit the nursery and bring me word that my son is in good hands and is well. Then go and tell the Keeper that I want to speak with him at once."

She bowed again and retreated to the door, but a thought struck me and I called her back, pointing to the meal she had set out on the table. "Wait. Please taste my food." I watched her carefully as she lifted the soup to her mouth, took a tiny portion of the bread, bit into the fruit, swallowed a little beer. Her hands were trembling, more, I think, from shyness than from fear. We both waited. I knew that the exercise was futile if a knowing hand had decided to save the palace the inconvenience of a trial, for there were many poisons that worked slowly and insidiously when ingested, but I did not believe there was anyone but myself and Hui who had such a knowledge in Pi-Ramses. The girl stood steadily, eyes downcast, and in the end I dismissed her and pulled the table to the edge of the cot. The guard let her out and I ate my simple meal in heat and silence, serving myself.

Once more I waited. After a while a few flies found their way into the cell through the small window in the door, lured by the swiftly decaying remains of my food, and I watched them settle and explore the dishes. I had no whisk with which to flick them away. My guards occasionally exchanged a casual word or two. Leather creaked as one of them shifted position.

At last I heard them spring to attention and I tensed. The door was unlocked. Amunnakht entered and bowed, and behind him came the servant girl. Her arms were empty. Executing a clumsy reverence she picked up the tray and went out. A cloud of flies followed her.

I turned to the Keeper. "Where are my belongings? Surely I am not a common prisoner, Amunnakht. I cannot be denied some comfort." He inclined his head. I could smell his perfume. His linen was dazzlingly pure in this place. His gems winked at me dully. His facepaint had been impeccably applied. Already I was painfully aware of the gulf that separated us, particularly as I was still unwashed and wore a sheath from the night before. It has been planned this way to make me feel at a disadvantage, I thought mutinously. Well it will not work.

"My most profound apologies for your continued inconvenience, Lady Thu," the Keeper replied. "Of course you may have your things, as soon as a thorough search of your quarters has been accomplished. You stand accused of a very serious crime, but until your guilt has been established I may do all I can to ease this experience for you." Fear shook me. The cushion. Would they find the scroll?

"This cot is not even made up," I protested. "I cannot lie on it. Can I not even have my linens and cushions? And my totem, Wepwawet. Is it forbidden to pray before the likeness of my god as well? Who is conducting this insulting search?" Amunnakht smiled reassuringly.

"Your case has been placed in the hands of the Prince Ramses. You may be certain of a fair hearing, Lady Thu. He is an honest man. I have already made enquiries as to when you may have your belongings restored to you, and he has promised them by this evening."

By then his minions will have rifled through all my chests, fingered my cosmetics, handled my jewellery, and torn apart my mattress and my cushions, I thought cynically. Will they find the scroll? Naturally, for the man in charge of the rape will have been secretly commissioned to look for it, and he will know the difference between the hand of his Prince's scribe and the hands that recorded prescriptions, letters and my Overseer's reports on the other pieces of papyrus in my chests. I should have foreseen this eventuality. I should not have been so confident.

"In that case I suppose I must be patient," I said smoothly. "I would like to see my son, Amunnakht. Will you have him brought to me?" But once again he gracefully shook his head.

"I am sorry, Lady, but it is not allowed. I have personally made sure that he is not being ignored in the nursery. His wet-nurse will see to his feeding, and I have made Eben responsible for his welfare." My eyebrows shot up.

"Eben? The concubine I supplanted in Pharaoh's affections? That was a stupid choice, Amunnakht, and I protest it vigorously! She will neglect Pentauru! She will treat him badly out of her jealousy for me!"

"I do not think so," the Keeper contradicted me gently, "for are you not now in a worse position than she ever was? She has some sympathy for you, and has promised to give Pentauru the best of her care." I bit my lip and clenched my fists behind my back. To be forced to accept help and sympathy from that woman! To find myself humiliated and abased in her eyes! It was too much. I tasted blood, and dabbed at my mouth.

"I must trust your judgement in this matter, Amunnakht," I said, "but please watch her carefully. There is much malice in Eben's heart."

"There used to be," Amunnakht corrected me. "But Eben has learned many lessons since she was put in charge of Pharaoh's younger children. She has grown up. She has changed. I would not give her Pentauru if that was not the case." I did not like his choice of words. It made me shiver.

"I hope you are right," I said grimly. "Now what of Disenk? Send her to me I pray you, Keeper. She has been my right hand for years. Why are you preventing her from attending me?"

"I am not," Amunnakht said forthrightly, "but the Prince is. She is being detained for questioning."

"About what?" I burst out in both anger and the fear that was now overwhelming me. "This whole accusation is insulting at best! I am innocent of any wrongdoing! What proof can possibly be supplied by ransacking my quarters and subjecting poor Disenk to interrogation?" The Keeper stepped to my side and began to stroke my shoulder as though he was gentling a nervous horse. I jerked away.

"Calm yourself, Thu," he said quietly. "If you are indeed innocent then you have nothing to worry about. A trial will be arranged and in the course of it you will be exonerated."

"A trial? Then they must have discovered something. Someone has provided the Prince with lying evidence! Oh gods, Amunnakht, which of my enemies will sit to pronounce sentence upon me? Do not desert me, Keeper of the Door! You have always been my friend. Do not let them destroy me!" He turned and approached the door.

"You came to the harem with great promise," he said as he rapped for the guard to let him out. "You were beautiful and strong-willed and intelligent. In you I saw a chance for my King to be happy and I advanced your cause because of it. But you were also cunning and cold, and it saddened me to see how you tried to use my Master, whom I love and serve. I deal with the affairs of many women. I praise and punish, comfort and reprimand. Most of my charges are nothing but wayward children, but you were different. If you are found guilty but are indeed innocent, I will do whatever is necessary to discover the truth and have you reinstated in the King's favour. I have that power. You may expect to have your belongings restored to you by sunset." The guard had opened the door and was waiting. Amunnakht bowed, and the door thudded shut behind him.

I retreated to the cot, lowered myself onto the stained mattress, and folded my arms. The serving girl had left the jug and one cup but I did not fancy the small amount of beer I had not drunk earlier. I began to rock and frown in thought and in deepening distress. I was guilty. Of course I was guilty. But as long as no evidence was found I would be freed. There was no doubt that the scroll would be discovered and the Prince would burn it immediately. His men were probably tearing my cushions and slitting my mattress at this very moment. Its contents could be seen to implicate him with me by inference and if he wanted to be eventually named the Hawk-in-the-Nest he could not afford to be even lightly brushed by the shadow of suspicion.

But that was all the evidence against me. That was all. And could I be condemned for a simple agreement to put forward the Prince's claim with his father in exchange for a promise of advancement? Once Ramses the younger destroyed the scroll, there was nothing at all to point to me as Hentmira's murderer or the one who almost took Pharaoh's life. As long as that arrogant Paibekamun played his part... I sighed and, rising, walked to the door. "I would like water, and a little incense to burn in here, if it is permitted," I said. "The stench is becoming overpowering." One of the guards turned his head.

"Our watch is almost over," he told me, "and when our replacements arrive I will send water to you. Perhaps by then you will have your incense burner also." He looked away, out over the blinding expanse of rough ground, and I retreated to the cot once more.

I must have dozed, for I came to full consciousness to find myself curled up on the foul-smelling mattress with one stray shaft of red sunlight falling across my hip. There was a commotion outside, and, confused for a moment, I presumed that the guard was changing, but almost immediately I realized that it was sunset and a new face under a forbidding helmet was pushing open the door. Stiff and thirsty, I came to my feet.

The room began to fill with men. A scribe stalked to the far wall, and after a disdainful glance at the floor he laid down a reed mat, sank cross-legged onto it, and began to arrange a palette across his knees. After him came four figures I did not recognize. Their gaze swept over me, curious, disapproving, eager, and after them the Prince himself shouldered forward. He held a small object wrapped in linen, and my heart turned over. As I extended my arms and bowed very low my breath caught in my throat and I fought to regain control of it. It could not be. Could not!

I straightened and met the eyes that had once turned my body into a furnace and made my dreams feverish with lust. He was as handsome as ever, filling the small space with his virility and good health, but I no longer wanted him. He was a pretty toy whose brilliant colours had obscured his lack of substance. His voice, when he spoke, gave me a tremor that faded almost as soon as it had come. "Let me introduce the men who will be your judges, Thu," he said, and his jewelled fingers moved from one to the other. "Karo, Fanbearer on the Left Hand of the King; Pen-rennu, Royal Interpreter and Translator; Pabesat, Royal Councillor; Mentu-em-taui, Royal Treasurer. All honest servants of Pharaoh and of the gods, who have sworn to render an impartial verdict." I was trying to keep from glancing at the thing the Prince held in his other hand, trying to find within myself a composure that would cushion me against whatever shocks might come. What role should I play? I was not yet sure. Respectfully I bowed to each of the ministers in turn.

"I greet you, Lords of Egypt," I said. "Forgive me for not doing you the honour of receiving you correctly but I no longer have the facilities to do so. And as you can see, I have not been able to attend to my personal needs today." I pulled at my hair with a rueful smile. "I am disgracefully unwashed." One of them, Karo the Fanbearer, smiled back at me, but the others went on staring solemnly as though they were half-witted. I swung to the Prince. "I have read the wording of the charge against me, Highness," I said. "You speak of judges and verdicts, yet is such talk not premature? Where is the evidence that I had any evil designs whatsoever against my King? Or is this an attempt to discredit me because you grew to fear the contents of the agreement that was signed between us that would grant me royal status if your father named you his official heir?" Attack first, I had thought while my mouth had been engaged in a play for the ministers' sympathy. Be the scorpion of Ramses' imaginings. Try to sting this perfidious Prince. I had the satisfaction of seeing him flush and blink rapidly but he recovered at once.

"Such an agreement exists only in your own corrupt and ambitious mind, my Lady," he rebutted me loudly. "It is well known that you came to my quarters late one night and threw yourself at me in a clumsy attempt at seduction." I think he would have gone on, but he saw the trap into which I had hoped he would fall and he changed the subject, grasping visibly for control of himself. He held out the object, folding back the linen as he did so, and I knew I was looking at my executioner. "Is this your jar?"

"No. It is not."

"That is odd, because many people, women of the harem and servants alike, identified it as one you often took out of your medicine box when you wanted to treat a stiff limb or massage a sick patient." I shrugged.

"I had one like it, Prince, which has since disappeared. There is nothing unique about this jar. The potteries produce them by the thousands."

"Disappeared?" he pressed. "Why would something from your medicine chest disappear? Are you not careful with your medicaments?"

"Of course I am, but the blend of oils I used was particularly efficacious and brought relief to every person on whom I used it. It was probably stolen. The inmates of the harem are not always honest."

"It did not bring relief to my father, or to poor Hentmira," he replied grimly, and I flung up my arms in simulated disgust. I was very aware of the unwavering attention of the other men who stood motionless, their eyes going from one of us to the other. The soft rustle of the scribe's papyrus could be plainly heard.

"So that is what my arrest is all about!" I said hotly. "Someone stole my precious oil and massaged Hentmira to death? Do not be ridiculous, Highness!" He smiled thinly and extended the jar.

"Take it, Thu. Hold it in your hand." I backed away.

"I will not! Am I correct? Did someone add a poison to my oil? Is that how Hentmira died? But what of Pharaoh? If I touch it will I become ill also?"

"You should know the answer to that better than anyone," the Prince observed. He continued to stand with the jar nestling inoffensively on its bed of linen. "You mixed arsenic into the oil. You gave it to Hentmira in the belief that she would use it on my father and he would die. But she died instead, and the gods protected one of their own. My father is already out of his couch and grieving at your betrayal of his kindness to you."

"How do you know that there is arsenic in the oil?" I asked him in a low voice. "You are no physician, Prince. Who told you this? And who has fed you such a foul and evil story?" The panic was creeping closer to the surface of my skin now. I could feel it begin to prick along my spine and dry out my mouth. Even as I faced the Prince with boldness it was picking at the cloth that covered my eyes and soon it would rip it away and I would see everything. Everything...

"After Hentmira had died and the King was still ill," he began, "Paibekamun came to me. He had this jar in his hand, a hand covered with an angry rash. He told me that on the last night Hentmira had waited upon Pharaoh he had found it under Pharaoh's couch. He knew that Hentmira had used its contents to give my father the massage he loved, for as usual he had been in attendance upon his Master throughout the evening. He recognized the jar as yours because the oil you blend yourself has a particularly rare aroma. He presumed that Hentmira had asked you for the oil because Pharaoh had always like its effects. He did not presume that the rash he developed had come from the few drops of oil left on the lip and sides of the jar until later when he was ordered to investigate Pharaoh's food and drink on suspicion of rot or poison. That investigation showed nothing amiss. Then he remembered the jar, and brought it to me. By then he suspected that his malady had been caused by his contact with the oil."

"So Hentmira stole my oil!" I interrupted. "But why would she poison it? To disgrace me, her only rival? Was she so insecure in her position as favourite? She knew nothing of poisons, Prince. It is no wonder she ended up killing herself!" I was an animal at bay, cornered and terrified. Sweat had begun to pour down my face, yet I still had a shred of authority over myself. "How do you know it was arsenic that she added to the oil?" The Prince smiled, the grimace so full of triumph and contempt for me that a fresh spurt of dread flooded my body.

"She did not add it," he said. "You did, my Lady Thu. I have spoken to many people today, beginning with your servant Disenk and ending with the Seer. You may sit. You look as though you are about to faint." I found myself slumped onto the cot, with no recollection of bending my body to get there. I knew then that the end had come, that there was no hope for me, that I had been cruelly betrayed. I was entirely alone. I almost heard the sound of the cover being torn from the eyes of my mind but I did not want to see everything, not yet. The truth would be too much to bear.

Slowly I straightened, and with a supreme effort I looked into the Prince's matchless face. "And what did they say?" I managed. "It can be nothing accusatory, for I have done nothing wrong."

"Disenk tells me that she woke two nights before Hentmira took the oil into my father's bedchamber, to find you alone in the lamplight, pouring a white powder into this jar," he said. "When she asked you what you were doing you told her that you were unable to sleep and thought you might mix a fresh supply. She was puzzled by the powder, but as your knowledge of herbs and remedies is great and hers is not, she did not question you further."

"It is a lie," I said dully but could not go on, for was not the truth of that small encounter even more damaging? The Prince hardly paused in his story and I had the impression that he was enjoying building the circumstances that would damn me. Was it because I had failed him? Or because I had torn myself from his arms with an effort he could not possibly understand on that night I remembered so well, and so wounded his masculine vanity?

"On the following day you prepared a basket," he said. "In it you placed, among other innocuous things, the jar of oil. You went to visit the Lady Hunro, your old friend and the woman with whom you once shared quarters, and once there you made yourself very agreeable to little Hentmira, the concubine who had taken your place in my father's bed. Why did you do that? To win her confidence of course. She was a trusting child. She was very happy to receive from your hands the oil that would most please the King. The Lady Hunro tells me that you pressed it upon her with many words of friendship and exhorted her to use it liberally and as soon as she wished."

"That is also a lie," I put in monotonously. Hunro, who had guided me during my first weeks in the harem. Hunro who according to Hui could be completely trusted. Hunro, who had taken me under her wing and professed to admire me. Her defection did not hurt as badly as Disenk's but the blows were coming fast, each one finding a target, and I was reeling like a drunkard from the pain. "You have tortured them, Prince, to make them say whatever you wanted." One of the judges spoke up.

"Unlike the barbarians, we do not use torture in Egypt to obtain confessions or information," he said primly. "His Highness's investigation has been conducted with the utmost tact and kindness." I did not know which one had lectured me. I did not bother to look about and see.

"Hentmira took the oil into my father's presence and anointed him with it," the Prince went on. "She began to suffer the effects of the poison almost at once and so did Pharaoh."

"Hentmira added the poison and then took the oil into your father's presence," I corrected him without interest, and he shook his head firmly.

"Hentmira had no knowledge whatsoever of poisons and no way to obtain one," he objected. "Moreover, she had no reason at all to do Pharaoh any harm. Was she not the favourite? Could she not expect many blessings to come? No, Thu. The poison came from the Seer. He gave it to you himself. Mad with rejection and the desire for revenge, you used it on the Divine God as surely as if you had smeared it on him yourself." I passed a shaking hand over my features. The room was now unbearably hot, although the light was fast fading. I felt filthy and tired and my jaw ached.

"So my mentor is also charged with attempted murder?" I asked with as much sarcasm as I could muster. The Prince looked shocked.

"By all the gods, no! But it is typical of you to suggest such a thing. I myself made the short journey to the Seer's estate early this afternoon. He was immeasurably horrified to hear the charge against you. He feels in some way responsible, seeing that it was he who trained you in the healing arts and introduced you to the palace. He says that you often visited him to replenish the supplies in your medicine box, and the last time you did so, just before he left for Abydos, you asked for arsenic, to rid a patient of worms in the bowel. He cautioned you to be very careful with the powder, as you did not have experience in its use and had not asked for it before. You requested what he considered to be an exorbitant amount, and when he protested, you laughed and reassured him, adding that any left over from your potion could be mixed with moistened grain and set out to kill the rats in the harem granaries. So you lulled him, and returned to your quarters. Needless to say, no arsenic remained in your medicine chest when it was searched earlier. You are guilty, Lady Thu. These men will verify my words before pronouncing sentence upon you, but I have no doubt that they will agree with my conclusion."

I wanted to stand, to conjure up enough pride to defy this impossibly beautiful, this extremely self-righteous Prince who had seemed so wonderfully benign and who had deserted me in the end like all the others, but my legs refused to do my bidding. I knew how I must look, with my dirty sheath plastered to my wet skin, my hair straggling damply against my neck, and my feet coated in grey dust from the floor of this accursed cell. In spite of the mingled perfumes of the five men, the air was foetid with the stink of my ordeal and they could smell it. I was ashamed but I was not entirely cowed. "I want to speak to Pharaoh," I said. "Am I not owed a chance to put my case to him? To attend my own trial?"

"You may dictate a petition to the One," the Prince replied. He had begun to rewrap the jar, being careful not to touch it. "I will send a scribe to you tomorrow. But you know Egyptian law, Thu. You may not be present at your trial. All evidence will be heard, and Pharaoh wishes that it be heard fairly. You do not need to worry on that account."

"My belongings?"

"They are even now outside the door."

"And Disenk? Is she outside the door also?" She had betrayed me, but I still hoped that it had been out of the fear of an underling for an awesome authority, and in my misery

I wanted to be ministered to by familiar hands. But the Prince once again shook his head.

"She has petitioned the Keeper of the Door to allow her to return to her old mistress, the Seer's sister, the Lady Kawit. Her request has been granted."

"So I am entirely bereft." Now I was desperate to see him go so that I could cry in private, but I had one more thing to say. "What if I told you, Highness, that I have been used by many very powerful people who wish to see your father dead so that they can place a man of their own choosing on the throne? What if I name them?" I had caught his attention.

"Name them then, Lady. The hour grows late and I am hungry. Can you supply me with proof of their treasonous intentions?" I subsided, defeated. Of course I could not give him any proof! They had been too careful for that.

As I looked back down the months I had spent in the harem, in Hui's house, as I remembered the men I had met, their questions, Kaha's lessons, Disenk's story of her life in the High Priest's household, the way in which Hui had brought me into Pharaoh's view, my place in those events became suddenly completely clear. My perception changed. I had thought the hand of fate benign. I had believed that I had begun on the periphery of Hui's life and been drawn into its centre because of his slowly blossoming affection for me, but I had been at the centre all the time, an unsuspecting victim around whom a long, laborious plot had unfolded.

It had failed, therefore I was expendable. Indeed I must be disposed of as a liability so that the plotters could formulate a better plan. How often had they tried before, always cautious to protect themselves, cover their tracks? How often had they failed? They were clever, patient men and women, not likely to make any fatal mistakes. With my execution they could wipe the record clean and begin again.

No wonder Paibekamun kept the jar! If Pharaoh had died

it would have been better for them, but either way I must not survive to threaten them in a future into which they were always peering with infinite discretion.

"I can name them, Highness," I said, "but I cannot prove my words."

"Then I will bid you a good night." He strode to the door, and called sharply to the guard. Without glancing my way the Prince went out and the other men followed, Karo giving me a swift parting smile.

They had scarcely disappeared into the gathering gloom when the serving girl came in carrying a lighted lamp. Behind her several more servants struggled under the weight of my bedding and chests. It took them some time to place everything on the floor and leave, and even more time for the girl to make up the cot and arrange the few cosmetics that were mine and not Disenk's on the table together with my wigs, my lamps, and other trifles. All at once I missed little Pentauru. He at least loved me. He was my son. Would they speak of me to him with respect when I had gone, or would they poison his mind against me and make him ashamed of his parenthood? The thought of my imminent death was entirely unreal and I pushed it away.

"I have prepared the room, Lady Thu," the girl said shyly. "Shall I now bring food and drink?"

"No." I had eaten nothing since the morning but the thought of forcing anything past my swollen throat was unbearable. "You may go now. Wait upon me in the morning." Obediently she knocked to be let out, and as soon as I was alone I reached for the cushion in which I had secreted the Prince's scroll. It had been torn and re-stitched. I felt it thoroughly. It no longer held anything but stuffing.

Moving on to my medicine box I examined it. Nothing was missing but the phial that had contained the arsenic Hui had given to me. Setting the chest aside I opened the cedar box my father had given to me, and lifting out my statue of Wepwawet I set him on the table. "You have betrayed me too, O God of War," I said to him. "There is no one left to stand by me." But then I snatched him up, and cradling him fiercely I sat on the edge of the cot. The fresh linen the girl had placed there smelled of happier days, of myrrh and saffron, of Pentauru's body, and in a moment the tears engulfed me. I was lost, I was doomed, and I gave myself up to my grief.

I did not expect to be able to sleep, but the powerful emotions of the day had exhausted me and I fell at last into a heavy unconsciousness, waking at dawn to a full awareness of my surroundings and a fresh flow of tears that continued now and then throughout the day. I could not control them. I felt bereaved, abandoned, and a tiny part of me did not believe that the rapid events of the last two days had happened at all so that I spent the hours in a dislocated daze. Surely I had fallen ill and was in a coma. Or I was in the middle of a visit to Hui who had put me into a trance from which I would presently wake to embark in my elegant little skiff and return to the harem.

But layered over that illusion was a stifling cloak of pain. Hui, Hunro, Disenk, they were my enemies. I had never achieved any recognition in their eyes. While they pretended to admire and respect me, they were using the gullible little peasant from Aswat, and now, their aim deflected, they had forgotten her and were moving on to more absorbing things. She was flotsam. She was a cracked and discarded pot, a piece of torn linen, as disposable as the crumbs and rinds of fruit left on a plate when the meal is over.

I had been awake for a long time when the girl was admitted accompanied by a slave who placed a huge bowl of warm water on the floor and withdrew. I greeted them both, noting how their eyes flicked to me and then as quickly glanced away. The marks of my ordeal were all too evident on my face. I stood gratefully while the girl washed me and sat still while she did her best to braid my wet hair and apply my cosmetics. She did not have Disenk's sure, professional touch but somehow I preferred the feel of her clumsy, well-meaning fingers.

As she was rubbing saffron oil into my neck and the reassuring odour of the perfume I loved began to fill the air, the door was again opened. A meal was set for me and I discovered that I was hungry. The girl had dressed me in my yellow sheath, placed my beaded sandals on my feet, pushed golden bracelets onto my forearms and slipped jasper earrings into my lobes.

I began to recover. Waves of disbelief and anguish rolled over me from time to time but I was able to dry my eyes and fortify my inner self. I was the Lady Thu, no matter what. I would bury this agony. Already I was digging the hole into which I would tip it, cover it with my own resilience, tamp it down with my ability to forget, if not to forgive. It was unthinkable that the judges should convict me when I had been only the gaming piece and not, as I had believed, the hand that moved it across the board. Looking at me, listening to me as they had yesterday, could they not see that truth?

Her tasks completed, the girl left. I tried to distract myself by reading the numerous scrolls I had collected, but when I unrolled an old letter from my brother by mistake and was shaken by such a strong feeling of despair that I almost cried out, I closed the chest and lay on the cot, staring at the ceiling. My eyes itched with tiredness and the tears I had shed. Already the heat in the cell was becoming noticeable. I thought of going to the door and engaging the guards in conversation, but was too indolent even to sit up.

In the early afternoon the same scribe who had been present on the previous day was admitted to take my dictation. I would have preferred to write to the King in my own hand, on my own palette of which I was still inordinately proud, but I saw the wisdom in making every move I made an official one. He sank onto a corner of the carpet that now partially hid the dirt floor, prepared his tools, muttered the prayer to Thoth, and waited.

I hesitated. These words must be entirely correct. Each one must have the power of an arrow to pierce Pharaoh's heart and stir his sympathy. "To the Lord of All Life, the Divine Ramses, greetings," I began. "My dearest Master. Five men, including your illustrious son the Prince Ramses, are even now sitting in judgement upon me for a terrible crime. According to law I may not defend myself in their presence but I may petition you, the upholder of Ma'at and supreme arbiter of justice in Egypt, to hear in person the words I wish to speak with regard to the charge against me. Therefore I beg you, for the love you once bore me, to remember all that we shared and grant me the privilege of one last opportunity to stand in your presence. There are circumstances in this matter that I wish to divulge to you alone. Criminals may make this claim in an effort to avert their fate. But I assure you, my King, that I am more used than guilty. In your great discernment I ask you to ponder these names."

Briefly I considered the fact that the petition would be read aloud to Ramses as he sat in his office to deal with the business of the day, and then decided that it did not matter if one of the plotters happened to be there. He would appear mystified. He would point out, as I had, that an accused person will say anything to save himself from his rightful fate and that I was talking nonsense. But I was counting on Pharaoh's undoubted intelligence and on his memory of me as a woman who was far from stupid. Had I made him uneasy enough, had I intrigued him enough to win myself an audience?

Carefully I listed the men who had held me in such secret

contempt. Hui the Seer; Paibekamun the High Steward; Mersura the Chancellor; Panauk, Royal Scribe of the Harem. Here I saw the hand of the scribe taking my dictation falter before resuming its work. Pentu, Scribe of the Double House of Life; General Banemus and his sister the Lady Hunro; General Paiis... Now it was my turn to hesitate. I liked General Paiis. He had flirted with me, found me attractive. He had been kind to me. Oh, Thu, you shallow idiot, I told myself sternly. He used you too. In fact, if he could he would have used your body and not just your mind. I spoke his name without another qualm.

I did not list the servants, although my tongue trembled with eagerness when I thought of Disenk. She had lived beside me hour after hour for years. She had shared my hopes and disappointments. She had taught me to trust and rely on her, consider her a friend, while all the time she, a mere body servant, was looking down her perfect little nose at me, at my peasant roots, my lack of social ease, and was conferring with my mentor in the matter of my manipulation.

Quickly I ended my dictation in the usual way, read over the scribe's work to make sure that he had honestly reproduced my words, and sealed the petition with the hieroglyph for "hope," pressed into the wax by my own hand in such a way that it would be very hard to copy. "I do not know what master you serve," I said to the scribe as he closed his pencase, capped his ink, and prepared to leave, "but I beseech you to go to Pharaoh's personal scribe Tehuti and place this scroll directly into his hands. It is not addressed to the Prince but to the King himself. As you heard, it does not contain anything insulting or injurious to the Prince. There is no need for him to see it at all, though of course you must tell him that you have fulfilled your duty in taking my dictation. I thank you."

The act of doing something, however small, to mitigate my plight had lightened my mood considerably, and I spent the next few moments trying to persuade my guards to allow me to take some exercise on the ground outside the cell. But they adamantly refused, and so I retreated to the cot, drank some water, and lighting a few grains of incense in my burner from the lamp that was now kept burning on the table I said my formal prayers to my totem, Wepwawet, and settled down to wait.

The day dragged to its close. The guard changed. I slept away the hottest part of the afternoon, attempted to play dogs and jackals against myself, and then found myself again fighting a feeling of being smothered that closed in without warning and had me crouched by the cot, desperately trying to draw breath into my lungs. In my mind I flew at the door, pounded on it, screamed to be let out, but in reality I squeezed my eyes shut and forced myself to remain calm. In the end the peculiar fit passed but I lived in dread that it might return.

At sunset my girl returned with food and wine which she set out on the table, her movements now more assured as she grew accustomed to the chore. Grimly I remembered the lessons I had endured with Disenk when I had first entered the Master's house, how I had sat at the table in my room while she showed me how to eat, how to drink, how to behave. I asked the servant to eat with me, for I was becoming lonely, and she did so with an awkward selfconsciousness. To her I am a titled lady, a noblewoman, I thought with sad amusement. She does not yet know that I am a peasant. Will she lose her awe of me when she discovers the truth?

I was glad of the lamp when darkness fell. I lay for hours, watching its glow and listening to the dead silence caused by the thick walls that muffled almost every sound. At times I would come to myself, suddenly aware that my mind had wandered into distant fields, and I did not know whether I had slept or not. I tried once more to pray, but every word I spoke to the god had been spoken by me before. The petitions felt stale and old in my mouth and in the end I let my mind drift.

Two days later the blow fell. Freshly washed and dressed I had just seen the girl go out to fetch my morning meal when the door opened again and the four judges filed into my tiny space. With them was a royal Herald, and over his white linen he wore a gossamer cloak of blue. The colour of mourning. The colour of death.

My bowels turned to water. Oh gods, I thought hysterically as I rose to face them. Oh gods, no. No! Panic-stricken, I scanned their faces. They would not look at me, all but the Herald, who gave me a cool glance and unrolled a scroll. I did not want to hear his words. For a moment all control left me and I covered my ears with both hands, shaking my head from side to side in a paroxysm of terror and uttering sharp cries, but they waited impassively and the hysteria died. The Herald cleared his throat.

"Thu of Aswat," he read. "You have been judged and found guilty of the murder of the concubine Hentmira, and extreme blasphemy against the Divine God Ramses User-Ma'at-Ra meri-Amun. This is the sentence of the court. Your title is void. Your belongings shall be distributed among the women of the harem. The estate in the Fayum deeded to you by the King shall revert to him and become khato-land. You will remain in this cell without food or drink until you die, but Pharaoh is merciful. He will allow you to take your own life by whatever means you choose if you so desire."

Choose...wish...desire... They were words of life, words of love. The other words impinged themselves on my consciousness only slowly.

...until you die...

...take your own life...

I tried to make it real and failed.

"But I submitted a petition to Pharaoh!" I protested loudly. "Did he not read it?"

"He read it," the Herald said. "In his divine wisdom he chose not to intercede for you or to interfere in any way with the course of justice."

"It is a trick!" I shouted. "Ramses would never let me die!" I snatched the scroll from the hand of the Herald and stared at the signature at its foot. There was no mistaking the King's hand, strong again now, definite and cold. He had signed my death warrant. "What of my son, my child, his child?" I blurted. "What of my little Pentauru?" Deftly but politely the Herald took back the scroll.

"Pharaoh has repudiated the paternity of your son," he said. "He no longer acknowledges any responsibility for the boy, who will be placed in the care of a family of merchants in Pi-Ramses and raised as one of their own."

"I cannot take him with me?" I said stupidly, uncomprehendingly, and for the first time I saw pity in the Herald's eyes.

"I do not think that you would wish your son to go where you are going, Thu," he replied.

At that the full import of my fate crashed down upon me. With a shriek I collapsed upon the floor, curling in upon myself, hands over my face. Vaguely I heard the door open. Someone said, "No. Take the food away. She is to eat and drink no more." The judges, still dumb, went out.

Then rough hands picked me up and put me in a corner. Servants were already stripping the cot and tossing my fine linen out onto the ground beside the guards. Others were piling my sheaths and sandals, my wigs and jewellery, even my lamps, into chests. I saw my medicine box go flying to join the confusion. In a cloud of dust the carpet was snatched up. A man bent to pick up the lamp on the table and I flung myself on him.

"No, not that lamp! I cannot die in darkness! I cannot endure the night without it! Please!" But he pushed me away and I saw the lamp go hurtling through the doorway.

They even took the cedar box my father had given me. By the time the door closed behind them the cell was empty. They had removed the sandals from my feet, the ribbons from my hair, and the sheath I had been wearing had been replaced by a coarse shift with a piece of cord to tie it to my waist. I had hardly felt the shame of my nakedness as the linen was indifferently ripped from my body. Only Wepwawet remained, standing on the table beside the denuded cot and staring at me with an unwinking, lofty gaze.

Stunned, I was unable to move. Like a woman carved from wood myself, I remained in the centre of the cell, encased in shock. After a while I felt the first intimation of thirst steal over me, and with it the knowledge that the next liquid to caress my mouth would be the water used by the sem-priests to wash my lifeless flesh. My story was told. My luck had run out. The nameless grave of a criminal would claim me, and I would be forgotten.

Chapter 25

No one came near me. Morning became afternoon, and the fury of Ra beat upon my prison walls, turning my breath fiery and my body wet with sweat. Slowly the afternoon dissolved into a sunset I both longed for and feared, for with the coolness would come darkness and I had no lamp to keep at bay the phantoms that were waiting to torment me.

Once I left the cot, and going to the door I tried to speak to the guards. I had the muddled idea that I would plead with them to summon someone, anyone in authority, to whom I could explain the grave error that had been made, but the soldiers ignored me completely, although in the end I yelled and cursed at them through the small slit in the thick mud brick. The gesture only served to intensify my thirst and I returned to the cot where I lay trying to woo sleep to come to me.

In the end it did, but I woke to full darkness and a complete and final understanding of my sentence. No one would come. No one would bring water, or a covering to keep me from shivering in the night chill, or even a face, however hostile, with which to ameliorate the loneliness of my dying. No one would wash the sweat and grime from my body or give me medicine if I became ill. But that was a stupid thought. Of course I would become ill. And then I would weaken until I died. How long could someone live without water? Did they go mad first? Did they become consumed with fever?

Oh, water! I could feel it against my lips, slipping over my limbs, rippling in my hair as I struck out into the river

with the moon high overhead. I could taste it as Disenk
passed me a cup and the blessed contents slid over my
tongue and down my eager throat. I could see its surface
break as I dipped my hand into it before turning to the next
course of my meal. Water, from which the first mound that
was to become Egypt rose in the first days of creation.
Water, that flooded the land and brought fertility to this,
the most beautiful corner of the earth. Water, for which I
would murder again and again if I could be granted just one
sip.

I came to myself in a darkness that seeped into my nose
and pressed relentlessly against my skin. Thirst cried out
from every pore. My head throbbed. I ached with cold, for
the cell did not retain the heat of the day but gave out a
stinking dankness without the sun. Rising with difficulty I
went unsteadily to the door. I could sense but not see the
presence of the two guards to either side, and I strained to
perceive what was beyond, but there was no moon and I
had to imagine the rough ground, and the stables and perhaps even a row of palm trees beside the Waters of Avaris
that flowed deeply to join the Nile and from there to the
limitless expanse of the Great Green. I had never seen the
Great Green, and now I never would. Not with the eyes of
my body. But perhaps with the magic eyes of my coffin I
would be able to look upon that miracle.

Coffin? Criminals did not receive coffins. They were not
embalmed. Their bodies were buried in the sand, and only
by diligently searching would the gods be able to find them.
And then what? How would I fare in the Judgement Hall,
providing the gods were able to put a name to my withering
body? My heart would betray me. There would be no scarab
placed upon it to prevent it from telling the truth about the
evils I had done, and when weighed on the scales against
the Feather of Ma'at it would sink with a damning speed.
You are twice condemned, Thu, I told myself. Once by

mortal judges and once by the verdict of the gods. No happiness at the feet of Osiris for you. Only more darkness, more despair, an eternal cry for light in the lightlessness of the Underworld.

My hands and feet were beginning to swell. With fumbling fingers I lifted Wepwawet and lay on the cot, at first whispering prayers of contrition and remorse and pleas for clemency but then simply saying them in my mind, for my tongue was becoming fat and unwieldy and the effort of drawing breath hurt me. The air rasped over my parched throat.

I slept, oblivion coming upon me with horrifying swiftness, but to my dismay I woke again to daylight and a raging thirst that had me crawling to the door and begging incoherently for water. But my jailors were deaf to my increasing frenzy. It was as though I were already dead. At last one of them spoke without looking at me, without even turning his head. "You may ask for a sword if you wish to end your misery," he said brusquely. "That is allowed."

I clung with one hand to the lip of the window as panic finally overtook me and gave me a moment of renewed strength. Screaming and crying and beating at the door with one fist, I gave myself over to madness, and to that fear of the unknown that lurks waiting for everyone doomed to grow old and for whom a last breath is a terrifying certainty.

I do not remember much of the third and fourth days. I cannot describe my desolation, the bouts of delirium, the violent protests of a young and healthy body in the process of extermination. I know that once a face loomed over me and I came to myself sufficiently to recognize one of the guards, but I did not hear him retreat and close the door again. I was sporadically aware of the quality of light in the cell, grey at dawn, dim at noon and briefly red at sunset. The air seemed full of noise until I realized that the sound came from me, it was my breath panting like a suffering dog, and in my lucid periods I tried to concentrate on it as proof that I still lived, that I was still Thu, that time still held me in its grip.

I began to imagine that Kenna was bending over me. He was a pale oval floating in the darkness, his features shifting. "She is far gone," he whispered. "I do not know if this will be enough."

Oh, Kenna, I thought. It is enough. Is it not enough? Have I atoned for what I did to you, to Hentmira? Is she here also? I felt his hand beneath my head. A ghostly cup bumped gently against my mouth. My cracked lips opened. The waters of paradise gushed past them. My stomach heaved and I retched.

When next I opened my eyes Kenna was still there, and this time he had more substance. His features did not swim but cast long shadows over his face. The light of Ra haloed him. Once more he raised me and I drank, but before I could ask him if I had perhaps already traversed the Judgement Hall unconsciousness claimed me again. As I plunged into the void I heard Osiris say, "The stench in here is unbearable. Have her washed at once."

A third time I surfaced, and now there was a lamp on the table and I was drinking, drinking the sweetest water I had ever tasted. It was running down my chin and trickling between my breasts and soaking the filthy mattress on which I lay and I wished I might drown in it. Amunnakht withdrew, carefully lowering my head and placing the cup beside the lamp. I stared up at him dumbly. He dissolved into the shadows and another face took his place. Round cheeks, a full chin, a high brow under a soft linen helmet, bright brown eyes that surveyed me shrewdly. I swallowed several times before I could find enough saliva to form a word. "Majesty," I croaked. He nodded.

"I see that you are now in your own mind," he said, "and

can understand me well enough. You are an evil and cunning woman, Thu, and you deserve the death that was to be meted out to you. Yet in my divine mercy I have decided to spare your life. I signed the warrant for your execution but I was troubled. I did not sleep well. Memories came to afflict me, and the contents of your petition whispered in my thoughts. I ordered it burned, but I will not forget the list of names. It is possible that you dictated to me the truth. If that is so, and I let you die, I will have committed an offence. Not as great an offence as yours, to be sure, for in your wickedness you sought to destroy your God, but a small tear in the fabric of Ma'at all the same. Time will reveal all. I have decided to send you back to Aswat and there you will stay. I have spoken."

I struggled to form words, to thank him. I tried to touch him but my hand trembled when I had managed to lift it and besides, it was too late. He had gone as quickly as he had appeared. The Keeper replaced him in my vision, helping me to drink again, wiping my face, drawing a blanket higher over my shoulders, and I found myself crying helplessly like a child. "He is a good God," Amunnakht said, and I moved my head once in assent, listening. I could no longer hear the laboured panting of my breath. I was going to live.

A week later I was taken from the cell that would have been my tomb, and chained to the mast of a barge bound for the granite quarries of Assuan. No one but the soldiers detailed to secure me to the craft bade me farewell, and when I had woken on the morning of my departure I had been alone. Amunnakht had himself tended me until the night before. I had pressed the statue of my totem into his hands and begged him to see that it was given to little Pentauru. I could no longer cherish and protect my son. Wepwawet must become his mother, guiding and guarding him as the god had done for me. Perhaps the passing of the statue from my hands to his would forge a link between us. Perhaps Wepwawet would draw him to Aswat one day to see the temple of the deity whose likeness had mysteriously companioned him from the cradle. I could only hope. The Keeper agreed to do as I had asked, but when I pleaded further with him to send me word now and then of how the boy was faring he refused. "It is forbidden," he said firmly. He did not return to see the shackles go around my ankles and wrists. I was sorry, for I had not taken the opportunity to thank him for his care.

I was taken in a closed cart to the docks of Pi-Ramses, fed a meal of sesame paste and bread, and assisted to my place on the enormous craft. The captain, a burly Syrian, watched while my guards secured my chains. He received a scroll from one of them for the mayor of my village then went away without a word. The soldiers also departed, and I was left to watch the mighty city slowly vanish into the pearly glow of early morning.

I was not sorry to leave it behind. I had never known it well. I had come as a captive and I was leaving as one, and my life had been spent within the cocoons of Hui's house and then the harem. Even the thought of my baby did not conjure regret. That would come later. For the present I sat, ate and slept on a thin pallet under a wide canopy, and for the rest of the time I was content to savour the breezes that caressed me, to hear with an almost overwhelming delight the slap of the Nile against the sides of the barge, to let my eyes explore the glory of a slowly passing vista I had never thought to see again.

I had nothing but the rough shift I wore. A few short months before, I would have been horrified at the prospect of venturing out without my litter, the soothing creams for sunburned skin, a parasol if I should decide to walk, sandals to protect my soft feet, some fruit if I should feel hungry, and of course the guards to keep away curious onlookers.

But now, as I crouched at the foot of the tall mast with the canopy flapping over my head, my hair whipping in my unpainted eyes and my cheeks already reddening with the sun, I experienced a surge of freedom such as I had never known. The chains chafed my delicate ankles where once there had been golden links. I eagerly and with conscious enjoyment ate the plain fare and drank the strong peasant beer placed on the deck for me twice a day, and washed with reverence in the tiny bowl brought to me each dawn. At night I lay watching the stars sparkle in the immensity of the sky while the sailors sang and laughed and the mast above me seemed to reach up and up and spear the brilliant points of light themselves. I had returned from the dead. I had stood on the edge of the chasm of nothingness and had been reclaimed. I could savour life as no other.

We churned past the entrance to the Fayum in the dark, and though I knew it was there I did not sit up to see the channel wind away towards the home I had never inhabited, the fields whose bounty I would never see. I had not been allowed to make any dictations, but Amunnakht had promised to see that the Overseer and his men were paid before the estate passed into other hands. I felt a deep sadness when I remembered how Ramses had surprised me with the deed and how we had journeyed there to see it. My fields had not betrayed me. They had faithfully and obediently yielded their fruits. It was I who had let them down and I grieved quietly while the Fayum dropped away behind me and the dry air of the south began to stir in my nostrils.

Eight days later at noon the barge dropped its two anchors in the middle of the river opposite Aswat. The craft was too large to negotiate the shallows but the captain lowered a small raft and poled me, still in chains, to the bank. The heat was unremitting at that hour. The stiff palms I remembered with a jolt, the configurations of the growth that overhung the muddy water, the haze of white dust hanging in the burning air, all incandescent in the increasing fire of Shemu, reached out to draw me back into their timeless embrace.

As I stumbled up onto the sand beside the small bay where my mother and the other women washed their clothes, the village itself came into view. It was smaller than I remembered, its houses merely mud boxes, its square that I had thought so vast nothing but an uneven patch of earth. Dirty and impoverished, I saw it for the first time as I saw myself, sturdy, strong, indomitable, surviving the vagaries of rulers and the depredations of war with its roots sunk deep into the soil and its nourishment the hallowed traditions of antiquity. I had expected to find an end, but Aswat greeted me with mute promise.

My mother, father and brother were standing on the edge of the square, together with the mayor. The Keeper had sent a message to them and doubtless, in the way of the village, the word of the barge's approach had spread long before it had appeared. They did not speak and I did not look at them as the captain struck off my chains. The flesh of my ankles and wrists had been rubbed raw. My face was red and peeling from the now unaccustomed exposure to the sun I had endured. When the man had finished, he thrust the scroll my guard had given him at the little group, picked up the chains, and waded back into the river. It was done.

No one spoke. A lizard skittered across the square and flicked into the thin shade of a bush. I saw movement within several of the doorways and I knew that though my father had probably requested the other villagers to let me disembark in peace, they were watching me from the shelter of their houses. I looked at him. His face was etched with deep lines that the sun had hammered home and his hair was greying, but his eyes were as clear and warm as ever. "Welcome back, Thu," he said. As if his words had broken a dam, my mother stepped forward.

"You have forever disgraced this family," she said in a low voice. "You are a wicked girl, and I can hardly hold up my head with my neighbours because of you. Even if I wanted to take you back as my assistant, the other women will not let you near them for fear you might do them harm. How could you? Did I not raise you well?" She would have gone on, but my father silenced her abruptly.

"This is not the time for recriminations," he said. "We must hear the Good God's instructions regarding Thu's future, then we will take her in out of the heat." I glanced at Pa-ari. He had neither moved nor spoken. The mayor was pursing his lips officiously. Then he blushed and passed the scroll to Pa-ari. I noticed that my brother's hand was shaking as he began to read it aloud.

"To the honourable mayor of Aswat and the High Priest of the God Wepwawet, greetings. The following dispositions shall be made of the criminal Thu. She shall regard herself as an exile from the whole of Egypt but for the village of Aswat. Such men of the village who are willing shall build for her a hut against the wall of the temple of Wepwawet and she shall live there, earning her living by performing such tasks as the priests of Wepwawet shall assign to her. She shall not own any land, jewellery, a boat, or any goods other than those the priests deem necessary for the sustaining of her life. She shall not be allowed to possess any herbs or medicines, nor may she treat any illnesses or diseases within the area of her exile. She shall go barefoot at all times. Once a year the High Priest of Wepwawet shall dictate to me a scroll describing her state. It is to be remembered that she is still a possession of the Horus Throne, and as such may not be betrothed or engage in any sexual relationship with any man other than Pharaoh himself. She may swim in the Nile whenever she wishes, and she may cultivate a garden for her own use and for the ease of her ka." Pa-ari let the scroll roll up and handed it back to the mayor. "It is signed by Pharaoh himself," he said. Then he stepped forward and enfolded me in his arms. "I love you, Thu," he said. "There is lentil stew and Mother's beer waiting for you. It could all be worse. The gods have been kind." Yes, they had been kind. They had chosen to forget me after all. And as I held Pa-ari's hand and walked with him across the village square I suddenly realized that in one month I could celebrate my birth. I would be seventeen years old.

My father and Pa-ari built a two-roomed house for me in the shadow of Wepwawet's wall and I took up residence there, going every day into the temple to sweep or clean, to carry away baskets of priestly linen which I would wash in the river, and sometimes to take such mundane dictation as an inventory of the god's utensils or lists of supplies to be sent for from Thebes. I dug and planted a garden. Dutifully I visited my mother, although she remained ashamed to acknowledge me and I was always careful not to appear at her door when she was entertaining her friends. My father often came to sit at my door and talk, or drink the foul beer I made. He had fashioned a cot, a table and a chair for me and I had woven for myself two sheaths to wear, a covering for the cot and two cushions. I had begged dishes from the priests. Other than those simple things I was destitute.

Isis had produced a girl, a daughter for Pa-ari. I did not see as much of him as I would have liked even though we both worked in the temple, for his world was bounded by his new family and I was on its periphery, but sometimes he would appear at sunset and we would talk of the old days, of our childhood. Only once I told him of my life in the harem and of the terrible thing I had done, and I did not mention how Hui and the others had used me. It was not shame that held me back. Sometimes I grew afraid that Hui would send an assassin to kill me because of all I knew, and I did not want Pa-ari to be a victim also.

When I had been in Aswat for six months I began to think of my son. My life in the village was so divorced from everything I had known in the Delta that for a long time the harem and the palace and all that had passed there seemed like a particularly vivid dream, but gradually Pentauru regained his reality and my heart ached for him. I spent much time wondering how he was. Were the members of the merchant's family treating him well? Was it possible that one so young could retain any memories of his true mother, perhaps flashes of her face? Would a certain perfume bring back to him an unease, a feeling of discontent that seemed to have no root in his present? Would the sparkle of light on a gem, the flutter of fine white linen, bring a sadness brimming into his heart? Had Ramses forgotten him altogether, or did his thoughts sometimes stray to his beautiful, fractious concubine and the child he had fathered on her?

I no longer felt beautiful. My hands became rough and calloused. My feet, forbidden any protection from the elements, grew splayed and hard. No kohl surrounded my eyes, only a fan of tiny lines as I squinted day after day against the sun, and my hair lost its sheen and softness and grew brittle. Yet for many months I was content to revel in the sheer miracle of my continued existence. Though I worked like the lowest harem servant, though the villagers at best ignored me and at worst threw dung at me for marking their village as the place from which a murderess had sprung, I was happy.

I took to wandering in the desert during the night hours while the village and the temple slept. I would rest for a while after sunset, and then I would creep out behind my hut to where the cultivation ended and the sand began. There I would tear off my sheath and run naked under the moon until I had exhausted myself, shouting and laughing, drunk with my isolation and the exhilaration of the endless horizon that stretched, stark and starlit, for as far as I could see.

Stripped of everything, I remembered the moment when waiting for word that Pharaoh was dead I had almost succumbed to the peculiar urge to walk away, out of the harem, out of the city, until I came to the desert where I could begin my life again, innocent and free. That urge had been satisfied. Dancing with the cold, shifting sand under my bare toes I was indeed innocent. I was free.

And I began to wonder what was happening in the palace. Was Pharaoh quietly pursuing his investigations into the lives of the names I had given him? Were his men watching the plotters as they hatched a new scheme? Would I ever have the satisfaction of seeing Hui's smug, cold world dismembered?

Then Ramses would remember me. Then he would send to Aswat. He might even come himself. His Herald would approach my hut. I would be invited aboard the royal barge but of course I could not go in such a state, so Ramses would send his serving women to bathe and oil me, massage soothing creams into my poor feet and abused hands, dress my hair and paint my face, clothe me in shimmering linen and put precious gems about my neck and arms. Then, with new sandals on my feet, surrounded by an aura of saffron, protected by a sunshade, I would leave the hut and walk proudly, so proudly, to Wepwawet's watersteps and up the ramp into my lover's embrace.

Until then I will continue to play the dutiful servant of the servants of my totem. I will continue to dance alone at night among the dunes of the desert. And I will continue to write this, the story of my rise and fall, in secret, on papyrus I am able to steal from the temple storehouse. When I am finished, who knows? I may give it into Pa-ari's keeping as a legacy, so that one day it may find its way to my son. Or I may entrust it to one of the royal Heralds who ply the river on the business of the crown and it may appear on Pharaoh's desk some bright summer morning. The future is a perilous adventure, after all. Who knows?

THE END